Sweetened
SUFFERING

Sweet Treats
Book Two

CHARITY B.

ISBN: 978-0-9993575-2-1

Editor: Joanne LaRe Thompson
Cover Design: Murphy Hopkins

Author's Note

This is the second book in a trilogy. To understand the story, it is best you begin with *Candy Coated Chaos*. This novel is considerably darker than the first in the series, so please be prepared for that. Thank you so much for continuing to read. I appreciate each and every one of you. Your love for these books means so much to me.

This story is very close to my heart and I hope you enjoy the journey.

Trigger Warning
This novel contains drug use, explicit sexual content, violence, child abuse, and sensitive subject matter which may be triggering to some readers.

Dedication

To my husband : You have had faith in me from the very first day. You never once doubted my ability, even when I doubted myself. You've made sacrifices for me and my dream and I will always be grateful for that. I love you.

Celebrate your scars, sweet soul. They are a sign
you have lived beyond your suffering.
—*S. C. Lourie*

CHAPTER ONE
Gone

Tavin

ALL THESE YEARS, AND I STILL HATE ELEVATORS. The *ding* of the doors opening makes my breath push out of my lungs as I follow Sasha down a long, white hallway.

Run! Turn around and run, you stupid cunt!

Our footsteps are quiet against the tan carpet, before we stop at a brown door where *13B* is written in silver. "Home sweet home," she sighs.

With my bag over my shoulder and my stomach in my feet, I follow her inside. Her ceiling is high, making her apartment look larger than it really is. Her boyfriend, I mean fiancé—she gets mad if you don't call him that, is drinking a beer on the couch and watching TV.

Without looking away from the soccer show he's watching, he brings the bottle to his lips and grumbles, "So what the hell is going on over there, now?"

"Drew," she snaps. When he finally turns to look at her, he sees me and frowns.

"What's going on, Sash?"

She walks toward the hallway directly in front of us, and I make sure I am right behind her. This is awkward, and Drew is making me nervous, so I focus on the things around me.

Her living room has lots of decorations on the pale-yellow walls, and there are colorful mix-matched pillows tossed on the couch and chairs. I can feel his glare on my skin, so I avert my eyes to the opposite direction.

The kitchen and living area are one giant room with nothing separating the two spaces, not even different flooring. Her cabinets are light blue with white doors and I like her pink elephant cookie jar on the counter. I think it's cute and pretty that none of her canisters match. Even the chairs around the kitchen table all come from different sets. This is nothing like Alexander's house. His house is always so perfect. Everything matches, and Cara Jo is constantly cleaning it.

"I'm gonna show Tavin her room," she tells him. "Then we need to have a conversation."

He doesn't say anything and he doesn't need to; it's obvious he wants me to leave. Well, that makes two of us. I see her mouthing something to him, out of the corner of my eye, and I want to crawl inside myself and disappear.

I follow her down the hallway that curves to the left, and I'm so grateful to be out from beneath Drew's view. She opens the first door on the right and momentarily flips on the light.

"Here's the bathroom. Drew and I have our own so this one's all yours." Pointing to a set of glass double doors on the left, she says, "That's our room, and…," she turns the knob to the door next to the bathroom. "This is my studio."

The light comes on and my eyes are instantly pulled to the rolls of fabric that are in every color of the rainbow, stacked along the back wall.

As she walks past me, she takes a cream-colored jacket off a rack and holds it up. "This is from my newest collection. Isn't it gorgeous?" She spins it around. "Look at the detail on the back."

I like how enthusiastic she gets about her clothes. Her energy is contagious and I get excited with her. Right now though, I'm struggling to feel anything other than sad and scared.

I smile at her. "It's beautiful, Sasha."

Buckets of buttons, zippers, snaps, and ribbons along with scissors and other utensils are organized in containers in the corner. I walk around the table in the middle of the room and stop myself from touching the sheer, blue fabric scraps lying across it.

On her desk is a photo of her and Alexander, and seeing his smiling face makes my heart sting. The bookcase next to her desk is covered in fashion books and magazines, while her walls are lined with photos of men and women in amazing clothes.

"You like my studio?"

At first, I think it's pride I see on her face, and while I'm sure she feels that too, it's more than that. She truly cares for all this stuff.

I pull out a long dress with lots of colors and a pretty pattern. "It's really neat. I wish I knew how to make things like this."

"Well, now that you're here, maybe I can teach you," she offers. It's fun to learn new things and I rarely get the chance, so while at the moment it's hard to wrap my head around excitement, if she does teach me, it would make me really happy. She waves at me to follow her. "All right, let me show you your room."

As we go back into the hall, I see there's only one door left at the very end. She pushes it open and as the light flickers on, a smile is able to squirm its way onto my lips. It's the loveliest room I've ever seen.

Even though it isn't as big as the one I stayed in at Lex's, or the basement at my house, there's still plenty of space. Paintings framed in pale pink are decorating the walls, and I like the one with the rope swing in the garden, the most. The bed is the same size as the one at my house, and looks soft as a marshmallow with little pink and blue flowers sewn into the blanket. The best part, though, is the window. I like windows. It's lined in white crocheted curtains and has a seat with a blue and white striped cushion on it.

"There's room in the dresser and the closet for your clothes." She pushes open the door to show me all the empty hangers. "I'm going to have a talk with Drew, really quick, and then I'll go get you whatever you need." She lifts the side of her mouth in a sad smile and shoves her hands in her shorts pockets. "I promise we'll figure this out, okay?"

That's not a promise she can keep, she's just trying to make me feel better, so I smile back at her. "Okay."

You deserve everything coming to you.

The door *clicks* shut behind her and I fall back on the bed as Drew's yelling seeps through the wall.

"What the hell, Sasha?" I'm not able to make out what she says before he barks, "No, fuck that, I'm so sick of your shit! You didn't even think to ask me. She's not our Goddamn problem!"

I sit up and sigh. She's getting in trouble because of me. Partly, I wish I never would've gone to The Necco Room, the night of the Carnival. Then none of this would be happening. Sasha wouldn't be risking herself or getting yelled at for me, and Lex wouldn't be sad or angry; he would still be going about is life like he was before I messed everything up.

I'm too selfish to not be grateful for the time I had with him and the friendship I made with Sasha. The problem is, now I know what it's like. How am I supposed to go back to my life after these last few weeks?

The bed squeaks as I push off it to stand up. I'm wasting my thoughts because none of them matter. I can't stay here. Things will be better the sooner I go back. I don't know why I agreed to this in the first place. I can't let Logan find out about Lex or Sasha, and staying here risks both.

Oh, I feel sick. I rub my stomach before I hoist my bag back over my shoulder and go back into the hall. Taking a big breath, I cross the living room and march right past them arguing, to yank open the front door.

"Hey! What are you doing?" Sasha grabs my arm.

"What I should have done three weeks ago. I'm going home. This was a bad idea to begin with and now I'm making you fight."

She glares at Drew and grabs my hand to pull me back into the bedroom. Once inside, she shuts the door and combs her hair back with her fingers.

"Ignore him, he's manstruating. He'll get over it."

"It's not Drew. Me staying here is dangerous for all of us."

She takes my bag off my shoulder and digs through it before tossing my green shorts and Halsey tee onto the bed.

"Come on. I know you're worried about Toben, so let's just start with tonight, okay? It's too late to figure anything out anyway."

The tears build up, clogging my nose and I hate that I'm such a baby. "It's more than only being worried. You don't know Logan!" I'm yelling and I don't like to yell, so I force my voice down. "I can't leave him there."

She rests her hands on her hips with a sigh. "What are you trying to say?"

"Please, I just need to go see that he's alright."

Her face twitches as she bites her lip. "How do you expect me to respond here? I understand where you're coming from, it's just too dangerous."

I'm desperate. I need to know Logan hasn't hurt him.

"I won't even get out of the car. You can knock on the door and when he answers, I'll see he's okay and then we can leave. If Logan's car is there, we'll just keep driving, okay?" I clasp my hands together so she knows I'm literally begging. "Please?"

She drops her head forward and groans. "Will you stop fighting me about staying here if I do this?"

I'm not used to making my own choices. I'm as scared to go home as I am not to. It's not as if I want to go back, the idea makes the nausea wrap around my stomach like a bow. I just don't want any of us to suffer Logan's wrath. Neither choice is a good one. Confusion is one of my least favorite feelings. Ultimately though, the most important thing to me right now, is making sure Toben is safe.

My nostrils flare as I close my eyes and drop my hands in defeat. "Fine."

───

Her car slows as we pull up to my house, and I'm relieved there aren't any cars here. Sasha groans as she opens the door, causing the interior light to turn on.

"I can't believe I'm doing this." Her finger is inches from my face as she points at me. "Don't get out of the car."

I draw an X over my chest. "I won't. I promise."

Please let him answer... Please.

With a sigh, she leaves the engine running as she shuts the door, and walks in front of the car. The street lights are almost blinding, brightening up the whole block, while the houses remain dark, black boxes. The porch light flips on as she walks into my yard. Her pale hair looks so pretty the way it swings back and forth, while she jogs up the steps. She lifts her hand and...dang it!

She's ringing the doorbell and the doorbell doesn't work. I don't think it ever has. I let my forehead slam against the window and I feel like screaming because she's just standing there. Turning back to me, she holds her arms up in question.

"Knock on the door!"

I imitate knocking and a moment later, she finally gets it. I fall against the seat and watch as the seconds pass by. He isn't answering. Oh, God, why isn't he answering? She knocks again and tries the handle. The door is locked, allowing my breathing to slow. The door is only locked when we leave, and I'm not sure if Toben has a playdate tonight or not.

Sasha made me throw away my phone, so if Toben did call me back, I have no way of knowing. He could be with Christopher, or anywhere for that matter. I chew on the inside of my cheek as I turn up the music to erase the quiet.

She makes a good effort at least. She peers in all the windows and even tries to go around to the back of the house. Finally, she gives up and walks back to the car.

"There isn't anyone in there as far as I can tell."

Putting on my seat belt, I grumble, "He probably went out. There's no way to know without my cell phone."

With a tilt of her head, she raises an eyebrow. "Don't give me that tone. For all I know, Logan could have tracked you down with it. I did that to protect you."

Now I feel mean. It's not fair for me to take my frustrations out on her. She's one of the nicest people I've ever met and she just did me a huge favor.

"You're right, I'm sorry. Thank you for doing this. I'm just confused and scared about what's going to happen. Not that any of that's your fault…"

She shifts the car into drive and pulls away from the curb. "I know, hon. Well, I don't know. I can't pretend to understand what you must be feeling right now, but I do understand it's a lot. We'll figure this out, okay?" She holds out her middle finger. "I Sasha swear."

She grins at me and I return it as I hook my middle finger with hers. I never knew girls were like this. After everything, I can't imagine not knowing her or Lex. I could never regret that.

Looking out the window, I watch as we pass Toben's old house. I wish, so badly, he was here.

Alexander

The walkway lights are blurry and almost look like they're moving, which doesn't make it any easier to get to my front door. All that alcohol finally caught up and I think I might puke.

I try to unlock the door and the stupid key won't go in. Oh…because it's the wrong key. I fumble through the ring until I find the correct one, finally victorious in opening the door.

As I stumble into the entryway, I look into the kitchen and can almost imagine her standing there with her face lit up in a smile. The house is completely silent besides the clink of my keys as I toss them in the bowl. Finally, I wash the blood off my knuckles while Blind Mag trots in a circle around me. That little fucker is gone tomorrow. Drying my hands, I ignore the loofah with legs and walk toward the stairs. I make it to the second step before she whimpers and her nails begin scratching at the glass of the backdoor. I don't want her pissing on my floor, so I let her out before going upstairs. As I walk down the hall, I pass by her room.

Her room. It's not her room anymore.

I must want to keep torturing myself because I push open the door and flip on the light. As I walk inside, the painting from the art fair taunts me, along with the clothes she left in the closet. It feels like she's going to walk in at any moment. Everything she left is what I got for her. That equally hurts and pisses me off. They were gifts. She either didn't want the reminder and left me to deal with it, or she never saw them as hers in the first place. I look for the necklace and find it on the dresser next to her cell phone. Picking it up, I spin the carousel. I really wish she would have at least taken this. It always looked so perfect on her.

I despise feeling so weak and pathetic. After Carrie, I swore I would never let another girl make me feel this way again, yet here I am. Looking back, there were plenty of flashing warning signs that something like this would happen. I wonder if she ever once thought about giving it an honest shot at making it work between us. If any of it was real. Was it all some kind of game? I think she always knew she was going to go back, so what was the point?

The chain slides through my fingers as I drop the necklace back onto the dresser and open the drawers. I dig through it for a moment before tossing all the contents on the floor. I don't even know what I'm looking for. Finding nothing, I walk to the bed and pull off her pillowcase. It still smells like her and my chest burns as I press my nose against it. With a sigh, I toss it back on the bed before walking to the closet. The door rumbles on its track as I push it open and yank the clothes off the hangers, throwing each article over my shoulder, onto the floor.

Halfway through, a flash of bright orange catches my attention, so I push the remaining items to the end of the closet. My jaw drops as my eyes scan over the closet wall. It's a huge mural of bright stars and swirled lines, warped doorways and twisted, mutilated bodies.

She drew on my fucking wall? Who the hell does that?

I can't stop staring. It's bright and sweet, while at the same time, disturbing and haunting. While her artistic style is unique and beautiful, it has always made me feel sad. I snap myself out of it and slam the closet door shut. I cannot believe she did that.

Rage is the emotion I am clinging to for dear life because the only other option available is despondency. Part of me knows I have to move on from this, while a much larger part knows that it's impossible because I'm no longer the same as I was before I met her. What exactly am I supposed to move on to? Mindlessly fucking any remotely hot woman I can find? Or even better, meet a normal girl and have normal sex in our normal relationship? That's no longer an option for me. It was such a stupid move bringing her into this house. Everywhere I look, I see her. It's as if she left her imprint on everything she touched.

The screen light is annoyingly bright as I open my laptop and pull up the Google search bar. Though I have no idea how to go about speaking to someone in prison, right now her father seems like the best option for information.

I type in 'Visiting a California inmate' and click on the government site for the California Department of Corrections and Rehabilitation. My disappointment flares when I see it isn't even possible to see him without an official C.D.C.R. form that he has to sign. He has to allow my visitation and I can't even get the form without him sending it to me personally. I have no idea if he will be open to meeting with me. He doesn't know who I am, and I'm sure it's safe to assume he's less than friendly. Not to mention, he's been incarcerated since 2004 so he may not know much. It's still a door and I need to try to open it. I'm hesitant on what to write so I keep it simple:

Mr. Winters,

My name is Alexander Sørensen and I am writing to ask for your signature on the C.D.C.R. form 106. I'm aware that you do not know who I am and my request for visitation is unexpected. My reason for wanting to speak with you involves questions concerning your daughter, Tavin. If you would consider this meeting and adding me to your list, please include the form in your response.

Thank you,

Alexander Sørensen

I send it to my printer and enter the address into my phone. I'll drop it at the post office tomorrow. Closing my laptop, I roll my eyes as a playful growl vibrates by my feet. I glare at her and she tilts her head and whines.

First things first. This dog is gone in the morning.

Sunday, June 7ᵗʰ

Tavin

Knock. Knock.

I lift my heavy eyes and my stomach is snarly, making me queasy as I sit up. The door opens and Sasha walks in with two cups of coffee.

"Butterscotch creamer and a shit ton of sugar–just how you like it."

I take the mug as I try to make myself smile. "Thank you."

She sets down her coffee and carries my bag to the closet to hang up my clothes. "Come on, let's try to look on the sunny side, okay? I know things with Alex ended…well, terribly, but at least you're free of Logan. Doesn't that count for something?"

I almost laugh. She knows the whole story and she still doesn't get it. "Free? You think I'm free?" I push off the blankets and set my coffee on the nightstand. "I don't know what that even means, I just know this sure as heck isn't it. He will find me, Sasha. Sooner or later he always gets what's his."

She slides a hanger into my pastel pink dress with the lacy, peter-pan collar. "Look, since you refuse to let me tell my brother, I'm all you've got." She turns around and walks to the bed, placing her hands on the foot board as she gives me a look that reminds me of him. "I need you to try to trust me. At least a little. Give me some time to figure this out and come up with an actual plan. Until then, you are free of him, Tavin."

I fall back on the bed and huff. She doesn't understand and it's frustrating me. It's not that I don't want this 'plan' to work out. I wish it would, it just won't. If I go back home on my own without him having to come look for me, it will be better for me and Toben. The sooner I do, the less the punishment will be. If he has to come find me… who knows what he will do?

She sits on the bed next to me and crosses her legs. "It doesn't make sense to me why you won't tell Alex. I don't see how you can't trust him after everything he's done for you. He can protect you better than I can, and he's smart. He could at least think of something."

I can't believe she called him smart. She would never do that to his face.

Groaning, I sit up and lean against the headboard. "This isn't about trusting him. It's about his safety. He can't know.

You shouldn't know. I put you in danger by telling you, and that was selfish of me. I'm very sorry for that."

I lean over for my coffee and take a sip. It's so good. I lick the butterscotch from my lips and look at Sasha. Her eyes are glossy as she wraps her arm around me and rests her head on my shoulder.

"Your whole situation is so fucked up." She lifts her head to face me. "We need to consider the police. This is too big. It's what I should have done in the first place."

I almost spill my coffee as I grab her arm, so I set it down.

"What? No! The police will make things so much worse. And even if they weren't bad, Logan has people everywhere working for him. That's what I've been trying to tell you, there's nowhere to escape him."

She snorts and rolls her eyes. "Oh, come on, he's full of shit. There's no way this guy has that much pull. Besides, who told you the police are bad?" Her nose scrunches as she shakes her head. "It doesn't matter right now. Listen," she holds my hand. "I'm going to ask you this once and I want you to be completely honest. I won't be mad with your answer, okay?" I nod to her because I don't know where this is going. "Do you *want* to go back? Besides everything with Toben, do you want to go back to that life?"

Of course not, but Toben is the biggest part of the life she's referring to. I shake my head as she releases my hand.

"No."

"Alright, then believe me when I say we'll figure out a way to make sure you don't ever have to." Leaning back on one hand, she uses the other to comb back her hair. "Now, I'm still not fully comprehending all of this, so we won't get the cops involved. At least not yet. However," I glare at her. Why is there always a 'however'? "You just said it's not want you want, so if you ever go back to Logan, I'm going to tell Alex. All of it."

My mouth drops open and I can't believe she's black-mailing me. "What about Toben? I need to talk to him."

Her head drops back as she sighs. "Well, you can't call him, and we just established you can't go home, so unless you have some other way, I don't see how to do that."

A thought suddenly pops into my head and it's too fun-ny for me to push my smile down. Groaning, she looks at me sideways.

"What's that look for?"

"I can't go to my house, but you can." I point to her and her eyebrows raise. "Just because Toben knows who you are, doesn't mean Logan does. Toben always has random girls over, so Logan wouldn't think a thing of it if you show up acting like you're there for a hook up."

Her unease is a vapor seeping into me as she asks, "Is Logan going to be there?"

"I don't know."

She drops her hands on the bed and dramatically slouch-es her shoulders as she pretends to be grumpy with me. "You owe me big time."

I wrap my arms around her, almost knocking her over. "Thank you, Sasha."

Her laugh is so soft. As I release her, she flips her hair. "Yeah, yeah, just be grateful he's good looking or this would never be believable."

⌒

She hasn't been gone long. Still, I hate being alone. Crippling fear, sadness, and regret wash over me, choking me like a noose. I want to peel the skin from my bones like string cheese, dig my fingers into my eyes and feel the tendons pop as I tear them from my skull.

My mind begins to consider the reality of what's possi-ble, because of my actions. How did I ever think I could get away with this? If I go back now, then Sasha will tell Lex, and the outcome of that is not one I want to think about. Not going back means Logan might kill Toben, and he's suffering as much as anyone. Thinking of the things he might have done to him because of this, makes me want to scream so loud my throat bleeds.

You asked for this.

All this damage I caused, in less than a month. My actions have destroyed mine and Toben's already distorted lives, as well as Lex's and Sasha's.

I want you gone.

Those are the last words I'll ever hear in Alexander's beautifully unique voice. My insides twist so tight I hope it rips me in half. While of course I detest that he saw me with Logan, there's a part of me that's oddly relieved he did. He saw me for what I am.

A dirty, broken toy.

This feeling that I have inside of me, it's more than missing him. I can't place this emotion, this specific agony in my chest. I feel like I've been mauled and ripped open. More torn apart than my flesh could ever be. I can't do this; I can't feel like this anymore. I need something. Anything.

I know from already checking, that the cabinet in the hallway bathroom doesn't have anything useful, so I sneak into Sasha's bedroom and into her bathroom. My reflection stares back at me, but I refuse to look myself in the eye, as I pop open the medicine cabinet. It's full of bottles and tubes and not a single one will get me high.

Going back into the living room, I turn on the TV and mindlessly stare into a fictional world of cartoon people and talking animals.

I've been sitting here zoned out for so long, I barely hear it. *Click.* My vision clears as my bloody, torn up fingers come into focus. Jumping off the couch, I stare at the door and watch as it opens.

Toben's voice pushes the oxygen back into my lungs. "Did you have to kiss me? No one was even around."

Sasha scoffs. "Like you didn't love it. Besides, you said yourself you didn't know that for sure. I had to sell it, just in case."

He limps as he walks over to me and I ache at his wince. "Oh, God. He hurt you."

This is because of you, you selfish bitch.

His arms are already around me as he pulls me to his chest. Our fingers lace and we connect the physical remains of our memories.

"Oh, come on, it's not that bad. We both know I've had worse, and believe me, I got off easy." Our foreheads press together as his chopped-up breathing pushes small puffs of air onto my face. He cups my cheek and whispers, "What are you doing?"

"I… I don't know."

"Just come home," he pleads. "He'll forgive you, eventually. Then everything can go back to the way it's supposed to be."

Sasha slams the door making us jump apart. "How could you want her to go back? You're supposed to be her friend!"

He spins around and has her against the wall so fast, I don't see him move until it's done.

"Don't talk about things you know nothing about. You aren't capable of understanding, so if you want to help, then back the fuck off, bitch."

"Toben!" I yell at him.

She doesn't seem bothered as she pushes herself right back in his face. "You're right. I can't pretend to get it, but you're both desensitized." She waves her hand in the air. "Blind."

He tightens his fists and shakes his head. "You fucking people. You have no idea who you're dealing with. Logan James is more ruthless and powerful than you can imagine."

The color in Sasha's face slips away as she lets herself step back against the wall. "Whoa…Logan James? As in *Rissa* Logan James?"

What the heck is a Rissa?

"You know who he is?" His steps falter as he backs away from her.

Sasha keeps her distance as she steps around him to the living area. "Who the hell doesn't? Especially in this town. There isn't a kitchen in the country that doesn't have at least one Rissa product in it." Her forehead is scrunched with her frown as she looks at me. "Not to mention my father is his fucking chairman." Bouncing on the cushion, she drops herself on the couch. "I can't believe this."

"Now do you get it?" He's pointing at me while glaring at her. "He will find her. He'll follow me and he probably has men out looking for her right now. When he realizes she's here, because I fucking promise you, he will. He'll come for her. And if he has to do that…" He clicks his tongue at her. "Well, let's just say you don't want that."

She wipes her hands over her face, and I wish she didn't always remind me of Alexander. "All we need is enough time to get her out of the city, possibly the state. Then she can start a new life somewhere."

"No motherfucking way. That's not an option," he barks.

"How do you know he won't still kill her if she goes back?" Sasha yells.

"I don't. What I do know, is it will be a million times better than if he has to drag her there."

They argue between each other deciding my fate. Why does everyone get to choose how my life is lived, besides me? I am overwhelmed and sad and scared and they are driving me crazy! I take a deep breath so my voice is louder than theirs.

"Hey!" They back off each other and look at me. "Does anybody care what I want?"

Alexander

The sun shines over my closed eyes causing me to groan as I sit up. Glancing down at the foot of the bed, I see Blind Mag cocking her head to the side.

"Don't look at me that way, you furry little shit. You're out of here. Today."

She whines like she actually understands. I climb out of bed and it's as if standing causes the anger to wash over the sorrow. For the first time, I wish I had allowed myself to care for more girls. Maybe if I would have had my heart broken a few times already, this wouldn't be so intense.

I walk into the hall to go to my home gym and the damn dog starts barking. The further I walk away from her, the shriller it becomes.

"What the hell is your problem?"

She runs towards the top of the stairs where she continues the ear-piercing bark until I walk toward her. I follow her to the kitchen, where she paws at her empty bowl, making it flip over.

I guess I can't let the fucking thing starve, so I give her some food and she immediately starts scarfing it down.

I roll my eyes and open the back door so she can piss before walking back upstairs. It's been weeks since I've been to Benny's Boxing Gym and I know I should go, I just can't bear to listen to the twenty questions he's bound to ask.

Even with my knuckles cut and bruised, I don't feel a thing as I take my pain and anger out on the bag. I have no appetite to speak of, so, I skip breakfast and hop in the Alfa, driving the three and a half miles to the post office to drop the letter to Brian Winters in the mailbox.

Afterwards, I stop at Shadoebox Hardware for supplies. Her mural in the closet needs to be covered and I don't feel like waiting to hire someone. Wallpaper is a cleaner option than paint and doesn't sound that hard, so as soon as I get home, I grab my new bucket of tools and go upstairs to get this over with.

Giving the drawing one last look, I have a moment of weakness and consider snapping a photo before I realize how pathetic that is. The stupid dog comes in as I'm wetting the paper. It's not quite as simple as I originally thought. I get water everywhere and I swear Blind Mag glares at me before shaking out her coat. Cursing under my breath, I try to smooth out all the little bumps that are making my life hell.

I finally hang the last strip and back out of the closet to look at my work. Well, that looks like shit. Fuck it, I'll get someone to fix it later. At least the drawing is out of sight for now.

I let out the dog before going into the garage to search for something to pack up Tavin's things. I find a fairly large cardboard box, so I grab it, along with a roll of packing tape.

On my way back upstairs, I notice the bottle of booze on the counter. Not bothering with a glass, I bring it with me.

Opening the door to her old room, I sigh before taking a swig. The room is trashed and I don't expect Cara Jo to clean it up. What am I going to do with all this stuff? I look at her clothes strewn across the floor. Every piece has a memory attached. I sit on the carpet, nursing my bottle as I fold each item and place them in the box.

The gown from the fundraiser, the blue dress from the

art fair, the little black dress… She looked so beautiful in all these things. Sasha says people feel lovely in lovely things and now I understand what she means. Tavin would always glow a little brighter and smile a little bigger when she got dressed up. Groaning, I pull another drink from the bottle. This has to get easier. I just pray I fall out as fast as I fell in.

The painting I bought her is a beacon, from its place on the wall. That definitely needs to go. She loved it, and now it makes more sense as to why. It appears beautiful and sweet, when it's really full of darkness and anguish. Just like her. Pushing myself off the floor, I lift the painting from the wall hook and place it in the box.

I look around the room to see what else there is, as I slide the necklace off the dresser and shove it in my pocket. When I pick up her phone to toss it in the box, my thumb presses the unlock button. I'm already this far, so I tap on the envelope icon to open her messages and the only ones are from me. Same with the call log. She doesn't have an email setup or any apps downloaded so I hit the camera icon for videos. There's only one, and like an idiot I click on it, even though I know exactly what it is.

My dresser flashes onto the screen and when her raspy voice floats through the room, my stomach flutters at the sound. *Oh, he would die.* She laughs to herself and the camera shifts while she moves about. My former self walks into the room, filling the camera frame. I know what she's about to say and I smile in spite of myself.

Let's make a movie. Undo your shirt, but leave it on so I can see your abs.

So are you the director of our little flick?

Yup.

Then I'm the videographer.

That's when I take the phone and her smiling face comes into view. My eyes strain and my throat burns at the sight of her.

Refraining from throwing the phone against the wall, I shut it off and toss it in the box before kicking it into the closet.

I jog down the steps to remedy my empty bottle situation, and see the fur ball standing with her paws against the glass door, waiting to come inside. Fuck that little critter. I turn back to the kitchen and she barks before she whines, as if she's being tortured. I shake my head. and open the liquor cabinet. She doesn't let up, so for my own sanity, I relent and let her inside.

"You're lucky I'm already too drunk to take you anywhere today." She follows me inside, tail wagging and proud as hell of herself. "Yeah, you won this round."

I take my fresh bottle of bourbon and sit on the new couch Cara Jo bought last week to replace the one Tavin bled all over. Blind Mag jumps up, curling her body next to mine and I scoff at her.

Whatever.

CHAPTER TWO
C.D.C.R.

Monday, June 8th

MY BODY ACHES AS I PULL OPEN MY BEDROOM door and almost run into Cara Jo, smiling, in the hall. "Good morning, Alex. Is Tavin still asleep?"

My face heats up as I snap, "Her name is now off limits. Say it again and you're fired."

I know it isn't fair to treat her that way. I also know I can't bring myself to explain what's happened, so I suppose I'm being a coward and taking the easy way out. She backs away and gives me a look I can't identify, before disappearing into the bathroom.

After I hit the bag and force down a few bites of my omelet, I take a couple whiskey shots before getting dressed.

Cara Jo avoids me for the rest of the morning, and not even Kurt Cobain can comfort me as I make my way through morning traffic. All I want is to get in my office and submerge myself in work.

Walking through the Vulture lobby, I wear a plastic smile until I get into the elevator. My cheeks puff out with my sigh as I press the button, and irony can kiss my ass because right as the doors are about to close, Eric slithers inside like the snake he is.

"Good morning, Mr. Sørensen."

"Hello, Eric. I actually wanted to speak with you." Any promise I made to her in the past means nothing now. Turning to face him with a clenched jaw, I remind myself to try and remain professional. "Tavin Winters is not to be inside this building. If you bring her here again, I will terminate your position with Vulture Theaters."

His eyes are about to pop out of his head as his posture turns as stiff as a corpse. "What?"

"Tavin. Sweet Girl. Whoever the fuck she is." He sways as if he's going to pass out and I kind of hope he does. "Have your 'playdates' with her somewhere else." I face forward and will admit I'm enjoying his obvious panic. "I am curious though, how much do you pay for her?"

"Uh—s—seven an hour."

"Grand?!" I knew she was expensive, but Jesus Christ. He nods as I straighten my jacket. "Your job is on extremely thin ice. Do not schedule her during business hours and do not mention her name in this office."

"I understand, sir, and I won't. She's out of stock anyway." His mouth twitches and he's clearly kicking himself internally for that last bit.

"What's *that* supposed to mean?"

Rubbing the back of his neck, he releases a nervous laugh. "She isn't available."

'Out of stock'? She isn't a fucking pair of shoes. I shake my head as the elevator doors open, and when I step out, I add, "Check again, I'm sure she's back 'in stock' by now."

I may have allowed myself to go a little overboard with the bourbon, so by the time lunch rolls around, I could really use some fresh air. After locking my office door, I turn around and nearly knock Silas over on my way to the elevator.

"Hey, Slilas." Damn it, I'm slurring.

"Oh my God, are you…" He examines my face a little closer and glares. "Are you drunk?" He reaches for my trouser pocket. "What the hell, Sørensen? Give me your phone."

I back away from him and walk toward the elevator. "I'm fine." Somehow, my foot gets caught on the carpet and I stumble forward.

"Clearly," he deadpans as I push the button. "What's going on? Why are you wasted at twelve thirty on a Monday? Pretty sure that's grounds for A.A."

The doors open, and as I walk inside, I sigh and lean against the wall. Following me, he crosses his arms and awaits my response.

"I walked in on Tavin with someone."

"Wait, what?" He scoffs as he yanks out his phone. "That bitch. I'll call you a car."

"I'm fine, Silas, really. I've missed too much lately and it'll look bad."

"Yeah, and being more trashed than a freshman girl during Greek week is much better." He shakes his head and rubs his right temple. "Oh, God, this is starting to feel a lot like Carrie. You can't let this affect Vulture, Alex. It's okay to fall man, but do you have to do it so damn hard? These sluts aren't worth it."

As angry as I am with her, I still don't see her that way. "Silas, don't call her that."

He rolls his eyes as he leads me outside and waits with me for the car. When the driver pulls up, Silas opens the door and I fall into the backseat. He rests a hand on the hood as he leans down and hands me a joint.

"I'm sorry, I know you really liked her and I do understand how that feels." He doesn't though. He's never been in love with anyone. "I'm also gonna need you to suck it up at work alright? What was that crazy thing your mom used to say? You know, when she wanted you to get your shit together?"

"*Skjerp deg.*"

"Sk—Yeah, that."

I smile and pull on my seat belt. "Thanks, Silas."

He shrugs as he straightens and shoves his hands into his pockets. "What are best friends for, right?"

Cara Jo glares at me as I stumble my way into the kitchen and grab the bourbon off the island.

She wraps her hand around my wrist and holds it tight. "You've clearly had enough."

I jerk my arm free and back away from her. "I hired you to clean my house and cook for me, not to tell me how much you think I should drink." She flinches and turns back toward the sink. When I get to the stairs, Blind Mag is sitting at the top. "And get rid of this fucking dog."

I know I'm being an asshole. I don't even know why I'm treating her this way. She doesn't deserve it.

There's no response and when I turn back to apologize, she's gone. I groan and climb the steps. She's never been anything besides supportive of me my entire life. Most times she was more of a mother than my real one was.

Twenty-two years ago...

"Mom, look!"

I try not to crinkle the paper as I run outside. Since my mom is the prettiest lady in all of Shadoebox City, and probably even the world, I wrote a story all about her. I really hope she likes it. I've been working on it for three days.

My feet stay on the pathway because we aren't allowed to walk on the grass.

She's smiling in the garden with her friends drinking her 'adult drink'. She and my dad say I'm not old enough, but I tasted some once and it was so gross, I hope I never get old enough for it.

Her laugh makes me grin as I shove my story in her lap. "I wrote this for you! Will you read it?"

She doesn't seem happy with me as she laughs like she does when she is uncomfortable.

"Alexander, can't you see that I have company? It's rude to interrupt, now apologize."

Isn't she even going to look at it? It's so embarrassing to get in trouble in front of these ladies.

I don't look down even though I want to. Dad says it's important to always look people in the eye.

"I'm sorry, ma'ams."

I won't cry because Dad says boys don't do that. I'm so angry because she didn't even look at it! I worked hard on that!

The door slams behind me as I walk back inside and I stomp across the kitchen towards my room.

"Hey, young man, get over here right now." I roll my eyes, even though I hide it so Cara Jo can't see me. "Why are you slamming doors? That is no way for a gentleman to act."

"Because I'm mad at Mother."

She bends over in front of me and puts her hand on my arm. "Well, Mr. Grumpy, you can get glad in the same pants you got mad in. Today, I'm letting you and your sister decide where we go."

My stomach does the somersaults it always does when I get excited. "We can choose anything?"

"As long as it's in Shadoebox."

I know I'm smiling even though I'm still upset with my mom. Wrapping my arms around her neck, I rest my head on her shoulder. "Thank you, Cara Jo."

Mmm, she gives the best hugs.

"Alex!" We push apart at the sound of Sasha's enthusiastic voice, as she runs into the kitchen carrying one of her weird outfit creations. "Look at what I made! Aren't they bitchin'?"

Cara Jo's mouth drops open and her eyebrows do that thing where they scrunch together. I always wonder if she gets mad enough, if they will touch. "Sasha Sørensen! Foul language is not allowed, and I know you know that."

She covers her mouth. "Sorry, Cara Jo." The metal of the hangers clank together as she pulls them apart. "Check these out."

Sasha makes me laugh. She's so crazy with her 'fashion' design and trying to talk the way they do on Beverly Hills 90210. She holds up two shirts and I instantly cringe because I know the striped one with the drawn-on collar is for me.

Even Cara Jo can barely contain her smile. "Oh, well those are…lovely dear."

Sasha has a huge grin. She's so proud of these ugly things.

Cara Jo says sometimes people lie to make others feel better and that's okay. I think this is one of those times. "Yeah, they're, uh, great. Good job, Sasha."

"Thank you." She hangs the shirts on the chair and walks to the fridge for some grapes. "What are we doing today, Cara Jo?" Those grapes look good. I take a few of them out of her hand, and even though she pushes me, I still get to shove a handful into my mouth. "Hey, get your own!"

I swallow and laugh at her scowl. "She said we can pick."

Cara Jo dries off the sink before untying her apron. "So, what do you two think?"

I know exactly where I want to go and as soon as I look at Sash, I know she wants to go, too.

"The Walk!"

We point at each other. "Jinx!"

Cara Jo chuckles, "Well, I suppose that's decided."

I'm going to play at the arcade, and get some saltwater taffy, and look at the toy store! There is so much stuff to do at the boardwalk.

"Oh, Alexander! We can wear the shirts I made!" Sasha squeals and claps her hands.

No way, no way. I'll look like an idiot. I feel my head shaking and when I look at Cara Jo, her facial expression tells me I'm going to be wearing that terrible shirt in a few minutes. I better act like I love it, too. I just don't understand why they have to match. Is looking alike not enough?

I try my last chance at saving myself the embarrassment and give Cara Jo my best begging face. Her raised eyebrow is my answer.

"Greeaat."

Sasha shoves the shirt against my chest. "Hurry and get dressed!"

I groan as she sprints out of the kitchen. Cara Jo wraps her arms around me from behind and kisses the top of my head. "You are a good boy, Alexander."

I pull off my jacket as I walk into my room and lie back on my bed. I must fall asleep immediately because that's the last thing I remember when I wake. My clock says it's after eight and Cara Jo is gone when I go downstairs. She left me dinner in the oven, but eating doesn't sound that appealing at the moment.

Blind Mag is sitting on the couch and her ears perk up as I walk by. When is this dog going to be gone? I ignore her and get a beer before running back upstairs to shower. The thought of sitting here getting wasted by myself again, is unbearable, so I get dressed and grab my keys.

The Necco Room isn't a possibility right now, so I pick somewhere random. Ichiban, I think it's called. I sit up at the bar so I can get the quickest service and enjoy the fact that I don't have a single memory of Tavin here.

I'm drinking from my freshly filled glass when a short blonde scoots onto the seat next to me. I smile at her and she instantly returns it. I wonder if she will help. If I bury myself deep enough inside of her, will it numb this ache?

Pointing to her mostly empty martini glass, I ask, "Would you like another drink?"

She bites her lip and nods while I hold up my hand for the bartender.

We talk for a while. Well, she talks, but I can't tell you, for the life of me, about what. And I'm really trying. I'm not sure why it's so difficult to focus.

"Do you want to go?"

I snap out of my daze. "I'm sorry?"

"You know…somewhere more private?"

My head nods before I can consider declining. She grabs my hand and I follow her. God, why am I doing this? I mean, sure she's attractive, but I'm not into her at all. She leads me down the hallway, and I almost tell her to stop. Between the unreasonable guilt and the lack of desire for this girl, I don't think I can go through with it. It's not like I'm gonna ever call her.

I've always assumed the girls I've hooked up with were using me too, but what if I was wrong and trying to ease my own conscience? This girl could be sad or lonely, desperate for some kind of intimacy, and I'll be just one more guy that uses her and throws her away. Is that really the man I want to be?

The door of the club slams behind us as she pushes me against the wall in the alleyway. She kisses up my neck and her nails scratch my stomach as she slips her hand into my jeans. My body is having no problem enjoying itself and currently winning in the battle against my brain. A moan leaves my mouth before I can stop it. The hand that's stroking me is picking up pace and the longer I let this go on, the worse it's going to be.

She pulls my dick out. "Would you like me to suck your cock, Alex?"

No, actually I wouldn't. I just want to go home. I can't believe I'm going to decline this offer. As soon as I talk myself into stopping her, something moves in the alley, making us both jump as she whispers, "What was that?"

Whatever it was, I'm grateful for it and exactly what I need.

"Brooklyn, look, I—"

"It's Brailyn."

"Right, sorry…Brailyn. I'm gonna go ahead and call it a night." Even in the bad light, I can see I hurt her feelings. "Trust me, it's not you, you're… hot, I just have a lot going on and shouldn't be here."

She nods with a confused smile. "Oh…okay…well, it was, uh, nice to meet you?"

"Likewise."

This is incredibly awkward. I'm not sure if I'm supposed to shake her hand or hug her or what, so I opt for patting her on the head like she's a damn poodle. I shake my head at my idiocy and walk back into the club.

I can't believe I just turned down head.

Tavin

This place smells like sex and piss, and the wig Sasha got me itches horribly. I scratch as the blaring music and flashing lights start to give me a headache. I guess I better get used to it though, if I want to work here. I'm nervous and it's making me feel kind of sick. I've never tried to get a job before. Shaking out my hands, I take a deep breath.

First things first, I need a boost.

The girl icon is on the bathroom door to my right so I slip inside and go into the first stall. I pull the little baggie Toben gave me from my back pocket and hold it up. Dang it. I'm already getting low. Sprinkling some on my hand, I bring it to my nose and inhale deeply.

Ahhh, there it is. That's better.

Toben heard the club owner here won't ask questions if I tell him I don't have valid identification. If he likes me, he'll hire me. Hopefully he likes me. I shove open the bathroom door and look around until I see a black sign with white letters at the end of the hall.

MANAGER

I take in a breath and hold it until I tap my fist against the door. *Knock, knock, knock.*

"Yep?" A male voice calls.

I turn the round metal handle and poke my head inside. "Mr. Heder?"

He looks up from his desk and waves me in. "What can I do for you, little lady?"

My hands are sweaty so I wipe them against my shorts as I walk across the narrow office. "H—hi. I was wondering if I could apply…here."

As he smiles, he looks me up and down before bending over to open a drawer. "You're eighteen, right?"

"Yes, sir, I just…I have no way to prove it."

He sighs and closes the cabinet. "Then an application would be pointless." He pushes his glasses up onto his head. "So where are you from?"

"I'm from here."

He rolls his eyes. "Sure you are. If anyone asks, you have all your papers, alright?"

I nod. "Yes, sir."

He leans back in his chair and crosses his arms. "When can you start?"

Does that mean I got the job? Even biting my lip doesn't stop the grin from spreading across my face. I did it!

"Now?"

He chuckles, "Young and eager. I like that. What's your name?"

"Tavin Winters."

He laughs again as he reaches across the desk and grabs a pen. "No, not your real name. What's your stage name, doll?"

Stage name? I have no idea what that is. "I…I don't know."

"Well, what do you like?"

I say the very first thing I think of. "I like candy."

He strokes his beard. "A bit on the cliché side, but it kind of fits you." With a click of his tongue, he holds his arms out. "'Candy' it is. Why don't you get a feel for the place while I tweak the schedule? It won't take long."

I give him my biggest smile. "Thank you so much, Mr. Heder!"

He grins back. "Call me Keith."

Nodding, I back up and leave his office. That was so much easier than I thought it would be. I can't believe I got my own job! I've never done anything other than being Sweet Girl.

I walk in the aisle between the booths and tables, as I count six different stages. Flashing lights make me worried I'll bump into something, so I take careful steps.

The men don't even notice me as they keep their hungry eyes on the dancers. Each girl has her own stage that's littered with money, but there's one girl I can't stop watching. Her short, pink hair reminds me of cotton candy and her body moves like the music is coming from her caramel skin. She has the biggest crowd by far. As her fingers caress her breasts and trail down to her diamond studded belly button, I become self-conscious.

I don't dance like that. Is that how I'm supposed to do it? What if nobody likes my dancing?

"Candy?" A hand touches my shoulder and I turn to see Mr. Heder holding out some papers. "You start tomorrow. I've included the employee handbook along with the schedule." He holds out his hand. "I'm glad you came in. See you tomorrow night at eight."

I slap his hand with mine and I hear him chuckle as he walks away. Looking at the first piece of paper he gave me, I see the name 'Candy' written in little boxes next to the times eight through two, for tomorrow night. My heart thumps with the thrill of knowing I did this all by myself. I turn to the next page and see the rules. I'm really going to get paid to dance. Just dance. That's it. Obviously, I'm expected to take my clothes off, but according to these rules, if anyone touches me, or even makes me feel uncomfortable, they get thrown out. The men aren't even allowed to touch me? Oh yes, I will be perfectly fine here. I'm sure I can learn how to dance like the girl with cotton candy hair. Soon, I will be able to make enough to do…well, whatever it is I decide to do.

Now, maybe, Drew won't be so mean to Sasha. I feel like she gets in trouble a lot because of me. I feel guilty about it, and I don't like him, really. He's mean and he yells at her all the time. I've caught her crying a few times, when she didn't know I was watching.

Sliding my finger beneath my wig to scratch my scalp, I leave the club. The excitement from finding a job wears off, and I hate that the constant uneasiness is back. I haven't stopped feeling nauseated since Friday. At least I have the drugs. As long as it isn't heroin, Sasha won't try to stop me. Speaking of… I take the baggie out of my pocket and inhale a bump.

The strip club is in Shadyside Slums which is good because Logan would never come to this part of town and neither would any of the Clients. It's one of those nights where I can smell the ocean, even this far into the city. I am coked out of my mind, so I decide to walk downtown instead of taking a cab.

Eltsen Street is a popular party scene for Shadoebox, and is lined with bars, restaurants, and shops. Since it's after midnight, I'm thinking walking in the alleyway will minimize my chances of seeing someone I don't want to. I snort one more quick line and make my way down the alley.

It stinks back here with all the business' trash bins, and the street lights are spotty. This has got to be the hundredth building I've passed. I should be getting to the end of the street any time now. It's quiet and I thought I was alone back here so my heart jumps at the sudden movement in the corner of my eye. Stopping in my tracks, I slowly turn my head to watch a couple making out under a streetlight. It's obvious she's jerking him off, for anyone to see. Going back isn't really an option, so being as discreet as possible, I hurry past them.

"Would you like me to suck your cock, Alex?"

It's like an explosion goes off in my brain making it

impossible to move. My feet won't lift off the ground and it sounds like a tornado in my ears. Surely it's a different Alex. That's kind of a common name, right? I scoot a little closer. I don't know why I need to make sure it isn't him. I'm being as quiet as I can when my elbow hits a pole leaning against the trash bin, causing a loud *clang* to echo through the entire alley.

"What was that?" the girl asks.

I move deeper into the shadows, so even though they can't see me, I'm closer than I was, and I see it's definitely Alexander.

My heart falls to the pavement. She's feeling the touch I have ached for. Something's in my throat and hot tears burn my eyes. I don't have a right to the tears, I never have. What is he doing here anyway? I thought he always went to The Necco Room.

My chest is closing and there isn't enough room for the oxygen. I want to go to him. I want to pull that girl off of him. I want to tell him that I'm scared and confused, and that he makes me feel more special than anyone else has ever made me feel, that I never wanted to hurt him, and that I do love him. I want to tell him that I'm sorry for what I am, and that I wasn't strong enough to let him go before this went too far. I want to thank him for everything he's done for me.

As quickly and silently as I can, I slip into an adjoining alley. I know he needs to move on. It isn't fair to not want him with other girls, because it will help him not be sad. He's sad because of me and I hate myself for that.

The thought that maybe I could watch him from afar has come across my mind. Simply knowing that we were breathing the same air would somehow help satisfy this...longing.

Tonight proves that isn't a possibility. I can't watch him with other girls. While I truly do want his happiness, I'm nowhere near strong enough to witness it. I want him to miss

me and think about me, and that's terrible because being
with him isn't an option.

Right now, I need to focus on figuring out what I'm going to do.

Going back with the Clients feels impossible. Even being with Master isn't something I can ever do again. I would
rather die than feel the crawly, terrifying, slime filling my
pores.

If I'm completely honest with myself, I know I'm scared
to never see Logan again. What will it be like to not have
him in my life? More than anything though, I'm terrified
of what he'll do if he finds me. What he'll do if he finds out
everything about Lex.

Then there's the fact that Toben has never once said he
would come with me if I leave Shadoebox. I don't understand why. We finally get an actual opportunity to get away,
and he refuses to discuss it. I don't know what to do.

Entertaining the idea of telling Lex has been fleeting. It
won't accomplish anything besides make everything worse.
I just miss him. I can't get the picture of him in the alley out
of my brain.

The tears won't stop falling even after I get back to Sasha's
and lie down to go to sleep.

*You brought this on yourself. Be grateful you got to feel his
touch at all.*

Wednesday, June 10th

I'm clean out of the coke Toben gave me and I don't think
my stomach can get any twistier. I don't want to do this and
Sasha isn't letting up.

"Good Lord, I'm done arguing with you, Tavin. Call
her." She holds out her phone.

"No." She can't actually force me. I cross my arms. "Don't

you know any other doctors?"

Her nostrils flare. I'm frustrating her, but I don't want to see Marie the Doctor. She'll ask about Alexander and I don't want to talk to her about him.

"Not ones that make house calls and don't ask questions."

I scoff at her. "Marie the Doctor asks plenty of questions."

She looks at me funny and snorts. "I'm sure she's good with plain 'Marie.'" She pushes my legs open so she can see the cut. "You need to get these stitches out. We can't afford to add infection to the list of shit we're dealing with."

Sasha is the first girl I have ever been friends with. I guess there's Misty, Master's assistant, and she's very nice, she isn't really my friend, though. With Sasha I feel like she sees me as the same as her. She knows everything and still wants to be around me.

"I don't think she really likes me."

"She likes you fine. For some reason, she's always had this mother hen thing for Alex. That's how she is. She can be a bit overprotective." She looks at my crossed arms and rolls her eyes. "What if I call her for you?"

We've been arguing forever and I don't like fighting with her. If Marie the Doc—I mean Marie, takes these stupid stitches out, then maybe she'll tell me if she's seen Lex and knows if he's okay. He hasn't texted Sasha or returned her calls. Other than what I watched last night, I have no idea how he is or if he's still sad.

I groan. This is going to suck. "Fine."

She sighs and swipes at her phone. "Thank Christ."

Marie comes over when she gets off work. When she walks in, she looks straight at me and even though she supposedly 'doesn't ask questions', I can tell by her face she's about to start asking them.

"What are you doing over here? Why aren't you at Alex's?"

Told ya.

Placing her bag on the couch, she takes out a pair of blue latex gloves. Her hand presses on my knee to push apart my legs and inspects my cut.

"We, uh…broke up."

I guess that's what you would call it. 'I'm a selfish liar that smashed his heart' is much more accurate, though.

She kneels in front of me and lays down a towel before lining up silver implements on top of it. "I'm sorry to hear that." That's what she says, but it kind of loses its effect when it's said so cheery. She obviously hasn't talked to him if she doesn't already know. "Are you alright? What happened?"

I have to lie all the time and though it may seem like it, I don't actually like to. I'm starting to feel exhausted from it all. Taking a deep breath, I avoid her eyes when I say the words.

"He saw me…with someone else."

There's no response, so I lift my eyes to see her shock. "What?" She glances at Sasha before turning her scowling face back to me. "After everything he did for you?" She's nearly yelling and it makes me involuntarily push myself further into the cushions. I don't know what I should say. "I warned him you were bad news." Her eyes look like they could burn a hole in my face, as she continues setting up. "Alex is one of the best men I know. You have no idea what you fucked up."

The way her eyes get a little brighter when she says his name, her defensiveness of him, and how she looks at him differently when he isn't paying attention… I should have been able to tell before. She'll drop everything to help him no matter what.

She loves him.

She's *in* love with him.

My eyes start to sting with tears because she's exactly the kind of girl he should be with. She's been friends with him for a long time and truly cares about him. She has every right to hate me for what I did and everything she's saying is true, except, I absolutely do know what I fucked up, it's just that it should have never existed to begin with.

My voice is hiding. I try to push it out, and all I can do is squeak, "I know."

She scoffs as she cleans my cut and Sasha leans up against the couch. "Marie, ease up, okay? You don't know the situation."

"Oh? Enlighten me then. I'm sure there is a perfectly valid explanation."

She's using tweezers to lift the string of the stitches, and the scissors are cold as she slides them beneath the string. The sound of the blades closing as she cuts is harsh in the silence. She isn't exactly rough, but she definitely isn't gentle about it.

Sasha sighs and sits next to me as Marie continues her process down the wound. When she tugs on the thread to pull it out of my skin, I swallow back my moan.

"I know we haven't been close in a while, and I know I went off the deep end there for a bit... just please believe me when I say Tavin isn't completely at fault." She glances at me. "She's made some stupid choices, it's just not as clear cut as you think."

Marie rolls her eyes as she places a clear sticky strip over the healing skin. "Yeah, its Alex's fault she can't keep her legs closed."

"Hey!" Sasha snaps.

Marie gathers up her tools, placing them back in her bag. "She screws around on your brother and you put her up in your apartment?" She shrugs. "I guess junkies tend to stick together."

Sasha shoots off the couch. "What the fuck, Marie?" While it's clear she's angry, it still doesn't hide the tears in her voice.

"I'm finished." Marie stands to face Sasha. "You need to find another doctor. She isn't my patient anymore."

"And you need to get out of my apartment. I thought we were friends. You obviously still just see me as needle trash." Sasha shakes her head and all her sadness evaporates. Now she's flat out pissed. "Two years. Next month will be two years, so fuck you."

Marie's face falls and I think she's going to apologize, when instead she turns and walks out. Sasha goes to the door and locks it before slamming her hand against it. She spins around and walks past me.

The light shimmers off her cheeks, from tears. "If Drew gets home, tell him I'm taking a bath."

"Okay," I murmur, even though she doesn't hear me, she's already gone down the hall. Sighing, I sit at the kitchen table and rest my chin in my hands.

Am I ever going to stop messing with these peoples' lives?

Alexander

Cara Jo hasn't spoken to me much the last few days and I still need to apologize. She wants to be here for me and I know I should let her. Right now though, the last thing I want to do is talk about my feelings with her.

I drop my keys in the bowl as I walk into the kitchen.

"Hi. Did you have a good day?"

"I did. Thank you." Her arms are full, so she shuts the re-frigerator with her foot. "There's mail for you on the counter."

She places the items on the island and turns down the hall. Her abrupt responses, short tone, and failing to ask me about my day are all pretty big clues she's still upset. I sigh as I flip through the envelopes, when six words become clearer than the rest.

California   Department   of   Corrections   and Rehabilitation

I'm suddenly conflicted. I want to know what Tavin has lied about, what her story really is. So why is part of me hop-ing he declined my request for visitation?

Tearing open the envelope, I find the signed form and a handwritten note.

Friday, June 12th, between one and four p.m.

Okay, I'm guessing that's when he wants me to visit? Relief battles with trepidation as I walk to the cabinet for a glass. Talking to him will bring me one step closer, but to what exactly?

As I take my drink upstairs, I hear the one-eyed demon's collar jingle, while she follows me to my room.

"Are you ever going to be out of my house?"

Friday, June 12th

Marie gives me an STI test every six months, since I hav-en't been able to keep women off my cock since college. The cute nurse seems to be enjoying herself as she checks my blood pressure and gives me a flirty smile. If this were a few months ago, I would ask her out. Now as it happens, the idea of being inside another faceless girl has completely lost its appeal.

She bends over as she types a few things into her computer. "Dr. Forge will be in shortly."

I nod at her and check the time causing a twitch of slight anxiety at the fact I'm leaving for the prison in a couple of hours.

There's a soft tap on the door before Marie comes in. "Hey—" Walking straight up to me, she wraps her arms around my neck, squeezing tight. I chuckle at her enthusiasm. "It's good to see you, too."

"Oh, Alex, I told you she was messy."

"Whoa, what?" I push her back. "You know about Tav?"

She's gnawing on her lip the way she used to before her track meets. "Her stitches needed to come out."

I completely forgot about her cut. Why doesn't she call her own damn doctor and leave mine out of it?

"Oh, right. Of course."

I want to know how she is and what she said, if she's doing her Sweet Girl thing again. I don't though, because it doesn't matter. My interest is in her past not her present.

Sitting on her stool, she places her hand on my knee. "How are you doing?"

Terrible. I wave her off to add to my convincing factor. "I'll be fine."

With an apologetic smile, she rolls her chair to the computer on the wall. "She's obviously special to you, I just don't really understand why. I know she's pretty and she's adventurous in…" she glances away from me as her cheeks redden, "the bedroom, but she's a drug addicted prostitute with Tourette Syndrome." She chuckles, "And I mean you're…you know…you."

"She has Tourette Syndrome?"

Her nostrils flare as she exhales out her nose. I don't

think that was the part she wanted me to latch on to. "What do you think that little head jerk she does is? It's a tic."

I've noticed it, especially when she's upset or anxious, though I never gave it much thought. It almost seems obvious now.

"Is there anything you can give her for it?"

"There's no need to. It doesn't hurt or affect her. I doubt she even knows she does it. Anyway, she isn't my concern anymore."

The smell of sanitizing solution fills the room as she coats her hands with it.

"You know, I could really use a refill on that Valium prescription…" I mention as casually as possible. She gives a bitchy eye roll and pulls on her blue latex gloves.

The alcohol swab is freezing when she wipes my arm with it. "Okay, Alex, I'll give you one refill so make it last." She pricks my skin with the needle and I watch my blood fill the tube on the syringe. "For what it's worth, in my opinion, she's a sick, young woman. And there's something unsettling about her, it's like I get an odd feeling."

I hate to admit I kind of know what she means. There are times when Tavin can creep me the hell out. She'll say something completely fucked up or will laugh at the most unsettling times. God, I hate that I miss her.

I get a bite to eat and pick up my Valium prescription on the way to the correctional facility. The pills aren't even down my throat when my phone rings.

"Hello, Mr. Sørensen, William Morrison here."

I've been wondering when I was going to hear from him.

"Yes, hi. Do you have anything for me?"

"I'm not sure how much you know already, so I apologize if this is less than informative."

"We can operate under the assumption that I don't know anything."

He grunts. "Okay then. The boy, Toben Michaels. Twenty-three years old…his mother, Korin Michaels, passed away in October of '91 and his father, Jarod Michaels, was most recently seen in Florida." He rattles off the information as I hear his keyboard keys clicking. "He was enrolled in the Shadoebox City public school system until March of 2002, when he was sent to River Forge Academy; a boarding school for troubled youth, in Michigan. He dropped out on his eighteenth birthday."

Wait. Toben went to school in Michigan for seven years? That doesn't make sense. Tavin never mentioned that, and some of the pictures I saw on their fridge would have to have been taken during that time.

His voice changes from reading off the screen as I hear a chair squeak. "Something is peculiar though. This week alone, he's visited three separate corporate establishments and two hotels. I haven't been able to find out why, yet."

"I don't need you to. What about Tavin?"

"She's tough. I can't find a single piece of information on her. Are you sure that's her real name? There was a Brian and Lacie Winters that lived at the address, before Mrs. Winters' death in 2004. Mr. Winters was incarcerated that same year for her homicide. There's no mention of a child anywhere. She also hasn't been at the house. I have yet to see her at all."

She hasn't been home? After the big deal she made about needing to go back?

"That's it?"

"There is one more thing that I found interesting. Did you know the house is currently owned by Logan James?"

All the air seems to get sucked into the vents making it a miracle that I am able to speak. "Logan James of the Rissa

Corporation?"

"Yep. What I find odd though, is that it's owned by him personally, not Rissa."

I'm sweaty, so I crank up the A/C. How is this possible? So many times, my father has tried to get me to meet Logan James, and I avoided it at all costs because of his reputation for being ruthless and crooked. Maybe if I'd agreed to one of those meetings, I would have recognized him at Tavin's house.

That explains the twenty-thousand dollar suit. He's one of the richest men in the world. Why would the chief executive officer of a multi-trillion dollar food distribution company risk dealing in the sex trade?

This isn't adding up, and Tavin not going home doesn't sit right, either. She left me to go back. If she isn't there, where is she? With Logan?

"Is Logan married?"

"Uh…" I hear the *click, click, click* of the keys. "Let's see…Logan James, fifty-five years old…oh, here it is. Yes. Been married for…twenty-five years to Victoria James. They have a boy, Beau, and a girl, Bethany, together."

I wipe my hand over my face as I get off on the exit for the prison. "Okay, thank you, Mr. Morrison. Is there anything else?"

"No, that's it, for now."

Well fuck. Every answer I get brings up fifty more questions. Where the hell is she? I'm trying not to worry, but regardless of how I feel towards her, the idea of her being seriously hurt or worse, is still terrifying.

He's seen Toben though, and if I know Tavin, she isn't far from him.

⌒

I've never been to mall jail much less an actual correctional facility, and meeting Tavin's father is bound to be interesting, so my curiosity is significantly piqued. Visually, the facility isn't far from how I imagined it.

I stop at the gate as an officer signals for me to roll down my window. "ID, please." I hand it to him and he gives it to the man in the booth behind him. "Visiting an inmate?"

"Yes, sir."

The man in the booth brings out what I presume is a drug dog, and then returns my ID. The dog walks around the Alfa as the officer directs me to the visitor's parking. Once I'm cleared, I follow his directions to the correct lot.

As I walk through the entrance, I'm a little surprised at how normal it looks in here. There's a front desk with a female officer and I smile at her as I hand her my ID. Her gaze lingers a moment before clicking the keys on her computer.

"Name, please?"

"Alexander Sørensen."

She smiles at me and holds out my ID with another card. "This is your pass card. Be sure to hang onto it until you leave." A few more mouse clicks and she points behind me. "All right, hon, go ahead and take a seat in the waiting room. They'll call you when it's time for processing."

I nod and sit down. This could be a waiting room anywhere if it wasn't for the metal detector and the interesting posters. You wouldn't believe the things people can transport anally, Jesus Christ.

"Alexander Sørensen?" I jump as I hear my name. I've been waiting for so long, I almost dozed off. I stand and walk to the officer as he lists off a few other names. Once he seems satisfied, he leads us to the metal detector. "Take off your shoes, empty your pockets, and put it all in this bin."

While I don't have any issues, the third woman behind me must have something because the next thing I know, she's being escorted away by two officers as she screams about it being a mistake. Once that little ordeal is over, an officer takes the group down a long, straight hallway lined in doors.

Abruptly, he stops right in front of me and turns. "Inmate's name?"

His gaze isn't directed at me, so I look over my shoulder to make sure I'm who he's speaking to. "Brian Winters."

He holds his hand out behind him. "Second to the last door on the left." I nod and follow his direction.

This hallway is a little more like I would imagine a prison to be, with the whitewashed, brick walls and worn flooring. The officer is guiding the other visitors to their appropriate doors as I wrap my hand around the handle of mine. Once inside, I give my pass card to another officer.

He looks at it and points behind me to a cluster of tables and chairs. "Sit and wait at one of the tables. The inmate is being notified of your arrival."

I do as he says, taking in the scenery of bars on the windows and the Plexiglas protecting the desk.

Yawning, I turn my wrist over to see the time. Christ. This is taking all damn day. I've been here for over three hours.

"A. Sørensen?"

I look up to see the corrections officer directing a man to my table. He's taller than I imagined and probably in his mid-forties. Gray streaks are scattered throughout his brown hair as his scowl appears comfortable in its location.

I stand and hold out my hand. "Thank you for agreeing to see me, Mr. Winters."

He doesn't take it. He gives no response at all as he pulls out the chair to sit. I do the same as I clear my throat and question if this was really the best idea.

Chuckling to himself, he crosses his arms as he leans

back in his seat. "You're telling me that little cunt is actually still alive?"

Shock forces my jaw to drop and I momentarily forget that I'm angry at her. "For the duration of this visit, I'm going to ask that you call her by her name."

"I'll call her whatever the fuck I want," he spats. "Who the hell are you, and why are you here?"

Biting my tongue and swallowing my pride, I remember that I don't have a lot of information resources to be exhausting this one. "Who I am is irrelevant. As I said in my letter, I have some questions, the first one being, why isn't there a legal record of her anywhere?"

He shakes his head as he wipes his nose. "Because Lacie didn't do what she should have and neither did I. One of my biggest regrets is not killing that little bitch when I had the chance."

"Just like you killed your wife?"

I kind of wish I could retract that statement when he flies up to standing, gripping his hands in fists. While I may be bigger and stronger than this asshole, I have the feeling he's a hell of a lot crazier.

"Inmate! Sit down!" The guard calls from behind him.

"I didn't kill Lacie," he bites out.

"Inmate, last warning."

He sits down while glaring into my soul.

"I'm sure you're as innocent as every other upstanding citizen in here."

God, shut up Alexander, just shut the fuck up.

He narrows his eyes at me. "You're here because you need something from me, right? So, I'd think about the next thing you say, if I were you."

I hold my hands up in peace. "Okay, fair enough." He waits for me to continue, and even though it isn't going to tell me what I need to know, curiosity gets the better of me.

"Can I ask what makes you hate her so much? I mean, she's your daughter."

He scoffs, "I loved Lacie, but she was a dumb whore." He reaches up to scratch his jaw, and little flakes of dry skin fall to the table, as he shrugs. "I never liked kids and definitely never wanted my own. When she told me she was knocked up, I was pissed. Abortions aren't cheap and she was too scared to let me use a hanger." He laughs, presumably at my expression, as his yellow fingers scratch his eyebrow. "We were young, she was sixteen and I was eighteen. She told me she wouldn't carry to term, and with all the drugs we were doing, I believed her." The chair squeaks as he shifts. "Needless to say, we were wrong. I found her in the basement one morning, covered in blood with an ugly, wrinkled baby sucking on her tit. *It's a girl*, she had said…" He holds his hands out in front of me. "I remember almost being able to feel her little neck snap as I imagined it. Lacie freaked out when I tried to take her, and the truth is, if I hadn't needed to get to work I may have gone through with it. I figured she was hormonal and exhausted and I thought for sure I would come home to a newborn in my trash can. Obviously, that never happened. She eventually got over the maternal thing, but she never was the same."

While I've heard of people like this existing, on the news and online, those stories always feel far away and detached. I'm sitting in front of a man that fantasized about killing a baby. Whether it was his own child or not, this is as close to real evil as it gets.

My jaw has become concrete. Opening it feels impossible so I grate through my teeth, "How does Logan James fit into this?"

His blue eyes darken as his lip lifts in a snarl. "I worked at the Wentworth Coffee factory in the industrial district downtown. It's a Rissa company." He pauses, raising his eyebrows as if he figured something out and laughs. "That's why you care about all this. You're fucking her."

"And why is that funny?"

"Because the last time I saw her, she was twelve. That's still how I picture her."

My stomach feels nauseated. This man, this life she's from, is so different from what I know as reality.

"You have five minutes, Winters." The guard yells from behind him.

What? No! Shit! I need more time. Brian pushes the chair back to stand up.

"Wait. Please. How did Logan get involved with her? Is he the one who hired her to be the Sweet Girl?"

His face squishes together in confusion for a moment before placing his hands on the table to lean toward me. When he speaks, I try not to focus on the black surrounding his teeth, as the stench of his breath makes me a little light headed.

"I don't know what you mean by 'Sweet Girl'. What I'm sure you want to know will be answered if you get the video tape."

"What tape?" My heart punches against my chest at the prospect of new information.

"Let's just say I never trusted Logan and I wanted something to hold over his head. He blindsided me when he killed my wife, and I never got the chance to use it before being sent here. If he hasn't found it, it's in the house. Upstairs in my old bedroom, in the wall behind the dresser."

"Why are you telling me this?"

"Because that fuck ruined my life and I can't do anything about it while I'm in here."

"Winters! Let's go." The guard calls.

Even after he's gone, I sit at the table for a moment. My father and I have never gotten along, but compared to Mr.

Winters, he's a saint. No wonder she's so fucked up. It doesn't excuse what she did to me by any means, but damn, he's intense. I can't begin to imagine what it was like growing up in a house with him.

Once I'm back on the freeway, my body relaxes. If I never see that man again it will be too soon, so I'm relieved it was informative. I press the call button on my steering wheel, for William's number, and after a few rings it goes to voicemail.

"Hello, William, this is Alexander Sørensen. I've been told there's a video tape inside the house and I need you to get it. It's supposed to be in the wall behind a dresser in one of the bedrooms. If you can't find it there, look everywhere. This is now your biggest priority. Call me if you have questions."

CHAPTER THREE
Gummy Bears

Sunday, June 14th

"A**W, DAMN IT. SERIOUSLY?**"

The trail of mud this stupid dog just tracked in from outside, stretches from the back door all the way to the kitchen. She stands on her hind legs and dances in a circle. "You're not being cute, now stay here."

I walk down the hall to the linen closet for towels. Since it's Sunday and Cara Jo is off, I'm going to have to give the little fucker a bath, myself.

Setting the towels on the kitchen counter, I take off my shirt, so of course when I pick her up, her muddy paws smear all over my stomach.

"Sure, I wanted another shower."

I glare at her and she licks me before I put her in the sink. As I get the water warm enough to spray her, she looks at me like I'm about to take her to slaughter. She isn't making this easy on me and she keeps shaking her body to throw off the water, soaking me in the process. I mumble my complaints as the last of the soap washes down the drain. She shakes as if she's dying from hypothermia and her expression is so sad and pathetic I almost feel bad.

"Oh, come on, you're being a bit dramatic, don't you think?"

I wrap her in a towel and she whines as she presses her body as close to mine as she can. I roll my eyes as I grab a treat from the cabinet. Her head pops out of the towel, and would you look at that—she's suddenly no longer shivering to death. Putting her down, I throw the treat and off she goes to retrieve her prize.

I grab some beer and a bag of pretzels before going downstairs. Even though I know it's been way too long since I've been to Benny's to spar, there's a fight about to start and staying home to watch that sounds much better.

It's still during the prelims when the theater door opens and I turn around to see Silas. I hold up my hand and look back at the fights. "Hey."

"Hey." He sits in the seat next to me and helps himself to one of my beers. "What are we doing today?"

"I'm getting drunk and staying right here. I don't know what you're doing."

He pops the tab and shakes his head. "Oh, my Christ, dude. I've tried to be supportive, but it's been days. I can't believe you are getting this way over a broad. A cheating one at that. You seriously need to get it together. And you look like shit, by the way." He gets up and turns off all my theater equipment. "So, get fucking dressed. We're taking out the yacht." I groan as Blind Mag runs through the open theater door and stands on her hind legs in front of Silas for attention. He laughs and picks her up as he rubs behind her ears. "I thought you said you got a dog? This thing is not a dog. It's a giant rodent."

Blind Mag's tongue is hanging out as she lies on the port side jump seat. "How did you talk me into bringing the fucking dog?"

Silas laughs at me as he polishes off his beer and flips the steaks on the grill. "You don't hate her nearly as much as you're trying to act like you do. Besides, look at her. She's loving this."

My smile makes its way onto my face without my consent. Her tail is wagging and she does look like she's living the high life. To be honest, I'm glad he dragged us out here. Being on the water clears my head and he's putting real effort into cheering me up, so I oblige.

My cell phone rings and William's name comes across the screen.

"I need to take this, I'll be right back." Silas nods and I slip into the galley. "Hey, William, I only have a minute, what do you have?"

"Not much, I haven't gotten inside the house yet. I did, however, finally see Ms. Winters last night. I followed Mr. Michaels into an apartment building he's been frequenting and she was the one to greet him."

"She has an apartment?" Unless Logan got it for her, I'm not sure how she pulled that off.

"No, not her. There isn't a tenant in the building with her name, so she must be staying with someone. I haven't gotten as far as to find out who that is, though. I checked the public records and Logan James neither owns the building nor rents an apartment there."

"Which Apartments?"

"Sinn Gates."

My fucking sister.

All Sasha was supposed to do was get her out of my house, not become damn roommates with her. I can't help feeling betrayed by this.

"That's my sister's place… Is that it?"

"Yes, for now."

"Okay, thanks. Let me know when you get the tape."

"Will do."

I go back up to the cockpit as Silas is taking the steaks off the grill. "Once we're finished eating, we need to go to Sasha's."

"Okay…why?"

"She's letting Tavin stay at her apartment. With Toben. Can you believe that?"

Shaking his head in frustration, he asks, "And how did you find this out?"

I debate lying to him. This reeks of desperation. "I uh… hired someone to look into Tavin."

His head snaps in my direction to glare at me. "I think I might actually kill you. Do you realize how insane that is? You need to let it go. I mean, God, she's literally a prostitute. That right there spells disaster. Be thankful you got out when you did."

"Fifteen years old, Silas. That's how old she was when she started working. How fucked up is that? Her father is a complete sociopath and there has to be more I don't know. There has to be an explanation or a reason for why she did it."

He rolls his eyes as he slaps the steaks onto our plates. "There is no reason. She wanted to get high and she opened her legs for it. The End. You want to believe there's this elaborate explanation because you see her as something she isn't. There are no answers, I'm sorry."

I grab a beer from the cooler and sit back in the booth seat. "How could Sasha let her stay there? With him?"

He slides my plate across the table and sits opposite of me. "Yeah, that part is pretty low. Still, I know the real reason you want to go is to see Tavin, and I'm not letting that shit happen. So forget it. Now let's eat, I'm starving."

Tavin

A sun ray kisses my face, bringing me out of sleep. Toben's arm drapes across my waist and I smile at the comfort of his shallow breathing on my neck. I'm making Drew angry with my nightmares, so they let Toben stay with me when he can. My fingers trace over his scar that's like mine.

When you bleed, I bleed.

Rolling over to face him, I kiss his nose and he scrunches it as he cracks open an eye.

"Good morning, Love." I stretch and it feels so good. It's one of my most favorite feelings in the world. He laughs as he trails his fingers over my stomach. "God, I miss you. Every morning I wake up without you there, I feel empty."

He's made it clear how alone he felt when I was with Lex, and I do feel guilty about it. I knew it would hurt him and I stayed anyway. I never wanted that. I wish he could feel what I did with Alexander, so he could understand.

It's confusing to love two people. I need another word besides love. What I feel for each of them is so different, that the same word can't possibly fit both relationships.

Toben wipes my tears and bleeds my blood. He has seen every corner, crevice, and deranged hallway of my mind, body, and soul. He has been my partner through hell, and my safe place when the pain was too much to bear.

Alexander opens me up and pours in new light. He's the color in Oz. His touch is fire and I could get high on his passion. He makes me want to laugh and sing and dance. I feel beautiful with him. He's a truly good man and those are so much rarer than you can imagine. His slight accent makes my stomach feel like pop rocks and soda and his smile warms my skin. He takes away the grime and filth and replaces it with peace and pleasure. He gives me hope, but for what I'm not exactly sure.

I betrayed them both. The only two people who have ever truly loved me. I've said it a thousand times. I could say it a thousand more and it will never be enough.

"I'm so sorry. For all of it."

His fingers brush over my cheek. "You can still fix it."

I can't give him what he wants. I would rather choke on my own blood.

Hot tears sit along the rim of my eyes. "I'm sorry, Toben, I can't do it. Not anymore." I press against him and hold his hands. "Sasha says we can start a new life somewhere once we get enough money and we can do whatever we want. We can have our own life away from him. What if we can really do this? What if we can really be free?"

He lets go of my hands to grip my face. "Why are you letting them fill your head with this bullshit? We'll never be fucking free, Tavin. We aren't like them. We can't be 'whatever we want' because it isn't up to us. We're his toys and it's what we've always been. It's what we'll always be. There's nowhere else to go and you're making this harder on the both of us."

How does he not understand? He of all people? "Please, don't hate me for this."

"Oh, come on, I don't hate you. I could never hate you." His lips press against mine before he softly kisses my hands. "I love you more than the drugs in my veins and you know that. Of course I would never want you to have to live this life. It's the safest option, Tavin. I don't think it matters where you go, he'll find you eventually. Then what do you think he'll do?"

I press my cheek against his chest; his worn t-shirt is so soft. "I don't know where I'll go or what to do when I get there. I just have to try, but I need you…" I have to know, even if I'm scared of the answer. "If I go, will you come with me?"

He doesn't speak for a long time. I'm about to look up at him when his chest lifts as he sighs. "I know you despise it, but to be honest I don't mind it much anymore. I get as much pussy and drugs as I want and I can buy pretty much anything. The playdates are just my job. So even though I'm not miserable, I would be without you. I'd leave it all to follow you anywhere, Love."

His words help untie the knots in my stomach and all the waiting tears fall at once. Wrapping my arms around his neck, I whisper, "Thank you. I love you so much, Tobe."

"And I love you. More than anything in this wretched world." He kisses me and rolls off the bed. "I have a Client at one so I need to head out, do you want to do a few lines first?"

I don't even know why he asks.

"Oh, yes."

I dry my hair with a towel as I walk out into the living room and see Sasha sitting at the table with a cup of tea. She's been crying again.

With a pretend smile, she looks up at me. "Hey." Her brows quickly knit together as she throws out her arm to point behind me. "Damn it, Tavin. Go put some pants on. I've told you twenty times already, I don't like you walking around in your underwear."

"Drew isn't even here."

"I don't give a shit. Go put on shorts or something."

I cross my arms and huff at her. Maybe if they wouldn't keep it so hot in here, I would wear more clothes. I scowl at her when there is a loud knock on the door.

My heart pounds so hard it cuts off my breathing. Did Logan find me?

We stare at each other for a moment before she marches over to swing open the door. A large *whoosh* comes from my mouth at the sight of Lex's friend, Silas.

"What the hell are you doing here?" she hisses at him.

"What the hell are you doing with *her*?" He points at me without taking his eyes off her. "You're his sister! Can't you stand by him for once in your life?"

"Silas, you don't have a clue about what's going on and neither does he, so just stay out of it."

I have done so much to destroy Lex's life. Yesterday, Drew told me that Bjørn and Caterina are getting divorced because of me. I need to know I didn't do permanent damage and that he's okay.

"Silas?" His head whips in my direction. Within a single stride he's glowering down on me and I can feel myself shrinking. "H—how is he?"

The repulsion in his expression flashes to fury as he takes another step closer. "Are you fucking serious? How the hell do you think he is? He's a wreck. It's been over a damn week and he's still constantly trashed. He barely does his job, or his damn hair, for that matter. He's hurt and confused at how you could do this to him." The clouds in his eyes clear when he leans forward causing me to take a step back. "You need to stay the fuck away from him, you poisonous whore."

"Silas Daniel Hamilton!"

Oh. She's using her super pissed voice.

Standing back up straight, he adds, "And if you decide to keep putting Eric's cock in your mouth, do it outside of the office."

You are a poisonous whore.

"Get out," Sasha grates.

Glaring at me one last time, he spins on his heel. "I'm

gone." As he walks past Sasha, he drops his voice. "And as long as you are helping that bitch, I'm staying that way." He slams the door and she throws up her hands.

"Ugh!"

I sit at the table and rest my chin on my fists. "Look at what I'm doing to your life, Sasha. His life. Your parents, your friends, each other. I'm tearing you all apart. Toben's right. He's always right. I don't belong here. This will never work no matter how much I want it to."

She throws her hand up to silence me. "Tavin, stop it. I don't need you fighting me, too. The only thing that you're doing wrong is not telling Alex. He won't look at you the way you think he will, and he's a big boy. He can protect himself. God knows he has the resources."

"I'm sorry, he won't ever know. You shouldn't know. I'm not doing anymore to ruin his life and that's what it would do if I told him."

"Oh, really? Because you're ruining his life by not telling him."

Well we're going to have to disagree on that.

I really like my job. I make my own money all by myself and the best part is there's absolutely no sex. They can look all day; they still don't get to touch me. I get to dance all night and I've even made friends with a couple of girls.

Sniffing from the coke, I look up at the busted Marvel sign. Some of the red neon letters don't light up and the *B* flickers.

MA VEL GENTLEMAN'S CLUB
EX TIC DANC RS

I push open the doors of the club and I am greeted with

Alia's pretty smile.

"Hey, Candy."

She gives me a quick kiss and holds my hand, leading me to the dressing rooms. I sit on her vanity as she sprinkles a few lines on her mirror, straightening them with her credit card. She opens her purse and takes a dollar from her wallet to roll up. The line vanishes before my eyes. Her nails lightly scrape my fingers as she hands me the dollar, and I bend over to take my hit. The jolt shocks my nerves and the tingles prickle my skin.

Her hand trails across my thigh as she asks, "Do you want to hang out tonight?"

Alia was the first girl to talk to me here and I've always thought she was so beautiful. She colored my hair for me so I don't have to wear the itchy wig and she's always so nice. Even though she touches me a lot, it doesn't bother me. I've never been touched by a woman and it isn't the same as with men. I don't feel dirty when she touches me like I do with the Clients. I don't feel on fire like I do with Lex, either. It never occurred to me that I could actually long to be physically touched. I didn't know how much I needed it until now because I don't remember the last time I was without it.

"Yeah, sure." The air conditioner blows on my shoulder as she stands in between my legs. She isn't as tall as Sasha, even though she's taller than me. Her cotton candy hair is straight and comes right beneath her chin in the front, but when she turns around, it's super short in the back. Her skin is gold and soft and she smells like chocolate. Blue tipped nails tickle me when she runs her fingers higher up my thigh. Silky lips that taste like bubblegum barely touch mine when her tongue softly dances across them.

"I want to taste you," she whispers.

I don't mind the kissing and the touching; I just don't want anyone…there. Lex is the only one I could ever allow to do those things. I kind of like doing things to her though. It makes her feel good and she's my friend so I want her to feel good. I hate to keep telling her no, so I help her forget her question by pulling the cup of her bra down and taking her hard nipple into my mouth. Her pelvis pushes against mine as she moans. I think it worked so I bring my lips to hers.

She knows how I feel and she knows I'm not gay. I don't think I am anyway. It's only about being touched. She brings my hand over her panties, between her legs. "Will you try?"

"O—okay."

The lace feels rough in contrast to her smooth skin. I slip my fingers beneath the fabric and they slide over slickness as I lightly rub her clit. Tenderly pushing my fingers back, I find her entrance and dip them in. It's so warm and slippery. It's like someone is grabbing and releasing my fingers. Alexander always made it feel so good when he did this to me and he did it rough. I push my fingers deep inside her before quickly pulling out and shoving back in hard.

"Whoa! Relax, hon." Taking my wrist she guides me. "Try soft and slow. Like this."

Once I find a tempo she likes, she rocks against my hand. It's fun to watch her wiggle around because I am making her feel so nice. After I do it for a few minutes, my fingers are soaking wet, her arousal dripping down my hand as she grabs my arm and moans.

"Candy, you're making me come," she whispers, as she slides herself up and down my fingers and finishes her orgasm.

The idea of another cock besides Lex's inside me makes me want to carve out my cunt. Sucking another dick seems less appealing than eating a bowl of tacks. A girl is different. I need to be touched by someone and for now, that's Alia.

Friday, June 19th

Alexander

I'm even beginning to depress myself, so I try to enthusiastically agree when my mother calls to invite me for dinner tonight. She's been through a lot and it's the least I can do.

She doesn't get excited about anything, yet she can barely contain her relief when I tell her about breaking up with Tavin. She wouldn't be quite so happy if she found out where she's living, nowadays.

Blind Mag and I have recently come to the agreement that we will, number one, just call her plain Mag, and number two, never, ever mention Tavin.

"So, what do you think, Mag? Green or blue shirt?" She cocks her head towards the green and whines. "Yeah, that's what I was thinking too."

It's not as if I enjoy having her around, she simply isn't a complete nuisance.

Heart-Shaped Box plays as I drive to my parents' estate. Well, I guess it's only my mom's now, since my dad recently moved into his own penthouse.

Baker greets me to park my car and I jog up the front steps, right as Bridget opens the door.

"Good Afternoon, Alexander."

"Hey, Bridget."

Muffled laughing comes from the parlor and Bridget gestures behind her. "Dinner will be served shortly."

"Thanks."

I follow the laughter and as soon as I walk in, four heads turn to look at me. My mother is sitting with a woman about her age, a man who I assume is the woman's husband, and a platinum blonde, twenty-something girl.

Please tell me my mother isn't setting me up.

"Oh good, Alexander, you're here." She sounds unnaturally chipper as she bounds over to me like she's about to fucking hug me. How much has she had to drink? She gestures to the young blonde. "This is Emily."

"Hello. It's a pleasure to meet you."

Emily's voice volume is at the perfectly polite level and her posture shows etiquette training. Controlling the urge to turn and walk right out, I take her outstretched dainty hand.

"Likewise."

My mother continues, "And I'd like you to meet her wonderful parents, Mr. and Mrs. Kempt."

Emily Kempt? No fucking thank you. This is not what I want or need right now. Or ever. She looks like she brings cookies to her church bake sale on weekends for fun. Not my type.

We stand there awkwardly listening to our parents talk for a few moments before Bridget finally calls us for dinner. Because my mother is watching my every move, I pull Emily's chair out for her and take my seat next to her.

Maybe it's because it's been longer than I thought since we've been in a social setting together, but it seems my mother has obtained the gift of gab since my father left. Not that I'm complaining, it allows me to sit here in silence and count down the minutes until I can leave, while she carries the conversation.

Glancing down at my watch, I see I've been here for over an hour. Their fake laughing sounds like nails in a blender, and if it wasn't for the alcohol, I may have shoved a bread roll down Mrs. Kempt's throat just to not have to listen to her talk about her champion poodle, anymore.

I'm thinking of an excuse to get out of here when my mom pipes up. "Oh, Alexander would enjoy that. Wouldn't you dear?"

"Uh, what?"

She narrows her eyes while maintaining her unnatural smile. Definitely one of her more terrifying expressions. "I was saying how wonderful it would be if you could take Emily out tonight to show her around Shadoebox. I think you two will find you have quite a bit in common."

Please. Like what? Having mothers who don't know when to shut the fuck up? I'm impressively believable when I feign enthusiasm.

"That's a great idea. What do you think, Emily?"

She smiles and nods. "Thank you, yes. That sounds lovely."

"Thanks for dinner, Mom. I'm gonna head out." I turn to Emily and do my best to be polite. It's not her fault I'm going through this. "I'll see you tonight."

She enters her number and address into my phone before I say my goodbyes and my mother walks me to the door.

"I really don't need you to set me up, Mom."

She waves me off. "You need to move on from that... *girl.* You won't be able to do that without getting back out there, and Emily is a wonderful, young woman. You can't keep your cake if you eat it all, Alexander."

I snort. "It's 'you can't have your cake and'—never mind. I get what you're saying...I think."

Kissing her head, I bee-line it outside before she gets anymore 'wonderful' ideas.

On my way home, I decide to stop in for a surprise visit at one of the local theaters. There have been some management issues and they won't be expecting anyone from corporate this late on a Friday night.

It's the busiest night of the week, so I go to the supply room until the crowd thins out between showings. I pull open the door to the back offices and run right into a kid carrying gummy bear boxes stacked three, too high. The boxes along with their contents, fly across the floor.

"Oh, damn it, man! Watch where you're going!"

I know my eyebrows fly up. He clearly has no clue who I am.

"I'll be sure to remember that," I look at his name tag, "Tom." Holding out my hand, I smile at him. "Alexander Sørensen."

I internally smirk when I get the desired reaction of a colorless face. I pat his back so he doesn't pass out before bending down to help pick up the candy. The blue boxes of gummy bears are everywhere, and as I reach for one flipped on its back, my eyes instantly snap to the logo. The room blurs around me and I can't pull my eyes away.

A lotus flower. The exact, same lotus flower burned into Tavin's chest and tattooed onto Logan's arm. Beneath it, the red Rissa ribbon logo stretches across the bottom.

This is a product of Lotus Candy Co.
Distributed by Rissa Corp.

What. The. Fuck.

⌒

I pick up Emily at her parents' house. Yeah, that's right, her parents' house. As if this date isn't going to be awkward enough, I have to stand here with her father as I wait for her to be ready. I thought I was done with this horrible part of dating when I graduated high school.

I never thought I would be so happy to see her when she finally comes down the stairs. At least her father spares me the gun jokes.

Once we're out in the car, I ask her, "So, did you have anywhere in mind?"

"How about we grab some drinks?"

For the first time, I give her an honest smile. She read my mind.

"There's a club that opened up a few months ago, I've heard some decent things about. Do you want to check it out?"

She buckles her seat belt and folds her hands in her lap. "You're driving."

We're able to get in and find a table, even with the place packed. I impress myself with my ability to carry on a conversation without the ulterior motive of getting her in bed. I have a feeling that would involve a key to a chastity belt, anyway.

She loosens up a little after a couple glasses of lubricant, and even though the conversation is substandard, it isn't completely boring. I remind myself that I'm doing this to make my mother happy and if I wasn't here, sitting across from Emily, then I would probably be drinking at home. Alone.

As I wait at the bar for our next round, I glance at the dance floor and my attention is caught by a girl dancing, who reminds me of Tavin. Even though my mind's probably playing tricks again, her little, bitty body moves exactly like Tavin's. Her long hair is a pastel purple instead of brown, and Tavin would never wear that outfit she has on. A black skull is on the front of a ripped-up, silver tank top tucked into a tiny, black, high-waisted skirt. Her clunky bracelets are going halfway up her arms and fall when she lifts her hands.

She spins around the guy she's dancing with and he's…
Toben?! Her fingers comb her hair back to pull it away from
her face and even though her makeup is dark and heavy, it's
definitely her.

My feet weigh a million pounds, my skin is damp with
sweat, and the room is spinning. Toben's fingers dig into her
hips and his lips brush against her ear as his hand flattens
across her stomach to press her closer. I can't make myself
do anything other than watch as he puts something next
to her face. She pushes a finger against her nose to inhale
the drugs before throwing her head back and returning to
dancing.

I forget the drinks and go back to Emily to take her
hand. "Let's dance."

"Oh…okay, sure," she says as I pull her from the seat.

Dragging Emily behind me, I watch them and the way
they are together. I've been an idiot to actually believe he
hasn't been giving it to her on a regular basis. He pulls that
terrible colored hair over her shoulder before pressing his
lips to her temple, as her half smile makes its appearance.
Toben lifts a vial from around his neck, unscrews the lid and
brings it to his nose. His head makes a slight jolt before he
hands it to that Christopher kid from their house. Watching
her shove that shit up her nose makes my blood run hot in
my veins.

I maneuver us closer until I'm facing Tavin and standing
behind Emily. All she has to do is look up and she will see
me. Tavin's hand slides into Toben's hair, her fingers clutch-
ing at the strands, and I remember how much I loved it
when she did that to me.

"Ow!" Emily yelps from my nails digging into her waist.

"Shit, sorry."

Tavin takes another hit from the vial and wipes her nose
as her eyes shift up to mine. It's as if the second that never

ends is on a continuous loop until finally, she breaks contact
and her gaze flutters to Emily. Backing up, she bumps into
Toben before turning to run. He starts to follow her, so I step
ahead of him and point a finger at his face.

"You stay here." Turning back to Emily, I tell her, "Give
me a minute. I'll be right back."

She nods in confusion as I follow after Tavin, through
the exit that leads to the alley behind the bar. I push open the
door and seeing her again makes my skin feel hot and clam-
my regardless of the cool night air. Her back is to me, her
hands are clawing at her hair and her shoulders are heaving
with panicked breathing.

"No. No. Shit. Shit!"

Her incredible voice is threatening tears. My pulse is
thrumming so hard I think I can see my skin move. I fight
every cell in my body to not reach out and touch her. I don't
know what I'm going to do when she turns around.

Then she does. I'm so close to her, she almost bumps
into me. Being here with her again brings up every emotion
I've ever felt for her. It's too overwhelming, so I pick what I
have the best handle on.

"Are you still actually expecting me to believe you hav-
en't been opening your legs for him this entire time?" I gesture toward the club when I notice the cocaine residue on
her nose. I reach up and wipe it off. "And I see cleaning up
your vomit was completely pointless." She doesn't respond
and she won't look at me. Does she just not care at all? I've
been a pathetic pile of depression and feeling sorry for myself over a girl who clearly doesn't give a shit. God, I'm a
complete idiot. "You seriously have nothing to say?" I might
as well not be speaking at all because she won't answer. "I
always thought there was something special about you." I
scoff at her and shake my head. "But you're just a fucked-up
mess in a pretty package."

Her gaze is on the ground and her head tics as she barely whispers, "I told you, you didn't want this."

She'll never throw that in my face again. I grab her chin, yanking her head up so she has to look at me.

"You better believe I'll heed that fucking warning next time. Fuck up someone else's life and stay out of mine." I release her face and turn around. "I want you out of my sister's apartment."

I'm glad I saw her. I'm done caring. Done drowning myself in memories that are nothing more than lies. I rip open the door and the music from inside blares in my ears as I pass Toben on the way to Emily.

"She's all yours."

He gives me a questioning glare before waving at Christopher to follow him and turning for the exit. Emily scrunches her eyebrows in question.

My mom was right. I need to move on from Tavin. Why shouldn't I try to do it with Emily? I place my hand on her cheek as I lean down to kiss her.

"Would you like to come back to my place?"

CHAPTER FOUR
VHS

Tavin

WHY DIDN'T I LISTEN TO THEM? THEY ALL SAID it was a bad idea. I just wanted to try to have some fun. I'm so sick of only seeing Sasha's apartment and Marvel. I knew it was a risk because of Logan, I just didn't think anything like this would happen.

I slowly breathe through my nose so I don't vomit. He's never looked at me this way before, not even the last time I saw him. He's seeing what I really am, and his words confirm it. I expected this, but I can still feel my heart cracking beneath my ribcage.

Every word I utter burns as it scratches its way out.

"I told you, you didn't want this."

His eyes take on a darker green as his hand flies out to squeeze my face. "You better believe I'll heed that fucking warning next time." His jaw twitches as he tosses my chin. "Fuck up someone else's life and stay out of mine. I want you out of my sister's apartment."

He hates me and I can see all the pain I've caused him, before he rips open the club door and disappears through it.

Once he's gone, my body heaves with bottled up tears. I

can't stop them. I know I'm being a baby. I knew all of this would have repercussions and the worst of them have yet to happen.

I feel two sets of arms hugging me from the front and the back.

"Are you okay, Love?"

I sniff and nod as Toben presses his head against mine. Christopher's chest is against my back as he rests his chin on my shoulder.

"Well, you know my opinion on the uptight douche."

"Christopher, he isn't a—"

"He has you out here crying in an alleyway. He's a fucking douche."

Toben nods in agreement and kisses my head. Christopher's arm wraps around me so he's holding the vial below my nose.

Thank God for cocaine.

Christopher drops us off at Sasha's apartment, and the girl he met at the club waves to us.

"It was nice to meet you."

I don't know if she's talking to me or Toben, but he doesn't answer her so I say, "You, too."

Christopher drives away as Toben reaches into his pocket, pulling out a works kit. "Logan thinks I'm at a playdate with Mr. Stride, so I can stay with you tonight."

"Whoa, what?"

I grab his arm and he smirks at me. "Mr. Stride likes to watch. I don't tell Logan when he brings friends along to play, and in return, he occasionally schedules fake playdates so I can get an extra night off."

Dang, that's a good idea. I wish I would've thought of something like that. He opens the kit and as soon as I see the spoon, my heart pitter-patters.

"Toben, I told you, you can't bring that into her apartment."

"Then let's go find somewhere to do it."

He's been giving me a hard time about the heroin. He misses being high together and I do too. It just feels like doing it again will make everything with Lex all final. It's already final though, and tonight made that clear. My reason for not using is gone and I've done everything else anyway. I'm tired. I don't want to feel anymore and I need to get his face out of my brain. Cocaine can't do that.

Toben grins because he already knows I'm about to give in. I try to frown at him, but his smiles have always been contagious. Looping my arm through his, I lead him down the street.

"Come on, there's a place back here."

We walk down the block a little ways to cut to the back of the apartments. There's an old couch by the dumpster, and I don't even think it's been rained on yet.

"Gross." He wipes at it like it will make a difference. I sit next to him and watch as he gets everything ready. "Logan would kick our asses for shooting up back here." He chuckles, "Look at us, junkies getting high in an actual alleyway. That's even worse than our parents." I have to admit, watching him prepare the fix makes me nearly salivate for it.

His smile slips away when he looks at me. "Have you thought anymore about what you're gonna do?"

I lean back against the couch and blow my bangs out of my eyes. "The more time that goes by, the more I know that leaving is my only option. I would rather die than go back to Logan and the Clients. I mean that with all my heart."

Sighing, he holds his lighter beneath the spoon. "Okay, so we pick a place…say, I don't know…Denver, Colorado. Say we get there and Logan doesn't find us. What will we do for money?"

"Maybe we could find someone who will let us work under the table, like at Marvel?"

"Okay, maybe." He takes off his belt and hands it to me. "And how long do you think that will take? Remember, we're in a town we don't know and need to stay low, so we don't alert anyone Logan might have looking for us."

Why is he trying to bring me down about this? Did he not hear me? I would rather die than go back.

"I don't know."

He sticks the needle in the mixture, careful not to touch the spoon. "What if it takes a week? A month? Two months?" He wraps his belt around my arm and pulls it way tighter than necessary. "Do you remember what it felt like to be hungry, Tavin? Dirty?" He taps my arm and slides in the needle to pull back the blood, as he stares into me with midnight eyes. "How long will it take before you finally let someone fuck you on a couch just like this one, so you can have a shower or a Goddamn burger?" I hate when he's angry at me. Before I can speak, he presses down the plunger. I look up at the sky, wishing I could see the stars as he snaps, "At least with the Clients we have the contract, and Logan to protect us. Think about what you're choosing."

…I choose to dance with the stars…
WHOOSH…
SWOOSH…I smell his laughter.
BANG…And death is love…

Saturday, June 20th

"Shit! What time is it?!"

Toben flies around the room throwing on his jeans as he shoves his wallet and phone into his pockets. I turn to look at the alarm clock.

"Um… six-twenty."

"Fuck! I have a playdate across town in ten minutes." He leans down and softly presses his lips against mine. "Please consider what we talked about." His eyebrows shoot up as he reaches in his back pocket and holds up a little baggie. "I almost forgot, I brought you something."

Oh, yes! I grin and jump up to give him a big hug. "Thank you." This will definitely help me get through the day.

Sasha is in the kitchen blowing into her blue mug as I lead him to the front door. Neither one of them acknowledges the other besides flipping each other off at the exact same time. I refuse to believe they hate one another as much as they act like, but they are both really good at acting.

He laces our fingers as we press our arms together. "I love you, Tav. I'll be back as soon as I can."

"I love you, too."

He cups my face and softly kisses me for a moment before he opens the door to leave. I close it behind him and when I turn back around, I jump at Sasha standing right in front of me dipping her tea bag in and out of her mug. I don't like how she has her eyebrow arched.

I cross my arms. "What?"

"For two people who aren't fucking, you guys sure are touchy-feely."

I roll my eyes. I need some coffee. "I explained that to you."

"Yeah, I guess." She pulls out a chair and sits in it, cross-legged. "You're looking kind of rough this morning. Are you okay?"

I blow out my breath as I pull the pink mermaid mug from the cabinet. "I saw Alexander last night."

She nearly chokes on her tea before she gapes at me. "No shit? What happened?"

My eyes burn, so I try really hard to keep the sadness

away from my voice. "He told me to go fuck up someone else's life."

She wipes her hand over her face. "Oh, Jesus."

"He knows I'm staying here."

"Shit."

"He doesn't want me to though. He told me to leave."

She scoffs. "He told you what to do in my house? He can kiss my ass."

I force a smile, more confused than ever. I don't know what to do. The things Toben said last night were true. What if my choices get us into an even worse situation? My eyes hurt, my head hurts, and my chest hurts. I'm confused, sad, and scared. I don't want to be here right now.

I think it's time I go on a little trip.

Alexander

Emily is safe and predictable. No scars, no prostitution, no drugs, no fetishes. Just good ol', plain Emily. She doesn't have secrets; in fact, she's an open book. She's the complete opposite of Tavin and exactly what I need.

We eat breakfast in silence while Cara Jo scowls at me and cleans. She'll learn to deal eventually.

Feeling nothing for Emily will protect me. I need to move on and she's who I'm going to do that with. I may not ever really be happy and I'm prepared for that. It sure beats going through what went down with Tavin again.

Oddly, Mag didn't come around at all last night and is finally making an appearance this morning.

Emily removes the napkin from her lap and places it on her plate before standing. "Well, I need to get going. Tennis lessons at two."

I stand to follow her to the entryway as her heels *click* on the tile. Mag trots out in front of her as we walk to the door, making Emily cover her nose and gasp, "Ugh, what's wrong with its face?"

I don't know what shocks me more. The fact that she said it or that it pisses me off she said it.

"Nothing's wrong with her, she just lost her eye."

Grimacing at Mag before kissing me, she asks, "Are we still on for brunch with my parents, tomorrow?"

I nod and let her out. Mag whines at me as I pass by her water bowl, to go back into the kitchen. "What? You don't like her?"

"I know I don't."

"Don't hold back, Cara Jo."

She maintains her glare as she cuts up the onions. "You can't imagine how much I'm holding back."

I need to get Tavin's things out of here, so I grab the box from the closet and carry it down to the garage to take out to the trash in the morning.

It's a nice day, so I throw on my swim trunks and take Mag out to lie by the pool. Sometime after she falls asleep on my legs, my cell rings and I lift my sunglasses to see it's William. I haven't decided what I'm going to tell him yet, all I know is, after last night, his services are no longer required. It doesn't matter anymore. I don't know why I ever thought it did.

"Hi, William, I'm glad you called."

"Hello, Mr. Sørensen. I got your message about the Lotus Candy Company, I'm just not sure what you're expecting me to find. It's a division of Rissa Corp. and was founded in May of '91. I could give you a bunch of facts, though it's all public knowledge. What I think you really want to know is, I found what you were looking for. Right where you said they would be. There are actually two of them, both unmarked. I can bring them to you if you can get a VCR."

I inwardly groan to myself, wishing I could tell him to forget it, because I still want to know. I still want answers to my questions and I still want to understand.

I sigh, "Yeah, I can get one. Go ahead and bring them by."

Mag jumps up as I move to go inside, following me all the way into the kitchen. I still have a VCR in one of the guest rooms, and while Cara Jo gives me a curious expression as I carry it downstairs, she doesn't ask questions. I hook it all up and it's all set by the time the doorbell rings.

Cara Jo has already let William inside and is grilling him by the time I get back upstairs.

"Thanks, Cara Jo, I got it."

She keeps her stare on us for a moment before disappearing back into the kitchen. She's only here to make up the hours for when she goes on vacation, and now I'm wishing I would have just paid her the difference.

"Hey, thanks for getting these. I know breaking and entering was asking a lot."

He hands me the tapes with a shrug that suggests this wasn't his first time. "Once I was inside, it was easy. I hope they're what you're looking for."

"Yeah, me too." I shake his hand. "Thanks again, and if I need your services again, I'll let you know."

"I would appreciate that."

Closing the door behind him, I walk back through the kitchen as Cara Jo inevitably asks, "What are those?"

"Hopefully some answers." She's obviously biting back her questions, so I take advantage of her silence to add, "You're good to go if you want. I'll pay you for the rest of the day."

She's caught off guard enough to forget her curiosity as she says, "Thank you, Alex."

Once I'm back downstairs, I turn the tapes over. There's nothing to tell them apart so I pick one and push it into the player. After a few moments of white noise, the times stamp reads *March 4, 2002*.

With my whiskey bottle in my hand, I sit back in the seat. Tavin's bedroom flashes onto the screen, and from the view, I would guess the camera is high on the wall or even on the ceiling, allowing me to see across the entire expanse of the space. The room looks the exact same as it does now, other than the missing washer, dryer, table, chairs, and dog cage. The camera is a little shaky and at first glance, the room looks empty, until the shot comes into focus and I spot her huddled in the corner behind a stack of cardboard boxes. Even on the grainy film of old technology, I can clearly see her little body shivering.

A rustling sound of the camera shifting is the only noise before her father's face takes up the view of the camera. Though he's much younger, as he backs away, I see his size and aggression haven't seemed to have changed much over the years. He screams into the seemingly empty room, *"Goddamn it, Tavin! Get the fuck out here!"*

I watch as little Tavin tries to back up further into the corner and ends up knocking down a few of the boxes, in the process. Brian's head snaps in her direction before he storms across the room to reach down, grab her, and toss her on the floor behind him.

"Every time with this, you stupid little cunt!"

He's screaming so loud at her, and I flinch when he brings a booted foot down on her back. She pleads through her sobs, *"Daddy, please! Stop!"*

This is incredibly difficult to watch. Though I had pretty

much assumed abuse, actually witnessing it is something else altogether. The sickness in my gut feels as if it's spreading throughout my whole body.

"I swear you like getting the shit beat out of you!" He kicks her in the ribs as her wails cause fissures in my heart. *"How many times do I have to fucking repeat myself?"* Dropping to his knees, he emphasizes each word with a punch somewhere on her small body. *"Do. Not. Call. Me. Daddy!"*

"I'm sorry!"

Her words come out strained and choppy as she curls her body into a tiny ball. Speaking with him at the prison made it clear he was a horrible person, but looking at her, so small and innocent… how could he hurt her?

She's shaking as his shadow consumes her tiny frame, and she flinches when he reaches down to pull her up by a fist full of hair. Dragging her to the bed, he picks her up only to slam her down hard on the mattress. She's struggling to sit up as he reaches into his back pocket and throws something at her.

"*Make it fucking quick,*" he snaps.

The mattress sinks beneath his weight as he sits down, causing Tavin to lower with it. He rolls up the sleeve on his right arm as she sprinkles what I presume is powdered heroin into a spoon. Brian ties off his arm while she holds a lighter underneath the mixture.

She can't be more than nine or ten when this was recorded and she knows exactly what she's doing. When I was ten, I thought I was special because I could belch the entire alphabet.

Once she gives him his fix and his limp body falls against the bed, she cleans up the paraphernalia. When she finishes, she sings and talks to herself like kids do, as though nothing had happened.

I fast forward a little more until I see Brian begin to stir.

Her head lifts up to look at him from her place on the floor before she gets up and runs out of the shot.

He becomes lucid, screaming for her and throwing things around before he gives up and climbs the stairs. Fast forwarding again, I reach the end of the tape and Tavin never comes back.

She's been exposed to drugs her entire life. It makes sense she would use as an adult. I release a big breath to give myself more room to breathe.

As terrible as that was to witness, it isn't really beyond what I had guessed already.

Ejecting the cassette, I switch it for the other one and shove it into the VCR. The date on this one is time stamped *March 6, 2002*. Only a couple days after the first.

Considering the disturbing contents of the previous video, I take a big swig of whiskey to prepare for whatever's coming with this one.

Her room once again comes onto the screen. She's sitting on the floor, singing to herself as she draws on one of the sparse pieces of sheet-rock behind her bed. Eventually, she gets up and pushes her bed to cover up her picture and turns on an old radio. *Blurry* plays as she dances around and sings along. Even though I'm angry and hurt, watching her makes me smile.

She grew up with an abusive monster of a father, yet she still found enough beauty in the world to sing and dance. After a while, I fast forward until I see child size Toben come into the picture. He had to have come in through the window-well because he enters from outside of the frame.

"Toben!" Her voice sounds completely different than it does now. Her young voice was much higher pitched. She hugs him as they sit down on her mattress. *"Look what I made!"* She reaches under her bed and pulls out two rags, holding one out to him. *"A prince doll for you and a princess*

one for me!"

"Tavin, boys don't play with dolls."

Her gaze falls to the floor as her shoulders slump. *"Oh."*

He puts his arm around her and scoots closer. *"Ah, come on, don't be sad. You need to practice reading first, anyway. Then I will play with the dolls, just don't tell anyone."*

She looks up at him with a pout. *"I don't want to read."*

"And I don't want to play with dolls, but I'll do it for you if you read for me."

She throws herself back on her bed and groans, *"Okay, fine."*

He smiles and pulls some books from his bag. He's incredibly patient with her and helps her sound out each word when she gets frustrated. Afterward, as promised, he plays with her rag dolls.

I'm enjoying seeing into her past in a way I never thought possible, when a creaking noise quickly transforms into banging. They both look up toward the stairs as two men enter from the stairway. One of the men is carrying the big dog cage while the other has a large duffle.

The moment I realize the identity of the man with the bag, I can't seem to move a single muscle in my entire body.

Logan must be in his mid to late thirties at this time, and while he's still tall and lean, his hair is darker and his skin is much smoother.

The other man in the shot, sets the cage on the floor as he places a tin coffee can next to it. He's similar to Logan in age and size, though he's significantly shorter. Logan drops the bag on the floor and strolls up to Tavin and Toben. With his hands on his knees, he leans forward to be eye level with her.

"Do you remember me?"

She nods. *"Yes."*

With a smirk, he asks, *"Do you know what it means to*

buy something, Tavin?"

"It means it's yours."

"That's exactly right." He playfully bops her on the nose. *"And you are my newest purchase."*

My mind catches up as I watch him throw her to the floor. Toben flies off the bed to attack him, and is abruptly knocked back by the other man punching him in the chest. It doesn't stop Toben though, he jumps up to fight them both. It's heartbreaking to see this little kid trying to protect her as Logan wraps his hand around his neck and lifts him by the throat. He carries him that way to the wall with Toben kicking and fighting the whole way.

"NO!" Tavin screams as she lunges after them. The other man walks up to her and backhands her so hard she's thrown back to the floor.

"Not the Goddamn face, Kyle!" Logan growls as he slams Toben's head against an exposed 2x4.

I don't hear the things he whispers to Toben. Whatever it is, immediately causes him to cease his fighting. Logan drops Toben's body to the floor and strides back to Tavin.

"Your life is about to change, my little Lotus." He yanks her to her knees by the front of her dress, causing her head to snap with the force. *"Put your hands on your thighs."* As she obeys, he smiles. *"You will become well accustomed to this position."* Kneeling down to her level, he continues, *"If you comply, things will be much easier for you. Now take off your clothes."*

My soul splinters as I watch her head tic. *"W—why?"*

"Because you are my new toy and I want to play."

I literally can't make myself react. It's as if I'm not able to process exactly what I'm seeing. I know what I'm watching, but this isn't real.

It can't be real.

How many times have I said I want to know her secrets?

This is what I thought I wanted. It isn't. I don't want to see this.

He doesn't wait for her to obey as he pushes her onto her back. She kicks and fights and I think she bites him because he pulls his arm back before he yells, and knees her in the stomach.

"*Tavin!*" Toben cries from across the room, as Kyle holds him back.

Logan whips his head around and barks, "*Come here.*" Kyle releases Toben as Logan adds, "*Hold her down.*"

Toben is crying and shaking as he kneels behind her and holds her arms over her head. He keeps his mouth next to her ear as his lips move quickly with inaudible words.

My eyes go back to Logan who's digging through the black bag. He takes out a stethoscope and kneels in front of Tavin, to press it against her chest. Her body expands as she breathes in as hard as she can. More than I've ever wanted anything, I want to climb through the screen and save her. To stop this.

"*This shit gets me so fucking hard.*" Logan grins back at Kyle, who chuckles in response. Dropping the stethoscope to the floor, he undoes his pants.

Fuck. Fuck. FUCK! I squeeze my eyes shut and push off the seat. I can't do it. I can't watch anymore of this.

I make my way to the bar as her little screams fill the theater. I wouldn't be able to stop the tears pouring down my cheeks even if I wanted to.

"*Look at me!*" He screams it at her over and over and over as she cries the most haunting cries I've ever heard.

"*Toben! Please Toben! Why won't you help me?!*"

She's pleading with him. She's so young and scared. She doesn't understand that he's as helpless as she is. Watching her thrash while she had her nightmares runs through my memory. She would always scream his name and this is why.

I'm only able to manage glances at the screen for seconds at a time. It feels wrong to fast forward through it when she actually experienced it. This is the closest I will ever come to understanding her.

Toben's face is twisted as his lips move feverishly in her ear. She continues to scream his name, and every time she does, Logan hits her. Kyle stands in the corner with his arms crossed, watching until Logan turns to him.

"Get it ready, but not too fucking much this time."

Kyle grins before bending over the duffle and removing a small bag. He empties its contents on Tavin's night stand and as soon as I see the spoon, I know what he's doing. He's going to inject her.

That's exactly what he does, and in a way, I'm grateful. The way she describes the high sounds peaceful, and this little girl needs some fucking peace. Almost instantly after he pushes the drugs into her body, she vomits all over Logan. His hands grab her ears as he slams her head against the floor.

"Fucking bitch!" He screams as he rips off his shirt and storms back to the bag. He wraps three small chains around his hand before returning to swing them down onto her limp body. I squeeze my eyes shut, and if anything, it intensifies the sounds.

For over an hour, they destroy her flesh. They cut, rape, and beat her. It's nothing short of a miracle that she lived through this. The bile burns my throat and I barely make it to the sink at the bar.

Finally, her body stirs as she regains some consciousness.

"We're almost done for today, little Lotus. Now it's time to exchange gifts."

Logan stands and once again returns to the black bag as Kyle kneels next to her. My eyes bounce between the two men, not knowing who will be the next one to hurt her. I look back at Logan and he's holding a long piece of iron and a blue blow torch, watching the flame lick at the metal.

Fuck. Her brand. This is how she got it. Kyle wipes her chest with a cloth, while the iron in Logan's hand begins to glow red. Glaring at Toben, Logan orders, *"Hold her tight."*

The hot metal touches her skin, and with surround sound, I can clearly hear it burn. She doesn't scream and she doesn't cry. She barely moves at all as Logan lifts his head toward Toben.

"Take off your shirt and get on your knees with your hands behind your head."

I'm horrified for him. He's a child living through what I can hardly watch as an adult. He obeys and he lifts his shaking hands behind his head. Kyle cleans off his right shoulder with the cloth before Logan uses the blowtorch to heat the iron once again. I didn't even know Toben had a brand.

His agonized bellows cause the glasses on the bar to vibrate. *"MOTHERFUCKER!"* His young voice screams.

Logan points a threatening finger and warns, *"Stay."* He picks up a knife from the bag and smiles at Tavin. *"You will always have a part of me. Now it's my turn to keep a part of you."*

He holds the blade over the flame for a couple minutes before he kneels down to pick up her foot. He's carving into her and she barely makes a sound. After a moment, he holds up a piece of skin to inspect it. His hand reaches into his pocket to pull out a silver locket and gently places it inside. Toben is rocking Tavin in his lap and weeping into her hair. I rub my hand over the sharp ache in my chest.

"Get in the cage." Logan's voice is calm and slow. Speaking as if he has all the time in the world.

"Fuck you!" Toben screams.

Smiling, Logan pushes open Tavin's knees as he holds the knife between her legs. *"You want to say that to me again?"* Toben frantically shakes his head. *"Then get in the fucking cage!"*

Toben scrambles to obey as Kyle kicks him inside and locks it.

Logan wraps Tavin's foot in gauze while she lies there unconscious. Once her foot is wrapped, he picks her up and puts her in bed. As he stands over her, he reaches into his pocket, and when I see what he's holding, I scoff and I rub my hands over my face.

It's a fucking lollipop.

Placing it on the pillow next to her head, he brushes the hair away from her face.

"You were a very good girl, today."

He kisses her forehead before picking up his bag and climbing up the stairs. Kyle follows behind him, and a moment later, the closing of a door sounds. Seconds of silence fill the room before Toben slams his hands against his cage.

"Tavin!" He's crying and shaking the cage trying to figure a way to get out. *"I'm sorry, Tavin. I'm so sorry".*

She never answers. She stays in the same position while he cries for her until finally the tape runs out.

Even when there's nothing other than white noise I can't move. I feel sick. I mourn for those children and the adults they've become. There's a physical heaviness in my chest pulling me to the floor. I'm so deeply...sad. I want to scream for these kids. I want to kill for them. I've never seen anything so heinous and obscene before. My feelings for Toben have changed one hundred percent, in the last hour. Their relationship, the way they are, makes exponentially more sense.

I'm not a crier. My father taught me that men don't cry, so it's been a very long time since I have, but in this moment, the tears won't stop.

How could she not tell me?

I know there's rage present for Logan and Kyle, I simply can't grasp onto it right now. I can't even think about it really. All I can think about is holding her as tight as I can. I want to kiss her and plead for her to forgive me. I need her to know that I'm not walking away from this. If she doesn't want to be with me, it will kill me, but I'll understand. I'm not going anywhere until I know she's permanently away from him. That she's truly safe.

No wonder Toben doesn't like or trust me. Who knows what they have been through these past thirteen years. To him I'm just another man who wants to use his closest friend.

My fist raps on the splintered wooden door and it's only a moment before it swings open. Toben stands there wearing nothing other than jeans and a stocking cap. There's a long, old wound that stretches across his chest and when I look to his forearm, he has almost the exact same scar as Tavin, right above their matching tattoo.

He glares at me through clenched teeth. "She's not here and that's because of you. So 'fuck up someone else's life' as you so eloquently put it, and leave her alone. She's not meant for you."

He tries to close the door when I wrap my arms around him. The raised skin of the brand on his back is smooth beneath my fingertips.

"What the f—"

His body tenses as he presses his arms flat against his sides. It's the most awkward hug I've ever been in. I just don't know how else to express what I'm feeling. Any words I think of seem inadequate.

"I've seen the tape."

He still looks freaked out from the hug. "Uh…what tape?" I don't know if he's playing dumb or if he really doesn't know it exists.

I slide past him to go inside. "I just need to see."

If I see her drawing from the video, with my own eyes, maybe this will all sink in and become real enough for me to process.

"Hey! What the hell are you doing?" He yells after me as I barrel down the stairs. As soon as I step onto her concrete floor, I notice the old blood stains scattered across it. Marching to her bed, I pull it from the wall. His footsteps are behind me when he snaps, "We don't let people down here."

Her art is here, though it's nothing like what was on the tape. There's such a small space to work with that she's drawn on top of what was already there, many times over.

"You were kids," I whisper it so softly, he probably doesn't hear me. "You were just fucking kids."

I can feel his glare even before he walks in front of me and gets in my face. "Tell me about the motherfucking tape."

He really doesn't know. "He recorded it."

Abandoning his anger for frustration, he throws his hands in the air. "Who recorded what?"

"Right where we're standing. This is where it happened, isn't it? The day Logan came down here with that cage and destroyed your lives." I shake my head to try and erase the images in my mind. "I can't believe he made you hold her down."

His chest rapidly rises and falls as he stands there staring at me. As I turn back to her bed, something on the floor catches my attention. At first, it looks like a regular belt, until I pick it up, then I see there are about a dozen little needles protruding from it.

I run my fingers over the sharp points as he says, "It goes around her thigh. The tighter the belt, the deeper the wounds."

He says it as if he's giving me facts about the history of

toothpaste. How can he be so passive about this? He's right though, it matches her dotted scars. The needles are spaced further apart on the belt then they are on her thigh, so it must have been used on her repeatedly over time in the exact same location.

"I don't understand. Why would she want to come back here?"

He shakes his head with a growl. "You keep asking your questions, you keep on digging. So while we're on the subject, how the fuck did you get a hold of a tape like that?"

"No, Toben. No more skirting answers. Tell me. Why would she leave me for this?" I hold up the belt before tossing it on the bed.

"I'm warning you, one last time. Get out. Leave us alone and go on with your uptight life. You don't want any part of this."

"Can you not hear through that beanie? I'm not going anywhere, Toben. I fucking watched it okay? Now tell me why you two are still with him."

His jaw twitches as he pulls out a cigarette and lights it. "Whatever you saw was only a piece. A snapshot. The very beginning, from the sound of it. You still have no idea what you're stumbling into."

"I'm sorry, this shit gets worse?"

His eyes take on a cast as a dark smile lifts his lips. "Oh, it can always get worse."

CHAPTER FIVE
Marvel

"HOW MANY TIMES DID THIS HAPPEN?"

He tugs on his beanie and shrugs. "How many hallways are in hell?"

"You're quite the cryptic little asshole, aren't you?" He laughs and takes another drag. "I will make them pay for this, Toben. I swear."

"Yeah, okay." He scoffs and rolls his eyes.

His patronizing tone makes me want to smack him over the head, so I take a deep breath and remember how much he's suffered.

"I know you don't trust me and that's fine, I just need you to understand that I'm not backing off until this is over."

He takes one last drag before snuffing it out on the concrete floor and turning around to climb up the steps without so much as a 'goodbye'. I kneel on the floor in front of her picture and trace my hand over the marker, crayon, and pencil marks. If I look closely, I can make out images. Faceless girls and body mutilation among rainbows, stars, and flowers. Resting my head against the wall, I whisper to her. Who she was, and who she is.

"Please forgive me. I'll never hurt you again. I swear."

The traffic is light enough that even though Sinn Gates apartments are on the other side of town, it isn't long before the apartment number *13B* is staring me in the face.

Tavin has to hate me. Those things I said to her were terrible. I need her to know that I'm behind her no matter how deep this horror show goes. She needs to know that I'm so fucking sorry and I don't care how long it takes, I will prove to her that she can trust me.

With a large breath, I finally lift my hand and knock. Sasha swings the door open so hard it blows her hair back. I'm impressed with how well she covers her surprise.

"What are you doing here?"

"I need to see her."

Her lips release a nervous laugh. "Now isn't the best time, Alex."

It's either the look on her face or how she says it, that makes me realize Tavin is here with someone. While I may not have a right to be angry about it, I sure as hell can stop it right the fuck now.

"Where is she?"

She sighs and holds her hand out to let me pass. "In the one on the end."

My heart is pounding so hard I can hear it while I walk down the hall. The glass doorknob creaks a little as I open the door to see her sitting on the floor. Alone.

Oh, thank Christ.

One of the knots in my stomach loosens as I slowly walk inside. She's in a sheer, purple t-shirt and panties, with her knees pressed to her chest, as she leans against the side of the bed. She ignores me as she focuses on her left hand, holding it out in front of her as if she's examining her nails.

"Tavin?"

Simply laying eyes on her puts a strain on my breathing. She survived that nightmare. She's so much stronger than I thought. I got angry that she wouldn't talk to me when she was trusting me as much as she could. She did love me and I fucked it up. After everything she's been through, she's still capable of love. Her life is filled with horrible people, yet her heart remains pure.

Kneeling in front of her, I reach out to touch her face. I miss her so damn much. Her gaze slowly lifts to me and her pupils are the size of pinpoints. She swipes her hand in front of my face.

"Look," she whispers, and lets out a breathy laugh.

What's she on now? I've always assumed her addictions were her choice, when in reality, they were forced onto her. And even if they hadn't been, after knowing what I know now, I can't blame her for needing an escape. I brush my thumb across her soft lip. Being able to touch her again does wonders for calming my nerves. I press a kiss to her temple and stand, before closing the door behind me. I'm obviously not going to get anything out of her right now, and my sister has some questions to answer.

Sasha's back is to me when I walk out from the hall. "What the hell is she on?"

Without looking up from the cup she's rinsing, she waves me off. "Oh, she dropped acid this morning."

My jaw drops at not only her statement, but also her lack of concern. "Fucking Acid? You allowed that?"

Her head snaps up at me and she waves a finger. "Oh, no. Hell no. You don't get to show up now and be conde-scending. You have no idea what it's been like over here." She dries her hands on a towel before resting them on her hips. "Do you want a beer?"

"Unless you have something stronger."

She opens the cabinet and takes down two glasses.

"Between the drugs, the nightmares, and the late nights, things have been a little rough." The bottle scrapes across the wood of the table as she pushes it towards me. "Besides, it's probably your fault she's in there like that anyway. I can only imagine how shitty you were to her last night."

I groan as I pour our drinks. "Believe me, I know."

Her fingers lightly tap the glass for a moment before she blurts, "Why are you here, Alex?"

Slouching in the chair, I rub my eyes with my palms. "I put together some incredibly disturbing pieces of her puzzle tonight. I need to talk to her and preferably when she's not on an LSD trip."

Her mouth drops open before she covers it with her hand. "Oh my God…what do you know?"

"What the fuck do *you* know? She told you?"

Softening her voice, she tilts her head. "Alex…"

She trusted her, not me. Why? What do I need to do to get her to let me in?

"How could you not have told me, Sasha? How long have you known?"

"If you haven't noticed, this whole situation is a bit convoluted. She's terrified and doesn't know what to do. Frankly, neither do I. According to her and Toben, Logan is as dangerous as he is rich. She's scared he's going to kill her and do the same to us if he finds out we've been helping her." She taps her temple and whispers, "There are things…going on up here, Alex. She thinks that if you know about her, you will see her the way she sees herself. All her self-loathing is so much more than low self-esteem. It's been drilled into her head as fact, her entire life." Her fingers wrap around my hand and squeeze. "She wasn't sober when she told me or else she wouldn't have." She's saying that to make me feel a little less hurt, but it doesn't work. "It was the night of the dinner nightmare at mom and dad's. She was an emotional

disaster, and it was like it poured out of her. Once she started telling me, she couldn't stop. I'm sorry I didn't go to you,
I was only doing what I thought was right. I honestly did
think she would tell you, eventually." She crosses her arms
and narrows her eyes at me. "How did you find out whatever
it is you know, anyway?"

I never realized how creepy this sounded, until Silas
found out that day on my boat. "I hired someone. A private
investigator…"

She snorts. "No you didn't."

"…And I went to the Shadoebox Penitentiary to speak
with her father."

Her eyes widen and her mouth forms and O. "No you
didn't."

"Yeah…that was a colorful experience."

She flaps her hand in front of my face to hurry me along.
"Well? What did he say?"

I debate whether to tell her. I don't want to lie to her, but
I don't want her telling Tavin because of her loyalty to her,
either. The words decide for me as they come out on their
own.

"He…recorded what Logan did to her. He was obviously
aware it was going to happen. He told me where to find the
cassette."

She gapes at me as she realizes what exactly that entails.
"Holy shit."

"You have no idea." I am wound up so tight that I pour
another drink. "Logan fucking James. I can't believe that's
who we're dealing with. Do you know everything? What
happened between then and now?"

She expels a harsh breath. "All I know is the cliff notes
version. It still doesn't feel right telling you anything until
she knows what you've seen."

"She can't know about the tape, Sash."

"Alex..."

I have zero energy to argue with her right now. This isn't up for a debate. "What do you think her seeing it, or even knowing about it, would do to her? Just do what I say and don't mention the fucking tape, alright?"

She holds her hands out in front of her chest. "Jesus, alright."

I'm so damn tired. I look at the clock on the microwave and it's only six fourteen. "How much longer is she going to be *Fear and Loathing in Las Vegas*?"

"It should only be another hour or two. She took it around six this morning."

"Holy shit." I look at my watch to make sure her microwave clock is right. "That was twelve hours ago!"

"Yeah, the little bitch waltzes into my room this morning and says, *'Hey, Sasha, I just dropped some acid, so I'll be trippin' for a while.'* Then she walks away like she told me she was going to take a shower."

I actually laugh. With Sasha mimicking her, I can picture it so perfectly.

No matter how many questions I ask, Sasha still won't tell me anymore than I already know.

We're still sitting at the kitchen table when I hear footsteps coming down the hall. My throat closes before I even turn to see her.

She's roughing up her pastel hair, that if I am completely honest, I absolutely hate, and hasn't changed from her underwear and t-shirt. She looks as gorgeous as ever while her drowsy gaze remains on the floor and she opens the fridge.

"Oh my God, Tavin!" Sasha yells. "Would you please put some damn pants on? How many times do I have to tell you? I don't like Drew seeing you like that."

Yeah, I don't like Drew seeing her like that either.

"Fine." Mumbling under her breath she adds, "It's hot and he isn't even here."

She slams the refrigerator shut as she gulps down a bottle of water. She lowers it from her lips and when she wipes her mouth, our eyes connect. Neither of us moves for a moment until a cloud of despair darkens her face. Let me tell you right now, you never want to see the girl you love, look at you like that.

She backs up a couple steps before turning around and sprinting back down the hall. I jump up behind her, catching up with her at her door.

"Hey, hey, hey, Tavin, stop." I hold her shoulders as I watch her shrink into herself. "Please, look at me."

She finally brings her eyes up to mine. While she isn't crying yet, she doesn't look like she can hold back much longer. I reach out to touch her and she fucking flinches. If I'm not feeling shattered enough tonight, that does it.

I have so much to say with no idea where to start, so I go with what I feel is most important. "I am so, so sorry. For everything I've said and done. All of it. I'm so damn sorry, Tav." I press my head against hers and whisper, "I love you. I never stopped loving you, I swear."

Her chest rises with choppy breaths as she looks at me with glossy eyes full of confusion. "Nothing's changed, Alexander."

Shaking my head, I cup her face. "Everything's changed." I take the bottle of water from her hand and lead her into the bedroom, closing the door behind us, and setting the bottle on the dresser. I lightly trace my fingers over her shirt where I know her brand is. "How could you not tell me?"

Her head ticks as the color in her face fades. "What are you talking about?" Backing away, she nearly trips over her own feet as she tries to get away from me. I wish I could kiss all of this away. I would do anything to take her pain for myself.

"You know what I'm talking about. What Logan did to you, to Toben. The heroin, the brand, the dog cage… God, Tav, you should have fucking told me."

She shakes her head violently as the tears finally break through. "No, no, no, no." Her eyelashes are drenched and her cheeks are shiny with moisture as she claws at her hair. She holds her arms out and screams at me through her sobs. She's crying so hard I can barely make out her words. "Well, this is me, Alexander. You wanted to know and now you do." She drops her face into her hands. "You probably hate that you put yourself inside me."

God, she's grinding me up raw. Standing in front of her, I cup the back of her head. "Tavin…please don't say stuff like that. I want to be with you right now."

She shakes her head and frowns at me. "No, you don't. You said it yourself, I'm just a fucked-up mess."

I really wish I could punch myself in the face. I'm such an asshole. "I didn't mean that. I didn't mean any of it. I was hurting and angry. You wouldn't trust me or talk to me and I had just finished watching you inhale a bunch of shit up your nose. You were touching him…and the way you danced with him…I lashed out, and I'm so sorry. You always have been, and will forever be, the most incredible girl in the world to me. I adore you, *Lille*."

"How can this not change how you feel?"

My hand moves along her wet jaw line and her chest rises to my touch. "I never said it didn't change. It has. I didn't realize who you were until now. That you fought your way through a world of nightmares and somehow came out with your heart intact." I kiss her and her breathing is shaky beneath my lips. "I've always known you were beautiful, Tavin. What I wasn't aware of, is that the strength of your spirit is what makes you so breathtaking."

Squeezing her eyes shut, she grips at my shirt. "I can't." She pushes me away as my heart free falls into my stomach. "This whole thing keeps going too far and then even further. He can't know about you. He'll hurt you. Bad. The way he'll see it, you never paid him to play with me and you kept me away from my Clients. You stole from him, and I'm so sorry I tricked you into doing that."

Her words should worry me, yet nothing compares to the fear I have of her pushing me away again. "All of this could have been avoided if you would have told me what was going on, in the beginning."

"What was I supposed to begin to say, Lex?" She pulls her hair away from her tear-streamed face. "None of it should have happened! I broke an endless number of rules and I never planned to stay. It was mean and selfish. You just…You make me feel things I've never felt before."

I want to feel her against my chest and to smell her hair. I hold my hand out to her. "Please, can I touch you?" Though she doesn't make a move to come to me, her head nods. I comb my fingers through her purple strands before I cup her face to make her look up at me. "There's nothing that will keep me away from this now. It doesn't matter what you tell me. Even if you don't want to be with me, that's alright. I'll be whomever you need me to be. I swear to you, you'll never have to go back."

She shakes her head. "You don't understand. Logan isn't like anyone you've ever met. He always gets what's his."

I logically know getting angry with her isn't fair, though rationality isn't high up on the list at the moment. "You are not a 'what' and you are not motherfucking his!" I tap her temple. "Whatever demented shit he convinced you of, is all a lie. You're a person. A human being with the fundamental right to be free." I pull her against me and at the presence of her scent, my throat swells and my voice softens. "I need you to trust me and I need you to be honest with me. I will keep you safe, Tavin. I promise."

She lets out a long, shaky breath while her little arms squeeze me tight. Pulling back, she gives me a sad smile. "I need to get ready for work."

Oh, God, what does that mean? "Work?"

"Relax, it's only a bar. I won't be putting any cocks in my mouth."

Jesus Christ, is she trying to piss me off?

"Tavin, don't say that shit. I mean it."

She sighs as she pulls on her jeans and slips into her pink flip flops. "I gotta go." She stands in front of me, and when she looks up at me I can see her contemplating something. "I…I really am sorry. You did so much for me and I…"

There are so many questions I still have, so many things that don't make sense, but right now I simply revel in being able to be with her again. I lift her chin and softly press my lips to hers, cutting off her unnecessary apology. Her tongue slips into my mouth and my heart beats faster as her fingers are back in my hair. Oh, I have missed this.

Our kiss deepens as I bring my hands around her little ass and lift her up, wrapping her legs around my waist. I kiss down her neck as I lie her on the bed. Finally, I'm kissing and touching her again. It feels like it's been so long. Sliding my hand beneath her shirt, I pull down her bra, exposing her breast. She arches her back offering me her body, and my mouth is on her, sucking and licking her perfect nipples.

My fingertips trace across her brand. I've always loved it, though knowing what it really is leaves me conflicted. Her moans bring more blood to the throbbing in my jeans. I pop the button on her denims and she pushes away my hand.

"I really have to go."

I groan and drop my head back. "No, you don't."

She sits up and straightens her shirt before she pleads with those big eyes. "Yes, I do. Please don't fight with me on this. I like this job."

I don't understand why she has some shitty job if she's supposed to be hiding from Logan.

"At least let me take you."

Her laugh is weak as she turns away from me. "No, I like to take myself. I'll call you when I'm done."

Even though I don't want her to leave, this has been an intense few hours. Maybe some time to calm my nerves won't be so bad. "As soon as you're done, okay?"

She wraps her arms around my neck as she touches her nose to mine. "Okay."

"I love you, Tavin."

Her arms squeeze me a little tighter. "I love you too, Lex."

I prop my feet on the ottoman as Sasha mindlessly flips the pages of her Vogue and fills me in on what life's been like with Tavin as a roommate.

"Now, you know I love the girl, but even when she tries to help it turns into a disaster. She nearly burned down the apartment the other night attempting to make us meatloaf." I chuckle as she tosses her magazine on the table. "She drives Drew nuts more than anything. Her shifts run late, so she comes home at crazy hours and is usually wasted."

"How does he feel about her doing drugs in the house?" I jab.

She presses her lips together and takes a breath before responding. "Keeping her from going back to Logan was my main priority. And I made it clear *H* was off limits. If she's been shooting up, it hasn't been here." She stretches out across the couch and crosses her ankles. "My biggest issue is with her lack of clothing." I laugh at her facial expression causing her grin to force through. She pokes my leg with her foot and the smile falls from her face as she suddenly goes somber. "What are we going to do about Logan?"

So much has happened today. While of course my natural response is wanting his head, I haven't had so much as a moment to think of a real plan of action.

I groan out my response, "I don't know yet. This is Logan James we're talking about. I still can't believe it. Our entire lives, Dad has worked for this man. We grew up on Rissa products and I fucking sell them in my theater. It's just so surreal." She combs her hair back and I push myself off the couch. "I'm gonna go. I want to check out this bar she works at. What's it called?"

She gives me an I-know-something-you-don't-know smirk. "Club Marvel."

I do not possess the patience for her games right now. "Come on, Sash. I really can't take much more today."

She laughs. "Sorry, this is too much fun."

"God, you're a bitch."

She blows me a kiss before she waves. "I love you, too, brother."

Silas doesn't attempt to cover his excitement when I call to see if he wants to go out. I pull up in front of his penthouse and he barely waits for the car to come to a complete stop before jumping inside. He rubs his hands together and is nearly bouncing in his seat as I pull off the curb.

"So where are we going?"

"Club Marvel, apparently."

He smacks the dashboard with enthusiasm. "Oh, hell yes!"

"Hey!"

Ignoring me, he drops the sun visor mirror and finger-styles his hair.

"Thank God, man, I was beginning to worry." He laughs, "But why are we going to skanky-ass Marvel? If you want strippers, let's go to the Kitten Caboodle."

I'm fucking sorry, what was that?

"Strippers?!" My speedometer starts rising along with my heart rate. "I'm going to kill her."

"This 'her' better not be Tavin," he snaps. The look on my face clearly responds because he shakes his head and points his finger at me, scolding me like a dog. "No! No!" He throws his head against the headrest. "Damn it, I knew this was too good to be true." He scoffs, "First she's a prostitute and now she's a stripper? How can you not get past this trashy bitch? Even your own dad got up in that shit."

Okay. Ooookay. I need to take a breather or else I'm going to kill him tonight, too.

"Silas, I'm aware that you have no idea what's going on, so I'm gonna let that one slide. You just need to take me very seriously when I say, do not ever speak about her that way again."

"What am I missing here?"

Tightening my grip on the steering wheel, I fight my desire to tell him. I want him to understand her. The thought of him or anyone else thinking of her that way makes me furious. I wish the whole world could see her the way I do.

Sasha's right though, they're her secrets, not ours.

"It's not my place to tell you. If she wants you to know, then that's up to her." I flip on my blinker to get off on the exit. "It's too fucked up for words, anyway."

Once we pass through the industrial district, the GPS says we've arrived. I'm about to ask Silas if he sees it when I spot the name on the building to the left.

We're smack dab in the middle of Shadyside Slums.

Well, that's fantastic. I've been wanting to scratch getting robbed off my bucket list.

The gravel crunches under our feet as we walk across the parking lot and the music volume rises once we pass under the awning. I wrap my hand around the door handle just to yank it back instantly.

"Ugh, it's sticky."

He scrunches his nose and laughs, "Nasty."

Touching as little of the handle as possible, I pull open the door and the smell of smoke and something repugnant swirls beneath my nose. I can't believe she left out the part about the word 'stripper' being in her job title. Actually, yes, I can. She knows I won't be cool with this.

It's dark besides the flashing lights so it takes my eyes a moment to adjust, but when they do, the inside isn't any better than the exterior. This is where velvet goes to die.

I scan over the separate stages to look for her and relief comes with the fact that while the girls are completely topless, I don't see any without their bottoms.

Small victories and all that.

This place is abhorrent. I can actually feel my shoes fusing to the floor. Maneuvering through patrons, I walk towards the stages in back, and finally, find her on the last stage. Thank Christ she has a bra on, even if her brand is out for the whole world to see. I'm trying to focus on positive things right now. She's having fun, which is clearly adding to her sex appeal, because she's gathered quite the crowd. Watching this would be insanely hot if she wasn't surrounded by these creeps. The dance she's doing isn't really all that bad, she's ju—

Okay, well, never mind.

She drops on all fours, crawls to a man at the edge of the stage, and basically puts her breasts in his face. She brings her lips way too fucking close to his before she flips onto her back and throws up her pelvis, leading the rest of her body back to standing. God, she dances like she fucks.

"Mmmm." The guy next to me groans.

Yep. She's done.

She's dancing at the edge of the stage as she tugs her candy necklace into her mouth, winking as she bites off a piece. Her fingernails glitter in the light as she trails them down her neck and plays over the clasp on her bra like she's going to unsnap it.

Oh, hell no, she isn't.

Tavin

He knows. How the heck does he know? Of course his questions didn't stop, he just stopped asking me. He's here, touching me. He knows what I am and he's still kissing me. The exhilaration from him being here and the terror of what that means are woven together like a braid. He was safe while he was gone, and now I know he isn't walking away from this. From me.

My body recognizes him and aches for his touch. His big hands squeeze my ribs before rubbing his thumb over my hard nipple. I want his mouth on me so bad it's agonizing. The pounding thrum in my core is so strong I have to focus intently to not thrust against him. Finally, his lips caress me as his hand brushes over the lotus. His summertime scent floats around me—that alone gives me a sense of warmth and comfort. Fingertips trace over my skin making my entire body hum. As my moan slides through my lips, I know I need to leave. If I don't, I may not have the strength to stop him.

His mouth is on mine, devouring me, while he undoes my jeans. It's getting late though, and I need to breathe for a second. "I really have to go."

"No, you don't."

God, he's so beautiful. I caress his soft lips and I soak up being in his presence again. While I want to stay, I don't know how this is going to play out, so I still need the job. If it's at all possible, I want to keep it.

"Yes, I do. Please don't fight with me on this, I like this job."

"At least let me take you."

Uh oh. That won't be good. Oh, jeez, can you imagine? Marvel is a topic I'll need to ease him into. Very, very slowly.

"No, I like to take myself. I'll call you when I'm done."

Surprisingly, I don't think he is going to argue. He looks sleepy. "As soon as you're done, okay?"

It's like his skin is vibrating. I feel it beneath my arms when I wrap them around him.

"Okay."

He looks a little different to me. I don't know, I can't place it. His accent peeks out through his words as he says, "I love you, Tavin."

I never thought I would hear him say that ever again. My heart twists, choking me up. I don't know what this means. Now that he knows, I want to believe that he can help me. I hold his face so I know he can see my eyes.

"I love you, too, Lex." I kiss him one last time and push off the bed. This feels kinda weird. Usually, he's the one saying goodbye so he can go to work. I'm flustered and nervous so my words trip over each other. "When I—uh, yeah. I'll call you… So…bye." I have no idea why I point my finger at him like a gun and click my tongue. He chuckles and looks at me like I've lost my mind, as I turn to leave and roll my eyes at myself.

Sasha's on the phone when I walk into the living room and quickly holds a finger to her lips so I'll stay silent. "Mom, I know how far away it is, and I'm telling you, *Farmor* doesn't want to come to my bachelorette party. The woman's almost eighty-five years old." I point to the door to tell her I'm leaving, as she nods and waves. I slip out as she's screeching, "No, Mother. You're absolutely *not* coming."

I give the cabbie his money and wave to my friend, Venus, as she walks inside. This is the time of night right before it gets busy. The patrons are sparsely scattered through the club and not as many of us go on at the same time. I push open the door to my dressing room and fall back in my chair. It's probably wrong to hide what I really do here, from Lex, but he won't understand. The only thing he'll see is that I'm taking off my clothes. I still can't believe he came back for me. The air *whooshes* from my lungs and I cut a few lines, moaning as I inhale, feeling it thrum beneath my skin.

My legs can breathe again as I push the rough fabric of my jeans to the floor and change into my dancing outfit. It's my favorite one. The bra is pale pink with lacy straps and a sheer ruffle along the bottom. The panties are the same color and cover most of my ass. They have a lacy waistline and the sheer ruffles make me appear a little curvier. I put on two candy necklaces and do another line before putting on the glitter lotion Alia gave me. I need to talk to her. I don't want to hurt her feelings, but I can't keep doing sex stuff with her. Hopefully, she'll still be my friend.

I smile at a few of the men as I leave my dressing room. The girls complain about how they are pigs and gross, but they have no idea. They would never be able to deal with the Clients. These men are different. They don't want to hurt us; they only want to see us naked. There's nothing wrong with that.

"Hey, Candy, when you up next, baby?"

A man steps in front of me and I instantly recognize him. He's in here probably three to four times a week. He's a decent tipper, too.

"I'll be over there in fifteen minutes." I show him my stage.

"Well, how about a private dance while I wait?"

"I don't do private dances… I'm sorry."

I turn to walk away when he grabs my arm. "My money not good enough?"

"I'm sure your money is real good, I just don't do them."

"Hands off the dancers!" Chaz, the bouncer, is right beside me as he glares down at the man. The patron takes his hand away and simply walks off. Oh man I love that.

I grin up at him. "Thanks, Chaz."

"You okay, sweetheart?"

I laugh. "Of course I'm okay. He only touched my arm."

He smiles at me before continuing his rounds. Chaz is so nice. He doesn't talk all that much, he keeps us all safe, and is a big help when some of the girls get into fights with each other.

I've only been here for a couple of hours and my tips have been great. It still kills me that these men actually pay money to only watch. Keith says that we have to get close to them sometimes, and we can touch them if we want to. I don't want to.

My song is almost over so I bend down to touch my ankle and allow my hair to fall over my face and do the move Alia taught me. Touching my fingers slowly up my leg, I roll my upper body, and pick a patron to smile at. I try to find the least-threatening looking ones, so I am pleased to see a boy that looks too young to even be in here. I keep contact with his widened eyes until the song ends and I gather the cash off the stage.

I organize my money into a uniform stack. It's nowhere near as much as I used to get from Logan, but I don't care, it's worth more to me this way. Fifi loops her arm through mine as we walk to the dressing room.

"Howd'ya do?" I show her and she whistles. "Not bad, not bad. If you'd do private dances you'd make a lot more. And not just money neither. I've scored diamonds, drugs, shopping trips…one guy even took me to Italy."

I shrug because I can get my own drugs and I don't want any of that other stuff. We walk into the dressing room and Venus is sitting on the couch doing a line. She pats the seat next to her for me to join her, and Fifi sits next to me. Venus gives me the rolled-up bill and I bend over the table. "Ahh, God." The cocaine runs to my brain as I rub my nose and give Fifi the dollar.

"Hey, Candy." Venus nudges my shoulder and pushes her cleavage up. "Are you fucking that guy that was in here last week? You know, the one that kinda looks like he hasn't slept since 2010?"

I laugh at her oddly accurate description. "Toben?"

She reaches across me to get the bill. "Maybe…scary-sexy in a beanie?"

"That's Toben. He's my best friend. I'll introduce you next time he's here." She snorts with her inhale as I stand up. "I'm supposed to be on again in a minute. I should get back out there." I put my money in my locker and Venus holds up the dollar.

"One more?"

Fifi scoots closer to Venus and cuts more lines as I grab it. "Sure, thanks."

This will be my third time on stage tonight and Alia still isn't here. Even though she's scheduled to go on in half an hour, she's late a lot. My music comes on and the cocaine beats in rhythm with my heart as I walk on stage. The men don't bother me. To be honest, I have to remind myself that they're there. This is when I free myself. When I dance. When the melody tells me its story, it moves my body to its words.

I wish I only had to do my routine, but the rules are, I have to engage. I wink here and there, lick my lips, and touch myself over the fabric of my panties. I fall to my knees and crawl to the man on my right. He smiles at me so I smile back. I get closer and I notice the come stains on his jeans. Who the heck can come just from watching someone dance? I pretend like I am going to kiss him and pull away at the last minute. They love that. At least that's what Alia told me.

My shift is going to be over in a few hours and I can't believe I'll be seeing Lex. While I'm trying not to think about it, there's a part of me that's angry that he knows. I never wanted him to and not just because of the danger of it. I never wanted him to see into that part of my life. I'm ashamed and embarrassed.

No matter how much I begged him, he wouldn't listen and leave it alone. Of course, I'm happy he came back. I'm also angry, hopeful, scared, hesitant, excited, and humiliated. What if he can't stick it out like he thinks he can? What if I end up not being what he wants? I don't know if my heart can handle losing him again.

Wads of cash are thrown at my feet as I make my way to the front and center of the stage. I find my target as I wink at him and I eat a piece of my necklace. That's my favorite part of my routine. It's time for my finale and the men really like it when I show my tits.

Suddenly, I lose control of my body. My head snaps back as I'm yanked forward by my arm and it feels like I'm falling. My face slams against something hard, and when I am able to pull back, Lex's furious green eyes are glaring at me.

"Uh oh."

CHAPTER SIX
Struggle

Alexander

"U H OH' IS RIGHT," I SNAP. She knows exactly how fucked she is. Something grips onto my arm as she yells, "No, no! It's okay. He's with me, Chaz!"

Oh yeah, you aren't supposed to touch the strippers. Well, she's not a stripper anymore now, is she? Still, I take my hand from her arm because I'd rather not provoke the giant, tattooed bouncer.

"No boyfriends, Candy. You know that."

I look at her with what has to be a gaping expression. "Candy? Are you joking?"

She knits her brows together and huffs as she turns to 'Chaz'. "Yeah, I know, just give us a minute. Please?"

He gives her a small smile, making him a lot less intimidating and nods toward the curtained area behind us.

On one hand, she's been through more than anyone should have to endure, and I probably should keep my cool with her. On the other, she deliberately kept this from me. She ultimately lied and that shit has to stop.

She pushes open the curtain and I follow her into a

room with a black velvet couch, a silver pole, and thick red carpet that hasn't been changed since Clinton was in office.

"Damn it, Tavin. You know I would never allow you to do this. Why the hell do you want to stay in this environment? You're not an object or a toy." She looks to the ground so I push her chin up with my finger until she lifts her eyes. "The lies and the deception stop now. I know about Logan so there's nothing that you need to keep from me. Now, get your shit. We're leaving."

"No!" Yanking her head back, she steps away from me. "I like it here. The men can't even touch me, Lex! Can you believe they pay me to just dance?"

Deep breath, deep breath.

"You're not just dancing! You're taking your clothes off!"

She scowls and mutters, "I didn't lie though. I *do* work at a bar."

"Tavin, I'm not it the mood for you to be a smartass. It's been a long and emotional day and all I want is to take you home. Now go get your stuff." Her eyes are rimmed in red and I just now noticed, high as hell.

Dear God, I can't even go there right now.

Through clenched teeth she snaps, "Fine," before jerking her body around throwing open the curtain.

I never thought I would say this, but she really needs to put on some damn clothes. She marches to the front of the club and I follow her to the end of a hallway. Her fist remains still for a moment before she knocks on the door that reads 'Manager.' A man hollers that it's open and when inside, she murmurs, "Keith?"

He looks up from his computer and scowls. "Why the hell aren't you on stage, Candy?"

If one more person calls her 'Candy' I might lose it. Her soon-to-be ex-boss is medium height and not much older than I am. He has the man-bun thing going on and not near as sleazy as I was expecting, considering the way he presents his establishment.

"I…um, uh…" She's shifting on her feet and can't form a coherent sentence. "Well, I just…um…" This is her first time quitting a job and she won't lift her gaze from the grotesque carpet.

"She quits." Grabbing her wrist, I lead her down the hall. "See? Easy as that, now go get dressed."

Her eyes are slits as she slams the door to her dressing room. I let out a big breath and lean against the wall before remembering where I am and what could be crusted along this hallway.

Where the hell is Silas? Looking for him from my vantage point, I spot him next to one of the stages enjoying the show.

It doesn't take her long to change and when she comes out, her anger has noticeably diminished. I take her hand and her body relaxes as I lace our fingers.

As we pass by Silas, I tap his shoulder and point toward the exit. "I'm getting her out of here. You can get a car, right?"

Holding up his phone, he says, "Already done." His shoulders slack as he looks at Tavin, while she is refusing to lift her head.

She's probably embarrassed and I am sorry about that. Still, she had to expect something like this was going to happen when she chose to be deceptive. I squeeze her hand and she doesn't say a word as I lead her outside.

"Come on, Tav, how long did you think you were going to get away with this? Did you really not expect me to come check out where you work?"

My car beeps as I press the button on my key fob and she pulls her hand away to cross her arms.

"I don't know, Alexander. I just wanted to make it last. This is the first thing I've ever done on my own," she points to the club before directing her finger at me, "and you just made me quit."

I truly do want to understand her sense of accomplishment. I also want her to understand my sense of not wanting other men to see her naked all the damn time.

"Then get a job wearing clothes."

"I can't!" Silas walks outside ready to say something, immediately stopping when he sees the state we're in. She ignores him and yells, "I don't know anything else! I've done nothing besides get fucked and high for thirteen years!" Her little fists are balled up and her head tics. "I have no identity. I'm not a real person. You know that."

I don't want to frustrate or upset her more, so I soften my voice. "Tavin, you are a real person. I can't imagine what this must feel like and I'm sorry, but you're not dancing. We'll work on getting your papers, a social security number, whatever you need. It's going to take time though, and you need to be patient."

She opens her mouth to respond, and right before her words can come out, a feminine voice yells, "Candy, wait!"

The three of us turn to the voice that's paired with an A-line pink bob. The girl shuts her car door and runs to Tavin. All I can do is throw my hands up in defeat when she cups Tavin's face and kisses her. To be fair, Tav does back away immediately.

"Alia, I...I'm sorry, I have to leave."

Does she have something going on with this girl? Silas' eyes are huge when the girl puts her hand on Tavin's stomach.

"Are you coming back?"

Tavin shakes her head. "I can't. I'm sorry. Thank you for being so nice to me."

The girl, Alia, brushes the hair from Tavin's face and leans down as if she's about to kiss her again. "Candy, I—"

That name is like sandpaper rubbing against my brain

and I'm way past ready to get out of this parking lot and Shadyside Slums.

Stepping between them, I face the stripper covered in kawaii. "Her name is Tavin. Look, Alia, is it? Thank you for being there for her and I'm sure you are a very nice girl, however, today has quite literally been the longest day of my life and I simply cannot take anymore of…this." I wave my hand implying generality.

Alia ignores me as she holds Tavin's hand. "Will you call me?" Tavin glances at me before she nods and hugs her for longer than I find necessary. I wait until Alia disappears inside the club before asking, "What the hell was that?"

Her chin lifts with her straightened posture. "She's my friend."

"She seems like a lot more than that."

Shaking her head, she looks away from me. "I don't know what to tell you, Lex. I needed affection and…she isn't a man."

The truth is, I'm not as mad as I feel like I should be. While I definitely don't like it, I understand it. After everything, her messing around with a girl while we were broken up doesn't seem that concerning.

She keeps stealing glances at me, gauging my reaction and all I want is her home in my arms.

"Just so you know, I left him alone. He's the one that came looking for me."

Is she talking to me? Her gaze has fallen to the ground as her fingers tug at the hem of her shirt.

Silas sighs, "Yeah, believe me, I know." He slides his hands into his pockets and rocks back on his heels. "I may have been a little harsh with you…I'm sorry."

"No, it's okay," she murmurs.

"What am I missing?"

As I look in between them, Tavin finally lifts her head.

"You don't have to tell him, Silas."

Crossing my arms, I scoff and face him. "Yes, he absolutely does. What did you say to her?"

He does that thing where he lifts his lip into a semi-smile and turns his head to the side as he rubs his nose. It means he's guilty as hell.

"You were a mess man. You weren't you and I was pissed at her for it."

"That's not what I asked."

He glances at Tavin before he drawls out, "I may have called her a whore."

No wonder she believes it so wholeheartedly. Everyone keeps calling her that. "Jesus Christ, Silas."

Tavin's soft hand brushes against my arm as she murmurs, "It's fine Lex, really."

"No, it's not fine, and you don't need to let people talk to you like that. Now can we please get out of this hell hole?" Crossing her arms, she nods while I glare at Silas. "Why are you even out here?" I ask him.

He gestures toward the Alpha. "My keys are still in your car."

The dome light comes on as I reach into the console and find his keys. "Here."

I toss them over the roof of the Alfa and into his hands. "Thanks. Later." He turns to go back inside and stops in front of Tav. "I really am sorry."

With a small nod and a smile, she climbs inside the car, while I give Silas one more glare before doing the same. As I turn the key, I lean back in my seat. The sound of the engine coming to life will always be one of my favorite auditory sensations.

She lifts her pelvis to reach into her pocket as I pull out onto the street, and I don't even make it to the first intersection, before the sound of her snorting jerks my head in her direction. Her hand wipes across her nose, and for a moment, I'm too flabbergasted to react.

"Seriously, Tavin? Right in front of me?!"

She doesn't even bat an eye. "You know what I am. Drug addict is included in the description."

I know my jaw drops when she sprinkles more on her hand and does it again.

She's pushing me on purpose. I don't know why and it doesn't matter. It's not going to work. I hold my hand out in front of her. "Give it to me."

"What?" she scoffs.

"Give me the damn bag, Tavin. I don't know where you got the idea that I would suddenly be okay with this."

She slams it in my hand as I lower my window to throw it out. My instinct is to reiterate everything I've already told her about the drugs and remind her that it's nonnegotiable, but I think she's trying to get a rise out of me and I won't give it to her.

All I want is a few moments of peace with her.

The idea of a double shot espresso sounds amazing right now, and there's a coffee shop on the way home. She would love their white chocolate, strawberry Frappuccino.

Reaching across the console, I hold her hand. "Do you want some coffee?"

Her shoulders shrug as she turns her head to look out her window. "Sure."

This feels weird. The tension's thick enough to choke on and I don't know how to break it. While I admit our reunion could have gone worse, it feels as if she's intentionally trying to make this more difficult than it needs to be.

We wait in the drive-thru line for our drinks and as much as I don't want them to, my thoughts keep going to what I watched this afternoon.

"I have some questions." Her shoulders tense as she continues to gaze out the window, making it impossible to see her face. She remains silent so I continue, "The first time Logan and Kyle came into your basement, you were familiar with Logan. Did you know Kyle too?"

She doesn't respond and I don't think she's going to when she finally says, "Initiation." Her fingers are tight and spread apart as she presses down on her thighs. Taking a couple of deep breaths, she slowly lets them out before speaking again. "The day you're talking about is called initiation." She turns her head and looks at me with an anger that's so unnatural on her sweet face. "How do you know about Kyle?"

"Initiation to what?"

"Answer me!"

She's naturally a soft-spoken person so her yelling startles me. I sigh and put the car in drive to move up the line. "It doesn't matter how I know."

She turns her body and pushes herself up as much as she can with her seat belt on, so she's closer to my eye level. "It doesn't matter?" She seethes, "This is my life. Not a way for you to get back at me!"

I'm in the day that never fucking ends and the last thing I want to do with her is argue. Why is she getting so mad at me? Is this all because of that disgusting job?

"Tavin, I'm not trying to get back at you. I can't tell you how I know, but I only want what's best for you." I grip the wheel ready to be out of this fucking drive through. "I've only ever wanted what is best for you. Now, for the love of fuck, will you please stop fighting me?"

Her anger melts away as her body falls back into the seat. "I can't believe you know," she whispers.

Her head tics and she looks so damn sad. I don't want her to feel this way. I don't ever want to be the reason for a moment more of her suffering. I cup the nape of her neck and pull her forehead to mine.

"Alright, no more talk about Logan, or drugs, or strip clubs tonight, okay?"

Her shoulders lift with her silent breathing as I feel her head nodding against my own. "Okay."

I rub my finger over her thumb as we listen to Nirvana and she annihilates her Frappuccino. The absence of words must calm us both because I can actually sense the energy loosen inside the car.

We pull up to my house, and as the garage door opens in front of us, her face falls once her gaze lands on the bare back wall. She attempts to hide her disappointment, turning her head toward the painting folded on the work bench.

I never had any intention of getting rid of that.

Her posture is stiff and her steps are slow as we walk inside, until right on cue, Mag and her jingling collar can be heard coming from around the corner.

"Oh my gosh, Lex! You kept her?"

Throwing her arms out towards Mag, she looks up at me, and her face is glowing with her gorgeous smile.

It's been way too long since I've seen that.

I shrug and lean against the island. "Yeah, well, she grew on Cara Jo."

Mag is almost more excited than Tavin, using the whole bottom half of her body to wag her tail.

"I don't think Cara Jo's the only one you grew on." She's talking to the dog, though it's clearly for my benefit. She crouches down to pick her up as she laughs and scratches behind Mag's ears. I allow her to pet her for a moment before taking the dog away and putting her back on the floor.

"Go lie down, Mag."

Holding up a finger, she corrects me. "Blind Mag. It's Blind Mag."

I chuckle at her and she grins. I am so relieved she's back here. Her lip is so soft beneath my thumb as I close the gap between us. "I missed you so much."

Forever I could spend looking at her eyes.

She stares at my mouth before crashing her lips to mine and wrapping her arms around my neck to pull me closer. The seams of her jean pockets are rough beneath my fingers as I cup her ass and pick her up to set her on the counter.

My kisses trail along her jaw and I feel her lips move against my ear as she rasps, "I missed you, too. So much, Lex."

The candy of her necklace is sweet as I take it into my mouth. Using my teeth to pull it from her neck, I bite off a piece before allowing the necklace to snap back against her skin. The sound of her quiet moan goes straight to my cock and I grind my erection against her body.

Her fingers are where I love them, while mine are slipping beneath the hem of her shirt. As her tongue slips into my mouth, I give her back her candy. She smiles against my lips and my stomach vibrates at the excitement of her being here again. I can't believe all of this has happened today. Her scent makes me strain against my jeans.

Pulling back to look at her, I don't get the chance before she's kissing me again with urgency. Her legs squeeze my waist and she yanks on my hair causing me to groan into her mouth. My hands wrap around her waist as I push up her shirt, feeling the bump of each rib.

I lift it over her head causing a break in our kiss. As the tee is discarded, she desperately grabs my face, and I see the shine on hers.

I rub my hands across her cheeks. "Hey, what's wrong?"

"I didn't think you would ever talk to me again." She laughs through her tears as she shakes her head. "I never wanted you to know about Logan, and now you do, and you're still treating me the same as you did before…I didn't think that would happen, either." More tears fall onto my hands. "This is a lot of emotions, is all."

Taking her hand, I silently guide her upstairs and her gaze lingers on her bedroom door. I know she's curious about her things. None of that tonight though. Tonight is about us—nothing and no one else.

I lead her into my room, releasing her hand to close my bedroom door to keep Mag out. I turn around to face her and she's looking at me in a way I've never really seen from her before. I would almost say predatory. She grabs my shirt and yanks it off with an aggression that makes it difficult not to laugh.

The violet of her eyes shines so bright beneath her lashes as she looks up to me and falls to her knees. I don't dare break eye contact while she undoes my button and unzips my fly. She frees me and tender lips continue to harden my dick with every kiss up my shaft.

I can't believe I almost lost her.

Watching this is just as enjoyable as feeling it. While my hands push her head down, her eyes refuse to break contact. Slowly I glide in and out of her mouth, seeing every inch as it enters those pretty lips.

I love her blow jobs. I always have. Right now though, I need my body to be inside hers. My finger runs along her jaw and she gradually releases me. As soon as I slide out of her mouth, I'm kissing it. I cup her nape and use it to lift her to standing. Our tongues touch while my fingers trace her lotus, until finally, I break our kiss and unhook her bra.

Her little breaths are on my neck as my thumb rubs over a perfect pink bud. I lean down to flick it with my tongue and bring it between my lips. She arches into me, making it easier to slide my hand down the front of her jeans. Smiling around her nipple, I slip a finger in.

"Always so wet." She's so cute with her pink cheeks and embarrassed smile. I remove my hand, and grip her waistband to pull her against me for a kiss. "Face the bed and place your hands on the edge."

As she does what I tell her, my arousal is suddenly traded for the realization that I don't have any idea how far I can go.

My heartbeat pounds against my eardrums and doubles in speed as I walk to stand behind her. I haven't even considered this aspect of our relationship. Knowing what I know now makes me question if she really likes it or if she's somehow warped into thinking she does. Then there's the fact that I enjoy hurting her and I don't know if that makes me like him, somehow.

Taking a deep breath, I focus on the sight in front of me. Her ass is adorable in those jeans so I spank it before I reach around the front to undo the button. My lips leave a trail of soft kisses across her shoulder and once I reach the crook of her neck, I bite down causing her pelvis to rock forward. She softly moans as I kiss down her back. This is probably the clearest I've ever seen it. It gives me a spark of hope because even though I've tried to not think about it, I still wonder if she's been with anyone besides 'Alia' since we split.

I crouch to slowly pull her jeans down her body, getting harder with every inch of milky skin that appears. She steps out of the leg holes and is wearing the same pink ruffled panties she was dancing in. I bite my way up her thigh, touching between her legs, over the drenched fabric. She pushes her body down on my fingers as I slip them beneath the material.

"Turn around," I tell her.

We're kissing again so fast, it isn't clear who kisses who first. I press my hand against her lower back, lying her on the bed and spreading her legs around me. My erection presses against the fabric of her lingerie, so I pull the panties to the side and nudge her clit. Lowering my jeans, I look up at her, and she's biting her lip while she watches my cock push into her entrance. I lift her chin to pull her eyes back up to mine, and as soon as I lock into violet, I shove myself completely into her body.

Her gasp becomes a moan as I increase my pace, moving her further up the bed with every aggressive thrust. My fingers intertwine with hers while I push as deep as I can physically go.

"The belt," she breathes. "Hit me with the belt."

Fuck.

I keep my pace as I trace a finger over her lips. "I'm sorry, Tav, I…I don't think I can do the belt anymore."

Her eyes flash before she completely stops moving and looks away from me. "Get out," she whispers.

"What?"

Her head snaps back as she glares at me. "Get out of me."

My stomach drops as I do what she says.

"*Lille*, come on—"

"I should have known." She flies off the bed and picks her jeans up off the floor. "I completely bought that 'strength of your spirit' crap. You pity me. I'm already sad and broken, right, Alexander? You wouldn't want to be responsible for any more damage." Snatching her bra off the rug, she storms toward the door.

For the love of Christ.

One of my strides is three of hers, so I'm in front of her in two paces. "Damn it, stop. You know I'll always chase your ass, but right now I'm emotionally strung out, so please don't make me. I don't pity you, Tav. I am angry for you. It's not that I'm scared to hurt you, exactly, I just…I can't get your fucking screams out of my head."

She narrows her eyes and her head tics. "What are you

talking about?"

It's so hypocritical to lie to her after I have told her endless times not to. I want our relationship to be honest and free of deceit, but she cannot find out about those tapes.

My personal shit with this needs to stay exactly that. Personal. I need to suck up whatever reservations I have if I want this to work.

With a scoff, she tries to push past me when I grab her neck and slam her against the wall.

"You want me to hit you?" I crash my mouth against hers, not caring that our teeth clash, as I slide my hand to the back of her neck and push her toward the bed. Shoving her face into the duvet, I rip my belt through the loops. "I'll whip the shit out of you."

She lifts her hips, silently pleading for me to pull her panties over and push myself back inside. The belt is folded in half when I lift it over my head and bring it down across her body. With her arching back and the hot, red line blossoming across her skin, I'm pretty sure I just pre-came.

This is what we were before all this. All she wants is for me to see her the same. I have to separate what he did to her from what she needs from me.

My chest hovers over her back as I lean forward and kiss down her spine. "Is this what you want, *Lille*?"

Her fingers clutch at the comforter as she turns her head to the side and gasps, "Yes."

CHAPTER SEVEN
Message

Sunday, June 21st

"WHAT THE HELL, ALEXANDER?"
Who the fuck is yelling? Jesus, what time is it?

I'm still half sleeping when I groan, "What?"

"We're supposed to be meeting my parents for brunch in an hour, and you're still in bed with last night's bar trash? We really need to discuss boundaries."

Wait what? I yawn as I force my eyes open and lift my head.

Oh no.

Shit! Shit! Shit! I completely forgot about Emily. I look over at Tavin and I can practically hear her heart crack. "Are you guys...together?"

Emily responds faster than I can open my mouth. "Yes, so if you would kindly get dressed and make your way home, we have places to be."

Situations such as this are one of the many reasons I don't cheat. How exactly do I explain this and not sound like an asshole?

The uncomfortable energy of the situation forces out an

awkward laugh as I try to cover my ass. "No—now see, I…" Maybe Sasha's right. I am an idiot. I can't even string together a damn sentence.

Tavin's teary eyes are glittering in the sunlight as she looks at me with disbelief and jumps off the bed. Grabbing her clothes on her way out, she stops in front of Emily and says, "I'm sorry, I didn't know," before slipping past her and disappearing into the hallway.

"Tavin, hold on!"

Oh, look at that, now I can talk.

I rip the duvet off my bed and wrap it around myself as I hear the bathroom door close. Bending down to grab my jeans off the floor, I stomp over to Emily.

"You think it's acceptable to walk into my house?"

She puts her hands on her hips and looks at me as if I'm being ridiculous. "I called and you didn't answer," her borderline insanity has me flustered because I'm not quite sure how to respond. Not that she cares, she's still talking, "and I didn't want you to miss our brunch. It's not true what they say, Alex. Second impressions are as equally important as the first."

I gave her every impression that we were a couple. Considering that, she's handling this pretty well. I feel like a complete prick. There's no way to avoid hurting her feelings.

As I run my fingers through my hair, I do my best to soften the blow. "Emily…I can't begin to explain myself. I swear I didn't plan this, and I know how this looks, but I never should have taken you to bed the other night… A relationship between us can't happen."

Her eyes go cold as she straightens her back and clasps both hands over her purse. "I see."

"I am sorry. She's my ex and—"

"There's nothing more to say, Alex, so don't make a fool of yourself." She shakes her head as she spins on her heel and lets herself down the stairs.

As bad as I truly do feel about that, I'm just grateful she's gone.

Walking down the hall to the bathroom, I rest my head against the wood of the door. "There's nowhere to go Tav, so open the door and talk to me."

The last word barely leaves my mouth when she swings it open and snaps, "Did you love her?"

I roll my eyes. "Don't be ridiculous, of course not. I met her two days ago. I may have led her on more than I should have, but I was angry and at the time, I thought I needed to move on." Her face softens a fraction and I capitalize on it. "Come on, I haven't even had coffee yet. Can we please have breakfast before we start on all this?"

She nods and laces her fingers in mine as I take her hand to lead her downstairs. The sun shines in the kitchen through the two large, front windows as I start the coffee and throw a couple bagels in the toaster.

"Do you want some strawberry milk?"

She gives me that half smile that she does when she isn't sure what she is supposed to be feeling. "Yes."

I hate that I've been with another woman since her. It was only two weeks and for once I'm ashamed I didn't keep it in my pants.

I go to the fridge for the milk and strawberry syrup. "It happened the other night…after I saw you at the bar." The spoon *clinks* against the glass as I stir. "I'm really sorry, Tav."

She doesn't look at me as she takes her drink from my hand. It's clear her feelings are hurt, no matter how hard she's trying to act as if they're not.

As much as I don't want her to have fucked anyone else, at the same time I wonder if it would alleviate some of my guilt.

"You were with Alia, right? Were you with anyone else?"

Her head snaps up to me and she furrows her brows. "No. And I didn't fuck Alia. We kissed and I touched her; she never touched me." She shakes her head and sets down her milk. "You're the only one, Alexander. Ever."

That makes zero sense. "I'm the only one what?"

"The only one I ever chose. I've never willingly let anyone inside me other than you."

Her words obliterate mine. I don't know what to say to that. Every time she's been touched it was forced upon her. I don't understand what makes me different. We didn't even know each other that first time. She starts toward the table when I grasp her wrist.

"Why me?"

She softly smiles as she leans against the counter. "When you asked me out, I never intended to have sex with you, I just wanted to go out with you so bad. I could tell you weren't like the Clients. You're just so warm. It's like the sun shines through your skin when you smile." She wraps her arms around my waist and rests her head against my chest. "Whenever I'm with someone, it feels like there are greasy hands all over me, suffocating me…it's like my skin is choking. Slimy fear crawls into my pores and it takes everything in me not to scream." I rub her back and I feel her head moving against me. "It's never been like that with you. You make it go away. You more than make it go away, you make it feel good." She looks up at me. "You make it feel good without the dirtiness."

A wrecking ball hits my chest every time she says stuff like this. I love that I can be that for her. In fact, it makes me feel incredible. However, why she needs me to be that for her at all weighs heavy on my soul.

I wrap my arms around her tight as Mag's telltale jingling comes down the stairs. "Mag has missed you too, ya know."

"It's BLIND Mag."

I laugh as she bends down to pick her up.

"Come on, you have to admit that's a bit of a mouthful."

She looks Mag right in the eye. "What do you think?"

Mag barks in response, and Tavin grins at me in victory while I glare at the dog. "Traitor."

With our coffee and bagels, we go back upstairs, her eyes staying on the guest room door as we pass.

"Do you want to go in?"

She nods, so I open the door and *Blind* Mag follows her inside. "Did you throw away the painting?" She asks.

"No," I shake my head at her, grateful I hadn't gotten to it yet and push open the closet door, "I did find your little masterpiece though."

She scrunches her nose and gives me a guilty smile. "Sorry. It's kind of a thing I do…" Sighing, she pets the dog. "I can't imagine how mad Drew is going to be when they move the bed in my room at Sasha's."

A deep laugh climbs up my throat as I back out of the room. "I'll be right back."

After running to the garage to get the box, I return to find her playing with Blind Mag on the floor. I place the box on the bed and she jumps up to dig through it, immediately removing the painting. She traces her fingers across it before she lies it on the bed and takes out the remaining contents. Once the box is empty, she looks inside with a disappointed stare.

"Are you looking for the necklace?"

"Did you do something to it?"

"I still have it. Would you like it back?"

"Yes."

I kiss her temple. "Eat your bagel."

I trot down the hall to my office and walk to the back of the room. As I lift my print of Salvador Dali's *The Elephants* off the wall, my safe comes into view. Pressing the keypad, I enter the date Vulture was established.

Beep **8**

Beep, beep **16**

Beep **7**

The *thud* of the safe unlocking sounds and I swing open the door. Pushing over the cassette tapes of Tavin, I reach in the back for the necklace. I rarely keep anything of real financial value in here. Everything inside is only worth the emotional attachment I have to it. Believe it or not, I can be quite sentimental. Wrapping my hand around the little carousel, I shut the safe.

She's sitting inside the closet when I return, so I hear her before I see her. "You covered it up."

I sit on the floor and lean against the wall as I hold up the necklace, letting the carousel spin. "I was pretty angry when I found it and I wanted it out of sight. I'm hoping we can get the wallpaper off and salvage it, because it was really incredible."

She crawls out of the closet with Blind Mag behind her, and sits in between my legs, pressing her back against my chest. I move her hair over her shoulder, hooking the necklace around her neck.

The dog crawls in her lap as her fingers fondle the charm and she eats her bagel. After a moment of silence, she whispers, "What are we gonna do, Lex?"

The truth is, I haven't the slightest clue. I don't have all the information yet, and the time I've had to think has been scarce. I don't have any idea how this is going to play out and I just want one more day with her before everything spins out of control.

"I was thinking swimming? It's a perfect day for swimming."

Panic is apparent in her large eyes as she turns to look up at me. "What do you mean? I'm talking about Logan! I need to talk to Toben about all this, and we have to be careful. Logan—"

I reach out and touch her arm to get her to chill for a second. "Toben already knows I know."

"What?" She flips onto her knees and poor Blind Mag is startled off her lap.

"I stopped by your place before I went to Sasha's yesterday."

Her eyes are wide with surprise and her voice has dropped to barely above a whisper. "What did he say?"

"Nothing immensely helpful." Sitting back on her feet, she suddenly slips into her own world. "Tavin." She looks back up to me and I want nothing more than to erase every bit of doubt from those eyes and to give her an honest sense of security. "I will figure this out. I promise. I want one day with you that's free of all this." I wrap my hand around hers and pull her up so we're at eye level. "Do you trust me? I mean honestly, one hundred percent, do you trust me to take care of you and keep you safe? If you don't, that's alright; however, if you do…I need you to, okay?"

I don't think I am going to get a response when she looks me in the eye and nods. "Okay."

"Good. Now put on that sexy as sin swimsuit and get your ass in the pool."

She grins and jumps up to dig through the box, with Blind Mag on her heels.

Blind Mag somehow loves to swim, yet every time I try to give her a bath she acts like I'm beating her. She paddles her little legs around the water with her tongue hanging out, while Tavin is personalizing her jumps off the diving board.

"I call this one the Tavin Tuck."

She jumps off and I look at Blind Mag. "Or as the rest of the world calls it, a 'cannonball.'" The next one is the 'Tavin Toe Toucher'.

The afternoon is so perfect, we're almost able to forget our troubles outside of the pool. I chase her back into the house to shower, and as she dries her hair, we weigh the pros and cons of Chinese or wings for dinner.

The muffled sound of *Fashionista* plays in my pocket and the picture of Sasha with her tongue sticking out, lights up my screen.

"Hey, Sash."

"You need to come get your piece of shit sister. She knew this was a deal breaker," Drew barks into the phone.

"What the hell are you talking about?"

Tavin's head cocks to the side, as Drew goes off in my ear. "I came home for lunch to find her fucked out of her head. I told her from the beginning: no drugs."

Though I should be feeling something along the lines of anger or disappointment, the only thing I feel is disbelief. This doesn't make sense. She was doing amazing and she was so proud of herself. Everything with Tavin should have been the nail in the coffin to keep her away from it, but maybe it had the reverse effect. What if it's all been too triggering and I'm the one that pulled her back in? What if this is my fault?

It's supposed to be my job to protect her. I swore it to her.

Twenty-three years ago…

I was supposed to be asleep an hour ago, and if Cara Jo catches me she'll take away my new comic. I just got it today and it keeps getting better and better! I had to wait a whole week for this issue, I don't want to have to wait a whole other day to finish it.

The beam from my flashlight shows the warehouse blowing up and I can't turn the page fast enough.

Click.

That was my door…uh oh, Cara Jo.

I flip off my flashlight and shove the comic beneath my pillow as I slam my head down on it.

"Alexander?" Oh whew, it's only Sasha. "I know you're awake reading your new comic…can I come in?"

I scoot to the edge of my bed and pull my blankets back. "Sure, come on."

She crawls into bed and lays her head next to mine. "I got scared."

"I told you not to watch that movie with me."

There's enough light from my X-Men nightlight to see her head shaking. "It wasn't the movie." She looks down and frowns. "Do you think I'm a big wuss for coming in here?"

I don't like it when she feels bad about anything, so I hug her. "Nope. That's what big brothers are for."

She giggles, "You're only three minutes older."

"Older is older." I shrug. "Do you want me to read you my comic?"

"No. Will you tell me a story? Not a scary one though."

"Okay… pick a color."

"Sage!"

She's so weird sometimes. "What kind of color is sage?"

"It's green."

"Okay, so there was a little girl who lived in Sageville, and when she woke up in the morning she would always brush her sage hair with her sage hairbrush before putting on a sage dress."

"She has sage hair? That isn't very realistic."

"Do you want to hear the story or not?"

"Sorry…keep going!" She reaches to the floor to pick up

my Charlie Horse doll, before laying her head on my chest.

"She got on her sage bike to go to the Sage River. On her way, she learned today was going to be a different kind of day. A clan from…pick another color—a normal one this time."

She taps her finger against her chin. "Um…orange."

I wrap my arm around her as I roll on my side. "A clan from Orangetopia was traveling by. The little girl saw them and hurried back home to tell her mother what she saw. The whole town of Sageville came to see these strange, new visitors that had odd, orange hair and orange clothes. The little girl's family, along with other families in Sageville, welcomed them and allowed them to stay in their sage houses."

"So, everything was just green and orange?"

"Stop interrupting and you'll find out."

"Sorry," she whispers.

"Well, one day, the little girl from Sageville and a little boy from Orangetopia were coloring a picture. She colored the sage leaves for the trees and he colored oranges to make it a fruit tree. Then something wonderful happened!"

She jumps up on her elbows. "What? What happened?!"

"Well, the orange and sage colors mixed together on the page and made a whole new color! Neither of them had ever seen it before and it allowed them to color a trunk to the tree and branches!"

"They made brown!" She claps her hands together. "Then what happened?"

I shrug because that was the end. "They all lived together forever and happy."

She squeezes Charlie Horse to her chest. "That was a good story, thank you, Alexander."

"You're welcome. Do you feel better?"

She nods. "Yes, but can I still sleep in here with you tonight?"

"Sure." I adjust the pillows so we both have enough. "If it

wasn't the movie, why were you scared?"

She breathes real hard and says, "Well...today when Jerich came over with his parents, he took my Skip-it. He wasn't playing with it right, so I told him to stop, and he said he could do whatever he wanted. I tried to take it from him and he used it to hit me and it hurt real bad so I cried. Then he said if I told anyone he would send the boogeyman to come eat me." She looks up at me with big eyes and hugs Charlie Horse tighter. "And I just told you!"

That dumb Jerich. I hate that kid. He thinks he is so smart and he's so special because his dad owns a baseball team. Well, I'll show him next time I see him. Nobody messes with my sister besides me.

"He's a stupid liar. He doesn't even know the boogeyman. Don't worry, I won't ever let anything happen to you, okay? I'll always keep you safe, Sasha. No matter what."

"Always?"

"Always. Promise."

Her breathing slows and I think she's starting to fall asleep. "You're the best brother in the whole, wide world, Alexander."

"And you're the best sister in the whole, wide world."

Since the Alfa is only a two-seater, I drive the Mercedes and park it in the Sinn Gates parking garage. I hold Tavin's hand as she carries the dog up the elevator. The closer we get to Sasha's floor the more fidgety and anxious she becomes.

"I don't understand, Lex. She was always so insistent that I not bring it around her. Why would she do this now?"

I wish I knew why she did it in the first place. I shake my head because I have no answers for either of us. She puts Blind Mag down as the elevator *dings,* and holds the leash as we walk to apartment *13B.*

I knock on the door and Drew opens it. "It's about damn ti—" I don't use full strength, probably not even half, but I still get plenty of pleasure from hitting him in the face. He grabs his jaw as he rights himself. "Argh! What the hell?"

"That was a love tap. Call my sister a 'piece of shit' again and you'll feel what it's really like when I hit you." I brush past him to see her, droopy eyed, on the couch. She's definitely high.

Shit, Sash.

"I have to get back to work. I'll separate her things later this week and mail them. I don't want her back here. Lock the door when you leave, you can send the key." Other than being a little stunned from being hit in the face, Drew acts mostly unaffected by the fact he's kicking out his fiancé. He's about to walk out until he remembers to add, "And don't let that dog pee on the floor, Tavin."

He shuts the door and Tavin situates Sasha into a more comfortable position on the couch, as Blind Mag does the same for herself.

"Where's Drew?" Sasha mumbles.

Tavin stands and rubs her arm. "I'm going to get her a blanket and a—" Her attention shifts to the floor as she kneels down and picks up a plastic wrapper. "This is the exact same packaging our needles come in."

I take it from her to look. There isn't anything unique or unusual about it. When I look back at her, she's frowning at Sasha, lost in thought.

"Tavin?"

Her eyes lift to meet mine. "I think this was Logan." I shouldn't allow myself to close my eyes because when I do, all I see is him shoving a needle into the ten-year-old version of my heart. "I think he knows I was staying here."

I collapse onto the couch and rub my forehead as if it will help me think. "We need to wait until Sasha can tell us what happened before we can know anything for sure."

Something dawns on her as she covers her mouth and gasps, "Oh, God…Toben! Logan will know he knew!" She pushes her palms against her temples before she gestures toward Sasha. "They've been pretending to date."

"Yeah, he wishes." Her eyes are pleading with me to fix this so I take her hand and pull her down to sit next to me. "Let's get Sasha sober, and get you both back to my place, then I'll go talk to Toben. Okay?"

She looks back at Sasha's stirring body and nods. "Okay."

I make us some tea and we sit on the couch watching Netflix while we wait. If someone were to look into the window, it would appear that we're an average couple being lazy on a Sunday afternoon, while Sasha could just as easily be napping.

Reality is not always how it appears, through a window.

Tavin

"TWO YEARS!"

I've never seen Sasha freak out like this. I'm worried she's going to pull her hair out if she keeps yanking at it like that. Her breathing is panicked as she paces the floor.

She's told me how hard she worked and continues to work to stay away from the needle, and because of me, all that hard work was for nothing.

"I'm so sorry…this is all my fault."

Her head whips over to me as she glares. "Not now

with that shit, Tavin. You didn't do this. This was that MOTHERFUCKER!" She screams as she keeps her hands in fists at her side. Alexander hasn't stopped looking at her like he wants to cry and she finally stops moving around enough to allow his arms to wrap around her. As soon as he pulls her to his chest, her shoulders shake as she weeps onto his shoulder. "I don't want to start over again, Alex."

He kisses her cheek as he squeezes her tighter and tells her, "I'll take care of you, Sash. Whatever you need, I'll get it. It won't be like last time, I swear."

She nods before she steps away and looks up at me. Not even trying to hide her disgust, she says, "I can't believe you were raised by that sick freak."

Even though I know she's sad and upset, her words still hurt. I know exactly who Logan is, but just like she said, he did raise me.

Alexander asks her, "What happened before he injected you?"

Her shoulders sag as she lets out a breath. "I was pretty sure it was him as soon as I opened the door," she gestures to me, "and since she wasn't here, I didn't think he would do anything. He greeted me as if we see each other all the time, it was really weird. There was another man with him and I figured proving I had nothing to hide was the way to go, so I let them in." She shakes out her hands and starts pacing again. I want to hug her so badly. "He told me he had a 'message' for you: He knows who you are, and if you wanted to play with his toy, all you had to do was ask." Alexander's body stiffens to the point I can't even tell if he's breathing. "He said if you return 'The Product,'" she sarcastically puts her fingers in air quotes, "in a timely manner, then this," she points to the red spot on her arm, "and a fair financial settlement, will be the only repayment required, since he holds our father in such high regard."

Alexander doesn't respond. He doesn't do anything besides turn his head to look out her window. I hate it so much seeing him sad. His brightness is dimmed and I'm the reason.

Doing my best to comfort him and make this easier, I take his hand to hold it. It's clenched so tight. I push his fingers open to slide mine between them.

Sasha's voice doesn't really sound like hers, other than her heavier accent, as she continues her story. "I thought that was the end of it, until he told the other guy to hold me down." The anger creeps back into her eyes when she looks at Lex and wipes her hand across her still wet cheek. "He touched my face. I don't think my heart has ever beat so hard. I was terrified. I didn't know what he was gonna do." Her voice breaks with hidden tears as she tries to regain her composure. "He was so close to me, I thought he was going to kiss me. Instead, he whispered, *'Aging is such a shame. You were an incredibly beautiful child.'* It was creepy as fuck, Alex." She walks to the sofa and falls against the cushions. "Then he gave me the shot. That's all I remember."

Alexander squeezes my hand so hard I wonder if I will hear the bones crack. When he finally speaks, it's cold. "What if dad knows? About all of it?" He asks her.

Just because Bjørn was an original Client, doesn't mean he knows anything about my life before then. Unless Logan told him, which I seriously doubt.

"I don't think so. I didn't meet Bjørn until our fifth anniversary."

Both of their heads snap in my direction as they simultaneously ask, "Whose anniversary?"

"Toben, Logan and mine."

"Are you telling me that you celebrated…it?" He speaks as if he's tasted something gross.

I pull my hand away. I knew he wouldn't be able to

understand. He's acting like it's horrible when I've always loved that Logan did that for us. Anniversaries were one of my favorite days of the year.

I cross my arms. "Yes. I looked forward to it, actually."

His face hardens and his Adam's apple bobs. I've clearly made him angry. "So how exactly does one celebrate rape day? Or as you call it, 'initiation.'"

He's making fun of me. Of my life. I feel stupid and embarrassed. I knew this would happen. I'm able to swallow down the tears before they come up too high for me to answer his question.

"After we played, he would give us presents and a big cupcake. Then we would all get high together."

It's like someone wipes something over his face because his fury is smoothed out as he looks to Sasha. "Pack what you can. We need to get going."

She chews the inside of her mouth before spinning around and disappearing down the hall. His hand is back around mine as he pulls me to the big chair and onto his lap.

"I'm sorry. I hurt your feelings and I don't want that. Honestly Tav, I have no idea how to go forward with this information. I've never experienced hate quite like this before. I want him to suffer an excruciating death and I know I can't kill him myself no matter how much I fantasize about it. I'm not perfect by any stretch, so I may not react to some of the stuff you tell me, in the best way, alright? Just please know I don't ever want to hurt you, okay?"

I want him to understand me, and my life, and my feelings, so I suppose that means it's only fair that I try to see his side. I know he cares about me and I do know my situation isn't good or normal. This probably is very difficult on him as well.

I nod and smile at him when Blind Mag jumps in my lap. "Okay."

We get her stuff together pretty fast with all three of us doing it. Alexander loads it all into the trunk while Sasha and I climb into the Mercedes. I tug the seat-belt strap across my chest as she pops her head in between the front seats.

"Give it to me straight. Should I stop planning this wedding?"

This is all my fault. She's been so excited about her dress and cake. She told me she's been dreaming of it since she was a little girl. I've barely thought about what a wedding is, much less ever wanting one.

"He was pretty mad, but maybe if you explain how it wasn't your fault, he won't be, anymore."

She reaches out and picks up Blind Mag from my lap. "What did he say exactly?"

I don't want to tell her. She isn't a 'piece of shit', she's beautiful, and my friend. "It wasn't very nice, Sasha, don't worry though, Lex punched him."

I expect her to be proud of him for standing up for her. Instead, her nostrils are flaring and her nails are going to ruin Lex's upholstery, so I don't think she is.

"He what?"

Before I can answer her, Lex gets into the car and looks at us. "What?"

"You hit Drew?!"

He playfully narrows his eyes at me. I didn't know she would get angry.

"He's lucky that's all I did. I've never understood why you let him talk to you that way."

She must be dropping it for now because she leans back in her seat and quietly pets Blind Mag.

They don't want me to blame myself, but how am I supposed to do that when this IS my fault? Absolutely none of this would be happening if I wouldn't have gotten involved with Lex.

His thumb presses a couple buttons on the steering wheel and ringing momentarily fills the car before it's replaced by Silas' distorted voice.

"Hey." He sounds like he's holding his breath. As he harshly exhales and starts coughing, I know he's smoking. A joint sounds fabulous right now.

"Hey, are you home? I need a favor."

"Does it require getting up? Because I just rolled a fatty."

Lex's lips are pressed together as he exhales through his nose. "This is serious, Silas. I need you to keep an eye on Tavin and Sasha while I run out for a bit. It shouldn't take long."

"Uh…okay, I guess." His voice turns bubbly as he asks, "Sasha's with you?"

"Yeah, it's a long story. Be ready when I get there and stop smoking. I need you sober."

"Ugh, fine. Somebody better be dying."

My heart cracks at the thought of Logan beating Toben to death. The horrible things he would do to him if he's angry enough. We need to hurry.

Lex takes my hand and kisses it. "Be there in a few.'"

I want so badly to go with Lex. I don't ask though because I already know what the answer would be.

He drops the three of us off at his house and when Silas shuts the front door, we all stare at each other, none of us knowing what to say without Alexander as our buffer.

Sasha puts down Blind Mag and I pick her up as Silas walks to the fridge and takes out a beer. "You guys want one?"

"Sure." Sasha sits at the island and I nod at him that I'd like one, too.

He hands them to us before he leans against the counter and pops the tab. Arching his thick eyebrow, he asks, "So, is anyone going to explain to me what's going on? Or why I'm babysitting two grown adults?"

Sasha looks at me so he does too. I feel hot and my stomach kind of hurts. I don't know what to say.

"W—well…there's someone after me. Someone bad. He found out I was staying with Sasha and he—"

"He threatened me and Alex," she finishes, as she glances at me, obviously not wanting Silas to know about something. I'm not sure if it's the heroin, Drew, or both.

"Um…yeah, so Alexander doesn't want us left alone. He went to go talk to my friend, Toben, to make sure he's okay."

"And how does he fit into this?"

I still shouldn't tell people. I don't want to do anything else to make Logan any madder than he already is.

"He's a prostitute that worked with Tavin," Sasha answers for me, and it's like my throat opens up allowing the oxygen to get back in.

"Ohhhh. So, the 'someone bad' is your pimp?"

"Uh, yeah."

He snaps his finger apparently proud of his ability to follow this. "Hold on, isn't that who you fucked?"

Sasha stands up and goes to the counter. "No more questions, Hamilton." When she turns around, she has two cookies in her hand and gives me one. Yes! Cara Jo's rainbow sprinkle cookies are the best. "You have to get your own cookie."

Did she wink at him?

His smile says she did. He lifts the lid to the cookie jar and grabs a fist full. Grinning, he asks, "So you guys wanna wreck the bong I keep here?" I keep myself from squealing as I nod at him, and he laughs, "Short stack's obviously down."

Sasha flips her hair over her shoulder and groans, "Ugh, stoner. You keep a bong here?"

"Yeah. I have some clothes and a few other things too. I keep them in the room I sometimes use when I…need to sleep it off."

"I'm sure," Sasha deadpans. "'Sleep it off' inside a chick, maybe." He shrugs and when her mouth falls open, he laughs at her while she punches him in the arm. "Fine, whatever. Let's go."

I hear something, causing me to look at the bedroom door. "Did you guys hear that?"

"No, just like the last three times you asked," Silas mumbles.

I shake my head. I heard something. "It's voices."

Jumping up to run out of Silas' room and down the hall, I ignore them calling after me. I burst into the kitchen and then I see them. The two people that mean more to me than anything.

Toben looks like he's alright, allowing my chest to slowly deflate and I want to cry with relief.

Silas and Sasha come behind me when Sasha asks, "Is everything okay?"

"We aren't dead yet. So yeah, sure, everything's fabulous," Toben spouts off as he laces his fingers with mine.

I examine him and he seems completely fine. "What happened with Logan?"

"Nothing, yet. He hasn't said a word to me." He cups my face with both hands. "So you've made up your mind about coming home then?"

There's anger in his darkened eyes and pain in his voice. I'm betraying the only person that has always been there for me no matter what. Am I being a bad person and a bad friend by choosing to trust Lex and wanting this other life?

Even though I really don't want to cry, the moisture burns so badly I don't think I can stop it. I was so sure, and now that I'm back with Toben, seeing what I'm doing to him, I'm suddenly not anymore.

He's endured so much pain at the hands of others, but this time it's me doing the hurting. I don't want that. I don't want that at all.

The tears pour from my eyes making things blurry. "Tobe, I…I don't know."

"What?!"

Sasha and Lex both yell at me.

I look up at Alexander, his chest rises with his deep breaths. "What the fuck do you mean you 'don't know'?"

Nobody understands. Nobody! I feel sick and slimy and I want to grab that potato peeler off the counter and shave the skin off my arms.

I pull away from Toben, from all of them. "What do you all want from me? Tell me!" I turn to Lex and Sasha. "You want me to put my best friend in danger. You want me to walk away from the only life I have ever known and expect me to instantly be something else." I look at Toben. "How can you not see that I may finally be getting the chance to be done with it? The chance to be free of the disgust, the Clients…Logan. You know how it is for me. Day after day, man after man, each getting to say and do anything they want, each making me dirtier and filthier! Why would you want that for me?" His face falls along with his shoulders. I don't want him to feel bad, I want him to see why. Why I need to get out. "I'm just…I'm so tired, Toben."

He comes closer and brushes his fingers across my cheek. "I'm sorry, Love. I don't want that for you. I've just always thought it was better that you're sad as long as you're alive."

Lex comes up behind me and places his hand on the small of my back. "You don't have to worry about her anymore. And even though I can't promise how long it will take, I will permanently free her from that fuck, one way or another. That much I swear."

Toben wipes his nose. "Well at least you believe it."

"I can help you too, you know."

Toben lets out a sarcastic laugh before straightening his beanie and crossing his arms. "Uh, no, I'm good."

Monday, June 22nd

Alexander

I trail my fingers over the scars on her back as she lies against my chest. When I look at the clock, I groan and lift her off me.

"I need to start getting ready for work." Pulling open my drawer, I take out my green basketball shorts and look over my shoulder. "Do you wanna let me watch you do yoga while I work out?"

With a grin, she hops off the bed to put on her shorts and tank. She's behind me as I swing open my bedroom door to find Cara Jo in the hallway. She glares at me with one hand on the vacuum and the other on her hip.

"Will Emily be staying for breakfast or do you already have someone new in there?"

I'm a little taken aback by her hostility. "Do you have something you want to say Cara Jo?"

She straightens her back and grips the vacuum handle. "Actually, young man, I do. You being my employer doesn't change the fact that I raised you from diapers, and that will always deserve your respect. Until now, I've never needed to point that out. I don't know the whole story with Tavin because you've decided to close me off, so I haven't said my peace about it. I spent a lot of time with that girl. Whatever you think she did, she must have had a good reason."

I didn't realize I hurt her so badly. While I knew I hadn't treated her the greatest, I simply assumed she would brush it off like she always does.

"It was never my intention to disappoint you and I don't ever want to make you feel that way. I lash out when I am struggling emotionally, you know that…not that it's an excuse. I should have come to you. I'm very sorry. Truly. Take Saturday off, paid, okay?"

She raises her eyebrow, turning her head to the side. "What's going on with you? Something's…" Her eyes widen as a huge smile brightens her face. "Tavin!"

I suddenly become invisible as Cara Jo pushes past me to hug her. A loud yawn makes us all look to see Sasha coming up the stairs.

"What's with the love fest?"

Cara Jo's joy is washed out by confusion. "What have I missed?"

I'm having a difficult time explaining the situation without being able to actually explain the situation. Cara Jo has always been good about giving me space, though her curiosity has its limits.

"Will you be staying here for a while then, Sasha?"

Sasha rests her cheek in her palm and nods. "Indefinitely."

"I'm very sorry to hear that, dear." Cara Jo pats her on the shoulder before she picks up her empty plate.

Sasha slouches down in her chair "Thanks, Cara Jo."

Tavin's gaze falls to her lap like she's feeling guilty again.

I squeeze her hand beneath the table to get a smile out of her, before I check my phone. It's almost six. The body guard I hired will be here any minute.

Casually, I try to inform Cara Jo. "I decided I needed to hire an extra hand around here." Her eyebrows lift up her forehead and I can feel a glare coming on. "He's only here for security. Don't worry, he'll stay out of your way."

Her irritation evaporates as she asks, "Security? What on earth for?"

"It's only precaution, there's nothing to worry about."

As if on cue, the doorbell rings. I open it only to be dwarfed by Dwayne Johnson's doppelganger. He holds out his massive hand. "Hello, Mr. Sørensen. My name is Timothy Shark."

Shark? Well, it's fitting. I wonder if he'll have to duck to get in the door.

"Hi. Come on in." He fills up the entire entryway as I lead him to the kitchen and gesture to the girls. "Mr. Shark, this is Cara Jo, Tavin, and my sister, Sasha."

His baritone voice rumbles as he clasps his hands together. "It's a pleasure."

Cara Jo gapes at his size as Sasha leans forward to rest her head on her hands, basically drooling when she says, "Yes, it is." She's so ridiculous it's embarrassing.

Tavin holds up her hand in a wave, and he nods to her before turning to me. "My portfolio has been emailed to you and I've been briefed on your file. Is there anything else pertinent?"

It's a little unsettling to know I'm leaving three of the most important women in my life, alone with a stranger. He's the agency's highest recommended body guard though, and that helps ease my anxieties.

"My main concern is that you're aware of Tavin's whereabouts at all times, and if you leave the house, she's not to ever be out of your sight."

"I understand completely, sir."

"If you need anything, feel free to call or text anytime. You have all my emails and numbers." I hold out my hand. "It's nice to meet you, Mr. Shark."

"Likewise. And Timothy is fine."

"Okay, Timothy, I need to get ready for work, so I guess I'll leave you to it."

As I walk up the stairs, I hear the small talk begin and on my walk back down, I hear laughter.

They seem to all be getting along just fine when I tell everyone goodbye. Tavin wraps her arms around my neck and she kisses me.

"Have a good day, Lex."

"You too. Try to have fun."

It gives me a mix of relief and excitement to know she'll be here when I get home.

As I pull out of my driveway and stop at the first stop sign on my street, I dial William's number. He hasn't called me back, and I've tried a few times since yesterday.

I'm about to hang up when the ringing is cut off by a woman's voice. "Hello?"

"Hello, my name is Alexander Sørensen. I'm looking for William Morrison, is he available?"

There's a long pause before she says, "I'm so sorry, William has passed on."

It's not as if I knew the man that well, and still, my stomach drops at the news. "I'm very sorry to hear that. May I ask what happened?"

She sniffles before I hear the creak of a chair. "Oh... well, I don't know if it's my place to tell you this..." Her voice drops as a sob escapes. "He shot himself." Alarm bells sound in the back of my mind as her breathing gets shaky, "I never had any suspicions that he could do this."

It may be paranoia, but with what just happened with Sasha, the timing doesn't feel coincidental. My heart beats a little harder as I consider the fact that William may have played a part in Logan finding out about Tavin staying at Sasha's.

"I appreciate you telling me, and I'm sorry for your loss."

Disconnecting the call, a shiver runs through my body. I know people can surprise you, but William always struck me as too selfish to kill himself.

My gut rolls at the thought of what could have transpired with Sasha if Logan had wanted to take it that direction. While I can't be certain he played a part William's death, the suicide isn't sitting right and hiring someone else to investigate could potentially get more people hurt. I wipe a hand over my face and crank up the air conditioner to cool myself down and slow my heart rate.

I'm going to have to figure this out on my own.

Driving a little faster than necessary on my way home from work, I finally pull into my driveway. I can't help it. I've been thinking about seeing her all day.

The kitchen is empty besides Cara Jo stirring away at the stove. "Hey, how did everything go today?"

She turns and wipes her hands on her apron. "It went fine, I just don't understand what's going on exactly."

"I know, and I promise at some point I will answer all of your questions." Taking off my jacket, I drape it over my arm as she pats my back.

"I won't ever push you, dear."

"Thank you." I wrap her in a side hug as I grab a fried potato off the skillet. "Where is everyone?"

She smacks my hand away and shoos me off. "They went downstairs about an hour ago. Maybe you should join them."

Laughing, I turn to go upstairs when she adds, "When you go down there, tell them dinner will be ready in a half hour."

Once I change out of my suit, I jog back downstairs. As soon as I open the basement door, music and laughter floats up the stairwell. I step onto the landing, and what's going on in my gaming center could easily be classified as disturbing.

Dance Dance Revolution is on the TV. Tavin and Sasha are in fits of laughter watching Timothy get down to a Britney Spears song.

I wait until the song is finished to let my presence be known. "That was impressive."

He laughs, "Peer pressure and pretty girls. I'm not invincible, you know."

Tavin bounces up to me and wraps her arms around my waist. I kiss her forehead and turn back to Timothy. "Are you staying for dinner? Cara Jo made plenty and I think she's expecting you to…unless you have a family you need to get home to?"

"That's very kind, and no, I don't have anywhere to be. I would love to stay."

"Great. Would you like a drink?"

I mix our drinks and we sit, watching the girls dance their little butts off. He seems like a pretty good guy. The short conversation we have before dinner tells me that he has recently split up with his fiancé, a girl named Melanie, because he met the love of his life, Todd. He told me that while he loves both of them, his heart belongs to Todd and he will always honor his heart. His story is rather sweet. His now ex-fiancé is completely supportive and they have been able to remain friends. By the time we head upstairs for dinner, any doubts I may have had about hiring him have vanished.

Dinner is a nice break from the constant tension that's been in my life, recently. Timothy is an intelligent and funny guy and has us all laughing over his tales of being a security and body guard. Over dessert, he mentions that he's always wanted to go to culinary school.

"I have some great tricks I could teach you, Cara Jo."

The awkward silence that follows her responding glare is broken by Tavin's chortles. "Cara Jo doesn't share the kitchen."

Cara Jo winks at Tavin and puts another small slice of pie on her plate. "That's my girl."

Sasha nudges her shoulder and loudly whispers, "Suck up."

Tavin swallows her huge bite, and points to her plate. "Maybe, but I'm the one with two pieces of pie."

Wiping my mouth, I chuckle as the doorbell rings through the house. Gesturing at Cara Jo with my hand, I tell her I got it.

I open the door to see the asshole who created me, standing on my front porch. "What are you doing here?"

He's definitely not coming inside, so I step out and shut the door behind me. His skin looks a little pale and the bags under his eyes are bigger than I've ever seen them. With shaky fingers he combs back his graying hair.

"I'm not sure what you know, Alexander. I've learned to not ask questions when it comes to Logan." Fear is not something I'm accustomed to seeing in my father's eyes, and as unsettling as that is for me, I won't let him see me waiver. "You've made a violent and powerful man very angry, Son. I can see you care about her and I know she's intoxicating—"

"If you want me to listen to another word you have to say, don't reference having been with her, again."

He closes his eyes while he shakes his head. "You need to

let her go, Son. The things this man is capable of doing… I should have warned you from the beginning. I'd hoped that maybe you were making the right connections in an unorthodox manner. I never imagined she was hiding with you."

"You're seriously suggesting I send her back to her captor and rapist?"

He wipes his hands across his face. "I didn't know anything definitive, though I had my suspicions. She always seemed as if she want—" He looks at my glare and is smart enough to stop himself. "He could destroy us all, Alexander. Please think this through. Is this girl worth losing everything you and those you love, have worked so hard for?"

I scoff. "Oh my God. He threatened your finances, that's why you're here." I don't even know why I'm surprised. "I thought maybe you knew about Sasha. Come to find out, all you're worried about is your money."

"What? What happened with Sasha?"

"Ask her yourself, I'm done with this conversation."

He grabs my arm. "*Tankene før hjertet*. Mind before heart, Son. Please, think about what you're doing. There will be other girls."

I pull my arm free and go inside. I haven't had much respect for my father for a long time and now I think I lost the rest of it.

Tuesday, June 23rd

It's not even seven and it's already so hot out that Sasha and Tavin barely let Timothy walk in the door before they drag him off to go swimming. It's days like this when I dread wearing a suit. I drape my jacket over my arm because I'm sure as hell not putting it on until I have to.

Splashing and laughing greets me as I slide open the patio door.

"Marco!" Timothy's eyes are squeezed shut and his giant arms are outstretched, while the girls try to throw him off by splashing and quickly swimming away.

"Polo!" They yell together as he lunges for Sasha.

I hold my hands up in a *T*. "Hey, guys, time out. I'm leaving for work."

Tavin doggy paddles to climb up the ladder and jogs over to me. Her lips are wet and her hair is dripping onto my shirt as she kisses me goodbye.

From that moment on, my day is packed.

I have a meeting as soon as I get into the office and a ton of paperwork that needs my signature. After my lunch meeting with a contractor to discuss some options for Vulture Sports, I'll need to focus my attention on a few financial issues.

It's almost three by the time I finally get back to the office. I barely step off the elevator when Jacob, my new assistant, comes rushing over to me. He's a dorky little dude with glasses way too big for his face, and so far, he's the best assistant I've ever had.

"Hi, Jacob." I take the files from his hands and he seems nervous. "Are you okay?"

"I'm sorry, I somehow missed that you had a meeting this afternoon. I never put it on your schedule and now he's waiting in your office. I apologize, sir."

"It's fine, Jacob. I know who it is. Hold all my calls and if you need anything, go to Silas until I'm done."

He nods and pushes up his glasses. "Of course, Mr. Sørensen."

We're considering a twenty-one and over Vulture location above a popular bar in Copetown, I just wasn't expecting the owner, Mr. Keller, until next week. Smoothing out my suit, I push open my office door and prepare to apologize for the delay.

The words never make their way from my lips because the man in my office is not Mr. Keller, and seeing him in the flesh makes my throat feel blocked with cotton. He sits behind my desk smiling as though we're old friends. A five second fantasy of grabbing the ice pick from the bar and stabbing him between the eyes jumps across my mind, when he stands to his feet.

"Hello, Alexander. Thank you for seeing me." Like I had a damn choice. Holding his hand out to the chair in front of my desk, he says, "Please." As if this is his fucking office. He wants it to piss me off, and while it absolutely does, I'm sure as hell not playing these games. I remain silent and standing as he sits back down and asks, "Do you know who I am?"

I focus on pushing all my weight through my feet to stay grounded, so I don't do something I'll regret. It feels as if I have lava burning through my vocal chords, so I'm relieved at the strength in my voice when I answer him.

"I know exactly who you are, Mr. James."

"Call me Logan. Formalities are a bit farcical at this point, don't you think?" I say nothing as I cross my arms. "Now, I'm sure Bjørn taught you that it isn't polite to touch someone's things without asking."

CHAPTER EIGHT
Purchase

REFUSE TO GIVE HIS PATRONIZING TONE THE satisfaction of any more than a scoff, as the facade of his friendliness slips away. Though his voice remains calm, I swear his hazel eyes brighten when he leans forward and clasps his hands on my desk.

"Where the fuck is my Lotus?"

My throat is as scratchy as sandpaper when I swallow, to make sure my words come out clear. "There's not a chance in hell I'm letting you anywhere near her again, you sick motherfucker."

Acting as if he didn't hear me, he reaches into his jacket and pulls out a clear bag of white powder, sprinkling it across my desk. Is this asshole serious? He straightens the line with one of my business cards and he speaks as if he's never been more bored.

"While your gumption may be a positive trait in most situations, I assure you this is not one of them." He leans forward and after one quick inhale, the powder is gone. Retrieving a handkerchief from his pocket, he rubs his nose and returns the drugs to his jacket. "I'm not a snake you want to poke, and my relationship with your father will not take you much further."

"You stole my sister's sobriety." Remorse is nowhere to be seen in his smug face. "You're welcome to do your worst. I'll never hand her over to a rapist and a pedophile."

For the first time, he bristles. His lip lifts into a snarl as the veins in his neck pulsate with silent fury. "I will get my toy back, Alexander. I've burned down bigger cities for less."

Everyone in my life that he could hurt, Sasha, Cara Jo, my mother…I can't protect them all. He speaks of Tavin as if she's his merchandise and the words slide out of my lips before I can process the thought.

"What if I pay for her?"

His eyebrows raise as his lips lift into a smirk. "You want to make a purchase? Now that's something else entirely."

"How much?"

He straightens his suit sleeves as well as himself, while he contemplates his answer. "You were in possession of Sweet Girl for a month, then of course the additional two weeks she spent with your little look a-like. The time, loss, and effort that has gone into the multiple missed playdates and my search for the product…Then of course there's the matter of the base financial value…" He does the math in his head and I'm in awe at how he can talk about her this way. "I've known your father a long time, and therefore I'm feeling quite generous. Let's just say an even six."

I don't have a clue if I'm able to hide the fact that my heart drops. This is going to be a huge financial hit. Of course it's not a question of being worth it, but damn.

"Done. I'll have it in your account by the end of the week."

He buttons his suit jacket as he stands. "I'll have a contract sent over by five this evening."

What's the point of a contract? I'm pretty sure that shit won't hold up in court. His nonchalance at this whole situation repulses me.

"Answer me one question. Six million is worth that, don't you think?" He tilts his head in curiosity as he nods at me to continue. "How could you do it? She was just a little girl, she was so young. How could you do those things to her?"

A slow, big smile stretches across his entire face as he chuckles, "You think she's tight now?" There's no possibility of covering up my horror as he laughs and walks to the door to leave. "Enjoy your new plaything, Alexander."

That's it? Yeah, it's a lot of money, but that went exactly six million times easier than I assumed it would.

"So that's the end of it? She's free?"

Once again, his body stiffens as his eyes flash. "That's entirely up to you."

He waits for my response, so I nod at him and four seconds later I'm alone. As he shuts the door, my body collapses into the chair he wanted me to sit in.

I can't believe it's really over.

⌒

As the day goes on, I get more excited about the Logan threat being eliminated. My chest loosens and I feel more relaxed than I have in weeks. I float through the afternoon and Silas even comments on my mood when he meets me at the elevator.

"Are you stoned or something? You seem really happy for someone who's supposed to be going through some kind of personal crisis."

Smiling at the receptionist, I walk toward the back hall for our board meeting. "Actually, there was an interesting development today that changed things drastically."

"Does any of this have to do with Sasha? She keeps skirting around why she's staying with you. This can't all be because of the pimp guy."

"She must have her reasons for not telling you, Silas."

He steps in front of me. "Come on. We've been best friends for almost twenty years. I've always been here for you guys, don't you think I deserve to know what's going on with you two?"

"Look, Sasha and I are finally getting our relationship back and I really don't want to piss her off, so let's just say she and Drew are having issues and leave it at that for now, alright?"

He huffs as I pull open the glass doors of the board room and he follows me inside.

The meeting runs long because Jefferson doesn't ever know when to shut up, and I still have some things to wrap up before I can head home. I open my e-mails, deleting what is unnecessary, when I see one with an attachment sent by Logan.

Bill of Sale
This bill of sale is made and effective June 23, 2015

BETWEEN: Logan James *(the "Seller")*
841 E. Blankenfort Ln.
Shadoebox City, California 95474

AND: Alexander Sørensen *(the "Buyer")*
286 E. Wharton Rd.
Shadoebox City, California 95475

The Seller hereby sells and transfers possession of the following product in their present condition and location to the Buyer.

(1) Sweet Girl – Tavin Winters
Ethnicity: Caucasian
Hair color: Brown

Age: 23 years old
Virginal: No
Use: Slight to moderate
Damage: Mild to moderate wear and tear

In payment of the sum <u>$6,000,000.00</u> the sufficiency of which acknowledged, the undersigned (the Seller) <u>Logan James </u>hereby sells and transfers to (the Buyer) <u>Alexander Sørensen </u>the described property above.

The Seller warrants that he has good title to said product, with full authority to sell and transfer.

The Buyer acknowledges examining the product and buying it "as is" at the Buyer's risk and agrees not to make any claims against the Seller based on alleged express or implied representations.

This bill of Sale is executed in duplicate on <u>6/23/15</u> signed and delivered to the Buyer.

BUYER

_____
Authorized Signature

_____
Print Name and Title

SELLER

<u>*Logan James*</u>
Authorized Signature

<u>*Logan James Rissa Corp. CEO*</u>

Seeing my name on this 'Bill of Sale' makes me nauseous. 'Slight to moderate' use? He's fucking insane.

I do what I have to do and sign the pointless contract before sending it back to him. The guilt over the fact that I just paid money for a person is tangled with the relief that he's agreeing to leave her alone.

I swear my heart is beating at double its normal speed, by the time I pull into my garage. This is huge. That's why I don't understand why there's trepidation still lurking in the back of my mind. I tell myself it's only nerves because this is nothing short of incredible.

The amazing smells that greet me as I walk into the kitchen have me licking my lips. Timothy is reading a Dean Koontz novel and Sasha's sketching at the island, yet Tavin is nowhere to be seen.

"Welcome home, Mr. Sørensen," Timothy says, as he closes the book and smiles.

"It's weird for you to call me that in my home. Please, call me Alex."

He nods at me as Sasha's pencil keeps swiping at the page, when she answers the question I don't even have to ask.

"She's upstairs changing out of her swimsuit, and showering." She adds a few final lines before closing her sketch book. "I'm actually gonna do the same." She playfully punches Timothy in the arm. "Later, Flounder."

I slip off my jacket and pull down a glass with a questioning grin. "Flounder?"

He rolls his eyes and smirks. "She's making fun of my name. She says 'Flounder' fits me better than 'Shark.'"

"She always thought she was hilarious." He chuckles as I ask, "Hey, would you and Todd like to come out with us tonight? I would like to meet him."

He stands and scoots the bar stool beneath the bar. "We would enjoy that. Let me talk to him and I'll let you know."

"Great. If you guys decide you can make it, meet us at The Necco Room sometime after eight."

He pulls his keys out of his jeans pocket and holds out his hand for a shake. "Maybe we'll see you later then."

He lets himself out as I pour my drink and wait for her.

I'm polishing off my second glass when I hear her coming down the stairs. She jumps off the last step with Blind Mag in tow and her face brightens into her beautiful smile when she sees me.

She breaks into a run and my tongue suddenly swells up. How do I tell her, that after all this time, she never has to be scared of Logan James again? My lips begin moving before my mind gets around to processing it.

"You're free of him, *Lille*."

She freezes in her path so abruptly, Blind Mag runs past her. She looks as if speaking is agonizing as she whispers, "What?"

Why is this so hard to say? I should be telling her in an excited rush. "He let you go."

Instead of the happiness I was expecting, her face reads only confusion. "That makes no sense. He wouldn't 'let me go'. That isn't how Logan operates."

This is the part. This is the part I didn't want to say, I just didn't realize it until now.

"I made a deal with him."

"What kind of deal?"

"I, uh…I…paid him."

Her eyes are the first thing to break my heart; the way her body sways back as if the words physically touch her, is the second. She falls to her knees and places her hands on her thighs. When she looks up at me, it isn't her looking into my eyes. Her body is hollow and Tavin is gone. The girl in front of me is a ghost.

My voice sounds furious, when what I really am is horrified. "Tavin, get the fuck up."

"Yes, Alexander." Her voice is monotone as she quickly stands to her feet.

No, she can't do this. She can't see it this way, see *me* this way.

I close the gap between us and pull her to my chest. I don't know what to do, how to help her. I cup my hands around her face so she's looking at me and smooth her hair back.

"I bought time, not you. I can't pretend to imagine how this feels for you. I didn't know what else to do. I just wanted you to feel safe. Please…" I softly press my lips to hers, "Please know this was just a means to an end. You are and always will be my equal." She stares at me as her mind is clearly processing all of this. "Say something."

"You're my…owner."

"I am not. I'm not your owner and you most certainly are not my plaything. I am your friend, your lover, and you…" I press my forehead to hers, "You are my *Lille*."

"Can I leave?"

It feels like a steel cannonball drops in my stomach. She's leaving me over this? What the fuck else was I supposed to do?

I stand straight without pulling away from her. "If that's what you want, then yes."

She nods and softly smiles when she wraps her arms around my waist. "Okay." Okay? What does that mean? "I believe you." She whispers it against my chest as she squeezes me tighter. "It just doesn't make any sense."

"What doesn't?"

"That Logan just sold me to you, easy as that. That isn't

like him." She shakes her head. "This doesn't feel right."

"It only feels that way because you haven't absorbed it yet. Give it a few days to sink in."

"I don't know…I don't trust him."

I pick her up and sit her on the island so we are closer to eye level. "You don't have to trust him, I'm asking you to trust me. We can finally be together for real this time."

She still doesn't seem completely convinced. "Okay, Lex."

I kiss her cute little nose. "After dinner, how would you like to go out?"

That brightens her right up. "Okay!" She jumps off the counter and picks up Blind Mag. "I better go change."

She bounces up the steps, and I'd bet the Alfa, that she's taking two at a time. She's been sober for the last couple of days and I'm sure she's more than ready to change that.

Maybe allowing her to drink when she has her drug addictions isn't the most intelligent choice on my part. However, if an alcohol buzz here and there is enough to keep her from looking for a high, then I'm all for it.

Sasha comes down a moment later towel drying her hair. "Tavin said you guys are going out tonight?"

"We have a lot to celebrate."

She raises her eyebrows. "Oh, do we, now? Two years sobriety was forcibly taken away from me by the guy who wants to kill your girlfriend, and let's see…oh yeah, I got kicked out of my apartment and have to cancel my wedding. So sure, I totally see your point."

As important as keeping Tavin safe is, Sasha is also high on my list of priorities, and even though she's handling this situation with grace, she has to be struggling.

"I know, Sash. How are you holding up?"

She exhales out of her nose. "Honestly, better than I expected and it's easier without my old connections. I'm just so angry those two years are worthless now."

I wrap my arm around her shoulder and pull her to me. "They aren't worthless, Sasha. I'm so fucking proud of you." She smiles and hugs me back. "What about Drew? Are you okay with that?"

She smiles the fake smile she used to use around our parent's friends. "I have to be. And I think it's true what they say about not knowing what you have until it's gone. I'm not nearly as heartbroken as I should be."

"Well, wait till you hear what happened today, it might cheer you up." She pulls away from me, tilting her head in question. "Logan came to Vulture this afternoon."

Her eyes widen as her hand covers her mouth. "Oh shit, seriously?"

"Yeah…we made a deal. I pay him a shit ton and he allows her freedom."

She looks at me like I'm full of crap. "That's it? Money?" She crosses her arms. "That's anticlimactic."

I toss back my whiskey. "Sorry I couldn't make it more entertaining for you."

She shoves my arm and grins. "Oh, shut up, you know I'm happy for you." She shrugs. "It just seems way too simple."

"Men like him operate on power. I presume that's why he did what he did to Tavin, it gave him some God-like authority over her. By making me purchase her, he not only beat the hell out of my bank account, he made it clear that it was his choice to allow her freedom."

She takes my glass and pours her own drink. "Maybe."

"If anything, it gives me more time to figure out how to go about bringing these charges against him. Now, are you coming out with us or not?"

As soon as she rolls her eyes, I know she's in.

"Fine."

Tavin

Lex smacks my ass as we make our way back to the kitchen for dinner. I love to see him dressed so casually in his Nirvana tee shirt and jeans. Things should be different between us now, but they aren't. Even though I'm his property, he doesn't see it that way and somehow, that makes me not either.

Sasha takes me into one of the bathrooms to touch up our makeup before we follow Alexander to the Mercedes. She sits in the backseat and lets me sit up front.

I like the way the blond hairs on Lex's arm show up in the light as the sunset shines through the window. I didn't know hands could be a sexy body part, but watching the way the tendons move in his fingers as he adjusts the dials on the stereo makes me want to put them between my legs. He turns the music down as he glances in the rear-view mirror.

"I texted Silas earlier, but haven't heard back. He's never not down for the bar, so let's swing by his place and pull him out of whoever he's inside of."

Something flies by my face as Sasha punches Lex in the shoulder and snaps, "God, you're such a pig!"

He chuckles, "What's your problem?"

She falls against the back seat as her pretty voice mumbles, "Nothing."

Silas' apartment building is one of the taller buildings down town. I've passed it hundreds of times on my way to playdates.

Alexander pulls open the big glass doors and waves at

the security guard behind a desk. He's in a black uniform and smiles as he nods to us.

"Good evening, Mr. Sørensen, Ms. Sørensen, ma'am."

I grin at him as Lex pulls me by my hand into the elevator. He slides a special key through the slot commanding the elevator car to take us to Silas' penthouse. My stomach tickles from the upward movement, until the bell dings at the correct floor.

The doors open to a huge living room and my jaw drops. He has the biggest window I think I've ever seen! The whole back wall is one solid window. His floors are black and shiny and it looks like the ceiling is being held up by two huge, white pillars.

Silas is sitting next to a dark-haired lady on one of those weird couches shaped like a peanut. They both turn to look at us and the woman's face brightens into a huge smile.

"Oh my stars! I don't believe it."

Lex instantly stops walking and laughs the funniest chuckle I've ever heard from him. It's almost a giggle and it's so awkward it makes me grin.

The woman stands up and gives him a big hug, squeezing him tight. "Look at you! My goodness young man, how you've grown!"

He rubs the back of his neck. "Hello, Ms. Hamilton."

Oh, this is Silas' mom? I look up at Lex. Is he blushing?

Her hand slowly rubs down his arm and she gives him a seductive smirk. "It's been awhile."

He does that weird laugh again. "Yes, ma'am."

I've never seen him act like this or seen him look so uncomfortable. He's usually bubbling over with confidence.

I think my jaw drops because between her flirty smile, her subtle excuses to touch him, his obvious fluster...they've had to of slept together.

"Oh, man," I can't stop my laugh, because honestly, I

can't imagine Lex with this woman and for some reason, knowing who she is makes it funny. "You guys have had sex, huh?"

Alexander's head whips down at me with his face full now of nothing besides shock. "Tavin!"

"What?!" Silas roars as he jumps off the couch. Uh oh. He's angry. Really angry. "You fucked my mom?!"

Lex glares at me and Sasha slaps her hand over her mouth like it will keep her laughing inside. Now I feel bad. I don't want to make them fight.

Alexander holds up his hands. "Look man, it was over ten years ago. You had gone to your dad's for the summer and it was right after I found out about Aslaug. I was upset."

Silas looks like he can't decide whether to yell or cry, when his mom puts her hand on his face. Her nails are long and red and they dig into his cheeks a little. "We were both adults, Sugar. He was sad and I was lonely. He made mommy feel good."

His face washes out like he might be sick. "Mom…"

I make the mistake of glancing at Sasha, who's completely red in the face from holding back laughter. I think laughing is contagious like yawning. Her face makes my own small snicker escape, and she looks like she's about to explode. Lex gives her a dirty look before trying to calm down Silas.

"Really, it's not a big deal."

"Well then, I guess it won't bother you to know I've been fucking your sister."

I look at Sasha's wide-eyed face and she's not laughing anymore. I wasn't expecting that part.

"What?!" Alexander barks.

"Yup, for more than a decade now, isn't that right, babe?" Sasha's mouth is hanging open and for the first time since I've met her, she's speechless. Silas looks back to Lex.

"I've always been curious if your twintuition tells you when I make her come, because that happens a lot."

Alexander's fists clench as he takes a step forward. "Oh, you motherfucker, did you forget I know how to box?"

Sasha rolls her eyes at them and grab's Lex's hand. "Alex, chill."

He glares at her. "Chill? You've been cheating on Drew and you both have lied to me for years. I mean fuck, is nobody honest or faithful anymore?"

I can feel myself getting smaller. Sasha stands up straight and lets go of his hand to point to Silas. "Drew treated me like shit and this bastard is never going to be monogamous."

Silas' mom drapes her purse over her shoulder and sighs. "I think it's time I head home. She softly pats Lex's arm. "It was good to see you again, Sugar."

"You too, ma'am."

Silas snorts. "Is that what you called her in bed?" Suddenly, his mom's hand reaches up and yanks down on his ear. "Ow! God!"

"I don't care how old you are young man, I'm still your mother and you will speak about me with respect."

"Sorry, Mom."

She kisses his cheek. "Call me once and awhile, would you?"

He nods and straightens as she gets into the elevator. We all wave at her and as soon as the doors close, Silas frowns at Alexander.

"I can't believe you slept with my mom."

"It sounds like we're more than even. Why didn't you guys tell me?"

"That was my call," Sasha says. "I've honestly never known what's up with us and I didn't need you getting all 'hurt my sister and I'll kill you'. I didn't want it to get in the way of your friendship. Besides, we first hooked up while he was dating Marie and I was with Roger Simons, and we felt horrible about it…and I mean, he's Silas."

"What the fuck is that supposed to mean?" Silas snaps.

This is beginning to feel weird standing here. Still, I kind of want to keep watching. I slowly back up until the backs of my knees hit a big, fluffy, white chair and I sit down.

Sasha sarcastically laughs. "Really, Hamilton? Do you even have standards or will you stick your cock into anyone who's female?"

Silas' face is pretty funny when he's frustrated. Pulling my feet under my knees, I glance to the coffee table to my right and I can't believe my luck. There's a bowl of saltwater taffy clearly there for anyone who wants some.

I want some.

Reaching out and picking a pink one, I unwrap it as quietly as possible before popping it into my mouth.

I never noticed how much Silas uses his hands when he talks. "Um, okay, so you don't want me to hook up with other women, yet you're the one who doesn't think we should be together. You've always said that, Sash. And I quote: *We would never work, Hamilton, we both know it. Now shut up and fuck me.*"

His impression of her is terrible and Alexander's look of disgust is adorably sexy. Both of which cause me to laugh to myself as I grab another piece of taffy. Blue this time.

"Well, was I wrong? I could never truly be with you because I would always wonder if you had just slid out of someone else. You can't be faithful to me."

"You never asked me to be, so how would you know? I'll take whatever you'll give me, Sasha, but I'm not putting my heart out on the line when you clearly aren't interested. So, I hook up with as many girls as I can, hoping it will make me feel better about not being able to be with the girl I really want to be with."

Oh, that's really sweet. I didn't know Silas could be like that. "Aww."

They all three look at me while Lex smirks and I chew my taffy.

Sasha turns back to Silas. "Is that true?"

He combs his hair out of his face and clasps his hands behind his neck. "And now you're going through with this wedding."

"The wedding's off." She rushes out her words and the way his face brightens makes me smile.

"Really?"

Lex holds up a hand. "Wait, so why would you even be with Drew, much less marry the guy if he was so terrible to you?"

She sighs and looks at the ceiling. "I had barely been clean three months when I met him. He was stable and in the beginning, he was really great. I don't know, I did like him a lot. I think I felt indebted to him for giving me a chance when I was struggling. Maybe I convinced myself I loved him because I knew he could never truly break my heart."

Silas steps to her and holds her face. "You almost ruined both of our lives, Sash."

Lex looks between them before he backs up to stand next to my chair. I hand him a taffy and he smiles at me before taking it and popping it into his mouth.

Sasha's voice is shaky when she says, "I'm so sorry, Hamilton…I didn't know."

He leans down to kiss her and it quickly becomes clear that this kiss is escalating. Lex is trying so hard to find somewhere to look that isn't at them. "So… are we still going to The Necco Room?" The only answer to his question is the soft, wet sounds kissing can make.

I stretch my fingers out to lace them with his as I look up at him. "I still wanna go."

He lets out a breath of relief as he pulls me off the chair. "Great, let's go." He drags me to the elevator and pushes the button. As we get in and the door closes in front of us, he shakes his head.

"Well that's not an image I'll soon be forgetting."

"I think they're cute together."

"I think I need a drink."

I choose the seat that I think of as 'ours' while he gets us drinks. It's so exciting to be openly here with him and not have to worry about Logan or Clients. It's impossible to stop myself from smiling when I look at him, and when he smiles back, my heart feels like it's stretched way out.

I still can't believe Logan sold me so easily. If I'm being honest with myself, it hurts me more than I want to think about. Master has been trying to buy me for years and Logan always says no. I kind of wonder if I'll miss him. I barely remember him not being there.

If I can change my life however I want, what will I do? I don't know how to do anything and now I can't even dance. I don't usually spend much time thinking about my future because it always makes my stomach hurt. Thinking about it now still makes me feel weird, just not in the same way. It's like I'm less than scared, and more than worried.

Alexander slides into the booth next to me and hands me my drink. It burns down my throat and I can't wait until the fuzziness takes this feeling away.

"What's wrong?"

I look up at his bright green eyes and wonder how things must look through them. "It's hard to believe we're really done with him."

He sighs and his shoulders press against the back of the seat. "We aren't done with him, Tavin. He's going to pay penance for what he did to you."

My heart starts thumping like a drum beating against my ribs. Just because I don't want to be Logan's plaything doesn't mean I want anything to happen to him.

"Why? He's going to leave us alone. Can't we just be together? Forget about him and move on?"

"No, I can't fucking 'forget about him and move on," he snaps, before he throws back his entire drink. Almost immediately though, he softens and brushes my hair over my shoulder. "He shouldn't get away with what he did and he can't be allowed to do it to anyone else."

His words are heavy as they fall over me. I never considered Logan would get another Lotus. Logan is my burden, no one else's, and I won't let another girl suffer for what's mine.

A lady in a short skirt stops at our table. "Hey there! My name is Cheyanne. Can I get you guys more drinks?"

Lex nods with enthusiasm. "Yes, you can. Surprise us, something strong."

She gives me a friendly smile as she picks up our glasses. "Gotcha, hon. I'll be right back."

I shake my head. This was all too good to be true. How can I live this perfect life with Lex if someone else has to take my place with Logan? I can't. The disappointment is sludge in my throat.

"I'm sorry, Lex…I know what you've done for me." I squeeze his hand and let my tears fall. I knew it, I could never have this life. "I have to go back. I didn't consider another girl and I can't let him do that."

Maybe if I beg his forgiveness and plead with him to take me back, the thought of replacing me may not have occurred to him yet…unless that's why he sold me in the first place.

His large hand yanks free from my hold to squeeze my

wrist. "Do not ever. Ever. Mention going back again. Do you understand?"

I narrow my eyes at his order. "Are you telling me as my boyfriend or as my owner?"

His nostrils flare as he releases my wrist to lean back. "I've already explained that to you. You can't throw it in my face when you're upset or to get what you want. It's not fair."

I want to crawl under the table because he's right. I know he doesn't think of me as property and that was a mean thing to suggest. I just can't bear the thought of Logan stealing someone else's life because I want my own.

"I—I'm sorry."

The features of his face relax as he laces his fingers between mine. "Hey, you don't need to apologize. I shouldn't have snapped at you and I didn't mean to make you worry. I have no idea if that's what he's planning. What he's already done though, he can't walk free from that."

I take a deep breath and wish our drinks were here. He has a point. What if there's no other girl and I throw away my chance at freedom for nothing? Logan has never been predictable. Lex only wants me to trust him, and I do. He's never given me a reason not to.

Cheyanne arrives with our drinks and they're both gone before she finishes asking if we want another round.

Once she walks away, he looks back at me. "Did Logan ever take you to his home or anywhere else that was his?"

Only once. "His jet."

The fall of his face tells me that wasn't the answer he was hoping for. "I don't want you to have to worry about anything anymore. Trust me to take care of this and to take care of you."

"I don't want you to take care of me. I want to take care of myself, for once."

"That's not what I'm saying. Taking care of you means making sure you're as happy as I have the power to make you. We'll get you the documents you need so you can get a job or go to school or do whatever it is your amazing little heart desires." He takes my hand and kisses it like you would a queen. "I'll help you get your own apartment if that's what you want. I just want to be with you, Tav. I'm not going to stop you from doing anything that might improve your life in any way."

My excitement gobbles up my worries at the idea of making all my own choices.

Cheyanne brings our drinks to us and leans her hip against the table. "Can I get you two cuties anything else?" I smile at her. She's nice. Alexander tells her to bring another round whenever she gets the chance and she winks at me. "Sure thing."

When she walks away, I look up to see Timothy smiling and holding hands with who I know is Todd, from the pictures he showed me. I wave them over and they sit across from us.

"Hey! I'm glad you guys could make it." Alexander holds his hand out. "It's nice to meet you. I'm Alex."

"Likewise, I'm Todd." He's even more handsome than the pictures. His dark hair is short on the sides and the long part on top is streaked in bright blue. In the pictures, his hair never looks the same in any of them. He grins at me. "You must be Tavin. Timmy was right, you're a cute little gumdrop." As hard as I try not to, I still laugh. Timmy? "It sorta feels like I've met you already." He looks around for a moment before he asks, "Where's the mouthy one?"

Lex laughs as he swallows his drink. "Sasha isn't coming. She's spending the evening with her…" He's acting as if it's painful to say the word, "boyfriend."

I think he's kind of being a baby about it, so I smirk at

him as Cheyanne sets our drinks down.

"Well, aren't you a lucky girl? Three handsome men all to yourself."

She brings enough for Lex and I to each have two, so we give the extras to Todd and Timothy. After Alexander gives Cheyanne orders to keep them coming, we all hold up our glasses and *clink* them together.

"Cheers!"

All of our empty shot glasses hit the table and the buzzing from the alcohol bursts through me. I love this song so I clasp my hands together. "Let's dance!"

Todd throws his hand up and grabs mine. "I knew I liked you." He lifts me out of the booth and bumps his shoulder against mine. "Let's go tear it up."

I grin. I like him too. I turn to Lex and he nods to me. "Have fun, we'll be out there in a bit."

I'm able to throw him a smile before Todd takes me to the middle of the dance floor. He's taller than I thought. Next to Timothy, he seems so small and he looks a lot younger too. I think his tan skin is so pretty and he's a great dancer. It's hard not to constantly smile around him. He has so much energy and keeps making me laugh with his facial expressions.

The music loosens my mind and I give into the hope. I'm choosing to believe that I'm finally done with all of it.

Earlier today, when I talked to Toben to tell him about Lex buying me, he told me Logan hasn't mentioned anything about it, or Sasha, or anything. All Logan has told him is that I'm not coming back, and that he's to continue with his play-dates as normal. It's so weird. This isn't how Logan usually works.

It's hard to release all my uneasiness, but the things Lex was saying…school, work, my own apartment. I've never lived on my own before. What would I do if I could do anything? If what he's promising is true, I can be anything I want to be.

CHAPTER NINE
Slumber Party

Alexander

ALLOW MYSELF A MOMENT OF WATCHING HER DANCE before turning back to Timothy. "They take to each other well."

He laughs, "Yeah, but Todd makes friends with everyone."

I turn the glass around in my hand. I don't want to bring down the evening with heavy conversation, so I try and keep my tone light.

"I'm glad you came out tonight. I want to talk to you about something. Obviously, your discretion is appreciated."

"Of course."

"Since you've seen Tavin in a bathing suit, I know you've seen her scars and the…marking."

"Oh, the logo?"

My back immediately straightens. "The what?"

He takes a drink before rubbing his thumb over his chest. "The scarred flower on her sternum? She calls it her 'logo.'"

Products. Logos. Sweet Girl. Clients. Playdates. I am so sick of this repulsive lexicon.

"Of course she does." I swirl the whiskey in my glass. "As far as I know, there's no immediate threat, however, I still feel the need for caution. She's allowed to go anywhere she wants besides her old house. If she wants to see her friend, Toben, she can do it anywhere other than there. As long as wherever she goes, you go with her. Ultimately, I feel much safer with you there and she obviously enjoys your company."

"As I enjoy hers. And Sasha's. I won't let anything happen to her on my watch, Alex. I don't care what the threat is. You can rest easy knowing that."

I hold up my glass in silent cheers. "Thank you."

"You're such a pretty girl, we really should do something about this." The alcohol clearly has an effect on Todd's filter as he scrunches his nose and rubs Tavin's lilac hair between his fingers. "Come by my salon, I'll fix you right up."

Thank God, I really miss her brown hair. "You have a salon?" I ask, as we walk outside.

"Yeah, it's the T. Acosta Beauty Bar, right on the boardwalk."

Damn, he's got a reputation. He is supposedly one of the best in California. "No shit? You're T. Acosta? Didn't you get an award recently?"

Todd rubs imaginary dirt off his shoulders. "Oh, I was just named 'Master Hairstylist of the Year' by *Salon Today* Magazine. And I was on the cover, no big deal." He acts as if he's shining his nails on his shirt, and grins.

"At least he's humble, right?" Timothy laughs, and adds, "We really should do this again. We both had a lot of fun"

"We would love that." I take Tavin's hand and pull her next to me. "We need to get going though, I have to work tomorrow and I happen to know Timothy does too."

While waving goodbye, we walk back to the valet to wait

for the car I called to pick us up.

Once we're in the back seat, I pull her dainty feet into my lap and make the most of the half hour ride by gently massaging my way up her legs. By the time the driver pulls up my driveway, my fingers have just found their way to the hem of her panties. I softly touch over the fabric before getting out and hand the man his tip. Reaching into the backseat, I grab Tavin's thighs to yank her out of the car and throw her over my shoulder. She squeals and her little ass is too cute not to spank. Her sweet laugh brings out my grin as I unlock the door and carry her all the way upstairs before tossing her on my bed. She sits up and slightly spreads her legs, only enough for her to reach down and touch her fingers over those sheer turquoise panties.

"What would you do for me Lex?"

I pull my gaze from her hand to look at her eyes. "Anything."

"Anything?"

"Anything."

She smirks. "Dance for me."

No way she's serious. I scoff at her. "What?"

"You watched me dance at Marvel. I want you to do that for me." She arches her eyebrow, daring me to refuse.

She's fucking with me.

"You want me to *Magic Mike* you?"

Her bravado falters for a moment with her confusion. "Um…maybe?"

"Tavin, I'm not doing a striptease."

She crosses her arms. "Oh. So, when you said you would do 'anything' for me that was a lie?"

I know my jaw drops. She's testing me. She wants to know if I mean what I say. If all these promises are real or just pretty lies. She needs me to prove it, but does it have to be in such a cruel way?

I place my knees on the outside of her thighs as I climb on the bed, forcing her to lean back. "You will pay for this."

Her eyes widen with her smile as she laughs and scoots back on the bed. She situates the pillows and crosses her ankles. She's enjoying herself way too much.

I cannot believe I'm about to do this. "Comfortable?"

"Very."

I roll my eyes at her and unsuccessfully keep the grin off my face. Scrolling through my playlist, I find the shortest song I can pull off dancing to.

The music starts and I kind of want to die.

"You cannot tell a soul about this."

Her finger traces an *X* across her chest as she smirks. "I swear."

I begin by lifting my shirt and feeling actual shame before I thrust my hip out. She shifts to her knees, biting her lip as she pulls her dress over her head. I drag this out as long as I can, while continuing to remove my shirt and… dance. Dropping my tee to the floor, I tug the leather strap of my belt through the loop. She smiles as she slides her hand down the front of her panties, her hand moving beneath the fabric as I unzip my jeans.

I don't have many places outside of my comfort zone, preferring to avoid the few that I have, and this one, is way out there.

You can't possibly understand how difficult it is to take off shoes while trying to dance. Her dimple appears with her smile as she pulls her panties to the side and shows me her fingers deep inside of her.

Okay, I can do this.

I lower my jeans enough to show her my erection and most of my underwear. Thank Christ the song is coming to an end. I stroke myself over the cotton before lowering the waistband and freeing my cock. She swings her legs off the bed, keeping eye contact as she walks to me and lowers to her knees. Her hands are on her thighs as she takes me deep into her mouth.

Fuck yes. Oh, fuck yes. My hands go to her head as I press her down further. Obviously, I passed the test. Now it's time to stay with the theme and keep my promise.

She's going to pay for that.

Friday, June 26th

Tavin

"Every time with this! Hold your head still." Todd straightens Timothy's head again. "I have four-year olds who sit better than you."

I decided to take Todd up on his offer to do my hair. Apparently, it's impossible to get Timothy to take the time to let Todd give him a haircut, so Todd's taking advantage of him being here and doing a quick trim.

"Alright, you're done. Let's go wash you so I can get started on Gumdrop."

Todd winks at me as he lowers the salon chair and I laugh as Timothy smacks his butt on their way to the shampoo bowls.

Once Timothy is styled and Todd sweeps up the hair, he turns the chair to face me. "You're turn." He puts a big, black cape on backwards and holds my hair in a ponytail as he brushes. "Oh, sweetie, she fried your hair."

He's running his fingers through my ends and I can see him looking a little repulsed in the mirror.

"No she didn't, she colored it."

He chuckles. "I'll need to cut a couple inches off, you

shouldn't really notice. This color though, it needs to go."

I don't mind the way it is, even though the need for it is gone. I only want it to look good. "You can do whatever you think will be best."

He claps his hands together and grins at me in the mirror. "Now that's what I like to hear."

Timothy goes to get us coffee as Todd puts the color on. It tingles, but not as much as when Alia did it. When it's been on long enough, he takes me to the shampoo bowls. It feels so good to have someone else wash your hair.

"Mmm. That feels nice."

Even with my eyes closed, I can hear the smile in his voice. "I have magic fingers, ask Timmy."

That makes me laugh every time he calls him that. He wraps my hair in a towel so I don't drip on the way back to the hair cutting chair.

I like the *snip, snip, snip* sound his scissors make. I don't even watch him, I just enjoy how good it feels to have him comb, and brush, and blow dry my hair. When he finishes, he turns me around.

It's shiny and so pretty. It's a little lighter brown than it used to be, and he put a whole bunch of different lengths in my hair. The ends are slightly curled, making it look full and thick.

He stands behind me and holds his arms out. "What do you think?"

"I don't think my hair has ever looked this good." I smile at him in the mirror. "Thank you, Todd."

"My pleasure, Gumdrop."

After the salon, Timothy brings me back to Lex's and when we walk inside, Sasha is sitting in the kitchen. She glances up from her phone as a big smile lifts up her cheeks.

"Look at you! The hair is gorgeous."

I like feeling pretty. It makes it hard to stop grinning. "Thank you, Todd did it."

She looks back at her phone and laughs. "Oh my God, look what Marie posted." She turns the phone to me and I walk up to it to see a picture of a bunch of little girls in pajamas. "It's one of our middle school slumber parties. God, that was forever ago."

"What's a slumber party?"

She puts her phone back in her purse and shakes her head. "I forget how many things you haven't experienced." She rests her cheek on her fist and smiles her pretty smile. "It's when friends stay the night together. The fun part though, is what you do before you fall asleep. Prank calls, truth or dare, tee-peeing houses, games like 'black cat scratch back' or 'light as a feather stiff as a board'…the list goes on."

I smile at her. Even though I can never do this stuff, I like hearing about it. "That sounds really neat."

Her face brightens. "Why don't we have one? I bet I can talk Cara Jo into it. We can get pillows and blankets to make a fort to watch movies in. We'll make popcorn and I have a Ouija board we can play. What do you say?"

I clasp my hands together and gasp in excitement. I get to go to a slumber party! I just found out what it is and I already can't wait. I don't know what a wee-jee board is, but I know my head is nodding.

"I say, yes!"

"So, you're telling me I can't go into my own basement?"

"Sorry bro, not till tomorrow. No boys allowed. Slumber party law." Sasha is sorting her nail polishes so we can give each other manicures tonight.

He laughs and combs his fingers through the strands of

my hair. He obviously likes it. His face lit right up when he first saw it.

"Are you excited?"

I grin at him. "Yes."

"Wait until you try my strawberry Jell-O popcorn," Cara Jo says, as she loads the dishwasher. It made me feel so good when she said she would come to our slumber party.

"Invited or not, I definitely get some of that." Alexander finishes his drink before he kisses me and whispers, "Have fun."

He disappears up the stairs and Sasha rubs her hands together. "Since this is a grown-up slumber party, I say we start off with drinks. Get rid of the apron Cara Jo, you're officially off the clock." She gets up and takes down three glasses. "I can make anything. Perks of being the daughter of an alcoholic. Chocolate martinis, anyone?"

Chocolate martinis are the most delicious alcohol drink I've ever tasted. I'm going to be drinking a lot of these.

I help Sasha carry all the pillows, blankets, and sheets we can find down to the theater room, while Cara Jo gets Lex's Christmas lights to line along the top of our blanket house. We crawl inside and get comfortable on piles of pillows as Sasha shows us where she stashed a bunch of snacks and drinks.

It's perfect.

The alcohol is making us laugh, and so is Cara Jo's story. She tells us about when she was in high school and some of the silly things she did for a boy's attention. One of which got her kicked out of school for three days!

Sasha laughs as she eats more pink Jell-O popcorn. They were right, it's delicious.

"Oh my God, we should prank call people. I haven't done that since I was a kid." Taking Cara Jo's phone, she chuckles,

"Hamilton's gettin' it." She puts her finger to her lips to tell us to be quiet as she puts the phone on speaker.

"Hello?"

"Congratulations, Mr. Hamilton, you have been cho-sen for the 'Sexiest Gay Bachelor of The Year' award!" She's changing her voice, so it's overly chipper, high-pitched and twangy. "Now, I just have a few questions for the article, but let's be honest, the answer everyone wants to hear is: Who is your ideal man?"

For a moment there's no sound, until eventually he clears his throat. "I apologize, there must be some kind of mix up… I'm not gay."

"Are you ashamed of your sexuality Mr. Hamilton? Or do you simply hate the LGBTQ community as a whole?"

"What?! No! Of course not!"

I grab a pillow to cover my face so he doesn't hear me laughing.

"So, to be clear, you do like homosexual men. Correct?"

"Yes, I have nothing against—"

"Thank you, Mr. Hamilton. I think I have what I need. You have a great evening. We'll send you the issue when it goes to print."

"Wait! What—"

Sasha hangs up and starts cracking up laughing as she gives Cara Jo back her phone. "Classic." Shoving another handful of popcorn in her mouth, she hands me her cell. "Do you want to try?"

"Um…okay."

I don't know who to call besides Lex and Toben and I don't know if Toben would think it was funny. I pick Lex's number and it rings. He answers and I don't know what to say. I guess I'm not good at prank calling.

"Sasha?"

"It's not Sasha."

I try to change my voice, but I don't think I do as well as Sasha did.

"Tavin?"

"It's not Tavin…um…you won! Congratulations!"

Sasha grins as she looks at Cara Jo.

Lex chuckles, "Oh yeah? What did I win?"

"Uh…an award! For…business."

"An award for business?" He sounds amused, so I don't think he's falling for it.

"Yeah…so just keep waiting for it." I think I'm done so I hang up and give the phone back to Sasha. "Did I do it right?"

She nods and laughs. "That was great." Leaning back against the pile of pillows, she takes a drink of her martini. "You guys wanna watch a movie?"

Cara Jo says she doesn't want anything sad, so we pick a funny one. I don't think I've ever laughed like this before. The girl in the movie is trying every horrible thing she can think of to make her boyfriend break up with her, and I kind of feel bad for him, except not really, because he's only with her to win a bet. By the end of it though, they fall in love for real and I clap my hands when they kiss.

That was such a good movie.

Cara Jo stands up to turn the lights on as Sasha scrolls through her playlist and lands on *Bubblegum Bitch*. Sitting up on her knees, she dances and makes me laugh as she lip syncs the lyrics. Cara Jo goes behind the bar to grab us sodas, as Sasha takes a thin, brown board from her bag and lays it on the floor. *Ouija* is written across the top in pretty black letters right above the alphabet. A picture of the sun is in the top left corner next to the word *Yes* and a crescent moon is in the top right corner next to the word *No*. It's so beautiful. I run my fingers over the numbers and the word *Goodbye* along the bottom of the board.

"How do you play?" I ask.

Cara Jo sits next to me and hands us our Dr. Peppers as Sasha places a heart shaped piece of wood on the board. It has *Ouija* carved into it and there's a hole in the top with a magnifying glass inside. She lifts my hands and gently places my fingers on the heart piece.

"This is a planchette. Keep your fingers on it, just don't move it." She and Cara Jo do the same. "Now we ask a question."

"Like what?"

"Anything you want." She shifts around and rolls her shoulders without moving her hands. "Here, I'll go first." She takes a deep breath and clears her throat. "Will my designs ever make it to the red carpet?"

Nothing happens. I look at Cara Jo and then I feel it move beneath my fingers. My heart thumps so hard I have to release a laugh. "Whoa!"

It continues to move across the board until stopping over *YES*.

"Sweet!" She moves her hand from the planchette long enough to throw more popcorn in her mouth. "Now you try, Tav."

"Okay...uh..." Even though there are a lot of questions that I could ask, I've had so much fun tonight, that only one question pops into my head. "Is Lex right? Will I really be able to do whatever I want, someday?"

It's moving slowly and I'm getting nervous. Closing my eyes, I wait until I can't feel it moving anymore. As I open them, I smile so big.

YES.

Saturday, June 27th

Alexander

The dinner reservations I made are in an hour and Tavin keeps eyeballing the rice crispy cookie cake Cara Jo made. Keeping her away from it before we leave is a task on its own. Once she's dressed in the killer pink dress she has on, she gets Blind Mag fixed up with food, water, and toys before we get into the car.

Merging onto the freeway, I see Tavin messing with something in my peripheral and when I glance at her she's downing a piece of cake.

"Damn it, Tavin, I told you to wait. You need to eat something not made only of sugar, and now you won't be hungry for dinner."

She scoffs and licks her fingers. "It's not only sugar. I watched Cara Jo put eggs in it, myself. Besides, I can eat both."

I actually believe that. The girl can put away some food. It's not that big of a deal, other than it's simply not good for her to eat so much sugar. I suppose picking my battles will be necessary with her, so for now, the crap food I'll forfeit.

"Jesus, fine. No dessert after dinner though."

"I was going to get dessert after dinner?"

Teasing her, I shrug and her glare is so adorable that I laugh. "Eat every single thing you order, and we'll talk."

Her expression turns smug as she leans back in the seat. "Oh, we'll be talking."

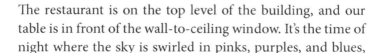

The restaurant is on the top level of the building, and our table is in front of the wall-to-ceiling window. It's the time of night where the sky is swirled in pinks, purples, and blues, with Shadoebox lit up in lights against it. Tavin must find it stunning as well because she's gazing out the window with a sweet smile on her lips.

My staring is interrupted by the bread boy with a warm loaf, water, and menus. We look over the wine selection and land on a bottle of *Armand de Brignac Rosé*.

Once we decide what food we're ordering, I bring up my trip.

"I need to fly to Tacoma, on Monday. As much as I would love you to come with me, I doubt your knock off ID will suffice." She shifts her gaze to the table while her lips form a subtle pout. "I know you're disappointed. It won't be like this forever and I'll only be gone overnight. I'll be back before you know it."

She quirks her mouth to the side in contemplation before she nods. "I know."

"Do you think you'd rather stay at Silas', with Sasha," Yeah… apparently she's staying there now, "or have Timothy stay with you at my place?"

"Can Toben spend the night when you're gone?"

I choke on the bread I'm eating. She wants him to stay with her in my house? Overnight? I'm not worried about her doing anything with him, it's not that…and I understand their relationship a little bit more now, I just still don't trust him yet.

"No drugs in my house, Tav. I'm serious. If he stays over, he leaves it all at home, okay?"

She claps her hands and does a little bounce. "Thank you, Lex. And I promise, no drugs."

I can't believe I'm allowing this. "Alright."

A victorious smile stretches across her soft face. I don't know if it's because I'm head over heels or if it's because she's getting healthier, but she seems lighter, as if she's glowing brighter. Regardless, happiness is beautiful on her.

Our server arrives to take our order and introduces himself as Chase. The waiters here are all fantastic. I hear they go through a brutal training process, and Chase isn't an exception as he shows off his knowledge of the menu, and informs us of the specials. Within moments of taking our order, he comes back with our drinks and appetizers.

Tavin asks him where the restroom is and he offers to walk her even though they're right around the corner.

I dig into the appetizer and, oh my God, these mushrooms are perfect. Tavin is taking so long that Chase comes back and I order my next drink. As I polish off my mushrooms, I keep glancing at the hallway. I'm beginning to worry she got sick.

Chase places my drink on the table. "Were the mushrooms up to par, Mr. Sørensen?"

"Absolutely. They were incredible."

"May I take your plate? Your food will be out very soon."

"Yes, thank you." He clears my space and I hand him a fifty. "Would you mind keeping an eye on the table? I want to go check on my girlfriend."

"Of course. Thank you, sir."

Dropping my napkin on the table, I walk to the hall around the corner and I freeze mid-step. Tavin's pressed against the wall as a large man hovers over her. My natural instinct is to react aggressively, though it's clear she isn't threatened or scared. She's sad.

"Tavin, what's going on?"

They both look at me and as soon as I recognize him, I'm sure my mouth falls open.

Cain Saxon. *The* Cain Saxon. He was in *The Song of the Dying* last year, and was amazing. I knew he lived in Shadoebox City and apparently, he's a bit of a recluse. He rarely does interviews and I never see him in tabloids or magazines, other than photo shoots. To be honest, I'm a little star struck at the moment.

"Look, kid, I need a minute. I'll repay you for your time," he barks.

Kid? Are you kidding me? That whole star-struck thing? Yeah, I'm over that.

"I'm her boyfriend, not a Client, you dick."

He backs away from her as if she struck him and frowns at her. "Boyfriend? Is that where you've been this whole time?"

She nods before looking up at him. "Yes, Master."

Did she seriously just call him…

"Master?!"

Tavin

It annoys Toben when I put all the little smiley face and heart pictures at the end of my texts. I don't care though because I like them, so he can deal with it. I push send on the text, telling him about staying over on Monday, as I pull open the bathroom door. Oh, I hope my caramelized whatever I ordered is there when I get back.

My face and body slam against something hard.

"Upmf!" Jeez. What did I just run into? I really should pay more attention. I see fancy shoes. Oh crap it's a person. "I'm so sorry! I—"

"Tavin?!"

My eyes stretch wide. I know this voice very well and I hesitate to look up because he's surely angry with me. I've missed quite a few of our weekend playdates.

"Master…I…"

He leans his body toward me as he walks, causing me to back up against the wall.

"Where have you been? I have been trying to hire you for weeks! Mr. James said you were 'out of stock." My head hits the wall. I can't move back anymore and his face is as close as it can get without touching me. "I don't even want to know what the fuck that means. The things I began to think... He has a reputation for viciousness, I was scared he..."

He was scared? Why?

"I'm sorry, Master. If I knew how to contact you I—"

His thumb softly touches my chin. "This is why I need you to be mine, really mine, Tavin. I miss you, and I've hated worrying about you these past weeks."

Why is he acting this way? He has his gentle moments, sure, but there was never any doubt who was in control. This is different. He isn't being aggressive or forceful at all. Is it because he hasn't paid for this time with me?

"Master, so much has happened."

He isn't like the other Clients, he never has been. He looks genuinely upset and I feel horrible that I didn't think about how he would feel. I thought he would be angry and then get over it. I never dreamed he would still care.

"Then tell me. I've always wanted you to talk to me. You're the one who's closed off. Even though I pay for you I—"

"Tavin, what's going on?"

Crap, crap. I shut my eyes because this is going to suck. I was hoping to get back out there before Lex started wondering where I was.

Master's shoulders drop like they do when he is irritated. "Look kid, I need a minute. I'll repay you for your time."

Lex hadn't really seemed too upset until now. He and Sasha do the same face when they get offended. "I'm her boyfriend, not a Client, you dick."

"Boyfriend?" Master looks at me in a way I can't quite recognize...pain? Why is he so upset? He's more than just mad—he's hurt. I don't understand. "Is that where you've been this whole time?"

While I want to be able to explain everything, this is completely outside of the realm of our normal relationship. I don't know how else to be with him. "Yes, Master."

"Master?!" Alexander's voice carries down the hall.

Now he's really mad.

This is getting overwhelming, I don't know what the heck is going on with Master, and I don't know how to explain him to Lex.

Master ignores him and when I look into his eyes, he's looking at me in that curious way he does sometimes. "We've been together for five years and you've never cared for me, have you? I was never anything more than a Client to you."

I don't know what he wants from me. "I never knew you felt this way...I'm sorry. I thought I was just Sweet Girl. You d—"

"I was working on that! I've been trying to purchase you for years. He's a stubborn bastard."

Glancing over at Lex, I can almost see the veins in his neck bulging. While he's clearly fuming, at least he's being silent about it.

"None of this was planned or intentional, it all happened so fast and—"

"Is he who you want?" He points to Lex as his Adam's apple bobs. "Would you truly rather be with him?"

I don't want to hurt him, but I know the answer more than I have ever known anything. "Yes, Master."

His eyes take on a cast as he transforms back into the man I know. "My name is Cain. I'm not your Master anymore." He turns his back to me and adds, "Apparently, I never was."

Without another look, he walks down the hall, past Alexander, and out of my life. Just because I never wanted to physically be with him, doesn't mean part of me isn't sorrowful at never seeing him again. I never knew he had real feelings for me and finding out this way makes me sad.

"You call Cain Saxon 'Master'?"

I can tell by his clenched fists that he's trying his hardest to keep it together, as he walks up to me.

"That's what he wanted me to call him."

"There's clearly more between you two than simply a business exchange. Why didn't you tell me about him?"

"I didn't know I was supposed to." I throw my arms in the air because sometimes, he frustrates me. "Even though there were times I had fun with him, I never would have been with him if I didn't have to. I mean, yeah, he was my favorite Client, and I guess over time we may have become friends, I just never thought of it like that until now."

My voice is raising and I'm getting angry. I feel like I'm always in trouble with someone.

His eyebrows smooth out before he wraps his warm arms around me. "Okay, relax. I'm sorry, I don't want to upset you. That was just a shock for me. I mean, Cain Saxon? Really?"

He takes my hand and leads me back to our table.

"You know him?" He sure didn't seem to know Lex. "I don't think he remembers you."

He laughs as he pulls out my chair. "I don't know him personally. He's an actor. A pretty big one."

Now it's my turn to laugh. "He's in movies? Can we watch one?" I hope he's in an old-timey one. It would be so funny to see Master as a cowboy.

He chuckles as he combs his hair back and smiles. That combination makes me so achy. "Yeah, I have a few."

I take my first bite of dinner and it's not what I was expecting. It's not sweet at all. "This tastes nothing like caramel!"

Alexander doesn't bring Master up again until we're back in the theater room deciding which of his movies we are going to watch.

"I'm guessing Cain was nice to you if he was your favorite. How long was he a Client?"

Even though I still don't like to talk about this stuff with him, I guess answering his questions is the least I can do after everything he's done for me.

"Five years. He wanted to wait until I was eighteen to hire me. And yeah, he was nice… in his own way. He would ask me my opinion sometimes and he gave me pretty dresses to wear at dinner. And he suspended me."

He turns from the reel case to look at me. "He 'suspended' you? What does that mean?"

I twist around in my seat and tap my shoulder blades. "He put big hooks through my back and used them to lift me into the air with chains. It made me feel so floaty." I turn back around and shrug. "It was fun."

"So that's where the holes are from." I nod and wonder if I will ever turn him off with these things; if he'll realize one day that this is all too much for him. "Huh. I've wondered that for a while." He's lost in his thoughts for a second before his attention is back on the reels. "What if we watch his newest one? It's really a fantastic film, it's a little sad though."

I look to the popcorn machine. "Sure. Can I make popcorn?"

He cracks that gorgeous smirk as he sets up the movie. "Yeah, and grab some soda."

Lex doesn't usually drink that much cola, and when he

does drink it, it's either out of a fountain or in glass bottles.

Going to the fridge, I grab two bottles of cherry cola and a gray and yellow striped tub with the Vulture logo on the side. I carry it all to the popcorn machine and fill up the tub with as much popcorn as I can. The previews start, and as the lights dim, he sits next to me and kisses my head while I grab a big ol' handful of popcorn. As I chew it, I realize there's something sweet and wonderfully different about it.

"Oh my gosh, this is delicious, what did you do to it?"

If the sun could laugh it would sound like Lex. "I thought you might like that. It's kettle corn. We recently added it to Vulture's concession menu."

I nod and hand him his soda. My mouth is too full to respond anyway. The movie starts and the music in the intro makes my heart beat in tune to it. When Master comes on the screen, he looks so different, I don't even recognize him at first. In real life, he's so well-groomed and put together. The character he's playing is not. I have to remind myself that I know him. That he's not really the man on the screen.

The final scene closes and as the credits roll, I can't stop crying. Alexander said it was a 'little sad' not that it was the most heartbreaking movie that has ever been made.

"He died? I... I can't believe it..."

Lights brighten the room as he flips the switch so I can see him smile. "He didn't die, we saw him a few hours ago."

"I can't believe he never told me he was in movies."

He clicks his tongue as he picks up our empty popcorn bucket and bottles. "Yeah, it sounds like you didn't do much talking."

I try not to get offended when he responds with that snip in his voice, I know this has been a lot for him. That doesn't mean I have to acknowledge it.

CHAPTER TEN
Drive

Alexander

I CAN'T BELIEVE THE ILLUSION OF NORMALCY THAT OUR life is taking on. The driver arrives to take me to the airport, and I hold Tavin's hand down the pathway to the car. He puts my bag in the trunk as I turn to her to take her face in my hands. Even though it's only over night, I still don't enjoy leaving her.

"Remember your promise."

"No drugs." She draws an *X* over her chest with her finger. "Promise."

"Thank you." I lean down to kiss her and she wraps her arms around my neck so I pick her up to bring her to eye level. "I'll call you tonight, okay?"

Her soft lips peck my nose. "Okay."

I watch her ass as she runs back to the house, until Timothy opens the door to let her inside.

I'm not a big fan of flying. It's not being on the plane that I hate, it's the pain in the ass of getting there. I love everything about Shadoebox City, besides this airport. The little bottles of liquor they give me on the plane don't do anything and I end up ordering four of them for barely an hour and a half long flight.

I didn't get much sleep last night, so once I get to Tacoma, I crash for a few hours at the hotel before calling a car to take me to the theater.

As the driver pulls up in front of Vulture, I look out the window and grin. There's a carnival in the parking lot across the street. The first night I was with Tavin, I made her a promise, and now it's time to fulfill it.

It takes me fifteen minutes to find it. The exact same pink and purple dragon. To win the game, I have to use a huge mallet to hit the target hard enough to cause the creepy clown face to ring the bell at the top. Third time must be the charm because the bell goes off and the carny asks me which prize I want.

"The pink dragon."

Tavin

I smile at Timothy as I walk inside. "So what are we doing today? Toben can't come over until this afternoon."

"Whatever you want, Little Miss. As long as I get a re-match in H.O.R.S.E."

I grin. I know he let me win last time. "You're on."

He follows me through the kitchen and it's sort of weird to not have Cara Jo here. She's gone on vacation to Florida for the next couple weeks. I lead him out back to Alexander's basketball court.

"Is Todd spending the night here tonight? We could have

a slumber party." I toss the ball 'granny style', as Timothy calls it, and it rolls around the rim before falling in. "Yes!"

He chuckles. "Lucky shot. And as much fun as that would be, I don't know how Alex would feel about that."

"Oh, he won't care. Want me to ask him?"

He smiles at me. It's a very nice smile. "Maybe. I'll think about it."

He shoots the ball making it bounce off the backboard and off the rim, missing the basket.

"Ha! Now you're the Hor."

"Tavin!" Why is he frowning? It was only a joke. "Why would you say that?"

"Because you missed and that gives you an *R*…which makes H-O-R."

He doesn't know about my past so I thought he would think it was funny. Narrowing his eyes, he changes the subject.

"What sounds good for lunch?"

The sun feels amazing on my face as I float around the pool eating my egg roll. I honestly keep waiting for this all to end. Nothing is this perfect. This isn't how my life works.

You don't deserve it.

Blind Mag swims by and I hand her a piece of the egg roll.

Timothy pushes down his sunglasses and squints at me. "You know Alex doesn't like you feeding her people food."

I shrug. Every once in a while, I think she deserves a treat.

"Hey, can I get one of those?"

My heart does little jumping jacks at the sound of his voice. "Toben!"

I cram the rest of the egg roll in my mouth and jump off

the floaty. Swimming to the edge, I climb out of the pool, and give him a big hug.

"Don't worry about it, I'll dry," he chuckles.

"Sorry. Do you want to swim? You can wear one of Lex's suits."

Tugging on his beanie, he shakes his head. "Uh, no, I'm cool."

"No, you're crazy. This is fun." I jump back in the water to chase around Blind Mag as Toben sits on the lawn chair and eats an egg roll.

Timothy stands up and grabs his towel. "I think I'm gonna go shower while you two kids hang out. I'll be back in a bit."

"Okay." I climb back out and dry my hands before picking up a fortune cookie and asking Toben, "Do you want to split the fortune?"

"Sure."

I hold on to one end and he holds on to the other and we break it apart. We each hang on to the paper and eat our half of the cookie.

"You read it," I tell him.

"It says, 'There is adventure in your future' and the lucky numbers are '8, 12, 64, 16, 50, 31.'"

"Ooh. What kind of adventure do you want to have?"

He reaches into his pocket and pulls out his works kit. "I can think of one in particular."

I understand, I do. It still upsets me that he doesn't support my choice to quit, for Alexander.

"I promised him, Toben. We can smoke some weed, that's it."

He huffs while he puts it back in his pocket and takes out his cigarettes. "Hardly an 'adventure', but okay."

Removing a joint from the pack, he lights it. As he hands it to me, I inhale and softly moan in comfort as its scent wraps around me.

"We could go to the boardwalk."

He shrugs. "Sure." Suddenly, his eyes widen and he grins. I don't think I like this look. "I think I have an idea for an adventure." He takes the joint and leans forward, resting his elbows on his knees. "Logan let me drive his car once in a parking lot. It really isn't that hard."

"So?"

He takes a long drag. "I really like that Alfa Romeo your boyfriend drives." Oh no. No, no, no. "He won't be back until tomorrow right? Let's take his ride to The Walk."

I cross my arms as I lean back in the lawn chair. "Are you nuts? He loves that car. No way, Toben."

"Come on, I'm twenty-three and I've never gotten to just drive somewhere. Especially not without Logan or in a car like that." He holds the smoking joint out to me and his eyes go sad. "Please? When will I ever get another chance to do this?"

I can't believe he's pulling the guilt card. I know he's been through so much, and lately it's all been because of me. I shouldn't let him do this, but I love him and I know that he should have had the chance to do this kind of stuff.

It is only to The Walk and I'll even tell Alexander about it when he gets back.

I narrow my eyes at him. "One hour. Borrowing his car without asking is bad enough and now I'm going to have to ditch Timothy. I can't be gone all day on top of it."

He grins. "Deal. Now, let's go get the keys before the Terminator comes back."

I'm actually grateful for Cara Jo's absence, as I take the keys from the bowl on our way to the garage.

We climb inside and he rubs his hands over the steering wheel and dashboard. What's so great about cars that I'm apparently missing?

"You're sure you know how to do this?"

Shoving the key into the ignition, he nods as the car roars to life. "Trust me. It's a piece of cake."

Other than backing out of the garage too fast, I'm impressed with how well he's doing. By the time we get onto the freeway, I'm able to sit back and relax in my seat. Maybe this isn't that big of a deal.

The blinker *clicks* as he gets off on the exit and I smile at him. "I gotta hand it to you Tobe, you're doing great."

"I told you. It's really not—"

My shoulder slams against the door and my head hits something as the breath is torn from my lungs. Everything's spinning and I can't focus on anything to know what's going on. As suddenly as it starts, it all abruptly stops, throwing my body in the opposite direction.

Owe...my head hurts. "Ughhh..."

"Are you okay?! Tavin?"

He's yelling way too loud. "I'm fine, just be quiet."

His hand wraps around mine and I can feel him shaking. "Fuck. I'm really sorry, Tav. That guy came out of nowhere."

"What guy? What are you talking about? Why are you sorry?"

My head is ringing...what's happening?

I lift my gaze and look through the splintered windshield to see smoke raising up from the left side of the car.

Oh. No. Oh, God, no. This can't be happening.

I press my hand against the pain in my chest that my heart is causing. Lex is going to be so mad. So mad. Why did I agree to this?

"You said you knew how to drive!"

"It was an accident!" He looks out the window and unbuckles his seat belt. "What are we gonna do? The police are gonna come."

I can hardly think through the vibrations in my brain. "I need to call Timothy."

My hands are shaking as I take my cell out of my jeans. There's a blue flashing light to let me know I have a text. I want to cry when I see it's from Lex. He's going to hate me.

Ignoring the message for the time being, I call Timothy.

"Tavin, I was just about to call you. Where the hell are you?"

There's already anger in his tone and it's about to get a lot worse. My throat strains as I speak. "We're on the exit for The Walk." The tears fall from my lashes onto my cheeks. "W—we crashed Lex's car."

Three seconds of silence tick by before he says, "Fuck."

～

I can't stop looking at what I did to his Alfa. He has always really liked it. He's tried so hard to be understanding of me and my past, but this is different. This has nothing to do with what Logan did to me. The Alfa wasn't mine to loan.

What if he doesn't want to be with me anymore because I did this?

"I should have never let you drive it."

Toben frowns as he holds my hand and squeezes it tight. "You've said that three times already. Are you okay?"

I shake my head because I'm definitely not okay.

Timothy's black SUV pulls up as we are waiting on the shoulder and he slams the car door before marching over to us.

"What were you two thinking?!" He lifts my chin to in-spect my face and his voice softens. "Your head is cut, are you alright?" I nod and he grumbles to himself as he pulls out his phone. "Alex is going to kill me. He's obsessed with this car." After he calls Todd to come pick us up, he crosses his arms and glares at us. "What the hell happened?"

My head feels stuffy and heavy.

I'm not really sure, so I'm glad that Toben answers. "I was getting off on the exit and just as I crossed the intersection, things suddenly went out of control. Whoever hit us, didn't stick around."

Cars are zooming by and I can feel the drivers looking at us and the crashed Alfa. I wish there was a way to fix it. I don't want to lie to Alexander and make it worse. He's begged me not to lie, I just don't want him to tell me to go away. I try to force back more tears and answer Timothy's question the best I can.

"I don't know. One minute, we were driving normal and then the next, we were crashed." Both Timothy and Toben look at each other before turning back to me. "Why are you looking at me like that? You asked what happened."

Toben stands in front of me to look in my eyes. "That was a few questions ago, Tav."

Timothy rubs his forehead and takes a breath so big I think his chest gets bigger. "You two are going to leave with Todd when he gets here. I'll tell the police I was driving alone and then we'll figure out what to do about her obvious concussion."

Even though I know he said other things, the only thing I care about is he's going to lie so I don't have to. "You're going to tell Lex you crashed it?"

"Oh no, little Missy. I'll cover for you with the cops, not Alex. He'd fire me for sure and I'm not too confident he still won't."

My heart falls all over again. I didn't think about him losing his job because of me. It was really selfish of me not to consider him in all this and he's been so nice.

"I'm so sorry, Timothy."

Sighing, his shoulders relax. "I know, Tavin." He points behind me. Go to that gas station and wait for Todd. I need to call the police."

I nod as Toben takes my hand to lead us across the street.

"I'm sorry you got hurt. Are you feeling okay?"

Everything is blurry through my tears. "What if he gets so mad he doesn't want to stay with me?"

His face goes hard before he pulls me against his chest. "If he's going to let you go over a car, then you don't want him anyway."

Tuesday, June 30th

Alexander

I'm so excited to give her this dragon. I wonder if she even remembers I promised her another one. I carry it under my arm, along with the bone I got for Blind Mag, at the airport gift shop.

The kitchen is empty with Cara Jo gone, and as I walk closer to the stairs, Blind Mag's collar *jingles* two seconds before she bounces around the corner. My smile has become automatic with this fur ball. Leaning down to pet her, I place the bone on the floor. With her tail wagging, she snatches it and carries it up the steps behind me.

I walk into Tavin's room, and I must commend myself for my incredible anger management skills. She and Toben are cuddling on her bed as they pass a joint back and forth.

She lifts her head, and while she smiles, her face doesn't light up like usual. "Lex! You're back."

Toben sits up and swings his legs off the bed. "I'm gonna head out. Call me later." He kisses her cheek and doesn't even look at me before he leaves the room.

Considering I've been gone, I'm a little hurt she doesn't

jump up to greet me. In fact, she's barely looking at me at all.

"I got you something."

I walk over to the bed to hand her the dragon, and instead of the smile I was hoping for, she looks like she's about to cry. "You got me the dragon... I can't believe you remembered. Thank you, Alexander."

I sit on the bed. "What's wrong?" I tuck her hair behind her ear and my eyes widen at the sight of a red cut with butterfly bandages across it. "Oh my God. What happened? Are you okay?"

She nods even though her eyes overflow with tears as she sobs, "I'm so sorry, I didn't think anything would happen to it. He's just never got to do the things normal boys get to and—"

She's spilling out her words in a shaky voice. I hold her face in my hands to keep her head from jerking. "Calm down. What are you talking about? Tell me what happened to your head."

She swallows and bounces her knee. She hasn't been this antsy in a long time. "I got a concussion."

My body temperature rises immediately at the thought of her being in danger, especially while I'm away. I look closer at her cut. "How the hell did that happen? Should I call Marie?"

She looks at me like she's begging me for something as she shakes her head. "I'm fine... I just...I let Toben drive your car and—"

"Whoa, what?!" I jump off the bed with my pulse pounding like a bass. "What happened to my car, Tavin?"

She chokes on her words and I know what they will be before she gets them out. "We crashed it."

Spinning on my heel, I storm down the hall and barrel down the stairs. I hear her behind me, but my only thought right now is seeing how minor or major these damages are.

I rip open the door to the garage and I suddenly want to cry.

My baby. My poor baby.

The windshield is completely cracked and as I walk around to the driver's side, the entire front end is bent and smashed. The front door doesn't even close right.

My fingers caress the dents as if I can smooth them out, when I hear Tavin walk into the garage. My Alfa…

"Why in the ever-loving fuck would you let him drive my car?!" It's completely totaled. There's no repairing this. I storm up to her as she shakes her head.

"I knew it was wrong and I knew you would probably be upset, but I never thought this would happen. He said he knew how." Her words are distorted by her tears and while I hate seeing her cry, right now I'm too furious to be swayed by them. "I'm so sorry."

"One day, Tavin. I left you alone for one Goddamn day," I bark at her before going back inside.

Timothy is standing in the kitchen with his hands in his pockets.

"Alex, I don't have an excuse. I shouldn't have left them alone."

I know this wasn't Tavin's idea and I also know how sneaky she can be when she's all on her own, so adding Toben is apparently the best way to be blindsided like this.

"I don't hold you responsible, Timothy. I'm just glad you got her back here, safely."

His relief is apparent as his body relaxes. "Of course."

"I'm sure you're ready to get back home to Todd. We'll see you in the morning."

"Thank you, Alex."

He pats Tavin on the back on his way out, while I pour a drink. You can't imagine how much I need one.

"Lex—"

"I need some time alone right now."

She intakes a quick breath and her head tics. "Do you still love me?"

I toss back my drink. There is a part of me that wants to comfort her, while the larger part is way too enraged to be capable of that right now.

"I will always love you, Tavin." I grab the bottle and my glass to head upstairs. "Tonight though, I don't want to be around you."

Wednesday, July 1st

I don't speak to Tavin before I leave. She stays in her room and honestly, it's a bit of a relief. I woke up this morning and the first thing I thought of was that I couldn't drive the Alfa. I'm still so pissed off that she did this and I don't know if anything I say to her right now would be beneficial.

It's such bullshit that I have to drive my Mercedes to work. I'm fully aware of how privileged that sounds and I don't give a shit. I only bought it for when I need to fit more than one person. It sucks all the fun out of the drive which puts me in a bad mood for the rest of the day.

"What the hell crawled up your ass? How did things go in Tacoma?" Silas helps himself to my bourbon before getting comfortable on my couch.

"Tacoma was fine, it was when I got back that things went south."

He rolls his eyes as he takes a drink. "Does this have to do with Tavin?" He scoffs, "What am I saying? Of course it does."

"She and her friend took out the Alfa and totaled it."

His eyes go wide. "Oh shit." He shakes his head. "Damn. Are you okay? There's gay and straight, then there's whatever the hell you were for that car."

I flare my nostrils as I take a drink. "I need to replace it tonight. Do you want to come?"

"Shit yeah! Why don't we grab the girls and get dinner together first? We'll make a night of it."

The idea cheers me up a bit. I know I have to forgive her eventually, and though most people hate the process of car shopping, I sure as hell don't. What's not to like? Spending an evening driving sweet-ass cars, and at the end of it getting to take one home? It's really more of a tradition with us now. Silas was with me when I bought the Alfa and I was with him when he bought his Porsche Cayman. It's just bitter sweet this time because I don't have a damn choice in the matter.

━━

After work, he follows me to my house and we pull up right as the tow truck is loading it up.

"Fuuuuck! Whew! He did do a number on it, didn't he? I can't believe nobody was seriously hurt." Silas walks around the car as he inspects the damage. "It sucks, the last time it was ever driven wasn't even by you."

I glare at him. "Yeah, thanks for pointing that out."

We walk inside and Timothy's sitting at the bar reading a book…wearing glasses. I hide my smirk. He doesn't look quite as scary as a book worm.

"Hey, Timothy, this is Silas."

He looks up and smiles. "Hi. I've heard a lot about you from Sasha."

Stretching his arms behind his head, Silas boasts, "It's all true."

Timothy laughs and takes off his glasses. "I'm not sure you want to be admitting to that."

Silas frowns and drops his arms. "What? Why? What did she say?"

I laugh with Timothy as he says, "Can't tell. I'm under the oath of pinky promises."

It's clear why he and Tavin get along so well. Speaking of… "Where's Tav?"

"She's in her room."

"I'll go get her and change, then we can pick up Sasha," I tell Silas, before turning to Timothy. "You're free to go. Say hi to Todd for me and I'll see you tomorrow."

Taking off my jacket, I bend down to pet Blind Mag. She's still working on that bone. I climb the stairs and take off my tie before pushing open Tavin's door.

She's lying on her stomach sketching in her notepad when her eyes travel to mine.

"Hi," she whispers so quietly it's barely heard.

"Hey." She bites her lip as if forcing herself to stay quiet. "We're going to go get dinner with Silas and Sasha and then I need to get a new car." I'm partially successful in keeping the aggression from my tone and add, "So get around and meet us downstairs."

She nods as I turn back into the hall. I know she's sorry. I don't like things like this between us. As angry as I am and as much as I loved it, it was only a car, a thing.

She's my *Lille*.

CHAPTER ELEVEN
Boardwalk

Tavin

MISS THE FIRE IN HIS EYES WHEN HE LOOKS AT ME. I HATE seeing the disappointment and frustration. I let him down and that's not what I want. I was just trying to be a good friend to Toben. For so long, it's been the two of us against everyone else. It's not like that anymore and I should have considered Lex more. I've always known how he felt about it.

As much as his words hurt, there was still comfort in them and that's what I've been holding on to since last night.

I will always love you, Tavin.

I slide my pale green dress with the puffy sleeves over my head and slide on my boots before going downstairs. Alexander gives me a small smile that heats up my chest and makes my heart race. I smile back and my lungs expand when he touches the small of my back.

Silas rubs his hands together as we walk outside. "Where do you guys want to eat after we grab Sasha? I vote for *Amai Gochis.*"

I'm happy Sasha is coming too. I don't get to see her as much now that she's staying with Silas, and I miss her. I'm glad she's with him, though. I like him way more than Drew. She told me at the sleepover, that Silas has been taking her to a group that helps her make sure she doesn't do heroin again.

I sit in the back seat and watch the trees pass in the window, while Silas and Lex argue about which movie made them more money, two years ago. A few minutes later, Lex drives up to the curb and we wait in the car as Silas runs into his penthouse for Sasha. I lean forward between the seats while he fiddles with the buttons on the console. I want him to talk to me again like normal.

"Lex? Will you please forgive me? I should have never let Toben drive, I know that. We just never got to do the kinds of things you did and sometimes it feels really unfair." He lets out a sigh and still doesn't look at me. "I want you to trust me too… I am so, so sorry."

His shoulders fall when he finally looks back at me. "I'm still upset about it, but I do forgive you, okay?"

I smile in relief at him as the car door opens and Sasha jumps in the back seat with me and wraps me in a big hug that feels so good.

The place we go for dinner is so neat you wouldn't believe it. The cook makes our food right in front of us and that's not even the best part. He does tricks with the food. He turns the onions into a train and flips an egg into his tall hat. He tells me he's going to try to get the food in my mouth by throwing it, so I open as wide as I can and a few seconds later a warm, yummy shrimp appears on my tongue. He sets things on fire and he's funny and nice. I don't think I stop clapping the entire time. On top of that, Alexander keeps smiling at me. The food is so good and I'm stuffed to the brim as we leave.

I rub my belly as Lex grabs my hand. "Did you enjoy

that, *Lille*?"

Every time he calls me that, it makes me want to laugh and cry at the same time. I love that he still sees me that way, after everything.

"Oh, yes, can we come back some time?"

I want to show Toben this place. He's gonna think I'm making it up when I tell him they throw food in your mouth.

"Of course."

I look up to him as we walk down the pathway. "Do you know what color car you want to get?"

He gives me another smile and I'm so glad he's not still angry with me. "The same. Yellow's my color."

I met this girl at a party once that told me I have a soft pink aura. She said it's the color my energy radiates. I can't see auras like she did, but if I could, I bet Lex's would be yellow.

"I think so too."

I'm excited to go see the car store. I've never seen one before. I bet there are aisles of cars in giant boxes on big shelves.

We pull in and it isn't at all like I imagined. All the cars are just parked in a big parking lot. There's a building, and when we walk inside, I see some cars in here, they aren't on shelves or in boxes though, they're just sitting in the middle of a big room. The man who helps us is so nice, he even walks around with us to help us look.

Sasha and I stay behind this time. As we walk around the lot, she tells me which ones she wants. They all seem fine to me. They will all take you to where you want to go and that's the point, right?

The engine is loud, so I hear it before I turn to see them coming back. Lex barely gets parked before jumping out and I'm so glad his big grin has made its way back onto his perfect face.

"I found it. I can't believe I found it. This is it. I need this car."

Silas climbs out and laughs as he shuts the door. "I bet you do. This is a serious upgrade."

Caressing his hand over the hood, Lex groans, "Fuck, I know. I'm so hard right now."

Sasha's eyes go wide as she scrunches her nose and slaps his arm. "Ewe, you're disgusting. How would you like to know how wet my pussy is?"

Now it's Alexander's turn to have the exact same expression, causing both me and Silas to snicker. "Oh God, Sash, point taken."

The man that's been helping us walks up to Alexander. "So, what did you think?"

Lex's smile is so wide, it makes me have one too. It feels good when he's happy.

"This is the one."

The guy punches his fist across the front of his torso. "The Lamborghini Huracan. Gets 'em every time."

Once we finish the paperwork, Lex is almost bouncing with joy and I'm happy because the guy that sold us the car gave me a sucker.

Lex opens the door for me and when I climb in, I smile because it's yellow on the inside too. The interior of the Alfa was all black and I don't think the seats were as comfortable as these. He jumps inside and slides in the key, the sound making him close his eyes and moan.

"Listen to that." He reaches his hand across the car to rub me over my panties and I grin.

He's definitely not mad at me anymore.

Silas' car is gone when we drive through the gate and Lex's

Mercedes is parked out front, so Silas and Sasha must have already left. The garage door opens and even though he pulls inside and turns the engine off, he still leaves the music playing.

Reaching over to me, his hand softly traces down my neck. "This is a brand new car." His voice is deep and husky which makes mine stick in my throat, so all I can do is nod. He trails his hand down my body until he reaches the hem of my dress. "I'm glad the Alfa can't hear me say this, because in some ways, I'm kind of glad I had to replace it." He murmurs.

His kisses are slow, and when I slip my tongue into his mouth, he lightly sucks on it while lifting my dress and sliding his hand down the front of my panties. He touches me softly and I ache for part of him, any part, to be inside me. I can't stop myself from grinding against his fingers when he suddenly shoves two of them in hard. I don't even know if I'm moaning or gasping when he pounds them in and out. It's shameful how loud the sound of my wetness is.

He breaks our kiss to unbutton my dress and pull down my bra. His kisses pepper my logo for a moment before he bites and sucks on my nipple.

"Every part of your body tastes so damn good." His hand slides out of my panties and he licks his fingers before he bites my ear.

Lifting his body, he hovers above me, making it easier to reach his jeans. His button can't come undone fast enough, and it gives me a rush to feel how solid he is. I pump up and down as he thrusts into my hand.

"I really want you to fuck me."

He grins as he yanks my panties to the side and lines the head of his cock up with my entrance.

"Say it again."

"Fuck me, Alexander."

He shoves himself inside and my body fights his size, taking a few thrusts before he's able to slide in and out easily.

There isn't a lot of room to be moving around, so he lifts my legs over his shoulder as he shoves in harder. God, he's so deep.

Reaching above me to the seat belt, he pulls it out far enough to wrap around my neck. He picks up pace as he tightens the belt until I am no longer able to get oxygen.

"Come for me, Tav." He says it just as the beautiful burn begins to fill my throat. The feel of his cock sliding into me is so much more intensified without the function of breathing. He squeezes the seat belt a little tighter.

The pain, the pleasure, his words, his voice…it's a plethora of sensations. The ache feels incredible and the tenseness of my building orgasm causes my legs to shake against his shoulders.

Finally, it takes me over and consumes me, as the little spots that I like to pretend are fairies, are all over everything. It rolls out of me in currents. Each one more overwhelmingly pleasurable than the last.

I hear his rough chuckle. I think he still gets proud of himself every time he gets me off. He lifts my head and suddenly the fire of air is rushing into my lungs as I gasp for it. The seat belt snaps back into place as my vision comes into focus.

He quickly pulls out and the sudden emptiness leaves me wanting to beg him to come back. Pulling up his body so he is inches from my mouth, he presses his hand against the back window of the car, using the other to guide his cock in between my lips.

I take it gladly. Tasting myself on him makes me want to suck harder. I feel so proud that it's my body he was just inside of. His hips push the tip against my throat and I try to get him even further in. I love the way he softly touches my hair and my face while violently fucking my mouth.

He groans when he slips himself out and kisses me on his way back down. His grin makes my stomach flip before he licks his hand and reaches in between my legs to my ass. He rubs his slippery fingers over my tight hole and slides one in. When he's satisfied that I'm ready, he scoots down and lifts my hips, giving him an easier angle.

The tip presses against my tightened orifice as the pain of the stretch forces me to moan. He grunts with the last push, getting him completely inside.

"Oh my God, you're so fucking tight."

I am, and it hurts so bad that when he begins to rub my clit, it doesn't take long for the heightened aching to begin again. He's about to come, so he's going harder and faster, and while it feels incredible, it's not enough pain.

As if he can read my mind, He leans down and takes a small piece of skin on my chest between his teeth. It's like he's biting out a chunk of my flesh while his fingers are expertly massaging me. Once I feel his teeth break apart the skin, I let the whimper fall from my lips and my body vibrates in pleasure at the same time he grunts and fills my ass.

His eyes are locked onto mine as he separates our bodies. He kisses me, and when he pulls back he touches my face and whispers, "Now I'm hungry." I laugh even though I kind of want something to eat too. Something sweet. I swear he knows what I'm thinking, because he asks, "How about ice cream?"

I can't nod fast enough. It's always a good time for ice cream.

⟋

His fingers lightly tap the yellow steering wheel to the

music as we drive to the ice cream parlor. He's in a good mood with the new car and us having sex, so now is a good time to talk to him about something.

I've been thinking a lot about him and Toben. I want them to get along and maybe even be friends, eventually. They both love me and I love both of them so that should make them want to try, right? If this is going to be my life now then they will have to accept the fact that they are both a huge part of it. Lex would have been easier to convince before everything with the Alfa.

"You know what would be really fun? If you invited Toben over for a 'guys night'. You could drink and talk about guy stuff."

His eyebrows drop and his mouth presses into a line before he says, "Yeah, about as fun as swimming in a boiling vat of oil." He parks in front of the ice cream parlor and turns off the car.

I'll give it a few days. I really want us to all be able to hang out together as friends, like me and Toben are with Christopher. I just think they need to spend time alone, without me there, to really do that.

The You Scream ice cream parlor is fun to just be inside of. The walls are white with a whole bunch of large brightly colored candy sprinkles painted all over it. The pink glittery tables have yellow and blue chairs, while the blue glittery tables have yellow and pink chairs. I really like the song that's playing in the background, too.

I walk up to the counter to pick my flavor and I can't believe my eyes. There's not only buckets of ice cream choices, there are also a ton of different candies and sweets. The best part? I get to do everything myself so I can get as many different ice cream flavors and toppings as I want.

"Just because it's there doesn't mean you have to get it.

I mean, Jesus Tav, Hot Tamales and caramel sauce? That's disgusting."

He'll be wishing he had this frozen treat masterpiece. The lady weighs our desserts and mine is almost twice as heavy as his. And twice as yummy.

As we pick a table, he says, "I'll seriously invite Toben over myself if you eat that whole thing."

"Pfft." Does he not know me at all?

We sit at a pink table and I stick my spoon into some chocolate chip cookie dough, taking a big ol' bite. Mmmm even more wonderful than I expected.

I point my spoon at him. "I'll give you his number."

He shakes his head and laughs. "I'm not worried. You're never going to be able to eat all that."

Ten minutes later my spoon scrapes across the bottom of the bowl to scoop up the very last bite. I shove it into my mouth and smirk at the open-mouthed expression of shock on his face.

"Where the hell do you put it?"

I shrug. "Toben really likes metal music, so if you play Slayer it'll get you on his good side."

"Shouldn't it be him trying to get on my good side?"

For some reason my emotions for him momentarily overwhelm me, forcing me to hold back my tears. I don't want to cry. I feel happier than I have ever before and I hate that I still can't completely trust it. I want to.

The fear of losing all this still sleeps beneath my skin. I will still save these memories and store them up in case the day comes when I can't make anymore.

"Thank you for the ice cream, Lex."

Friday, July 3rd

Alexander

As much as I don't want to do this, I made a promise and it's time to keep it. Toben's caller tune plays in my ear, or rather screams, as I wrap up a few things on the computer.

"Hello?" His voice sounds unsure and a lot less confident than normal.

"Hello, Toben. This is Alexander Sørensen."

His groan is long and dramatic. "Yeah. I was warned about this call."

I have to admit my relief that she prepared him for this. Maybe we can agree to grin and bear it for her sake.

"Look, Toben, she wants us to get along and I'm willing to try. My sister's taking her to an Independence Day fashion show tomorrow evening. What do you say you come by my place for drinks? I have a great view to watch the fireworks and I'll grill us some steaks."

I hear him inhale and exhale before sighing, "Fuck." I have no idea if that's a yes or a no. I'm about to ask him when he asks, "What time?"

"Will six work?"

"Yeah."

"Okay, see—" I hear the call end and I still check my phone. Well, okay then. At least that part's over with. Maybe we'll get drunk enough to forget we don't like each other.

I leave the office and my eagerness for the festival tonight increases as I get closer to home. This morning, Tavin asked if we could go to the boardwalk tonight for the Shadoebox Independence Day party. It's a two-day long event with a beer festival, live music, and a dance. I'll never pass up the opportunity to see her dance and now we both have plans tomorrow.

Music is playing as I walk into the house, and the view in my kitchen is a stunning one. The back of her pretty dress is the first thing I see. It's a cream sheer maxi dress that has soft ruffles caressing her shoulders. Her hair is loosely pinned up showing the neckline of the dress curving slightly across the top of her back. There are little buttons trailing down her slender frame to her waist where the fabric gently flows down in panels. She's holding a glass of white wine as she turns and gives me her angelic smile. The whole picture is so elegant.

"Wow." I kiss her neck and her smell adds to my desire. "You look gorgeous." Her cheeks pink before she softly presses her lips to mine and I lift her up to sit her on the counter. Pushing up the dress, I kiss her jaw and spread her legs. "Drink your wine."

She obeys as I remove my jacket, roll up my sleeves and loosen my tie. I pull a knife from the caddy before I get on my knees and pull her little nude colored panties to the side. She's holding the wine in one hand while the other is in my hair. I'm slow with my tongue and as I suck her clit, I do it softly. My fingers remain gentle as they move in and out of her. Watching her drink and rock her body onto my mouth makes me want to do this all night.

I have kept it leisurely up to now, but her wine glass is almost empty and we have a celebration to get to. I quicken the pace of my tongue and fingers until her grip on my hair threatens scalping. I don't like cutting near that artery, ever since last time, so I decide to move to the top of her thigh, closer to her hip. I swipe the knife across her flesh and she moans softly. I do it again, and she gasps as she grinds against my tongue, giving me her orgasm.

Once she's finished, I stand up and lick my lips before I kiss her. "I'm going to change, then we can go." Rubbing my thumb over her cuts I add, "Clean these up and cover them with a bandage."

She's still breathless when she jumps off the counter and takes my hand. "Wait, what about you?"

"Sometimes I just want to make you come, Tav."

I go upstairs to change and when I meet her back in the kitchen, her face is still rosy. Lacing my fingers between hers, I lead her to the garage.

"Ready?"

Her smile is soft and her eyes sparkle as she nods. "For anything."

The Walk is full of people and lined with American flags. It's never this busy unless there's an event going on. The stage is at the end of the pier and all the shops have their doors propped open with star spangled blue and red striped balloons tied to them. White lights are adorning the rooftops, and red, white, and blue streamers decorate all the stores. Many of the food shops, such as Tattletale Taffy, have stands set up outside, for people to try samples.

It's of course necessary that she tries every sample available.

Beach side communities, like Shadoebox, often have tourist shops that sell seashell and sand incorporated nick knacks, so we see a lot of that, along with Fourth of July themed merchandise, but there are also very unique items, and every store has their own style and flare. She's particularly drawn to the doll shop, so I lock that fact away for future use. The music volume gets higher, signaling the concert is about to start, so we head toward the food vendors.

"I want a funnel cake. Sugarville makes the best ones."

"We need dinner, Tav. How about taco salads? Or a corn dog?"

Burgers are her choice, so we eat our greasy dinner at one of the picnic tables while the first band starts up. She bobs her head to the music as she eats her fries. Once we finish, I lead us to the packed beer garden.

It doesn't take long for people to start dancing on Main Street with Tavin right behind them. She holds my hand until we are in the midst of it, letting herself get lost in the music. Three songs in and I hear her name being called.

"Tavin! Hey, Tav!"

She hears it too because she spins around and her face brightens. "Christopher!"

Now that I know who I'm looking for, I find him weaving through the crowd, toting a girl behind him.

His arms wrap around Tavin as soon as he reaches her. "Damn, Tav. Where have you been? I feel like I haven't seen you in forever." After he says it, his bloodshot eyes glare at me. "And now I know why…" He shifts his frown to her as he tilts his head. "Really? After what he said to you at the club?"

She shakes her head with a sigh, and I'm proud of the way she stands tall to him. "You know there's things we can't tell you, and this falls into that. Please don't hate me for choosing this. You're one of my only friends."

He lightly shoves her shoulder and blows a raspberry. "Always the dramatic one, aren't you? I don't care who you fuck, Tav. I just hate that it's taking you away from him. He loves you. He always has."

Her gaze falls to the concrete. "I know."

Sighing, he drapes his arm over her shoulder. "And I'll never hate you, you big dork. I care about you both. You're both my best friends. I just don't want to see our boy hurt, you get me?" She nods and gives him a small smile as he pulls her against him for a hug. "Text me if you need me."

She waves as he walks away with the girl that he never introduced. I stand behind her and wrap my arms around her waist as I rest my chin on her shoulder.

"Are you okay?"

She nods her head, though her earlier enthusiasm is no longer present. "I don't want to keep hurting people." I can't decide how to respond because everything I can think of feels self-profiting. I don't need to though. She turns to face me and holds my hand. "Do you want to get more beer?"

I squeeze tight as I gesture in front of us. "Lead the way."

Quite a few beers and three bands later, she's back in her original mood. The crowd has started to thin and I've noticed a couple vendors closing up shop. She's sweaty from dancing as she falls against me laughing.

"Did you have fun?" I ask, against her hair.

She squeezes her arms around my waist and grins. "Oh, yes."

As we walk back to the Lambo, I hesitantly bring Christopher back up, keeping an eye on her to gauge her reaction.

"How did you meet Christopher? You've known him for a while, right?",

"Toben used to go to school with him before Logan bought us." She's watching the store owner's close their doors and shut off their lights. "Then, when Logan let us out of the basement, we ran into him and we've all been hanging out ever since."

I still don't exactly know what all went on, and to be honest, I'm not sure I want to. Although, I do think the more I know, the easier it will be for me to understand and communicate with her. This isn't a random story on the news, this is her real life. I want her to open up to me because she trusts me and wants me to know her. At this point, though, I don't need to keep asking her questions.

Toben, however, I have no problem asking questions.

Maybe insight from a different source will be helpful. Perhaps I wasn't looking at this time with Toben in the correct perspective. Not to mention he owes me.

A fucking lemon-yellow Alfa Romeo 4C Spider, to be exact.

CHAPTER TWELVE
Guys' Night

Saturday, July 4th

S ASHA ARRIVES AT NOON WITH A BAG OVER HER shoulder, carrying a case of berry smoothies. She pulls off her sunglasses and hands me one of the cups, along with her keys, as she brushes past me. "The sandwiches and the rest of my stuff are in my car. Will you be a good brother and go get them?"

It isn't really a question considering she's already at the base of the stairs. I do what she asks, and when I open her car door, the smell of the sandwiches wafts beneath my nose, and my stomach reminds me how hungry I am. Grabbing the food, along with the garment bags, I carry it all up to Tavin's room where the beautification process has already begun.

Tavin's hair is pinned back and Sasha is lining hot curlers, nail polish, and a bunch of other stuff that I wish I didn't know what it was, along the dresser.

Sasha sees me walk in with the garment bags and jumps up to get them.

"Wait till you see this outfit I made for you, Tav. You're gonna love it." She takes out a pair of tan Mary-Janes that have little cut out patterns along the top. "Are these not the cutest?"

Tavin grins and reaches out for them. "These are for me?'

"Yes, nerd. Oh, and look at mine!"

She holds up black heeled sandals with long straps that tie halfway up her calf.

"Oh my gosh, those are so pretty!" Tavin squeals.

Their shrieks and estrogen are getting to be a bit much for me, so I take my sandwich and back up toward the door.

"Have fun."

They've been upstairs for over two hours and I think it's almost time for them to leave. I've never understood what girls could possibly do to themselves that would take that amount of time to get ready.

The doorbell rings and I answer it to find Timothy and Todd looking dapper. I let them in just as the girls are making their way downstairs.

"Thanks for coming today. I don't do fashion shows."

Timothy waves me off. "Are you kidding?" He points his thumb to a grinning Todd. "This one would have made me go regardless." His face lights up as he looks behind me. "Well look at you two!"

I turn and feel my own smile spreading. They both look adorable. Tavin's wearing a pair of ivory, crochet shorts with a sheer, cream tank and a lacy, sleeveless bolero. Her hair is curled and halfway pulled back with a ribbon. The best part is her cream thigh highs and they look so hot with those shoes.

Sasha's in a black and gold romper jumpsuit that looks great with her gold jewelry and black sandals. Her hair is down and curled, topped off with a black headband.

I still don't see how it took them more than two hours.

They leave in a cloud of excitement and I give Timothy an apologetic grin as he closes the door. While it's probably ridiculous to still have him go with her everywhere, my peace of mind is worth the possible over-caution. It helps that she likes him and doesn't seem to mind having a babysitter.

Blind Mag walks into the kitchen and drinks her water like she is dying of thirst.

"It's hot outside, huh? Want to go swimming?"

She gets on her hind legs in approval.

Toben should be here any minute, so I get the grill set up and make sure there's plenty of beer in the outdoor fridge. I decide to leave on my swimming trunks in case he wants to get in, and toss a t-shirt over my head as my doorbell rings.

"Hi, Toben." Not that I'm surprised, but it's obvious he's strung out on something. "Come on in, do you want a beer?"

"Sure, since I doubt you have any coke."

"I have Coke." It suddenly clicks. "Oh…you mean the drug."

He laughs and adjusts his beanie. "Beer's fine." Blind Mag prances up to him and barks for attention. He smiles before kneeling down to pet her. "Hey, Blind Mag."

I hand him his beer and Blind Mag follows us out back to the patio. He stretches out on a lawn chair while he lights a cigarette.

"I'm going to start the steaks." I lift the lid to the grill and point behind me. "There are a few extra suits and towels in the pool house if you want to swim."

Blind Mag just got situated on his lap when her ears perk up at the word 'swim'. She leaps off him to jump in the pool and paddles around with her tongue hanging out.

Toben chuckles, "Naw, I'm good, I swim all the time at Mr. Stride's"

"Mr. Stride?"

"A Client. A regular."

"Right…" I throw open the ice box to dig for the cuts I want. "How do you like your steak? Bloody?"

He gives me an odd smile and takes a drag. "Whatever you think."

I throw on the meat and sit next to him as I pull my sunglasses down. I don't really know what to say. I'm sure as hell not asking him how work is going.

"I appreciate you coming, Toben, it means a lot to Tav."

"Yeah, well, I did wreck your car so…"

"We don't need to talk about that."

He snuffs out his cigarette and when he opens his pack, I think he's going to smoke another one until he holds up a joint.

"You wanna smoke?"

Maybe some weed will take the awkwardness down a level. "Sure, do you want another beer?"

Nodding, he lights up. "You know, I do have to hand it to you. I don't know how you did it." He shakes his head and takes a long hit. He holds the smoke in his mouth for a moment before he exhales and trades me for the beer. "Logan told me he sold her to you. It doesn't make sense. I can't believe he let her go. Just like that." He takes a swig of his beer and watches Blind Mag climb the steps out of the pool. "I'm not going to lie, I fucking hate not having her home with me, but I've never seen her so happy. If she can actually be safe without having to be with the Clients, I want you to know I do want that for her."

I take a hit and hand it back. "I don't doubt you love her, Toben. I watched the video, I know you guys have been through a worse hell than I can imagine. I'm not saying that I understand what you feel, because I don't. Just know, the drugs and the Clients are her past now."

"You mean I'm her past."

I shake my head and get up to throw on the vegetables. "I don't want that, believe it or not. She feels like she needs you, and I respect that. If you and I can agree on anything, it's that we both want her happy. You make her happy and so do I. Don't pressure her into the drugs or put her in danger again and we'll be cool, alright?"

He leans his head against the lawn chair and pulls off the joint. "I really am sorry about that. I know it was stupid."

Oh, look, something else we agree on. I bite my tongue and change the subject to last night.

"We saw your friend, Christopher, on the boardwalk last night. Does he know anything about you guys?"

"Seeing as he's been my best friend since before I met Tav, I would like for him to not die. So no, I haven't told him anything. Logan made it clear what would happen if I did."

"He never asked any questions? Was never curious?"

He sighs and tugs on his stocking cap. "He was at first, and yeah, he asked a ton of questions. Then one day, he asked me where Tavin and I always go and I finally couldn't deal with making up lies to him anymore." He looks over the view of Shadoebox. "I bloodied his nose to make sure he kept it out of our business. Whatever he knows or thinks he knows now, he keeps it to himself."

I'm not sure how I feel about him beating the shit out of his friend to keep him safe. Thankfully, the aroma of the steak floats beneath my nose and creates a nice segue.

"I think the food's done."

Filling our plates, I set them on the table as the sun begins to set. Blind Mag has set herself on the foot of Toben's lawn chair to dry and he's careful to not disturb her when he stands up. I get us fresh beers as he cuts into the meat and takes a bite.

"Damn, dude. I'll give you this, you know how to grill

a steak."

His enthusiasm is a little out of character for him so I chuckle, "Thanks."

We eat in silence and I smirk at his gusto. He scarfs down the steak without touching his vegetables.

The plate scrapes across the table as he pushes it away and lights another cigarette. I polish off the last few bites of mine before pouring us each a whiskey.

"Can I ask you something?"

He blows out smoke as he nods and waves his fingers for me to continue. "Shoot."

"Tavin said he kept you in her basement after that first time, yet I found out through…sources, that you were at River Forge Academy until 2009."

He shakes his head. "River Forge is a front. I think the place exists, Logan must just pay off the Headmaster or something."

Wow, that seems extensive. I'm not so sure that Logan was ever sexual with Toben so it seems like a lot of hoops to jump through. "So, you were in the basement that whole time? You never left?"

He bristles as he shifts around in his seat. "Tavin didn't. I did sometimes. With Logan."

"Why?"

His body stills and he gives me a crooked smirk. "I'm not telling you that."

A vibrating chill runs through my skin and I fight the urge to scoot my chair back. "Okay… How long was she locked down there before he let her out?

He takes another long drag before answering. "Five years."

I'm surprised to say that I am actually having a decent time.

We're pretty buzzed and I swear he has an endless supply of joints. We lie back in the lawn chairs and watch the fireworks while swapping Tavin stories.

I explain how this little get together came to pass, and he laughs. "She's always eaten like that. When I met her, I thought it was because she was starving, but Logan always made sure we were well fed and she still ate her weight in food."

"How did you meet her?"

"Our parents were friends. I'll never forget the first time I saw her. She was so skinny and dirty. She asked me for food." He shakes his head. "I thought that was so odd. I didn't know she hadn't eaten in days." The kid smokes like a chimney. He pulls out another cigarette. "I could tell her things I couldn't tell the other kids at school. She was different, and sweet, and I wanted to help her. I would wash her clothes and bring her food. I even taught her to read." He looks at me and smiles. "She was my first kiss."

He isn't trying to taunt me or rub it in, he's simply recalling a happy memory.

"That's what I mean, Toben, you guys have this relationship I will never understand. I know you think I took her away from you, I—"

"Don't give yourself so much credit there, guy. You didn't take her from me, I lost her all on my own, let's get that straight, right fucking now."

I hold my hands up in compliance. "Fair enough. Can I ask what happened between you two?"

He shakes his head and murmurs, "You don't want to know that."

"Yeah, I do. I'm curious."

He stares at his beer bottle for an uncomfortably long time.

"I made her fuck me."

My head jerks back at his statement. Other than that, I can't move at all. I know he didn't say what it sounded like. He looks at me, waiting for my reaction.

"What did you just say?"

His chin juts out as if he's stretching his neck. "I think you heard me."

"And I need to make sure I heard you correctly. What did you say?"

He swings his legs off the lawn chair and rests his elbows on his knees. "You know, I still make myself come thinking about the way her body felt when I pushed into it... the memory of her tears moistening my cock as I shoved it between her lips..." He tilts his head and stares right into my eyes as the fireworks *boom* and *crackle* above us. "Is that what you want to know?"

Tavin

"It tingles! Is it supposed to feel like this?" I sit on my hands to keep myself from scratching it.

"Yes, it's a face mask, don't touch it." She pulls my hair up into sections and wraps them around hot rollers before putting it all inside a scarf. When she's done, she picks up a case filled with nail polish. "Here, pick one."

I fumble through the colors until I find a pearly pink one that I like, then I find a golden glitter one and I can't decide. "Can I have two?"

I'm so excited. I've never been to a fashion show, and even though Sasha isn't showing any of her clothes, she went to school with one of the designers who will be.

She smiles at my choices. "Very cute. Ooh, I might wear

the gold one too. Remember, if anyone compliments your clothes, tell them they were designed by me, alright?"

I nod. "I promise." Finally, she takes the junk off my face and I touch it. "Whoa, it's so soft!"

She's wiping her own off as she looks in the mirror. "Mmm, I know, it feels so good."

Once her face is clean of the mask, she spreads my fingers out wide so she can paint my nails. She does them all pink, except for my ring fingers, which she does with the gold glitter.

Staying perfectly still, I keep my hands on the vanity so I won't mess up my polish before it dries. I watch as her slender fingers maneuver around her light blonde hair.

"I can't believe you talked Alex into having Toben over. What I would give to be a fly on that wall." Rolling the ends of her hair onto the curlers, she laughs, "Actually, scratch that. It's probably going to be extremely awkward."

"It really bothers me that they don't like each other. They both mean so much to me, I want to be able to spend time with both of them, together."

"I get that, but you need to accept the fact that they might not ever like one another. If you ask me, I think you're lucky they tolerate each other." I shrug. Even if she's right, to me, it's worth a try. The last curler goes in her hair and she inspects her work before coming at me with a set of tweezers. "Now, hold still. I'm going to clean up your brows." She places them against my skin and stabs me with them.

"Ow!"

"Really, Tav? You want my brother to do all sorts of fucked up shit to you and you're moaning over an eyebrow hair? I don't think so. Now sit still."

I frown at her, even though I endure it until she's done. She holds up the mirror for me to see, and they do look nice. I don't know if it's worth that, but they look nice.

Even though it feels like she goes over the same area five hundred times with makeup, when she's finished and I see myself, I feel like I look much prettier. My skin is highlighted and glowing, and she did such a good job with my hair. I buckle my shoes and stand up to look in the mirror. My reflection is so cute that I smile. I really like this outfit.

I hear Timothy's voice as we walk down the stairs, and when we turn the corner, I see him smiling at us. "Well, look at you two!"

Lex's face is exactly what makes all this getting ready worth it. His smile is sweet and aroused as I walk up to him. He cups the base of my neck and whispers in my ear, "You look fucking incredible."

I press my thighs together at his words, and my cheeks feel warm. "Have fun with Tobe."

He makes a partial effort to look enthused. "I'm sure I will."

We go outside to Timothy's SUV and Todd turns on the radio once we're all inside. Even Timothy sings with us and Sasha starts dancing in her seat urging me to join her. The music and everyone's enthusiasm makes my stomach feel like it has a heartbeat.

We drive through a parking garage as Sasha points at people and tells us about their clothes. I'm so glad she made my outfit, so I know I'll fit in.

She loops her arm through mine as we get out of the car and walk across a big parking lot. The closer we get to a large building, the more people we see and the more interesting their outfits become.

The doors are big, and as soon as we walk through them, Sasha hands a man our tickets. He points to the set of wooden doors behind him and when Timothy opens one, it gets so loud. I follow them into a lobby with extremely tall ceilings. I can hear the thump of music coming from the main hall. My purple hair would have fit right in here. I see green, and blue, and even rainbow colored.

Sasha leads us through one of the sets of double doors and the music gets even louder. I have a pang of breathlessness as I look around me. There are HUNDREDS of people all in one insanely huge room. The runway is the centerpiece and is ginormous. Three boys are walking across the long, white stage in scarves and jackets.

Why are they in jackets? It's burning up outside.

Colored lights are blinking on the white stage and camera lights are flashing on the floor. People are sitting right up next to the stage and continue on back to the top of the room, creating a *U* shape. I have never seen anything like this and I've never seen this many people in one place before.

It's too loud to speak, so Sasha waves her arm for us to follow her to our seats. I hope they're close. We go down three levels until we reach our spots. We aren't on the floor, but I can still see perfectly clear. A whole line of boys, including the ones we just saw, all walk across the runway next to a man who doesn't match the others, and he doesn't really look like a model. He's waving at the crowd, and when they exit the stage, the music dies down and the lights get a little lighter.

Sasha pulls out a paper booklet and leans over next to my ear so I can hear her. "It looks like the spring/summer line by Leonora Synser is going to show next. I loved her swimsuits last year."

I'm not one hundred percent sure who or what she's talking about so I just smile and nod as the lights dim. A fun, upbeat song that I don't know, fills the whole room. A woman comes out and introduces herself and tells us the name of the line is called *Lilacs and Lace*.

I've never seen so many beautiful things all in a row.

Every girl who walks out is wearing something even more stunning than the last. There are similarities between each outfit while each of them are unique.

The very last girl is in a magical gown that I can't figure out how she's keeping on. The lace climbs up her chest and across her shoulders in a vine. Her hair looks as if there are pieces of lace woven throughout and continues onto her forehead. When all the girls come out again I see more things I like about each of them. The woman lifts her hand in a frozen wave, and I can't stop myself from clapping. That was so wonderful!

Every line we see has its own style and color theme. Todd and Sasha talk about some of the pieces like they're boring or ugly. I don't think any of them are ugly, and I definitely don't think any of them are boring.

Timothy says he wants to leave a little early to beat the crowd. As soon as we get in the car, Sasha pulls out her phone to post pictures on one of the internet sites she has. She somehow remembers all the designers' names.

I can't believe Lex wouldn't want to see that. Hopefully he wants to hear about it, though, because I'm gonna tell him all about it.

We pull up in the driveway and I jump out as soon as Timothy stops the car. I hope Toben is still here. The kitchen is empty when I run inside.

"Alex?" Sasha calls as she walks in behind me. There isn't a reply.

Suddenly, I think I hear Blind Mag barking.

"Wait, hold on." I listen harder and she's upset. Even though it's muffled, I can tell there's something wrong, she never goes crazy like this. I cross the kitchen to check out back. "Something's going on with Blind Mag."

The curtains are partially covering the open back door,

so I pull them back and see what has Blind Mag so riled up.

When I watch what's happening by the pool, my eyes don't believe it. Alexander's on top of Toben, and he keeps punching his fist onto his still body.

Sasha's hands fly up to her mouth as Timothy runs past us.

"Whoa, Alex, Alex! Stop!"

He throws Lex off of Toben and pushes him back. Lex's shoulders are heaving and he's glaring at Toben in a way that scares me. He wants to keep hurting him.

I run over to Toben to help him, and I whimper when I see his entire face is bloody. I can't believe Alexander would do this. The tears sting my eyes from the need to fall.

"Are you okay?" I whisper, and he winks at me. I turn back to Alexander and I hate the fury on his face. "Why? Why did you do this?" I scream at him.

He yanks himself free of Timothy and I can tell he's angry with me too. "You let him into my fucking house." His face is red with a darker rage than I've ever seen on him. "You let your rapist into my MOTHERFUCKING HOUSE?!"

He's screaming at me and my heart falls, taking my breath with it. Oh no... I look down at Toben. "Oh, Toben. What did you tell him?"

"No, Tavin!" Lex bellows. "Wrong question! The real question is: What didn't you tell me?"

I don't know what to say, I just want him to stop the way he's looking at me.

Scoffing, he shakes his head and turns to walk away. He feels like I lied to him again. I keep thinking he won't understand, when he's proved to be more accepting about all of this than I could have ever dreamt up. I need to start trusting him more and maybe he deserves to know.

I leave Toben to follow after him. "Please, Lex, it wasn't his fault. Logan made him do it... He was punishing us.

Toben didn't have a choice. Please don't be mad at me. I didn't tell you because I just want to forget about it."

"He needs to leave. Now!"

The sliding door slams shut behind him and I turn back to Tobe. "Why would you tell him that?!"

We've never really talked about the effect that day had on our relationship. I've tried so hard not to think about it, so I didn't consider that he did the opposite.

Sasha touches my arm. "Hey, you two need to have this conversation later." She nods her head toward the house. "You need to go talk to Alex. I'll give Toben a ride home." I look at the door Lex just stormed through. "Call me later if you need to talk, okay?" She gives my arm a squeeze.

"Okay." I hold my hand out to Toben to help him up, before hugging him tight. "I love you. You know that right?"

His lips lift into a half smile. "I know that."

Giving him a quick kiss, I take a big breath before going inside. Lex isn't in the kitchen, so I quietly climb the stairs to his room and slowly open his door. He's sitting on the edge of his bed with a bottle of whiskey in his hand.

"Alexander?" I whisper.

He looks up and as he sees me, the sadness in his eyes transforms back into anger. He shoots to his feet and for a moment, I think he's going to throw the bottle.

"How am I supposed to be okay with this? He…he fucking liked it, Tavin."

My own anger climbs up my stomach and bursts through my lips. "I know that! I was there! You have no idea what that was like for me. This is why I didn't tell you. You can't possibly get it."

"You didn't just not tell me. You lied to me about it."

"How was I supposed to tell you? I knew you wouldn't understand, and he's my best friend. No matter how you would have found out, you still would have freaked. You can't handle my life, Lex, just admit it!"

He marches up to me and grabs my face. "I love you. Do you get that? The idea of anyone hurting you does things to me, and this was done by someone you call a friend. So yeah, Tav, I am 'freaked.'"

How can I make him see? My life isn't black and white. It isn't even gray. It's every color of the rainbow.

"He's wanted to have sex with me for a long time, I just couldn't. It's Toben…I couldn't have something as horrible as sex dirtying our relationship. It was difficult for him, and he still never once pressured me about it. Then one day, I made Logan angry, worse than we had seen in a long time. He knew how I felt about sexual things, especially with Tobe, so that was my punishment, our punishment. It wasn't Toben's fault."

He shakes his head. "I don't want him back in my house."

"He's the only reason you ever met me! If it wasn't for him, I would have killed myself years ago!"

He sighs with frustration. "I'm going to need some time on this one, Tavin."

"Fine."

I turn around and shut the door. I understand why he's upset, I really do, but I'm the one who went through it. If I've forgiven Toben, then he should too. He isn't taking him from me, though. Lex not allowing him in the house won't stop me from seeing him.

All he's doing is making things more difficult. If he really wants to be with me, he's going to have to accept that my life has been filled with men using my body. A lot of men. What he doesn't see is, in a way, Toben was raped too. He didn't want to do it that way, he was forced to.

I go back downstairs and out to the patio, where everyone besides Blind Mag has already left. I walk over to where they were fighting and my heart aches when I see the blood on the concrete. Falling onto the lawn chair, I look over to see a few roaches on the table. I could definitely go for a joint right now. I scoop them up and tell Blind Mag to come on.

Stopping in the kitchen to give her a treat, we go back up the stairs to go to my room. I snatch my phone off the dresser before falling back on the bed and texting Toben. Lex made his face bloody, which is not going to be good when Logan sees him.

Are you ok?

I hit send and look at the nightstand. There's a magazine, so I grab it and pull open the drawer to get the papers. I start to break open apart the roaches when my phone dings.

Come on, I can take a few hits. Dude has an arm though.

I smile at the phone. He always acts so tough.

What are you going to tell Logan?

I scrape the secondhand weed into a pile and sprinkle it into the paper before rolling and licking it closed.

Don't worry, I won't tell on your boyfriend. I'll just say I got into a bar fight.

I sigh. Even though I didn't think he would tell, I still feel relieved at him saying it. I light the joint and take a long pull.

Thank you, Tobe. Why didn't you fight back? You were just letting him hit you.

Ugh. Pre-smoked weed doesn't taste the same. It'll get the job done though.

Because I deserved it.

My eyes burn as I press the palms of my hands against them, and push the 'call' button. There's background noise before his voice wraps around me. "Hey, Love."

"Tobe…you know I don't hold it against you, right?"

"I know. I hold it against myself. I should have fought harder, I—"

"You were trying to protect me. I'm older now, I understand it more. Please stop punishing yourself for it."

He's silent for a while and all I hear is him smoking, when he says, "I hope I didn't make too big of a mess of things."

I lean back and puff on the joint. "He's really upset. It wasn't fair of you to spring that on him. If I know Lex though, he'll come around, eventually."

"I don't know about this one. You didn't see his face before he flew out of that chair like a ninja."

I groan, "I really wish you wouldn't have done this." I can feel the high starting to float over my skin and I just want to enjoy it and go to sleep. "Use ice to get the swelling to go down, okay? Go get high and get some rest. I love you, I'll call you tomorrow."

"I love you, too. Sweet dreams, Tav."

"Sweet dreams, Toben."

CHAPTER THIRTEEN
Aslaug

Alexander

I TOUCH THE EMPTY SPACE IN MY BED. I THOUGHT I WAS done with the lies and the deceit. I thought I had proved to her she could tell me anything. Maybe if she would have told me herself, I wouldn't be feeling this way. Hearing it from him, the way he told me…I want to kill the little fuck.

I get out of bed and walk past her empty room. I still have the fear of her leaving. That one day she'll get too over-whelmed and bolt, so when I get to the top of the stairs and hear her talking to Blind Mag, I breathe a sigh of relief.

The dog is sitting on the island as Tavin feeds her bits of her muffin.

"Tavin, don't give the dog your food."

She jumps and gives me an unsure expression. I walk over to her and kiss her head before pouring a cup of coffee.

"Are you still mad?" She asks.

I pet Blind Mag and sit next to her, "I have to be able to trust you, Tavin. I have to know what you're telling me is the truth." Her head jerks and her eyebrows knit. "You told me over and over that you two had never slept together."

Her eyes get watery and her little fingers wrap around my hand. "I'm sorry, Lex. I honestly just wanted to pretend like it didn't happen."

"But it *did* happen."

"You're right, I should have told you, I…I don't know how to do this."

I hold her face so she's looking right at me, when I say, "No more lies. That's all I ask."

She nods and whispers, "I am sorry."

"I'll work on getting past this, okay? I do want to under-stand." She gives me a sweet smile before she sips her coffee. "So, what do you want to do today?"

She twirls a tendril around her finger and looks up at me with a raised brow. "Can we go roller skating?"

I burst out laughing. "Roller skating? What the hell made you think of that?"

Her eyes widen and she claps her hands together before spreading them out in emphasis. "One of the designers yes-terday had all the models on roller skates and it looked like so much fun."

I grin at her excitement. How can I say no to that? Hopefully I still remember how. It's been at least fifteen years since I've worn skates.

"Roller skating it is."

Her ass looks too perfect for words, in the shorts she has on. She's curling her hair and her reflection shows her eyebrows scrunched in concentration.

"What are you thinking so hard about?"

Her head jerks and I worry she'll burn herself. "Oh, nothing. It's just curling my hair always reminds me of one time when I got the wrong address for a Client and missed my playdate. Logan came over as I was doing my hair, He was so mad that he threatened to fuck me with the hot iron." The nausea rolls in my stomach as she releases the strand. "I actually wanted him to. I thought it might melt me closed or burn away the skin so I wouldn't be able to feel what they did to me."

"Oh, Tav…"

Taking the curling iron out of her hand, I place it on the vanity to safely wrap my arms around her. I wish I could drink up every ounce of her suffering. I bet even that would be sweet.

My skin jumps as my cell phone rings in my pocket. I take it out and Sasha's face fills up the screen.

"Hey, Sash."

"What are you doing right now?" She's talking in an excited rush and I can almost hear her jumping up and down. "Tell me you're at home."

I'm not even going to try to guess what's going on. She rarely gets like this, so whatever it is, at least it's good.

"Yeah, I'm here. What's up?"

"Just don't go anywhere. I'll be right over."

She hangs up before I can say bye. Tavin looks at me in question and I shake my head. "Who knows."

Sasha had to have already been halfway to my house because she gets here in record time. She's carrying a small cardboard box and is all grins as she shoves it against my chest. "Open it."

I chuckle at the girl who has possessed my sister. "Would you like to come in first?"

She pushes past me and sits next to Tavin who is asking, "What's in the box?"

I bite back the urge to quote *Se7en*.

"If he would open it, you would know," Sasha urges.

"Alright, Jesus."

I stick my thumb in the gap to open the lid. As soon as I see the pink heart gemstone, I choke on hidden tears. I can't believe it. I can barely form my lips around words.

"Aslaug's tiara…" I swallow, making my voice flow easier. "How did you find this?"

She's smiling so big her eyes are sparkling like the diamonds on the crown. "I've been looking for years. It was passed around quite a few times, and I met some lovely, shady people in the process, but today I had a meeting with a potential, and as soon as I saw it, I knew it was *it*. And it's still in perfect condition."

I haven't seen it in three years and I never entertained the idea of doing so again. It brings back so many emotions of sorrow, yet I'm overwhelmed with the relief of having it back.

"Sasha…thank you for this."

She waves me off as if it isn't a big deal, when we both know it is.

"Yeah, well, I stole it to begin with…" I place the tiny tiara on the island and pull her tight against me. She knows what this means to me. She laughs and squeezes me back. "You're welcome, Alex."

I look at Tavin's expression of misunderstanding and I know I should tell her about Aslaug. She's had so much bad stuff in her past, I think it's time I share part of mine with her.

Sasha pulls back from me and I can tell this helps absolve some of the guilt she's been carrying around. Letting out a shaky breath, she combs back her hair. "So, what are you guys up to today?"

"We're going roller skating," Tavin pipes up.

"Is this because of Maxwell Leonard's line?" Sasha laughs and Tavin smiles in admittance. "That kind of sounds fun. I haven't been to a skating rink in ages. Mind if me and Silas tag along?"

Picturing Silas in a pair of roller skates is nothing short of comical. "Of course not."

Sasha leaves to go pick up Silas and says they will meet us later at the roller rink. I walk her to the front door and when I get back into the kitchen, Tavin is staring at the tiara.

"It's so pretty. It's like a crown that a princess would wear. It's just so tiny."

I sit down next to her and gently rub my fingers over the gemstones. I'm in awe that it's really here. Taking a deep breath, I tell her what I've barely spoken of in years.

"Carrie and I started dating my junior year in high school. We took each other's virginity and to be completely honest, I thought I was going to marry her." Her eyebrows draw together and she chews on the inside of her cheek. While I don't want to upset her, I want her to let me in, so I need to do the same. "Toward the beginning of our senior year, she got pregnant. I loved her and wanted to be there for her, so I told her I would back whatever decision she made. When we chose to keep the baby, we told our families and friends, and began to do what needed to be done to prepare for a child. Naturally, I was terrified at first, yet after time, the only thing I became was excited. The day we found out we were having a girl was the day it really sank in for me. I remember watching her little arms move on the sonogram, like she was waving at us. That same day, I went out and bought everything for her to have the best nursery any baby could dream of. That's when I found this tiara. She was going to be my princess and I wanted her to have everything a little girl could desire." Her eyes look forlorn and it's only going to get worse because this story doesn't have a happy ending. "We decided to name her Aslaug after my *Mormor*. I remember wondering what kind of person she would be.

I fantasized all sorts of things about our life as a family." I take her hands to remind her that this is my past and she's still my present and future. "A couple months before she was due, Carrie called me in tears. She said there were complications with the pregnancy and she had lost Aslaug. Even though she hadn't been born, I loved her deeply. I heard her heartbeat. She was alive to me. I cried harder than I ever had, that day. Even though I tried to be there for Carrie, I struggled because I was so heartbroken, and she wouldn't open up to me. Over the next few weeks, I began to heal, however, Carrie and I were growing apart. A couple months after we lost her, we went to a party."

Eleven years ago...

"Hey, Carrie, you doing more shots, bitch?"

Why does she feel the need to yell? We're all standing right here. "Hey, Sash, maybe tone it down a bit?"

"Hey, Alex, maybe kiss my ass a bit?"

Silas laughs and I flip him off with the hand that isn't holding Carrie's.

She can barely walk the three steps it takes to get to Sasha. "Yeah, give me some Jack."

"Come on babe, you're wasted already and it's getting late. Your dad will kick my ass if you're out past curfew."

She waves me off. "My dad hasn't cared what I do since you knocked me up. He'll deal."

I hate how she talks about the pregnancy, as if it's nothing more than last week's drama. Marie holds up her shot in a toast, as Carrie and Sasha do the same.

"Whooh! We made it! I can't believe we're about to graduate! Here's to big dreams and bigger paychecks!"

Their glasses clink together before they all throw back the shots, and Silas shakes a bag of weed in my face.

"My mom will kill me if she finds this, and I can't smoke it all by myself so...who's in?"

The girls holler in agreement and we all head back into the hallway of whoever's house this is, to find a bedroom. I shut the door and Silas takes a little metal pipe out of his pocket, before cramming a bud inside. He hands it to Sasha first and as she lights it, her face is illuminated by the lighter in this dark room. She coughs and hands it to me. I light the bowl and feel the soft burn drift down my throat, as I pass it to Carrie.

We go around the circle. Marie has a coughing fit while trying to ask Carrie, "So is it true? Did you really get accepted to Stanford?"

She reveals a big smile and so do I, because I'm proud of her. She got the acceptance letter while she was still pregnant with Aslaug, so she was terribly depressed because there was no way she would be able to go. She didn't want to tell anyone. Now all that's changed.

"It is. Can you believe it? Fucking Stanford!"

Everyone has been tiptoeing around the subject, though our current lubrication makes their filters a lot less potent.

"Have you thought about what you are going to do now, Alex? Are you still taking next year off?"

I take the pipe from Sasha. "I suppose I'm back to the original plan."

Silas holds up his beer. "Berkeley!"

Before Carrie got pregnant, Silas and I were going to share a dorm together after we found out we were both accepted to Berkeley. Although I'm excited, the loss will never be worth it. Nobody understands, and the moping around got tiresome for people, so I've learned to put on my 'happy' face.

After my hit, I give Marie the pipe, as she says, "I can't believe we aren't going to see each other every day. None of us are even going to be living in Shadoebox." She turns to Sash. "When do you start at the Academy of Arts?"

"September third!" She squeals.

The bowl is cashed, and even though Carrie doesn't care, I would like to keep her dad from hating me anymore than he already does. I press my lips to her head to softly kiss her before I murmur, "I really think we should go. Give me your keys."

She rolls her eyes as she pulls the keys from her purse. "Whatever."

Stumbling out to her car, she proves she's way past trashed. She trips and falls right before she gets to the car door. "Ow! Shit!"

"God, Carrie, are you alright?"

I lean down to help her and she pushes me off. "I'm fine."

Sighing, I pull her up anyway. "Come on."

"Alex! I'm not fucking pregnant anymore so you can knock it off with the doting."

"How can you talk about it so casually? You'll speak of it in passing conversation, but you refuse to really talk to me about it! I love you, Carr. I want to support you."

She shakes her head. "Let's just go."

We drive the couple blocks in silence. If her arms weren't crossed I would hold her hand. I pull into her driveway and the porch light is on, though luckily, all the house lights are off.

"Do you need help getting inside?"

She opens her door and snaps, "No."

As soon as she says it, her knee bangs against the glove compartment, knocking it open and she falls from the car.

"Shit, Carr."

I jump out to help her and lean in to shut the glove box. There are papers sticking out so I pick them up and straighten them. Glancing down, I read the words at the top of the page. Suddenly, my knees feel as if they might give out.

Dilation and Evacuation Abortion Take Home Instructions.

The only part of my body I can move is my eyes as I keep reading. Even my lungs have stopped working.

Dilation and Evacuation (D&E) is a medical procedure consisting of opening the cervix and removing the contents of the uterus.

The 'contents'? Are you fucking kidding me? Did she... — no, that doesn't make sense, she was excited, too. This can't be right.

My tears are lining my eyes and I fail at keeping them from my voice. "You had an abortion?"

Her face falls as she begins to cry. "What were we going to do, Alex? I wasn't ready. I didn't want to give up on everything I had busted my ass for. My dreams. I couldn't let it all go."

"Then you should have made that fucking choice at the beginning when we discussed it! She wasn't a dress you could return! She was mine too!"

"Alex, I know you think you loved her, but you only loved the idea of her. We would have grown to resent each other if I would have gone through with it. She was still just a fetus."

"She had a Goddamn name! She was going to be here in a few weeks when you did this shit."

I throw the papers at her and she tries to touch me so I slap her hand away.

"Please don't hate me, Alex."

"I more than fucking hate you. I hope you burn in hell, bitch."

I toss her keys on the car seat and turn to walk back to the party. Tonight is apparently just getting started.

"Alex, please!"

She's nothing to me now. Her words, her thoughts, it's all irrelevant. I arrive back at the party and I realize I don't want to talk to anyone. I want to be alone and God knows there's *more than enough alcohol at my house.*

I'm impressed with myself that I'm able to back my car out of this fucked up parking system, and as I do, I blare the radio to attempt drowning out my thoughts.

As soon as I walk in my house, I grab a bottle of my dad's scotch, climb the stairs to my room, and pull the box from the closet to open it. I sit on my bed and take out the teeny-tiny tiara.

It's never going to happen. I'll never get to hold her, kiss her, or watch her grow up.

The tears are finally stronger than I am.

"I found out she never had a miscarriage at all and I've never been able to forgive her for it."

She shifts as if she's uncomfortable, and there's clearly something going on in that head of hers.

"Do you…do you still want kids?" She whispers.

"Yeah, someday I'd like to be a father." Her head jerks and she looks away from me so I softly touch her chin to turn her back to me. "What is it?"

"I can't give you that, Lex. I can't have babies."

"That doesn't matter to me. Really, it doesn't. Aslaug was already created, she was almost here, that's why it hurt so much. With or without children, Tav, I just want you." I smile as I tuck her hair behind her ear. "Now you have roller skating to get ready for."

Her sweet little grin comes out from hiding and her face brightens again. She hops down from the seat and I grab her hand to bring her against me. "You're everything I need, Tavin."

"Have you ever done this before?"

She shakes her head as she laces up her skates. "Nope."

I laugh. This will be amusing.

"God, how embarrassing, we're the oldest ones here." Silas looks around as if we would see anyone we know.

"Oh, come on, it'll be fun." Sasha grins at him as she pulls him behind her.

Tavin scoots her way across the carpet, and as soon as her skates hit the rink, she falls on her ass. She's cracking up, laughing as I help her up.

"Hold my hand until you get used to it."

She's possibly the worst skater in the history of all roller skating. She has to hang on to my arm for dear life so she doesn't fall every five seconds, but she's having a blast. Sasha and Silas skate around the rink twice before we even make it once.

"Okay, I think I can do it on my own now." She lets go of my arm and wobbles back and forth as she catches her balance. "I'm doing it!"

She's not really, she's basically standing stationary, moving forward a half an inch at a time.

"Are you hungry? Do you want to get some nachos or something?" She nods in approval and I point to the snack bar as we get passed by Silas and Sasha. "We're going to get some food."

"I could definitely go for a pretzel," Silas says, as he takes Sasha's hand. It's oddly not as weird to see them together as I originally thought. It almost seems natural.

We all go to the concession stand and I tell her to order whatever she wants, which consists of a cherry slushy, two bags of candy, and a hot dog.

We pick the cleanest booth we can find and pile in. Tavin immediately starts slurping on her slushy as she rips open her bag of candy and throws the sour chews in her mouth.

"Hey, I've had these before! I guess I didn't recognize them."

She rolls the bag over and instantly drops it on the table as if it burned her. Her face has lost all color and she sways as if she might pass out.

"Hey, are you okay?" Sasha asks.

Her chest is rising and falling so hard, so I hold her hand. "Tavin, what's wrong?"

She looks at me with wide eyes as she slides the bag of candy across the table. When my gaze follows her hand, I see she's pointing to the Lotus Candy Company symbol.

"It's my logo…and it says 'Lotus'. That's what Logan calls me."

I had assumed she knew what the correlation between her brand and the company was. The fact that she doesn't is just weird.

"You don't know? This is one of Logan's companies."

She shakes her head. "I don't understand."

"You really can't think of anything that would connect you to this?"

She's silent for a moment, her head jerking all the while. "He always gave us candy," she whispers.

"What?"

She looks up at me. "Every week, after he would play with me and Toben, if we were good, he would give us candy. It's how we knew we pleased him. When we started playing with the Clients, they did the same thing. If we did a good job, they gave us candy."

There's something so twisted about this detail. I really don't know exactly what makes it so demented, besides the lack of originality in a pedophile giving his victims candy. She takes my hand and squeezes it. "That's one of the things that meant so much to me when we met. You gave me candy before we had sex. Just because you liked being with me."

The cotton candy. Oh my God. Please tell me that's not

why she slept with me…because she felt like she was supposed to.

"Tavin, I bought you the cotton candy because we were
at a carnival and that's the kind of food you eat at those
things. It was never meant as some type of reward. You'd
never had it before and you wanted some. That's not why
you came home with me is it?"

"No. I went home with you because I wanted to, but the
candy just meant a lot and felt significant to me."

Silas' mouth is hanging open while Sasha doesn't seem
shocked at all, sitting there drinking her Slurpee annoyingly
loud.

From what I learned on my own, and from William,
the Lotus Candy Company was founded in May of 1991.
Twenty-four years ago.

"When's your birthday?"

I can't believe I haven't asked her this before. She said it
was a day she chose, I just find it a little odd that the company is roughly as old as she is.

"December eighth, nineteen-ninety-one."

If her actual birthday is anywhere close to her made up
one, then there's no direct connection between the two. Still,
the candy, the matching flower, and the name are too coincidental to completely ignore.

"Maybe Logan just has a thing for lotus flowers," I offer.

She shakes her head. "No, it's a symbol that I'm his."

My body heats up so fast when she says shit like that.

Sasha scoffs, "Uh, no. The lotus flower is a symbol, but
it has nothing to do with Logan James. It means rebirth and
purity." She knocks the salt from her pretzel. "Not possession and slavery."

Tavin leans forward toward Sasha. "Really?"

Her mind is working hard on something as her hand
rubs her shirt over her sternum. "Rebirth kind of means a

fresh start, right?"

It's too perfect for me not to smile at her. "That's exactly what it means."

Wednesday, July 8th

Tavin

"Come on, Timothy, he can't keep me from seeing him and he knows that. He doesn't want Toben to come over here, so that means I have to go see him."

"It may be none of my business, and I've tried to keep my mouth shut, but I must say I agree with Alex on this one."

I inhale deeply because he's frustrating me. Nobody's going to keep me from Toben, not even Lex.

"You can agree with whoever you want to. The way I see it, you have two options. You can come with me to see Toben, or you can stay here and I can go by myself."

He huffs at me. "You know that isn't really a choice."

"Good, then it's settled."

He shakes his head. "Fucking girls. Thank God I'm gay."

I snort at him. I know he isn't mad at me and only is trying to do what Lex wants, so I hug him and grab his hand to pull him outside. "Come on, slow poke."

I climb into Timothy's SUV and buckle my seat belt as he turns to me and raises his eyebrow. "Alright, where are we going?"

"*Gâteau* on Fifth and Eltsen."

His head whips toward me. "*Gâteau*? Damn, that place is pricey."

"Yeah, and the chocolate, gold flecked macaroons are totally worth it."

He turns out of Lex's driveway and whistles. "Todd's going to lose it. He's been bugging me to take him there for over a year."

"Invite him. My treat. I have some Marvel and Sweet money left."

"I don't really know what that is, and though it's kind of you to offer, he's at work right now anyway."

"Don't worry. I'll get him something good for you to take home."

He gives me a nice looking smile and I return it. "He would love that. Thank you."

Toben already has a table when we arrive at the restaurant, so the hostess leads us to him. He's so wonderful, he got us a seat right next to the window.

"I ordered you that drink you like."

I kiss him and take my seat. "Thanks. Oh, we should get the *crêpe au fromage* for Timothy to try."

I slurp my drink as the waiter walks up and takes our order. I tell Timothy to get whatever he wants and he fights me a little bit, until he smells the next table's food.

I'm starving by the time our meals arrive, and as soon as Timothy takes his first bite, his eyes roll into his head as he moans, "Oh God, this is incredible."

"And you haven't even tried the dessert yet," I tell him.

Toben's laugh stops so abruptly that it demands my attention. His eyes are wide and his body looks frozen solid.

"What's wrong?"

He gazes past my shoulder when the voice that will always make my blood run cold, sounds in my ear.

"Well, hello, Toben." His hand feels like a million pounds on my shoulder. "Tavin, dear, how are you? I'm assuming your new arrangements are going well."

I can't make myself move. I don't know what will happen

when I look at him. I haven't seen him in weeks and the last time I did, I was high. He moves to the side of the table and my heart hurts. It's beating so hard it burns.

"Hello, Logan." Toben's voice sounds perfectly relaxed. I know him though, and he's anything but.

I still don't want to upset him and I know not responding is one of the quickest ways to do that. Even though my words have to claw their way out, they can still be heard.

"H—hello, Logan."

"And who is your friend? I don't think we've met."

Timothy stands and holds out his hand. "Timothy Shark."

"Logan James. A pleasure." Timothy's expression fades into shock as Logan's remains smug. He turns his wrist over to glance at his watch. "I apologize, I must be going." His fingers lightly trail across the back of my neck making the little bumps cover my skin. "Charming as always to see you, Tavin."

I'm able to force my voice to speak once more. "Yes, Logan."

It isn't until he's completely out of the dining area that I'm able to get air back in my lungs. I wasn't sure if I'd see him again, and if I did, I had no idea it would make me feel this way. I'm not his plaything anymore and he was being nice, so why do I still feel like throwing up?

"Logan James is the Logan you guys talk about?" Timothy gapes.

I nod as Toben takes my hand. "You alright, Love?"

I'm not alright. I want to cry and scream. I've been living in this special world and it's so easy to want to believe that I could become the girl in this life. It still doesn't erase what I am inside.

Dirty, filthy, whore.

It was so stupid of me to believe I could just become

something else. I've wanted to get high on occasion, but nothing like this. I feel like I need it. It's the only thing that will push the fear and grime down to bearable, again.

Mostly for Timothy's benefit, I tell him, "Yes." Even though he knows me too well to buy it. I can't even finish my macaroons. "I need to go to the bathroom. I'll be right back."

I hope, hope, hope Toben has his works kit on him. I know this is wrong and right now, I don't care. I need this feeling to go away. I'll never truly be free of him. No matter what I do, he will always be a part of me. I take out my cell because this is the only way to ask with Timothy around.

I need a fix. Do you have any with you?

Hopefully he has his phone turned up because I can't be in here long or Timothy will come check on me.

I got you. I'll leave it in my seat.

I hug my phone with relief. I can always depend on Tobe.

Oh my gosh, I love you.

I feel a little better knowing it's coming. As I get back to the table, Toben is settling up the check, while Timothy rubs his belly.

"What do you guys want to do now?"

I know exactly what I want to do.

Toben looks at his phone. "I have a little bit of time before my playdate, I saw a new art supply store a few blocks down, do you want to check it out?"

As much as I want to see it, I can still feel my skin shaking. I want to scrub it clean with a steel wool pad. I take a deep breath. I don't get to spend near as much time with Toben as I would like to. For the first time, Timothy being here is a burden. I just want to go back to the house with my best friend and disappear into our private world.

I don't have that option though, so I smile and say, "Sure."

We get up to leave, and as promised, his little black kit is sitting in his seat. I shove it in my back pocket and Toben winks at me. He takes my hand, and when he does, I feel the plastic of a small bag.

My eyes go wide and I squeeze his hand tight to show him how grateful I am. He knows me so well, he knows what I really want to do. The coke will hold me over until I get back to Lex's.

I feel a pang of guilt because I know I promised him no drugs in his house, although if I want to get technical I only promised for that weekend.

Jeez, I'm not even convincing myself.

I quickly sprinkle a bump on my hand and take a wonderful inhale. I kiss him on the cheek and he wraps his arm around me as we walk to Timothy's SUV.

The art store is huge. I've wanted to try the different chalks and paints, I just always use pens and pencils because it was all I used to have access to. There are big white boards that you can draw on and a lot of other things that I don't really know what they are.

"Hey, check this out," Toben calls. I follow his voice to find him holding a piece of paper. "There's a whole list of art classes. Anyone can take them." He hands it to me.

Free Summer Classes Available to the Public:
1. Acrylics Basics: First and third Saturday in June.

2. How to Draw: Second and fourth Saturday in June.

3. Watercolor Techniques: First and Third Saturday in July.

4. Color Mixing and Blending in Painting: Second and Fourth Saturday in July.

5. Basic Skills in Oils: First and third Saturday in August.

6. Fabric Screen-printing: Second and fourth Saturday in August.

Even though I don't know what a lot of this stuff is, I bet I could learn, so I stuff it in my pocket.

"Thank you, Toben."

He takes out his phone and sighs, "Well, I need to go." Wrapping his arms around me, he pulls me close as he whispers, "I wish I could go with you, I've missed being high with you."

I kiss him. "Me too."

Timothy offers him a ride, but Toben says he would rather walk, which probably means he plans on getting fucked up somewhere first.

Timothy and I get back in his car, and as I buckle up, he tells me, "I have to tell Alex about who we saw today, you know."

"Yeah, I know."

The coke is wearing off, so I really wish he would drive faster.

I thought I was really getting a normal life and I started to truly believe I could have it. I'm so stupid, I can't change who I am no matter where I live. I'll always be his toy.

We get back to Lex's and Blind Mag greets us at the door. I pick her up to take her to my room. "I'm sorry, Timothy, I'm not feeling so well. I'm going to go lie down until Alexander gets home."

He narrows his eyes at me, so I don't think he really believes me, when he says, "Okay. Get some rest."

I hurry up the stairs, shut the door, and put Blind Mag on the bed. Unzipping Toben's kit on the bedside table, I set out the balloon, the packaged syringe, cotton, spoon, tourniquet, and lighter. Once it's mixed, cooked, and the cotton is full, I slide in the needle and pull back on the plunger. I close my eyes and take a deep breath. Alexander will be so mad if he finds out. He just doesn't understand, he wouldn't want to feel this way either.

I ignore the stab of guilt as I pull open the drawer to find one of his belts. Situating the pillows on the bed, I tie off my arm. The needle slides beneath my skin, making my heart pound. I remove the belt and Blind Mag whines.

"Come on, girl, I'll be back soon. I just need to stop the filth for a bit, okay?"

She lays her head on her paws while I pull my blood into the syringe, before pushing the drugs into my veins.

CHAPTER FOURTEEN
Remember

Alexander

ODAY IS A WEDNESDAY OF THE WORST KIND. I SKIP lunch for a meeting that's less than fruitful, and I'm running on coffee by the time I climb into the Lambo to head home. I just want to eat dinner, fuck Tavin, and spend the rest of the night relaxing.

Timothy's sitting on the couch reading an e-reader when I walk in.

"Finally broke down and got one, huh?"

He takes off his glasses and rubs his eyes. "Yeah, nothing will replace feeling the pages as you turn them, but a few bucks per book is hard to pass up." He stands and gives me a cautious expression. "We had a bit of an incident today."

I wipe my hands over my face and lean against the island. "What now?"

"Tavin and Toben wanted to meet up for lunch this afternoon, and while we were eating, we were confronted by Logan James. I don't ask questions, and I only know bits and pieces of what's going on, so while I'm only assuming he's a large part of why you hired me, I thought you should know."

Even if I have no reason to think he's still a threat, I

imagine seeing him wasn't easy on Tavin.

"What did he say?"

"Just hello, basically. I think it rattled her, though."

"Thank you for telling me." I slip off my jacket and back up to the stairs. "I'll take it from here, have a good evening."

"You too, Alex."

I climb the steps to her room and find her lying on the bed when I open the door. "Tav? Are you alright?"

She slowly turns her head toward me and her eyes are nearly closed as if she is half asleep. I make my way to her bed and my gaze shifts to the night stand. The blood beneath my skin instantly comes to a boil and there's a heavy pounding in my head.

She shot up in my Goddamn house?

I grab her arms and sure enough, she's smacked out of her mind. "Fuck!"

"I'm sorry..." she murmurs.

I don't know what the hell to do. She swore to me she wouldn't do this shit, much less bring it into my house. My fingers rake through my hair and I pace the floor. She can't keep doing this.

"You're letting that sick fuck have this control over you. You're giving it to him!"

She pushes slowly off the bed to face me. "That's what I mean. You think you don't see me that way, but you do. You think he's sick, my life is sick, and you don't want to admit you think I'm sick too."

"You're not what he's done to you. His...perversions are what's disgusting, not you."

"There isn't a difference, Alexander! You don't understand, I wanted him to do those things. I liked it."

She's trying to scream, and it's as if she physically can't. Still, her face is contorted in shame and I know she believes what she's saying. He's fucked her up so badly, I honestly wonder where he ends and she begins.

"You think you wanted it? Oh, Tavin…"

"I did! There was always a point I wanted him to keep going. Do you know how many times he's made me come, Lex? How's that for disgusting?"

I can't move, I can't speak, and I can barely breathe. I am so irate at this point, I feel if I take a single step I will explode on her, and she's the last person I want to be on the receiving end of it. There isn't anything I know to say that will undo the years of damage he has inflicted on her.

I have no idea if this is the right decision. Honestly, I'm out of ideas at this point.

"Do not leave this fucking room."

The door slams behind me as I walk down the stairs and take out my phone to call Silas.

When he picks up, I hear Sasha's fit of laughter as she hollers, "I love you, see you tonight."

"Yeah, you better run," he teases her, and a door shuts in the background. "Hey, what's up?" He chuckles into the phone.

"I need a favor."

He senses my mood because his tone quickly goes somber. "Sure, what's up?"

I go to the kitchen to get a drink. "I need you to go pick up Toben, I'll text you his number. Bring him here. Tell him there's something he needs to see."

"Okay… I don't really know the kid."

"Just do it, Silas."

I hang up the phone and text the number before tossing it on the counter. I down my drink and pour another. Going to the basement, I set up the theater for the VCR before retrieving the tape from my safe. I'm aware that this could do more damage than good. It also could open their eyes. Make them remember the monster he really is, not what years of abuse and drug use have transformed him into, in their minds. They need to go back to that day and see that he was never their savior or their friend. He's their abductor and tormentor. They owe him nothing and at this point they are freely giving their fear and their freedom to the man who stole their lives. They should hate and loathe him. I'm not getting that from either of them.

It takes Silas almost an hour to bring Toben here. Considering the last time I saw him I was punching his face in, I'm a little surprised that he doesn't seem fazed by me in the least.

"Go upstairs and get Tavin. She's in her room."

He tugs on his beanie as he shrugs. "Uh, okay."

Silas opens my fridge and takes out a beer. "So, what's going on with fucked up Hansel and Gretel now?"

Ignoring him, I walk to the counter. "I need another drink."

Tavin and Toben come back down the stairs and as soon as she looks at me she shakes her head and her eyes tear up. "Alexander, I know I messed up. I'm so sorry. I—"

"Are you sober?" I ask.

"Yes."

"Come on." I open the basement door and lead them to the theater. "Both of you, sit."

Toben crosses his arms. "What is this?"

"You both have become numb to what Logan James is. You've clearly forgotten and it's past due time you remember."

I press play and Tavin's younger self appears on the screen. Her eyebrows knit together as she sees child size Toben come into view. She looks at him, while he's glaring at me. I told him I wouldn't show her this.

She doesn't seem to understand or really know what she's watching until Logan and Kyle come down the stairs, then her head shakes violently.

"No, no, no." She covers her eyes and starts bawling, "No," over and over like a mantra.

I pull her hands away and hold them at her sides. "Watch it, Tavin."

"No, Alexander, please! NO!" She fights me with all her strength and I'm struggling with this decision.

Grabbing her face, I force her to look at the screen. Her little screams pour from the speakers. "You think you wanted this, Tavin? Does it look like you fucking wanted it?"

I'm screaming at her and I know I'm losing my cool as I feel a hand around my arm. Silas jerks me away from her.

"Outside, now," he grates.

Tears are flooding down her cheeks and she's shaking while Toben stares at the screen completely blank. Silas and I leave the theater and the screams are silenced once he slams the door. He rarely truly gets mad about anything. It's even rarer that he gets mad at me, and right now he is boiling.

"What the fucking fuck?! How could you not warn me about that? FUCK!" He's pacing the floor with balled up fists. "I want to hit you so motherfucking bad right now. How could you do that to her? How could you let her watch that, much less force her! That's FUCKED UP, Alex!"

My breathing feels shallow. What if he's right? What if I made things worse? I want to take this all away from her and I don't know fucking how! I feel so damn helpless.

"I…I don't know what to do, Silas." I fall in the seat and I can hear myself get choked up. "She's broken and I don't know how to heal her."

I honestly didn't even think about him seeing it and now I feel horrible about it. I know what that felt like to watch.

"I'm pretty sure this isn't how you do it," he snaps. "You need to get rid of that tape."

"I can't. I need it if I ever have a dream of putting Logan away."

He lets out a harsh breath. "Then use it for that, not to traumatize the girl you say you love."

I never wanted that and I suddenly don't want her watching another moment of it. Silas doesn't follow me back in as I shut off the projector. Her wails replace the screams of her past and I pull her to my chest, so immensely grateful that she allows me.

"Shhh, I'm sorry, I'm so sorry, *Lille*." I whisper in her hair, "I just wanted you to know that none of this is your fault, please forgive me."

She can't speak as she continues to weep against my chest. Toben hasn't moved an inch since I started the tape. When he does finally move, it's to look at me and I can't place what I see in his eyes.

He comes up behind Tav. "Will you give us a minute?"

I owe them that. I nod to him and leave them alone. I shut the door and pray that I didn't just do something irreparable.

Tavin

It was so long ago and yet in this moment, I feel all of the terror, the pain, the confusion, the wretchedness...I feel it all itch its way over my skin until I suffocate with it. The screen is blurry and I still know exactly what's going on. I want Toben to hold me, I just can't make myself move to go to him. Why is Alexander making me watch this? I don't want to! I don't want to!

The sound suddenly switches off and the screen goes blank and it still doesn't stop. I can see it and feel it.

Strong arms wrap around me and my mangled body is

consumed in warmth. "Shhh, I'm sorry, I'm so sorry, *Lille*." His voice calms me even though I don't understand why he would do this. "I just wanted you to know that none of this is your fault, please forgive me."

I don't know what to think or feel other than sad. I can't quit crying even as the tears soak his shirt against my face.

Toben's hand spreads across the small of my back as he asks, "Will you give us a minute?"

Lex's heat leaves me and I feel so cold, but I'm quickly comforted by the only person who has felt what I've felt, suffered how I've suffered, and bled how I've bled. We've been through everything together and survived together. It's only because of him that I lived to be this old. My protector, my best friend, the one who makes me a whole person.

"I forgot how that day made me feel," he says, as his forehead pushes against mine.

"I didn't."

"So much has happened since then…do you still hate him?"

"I…I don't know…he's Logan," I tell him.

More tears fall and he nods at my confession. "I know."

"I don't know how to feel about this…I just want to move on, Tobe. I want a different life."

"Do you want to make him pay? For everything he's done? Everything he's taken?"

I shake my head in frustration. I hate not knowing my own emotions. "I don't know."

"I do. I want him to suffer. I want to make him feel the pain and fear he's made us feel for thirteen years."

He holds me for a long time before he finally says he needs to leave. I hug him and kiss him goodbye, in the basement, so Lex doesn't have to see. I think it upsets him to see us touch and kiss. I walk him upstairs and I'm able to sneak past the main floor to my room before seeing Alexander.

I'm tired and conflicted. I knew it happened, but time has a way of smoothing things out and making me forget how things really are. The truth is, Logan didn't take me away from a wonderful life or anything close. In fact, I'm still not completely convinced that my life was any better before he came into it. I was just a different kind of dirty.

Saturday, July 11th

The sun is shining on my skin. I'm safe and warm.

"I love you. I love you." It rings out over and over. It's a song on my soul and a whisper in my heart. My body is wrapped in softness. "*Lille.*"

Lille...

It's him, he's here. My light, my sun, my comfort... His fingers are tracing along my face and as I feel them brush over my lashes, I lift them. His face is hard and creased and I reach my hand out to smooth the lines.

"I'm sorry," he whispers.

Last night rushes back to the front of my mind. He not only knows, he's seen it. That's what changed and that's how he knew about Kyle. He knows it all and he's still here with his arms around me. While I'm humiliated that he's seen the darkest part of my past, at the same time, I feel a knot loosen in my chest. If that didn't send him running away, nothing will.

Maybe I should be angry at him for keeping this from me and then forcing me to watch. Truthfully though, I'm too relieved at the fact that this is still real to find any anger toward him.

"I forgive you," I whisper back.

He kisses me slow and long. His fingers caress me softly as they trail down my ribs.

"I want to be good for you. I don't ever want to hurt you.

Tell me you know that." His voice is still quiet as his erection pushes its way into my body and I gasp at the sudden full-ness. "Tell me, please."

"I know Lex, I trust you."

He buries his face in my neck and thrusts as deep as he can go. The truth is, what happened on that tape was a lifetime ago, and he's right, I do feel differently for Logan now than I did that day. He's the closest thing to a father I have, and in an odd way, that's how I see him. He fed me, clothed me, cleaned me, and there are times I felt as if he cared for me. He made sure we had everything we need-ed, while he also took away everything we may have had. Especially Toben. I might not have ever had a normal life, but maybe he could have.

Lex takes my body slowly and for hours. He still feels guilty about last night and I still have a melancholy cloud following me. Watching myself in the past in so much pain, the vague memories, it leaves me a little grimy.

After breakfast, we take Blind Mag for a walk on the beach. The smell of the ocean opens my lungs and loosens my muscles. I think Lex's legs look really good in shorts and I find myself staring at them as he throws a piece of drift-wood for Blind Mag.

I've tried not to talk about last night because I can tell he still feels bad, but it's too much, I want to know.

"Lex? How did you know about the tape?"

He sighs and runs his fingers through his hair like he al-ways does when he's anxious or stressed. "I went to see your father." He gives me a sideways glance to see my expression.

"What?" I can't believe it. "He talked to you?" Lex's nod is stiff and curt. This is making my heart thump so hard, I can feel it when I touch my chest. "What did he say?"

"He told me about the tapes and where they were. He

wants me to use them to put Logan in prison."

"Why does he want Logan in jail?"

"He said he didn't kill your mom, that Logan framed him."

Logan killed Lacie? Why would he do that?

"Wait…you said tapes? There's more than one?"

He pushes his sunglasses up on his head. "Two."

Brian's always hated me and I still wonder if he ever thinks about me. The last time I saw him was the first time he ever called me 'his'.

"Did he say anything about me?"

Lex looks at me and his eyes are sad. "Tav…I spent ten minutes with him and that was more than enough to know he is a terrible person."

He is bad and mean, that's why I don't understand why I feel this desire to see him. I've always known where he is, it's just the thought of going to see him never occurred to me. I really don't know why he despises me so much. Why he's always wished I was dead. There's a part of me that wants to show him I'm still alive so he can see he didn't get his wish, even if it's silly and pointless. The time with him was so long ago I barely remember it. I do remember the constant fear, though. When he was home there was never a reprieve from it. That's one of the many things Logan gave to me. Six out of the seven days a week, I didn't have to be scared.

Suddenly, Lex's arms are around me, lifting me in the air. It makes my tummy flutter and I laugh when he puts me on his shoulders. He starts running down the beach and the wind lifts my hair from my back. Blind Mag runs right next to us and I can feel sprinkles of water getting kicked against my back. This is so fun. It would be so neat to be tall like this all the time. I feel his fingers against my thigh as he holds me tight, but I still wrap my arms around his neck so I don't fall.

"Whew, I'm exhausted." He pretends like he can't stand

anymore and he drops us both into the sand.

Blind Mag jumps up on us and tries to lick us clean and it tickles so much I giggle. Lex smiles at me, and even though he's trying to cover it up, he clearly has a lot on his mind.

"Are you going to do what Brian wants, with the tapes?"

He pulls me into his lap. "With the way technology is now, it's too easy to fake something like that. I honestly don't think they'll be enough on their own." His hand reaches to my foot, softly touching the missing piece. "Do you remember what happened with this?"

"I don't have an actual memory of it, no." I try really hard not to think of this stuff, so I dig around in my memories for details. "Toben once told me that Logan cut the piece out and put it in a locket."

I feel his warm breath against my neck when he murmurs, "Do you know where the locket is?"

"No…would that help?"

He softly laughs, "Oh, that would definitely help. As far as I know, there is no way to fake DNA. With the tapes and the locket, I think that would be enough to put him away for life. No matter how big his team of attorneys is."

I wish I could help him. The idea of Logan being locked in a cage and not being able to get Toben, me, or anyone else…it's so perfect. I want that so much, and if anyone can do it, it's Lex.

Alexander said he had to do some work in his office, so Blind Mag and I decide to paint our nails and listen to music. It takes a long time because I have to make sure each of her nails is dry before I paint the next one or else she will mess it all up. I think it's worth it because she's adorable with her pink and blue nails. I finish her off with a ribbon around her neck and she looks so perfect I have to kiss her.

"Wait till Lex sees how pretty you are!" She gets on her hind legs, twirling in a circle and I laugh at her. "Such a good dancer, too."

Toben's ringtone, *I Miss You*, jumps from my phone. I roll over on the bed and get it from the dresser.

"Hey, Tobe."

"Hey, Love. I'm about to walk into a playdate, but we need to talk about Logan. Can you meet me somewhere tomorrow?"

"Yeah, just text me. Is everything okay?"

"I don't know about okay. It's much clearer though, that's for fucking sure. I gotta go. I love you."

"I love you, too."

I don't have any idea what we could possibly talk about when it comes to Logan, that we haven't already discussed a thousand times. Whatever it is, it's clearly important or else we would just talk about it over the phone.

I need to figure out a way to get Alexander to let me meet Toben alone because whatever he wants to tell me, I doubt he would want to do it in front of Timothy.

It's pretty late by the time Lex finishes his work. Blind Mag and I are cuddled in bed while I play on the computer he lets me use. He climbs under the sheets and his fingers trail up my thigh.

"What are you watching?"

I turn the screen to show him the video of a kitten with an ice cream tub on his head and it's still so funny I can't stop laughing. "He keeps bumping into things. He can take it off, he just doesn't want to because of the ice cream."

He laughs and kisses my head. "You discovered cat videos, huh?"

"Oh, watch this one!"

We watch a few videos before he talks again. "So, Benny's Boxing Gym holds self-defense classes a few times a week, and I was thinking if it would be something you'd like to do, I could enroll you."

I hate not knowing what things are. It makes me feel dumb. "I don't know what that is."

"It teaches you to be able to protect yourself. There are tricks and techniques you can learn that can help you get away if anyone tries to hurt you."

Being able to protect myself and not have to depend on Lex, or Timothy, or someone else to do it, sounds exactly like something I would want. I like that he wants me to be able to take care of myself and I love that he believes I can. I grin at him and nod. "That's sounds fun."

"Perfect. I'll get you enrolled this week." He adjusts the pillows behind him. "Oh, and Timothy called me tonight. Apparently, Todd's out of town for a few days and I guess he's feeling a little lonely because he wants to hang out tomorrow."

I almost clap my hands with how perfect this is. If he and Timothy are together then neither of them can come with me to meet Toben. He has to give me one night without a babysitter.

"That's funny because Toben wants me to hang out tomorrow."

He tilts his head and gives me a don't-make-me-the-bad-guy look. "Tavin, the last time you went out with him you saw Logan, I don't think you guys should be out alone right now."

"Come on, Lex, please? Toben and I haven't spent any time with only each other, in ages. We'll be fine. We won't go anywhere Logan will be, okay?"

He sighs and brings me to his chest. "Fine. You're probably right."

Sunday, July 12th

Toben wants to meet at our favorite burger place, Fly Guy's Burgers and Fries. As I walk in, I see him waving me over to a table. There's a chocolate strawberry shake waiting for me and I grab it before I sit.

He leans over and kisses me. "I ordered our usual."

Dang, he looks really strung out, even for him.

"Thanks…so what's this about?"

He straightens his beanie and puts his elbows on the table. "I want you to know how sorry I am, Love."

I take a big drink of my shake. "For what?"

"For letting Logan do this to us."

He can be kind of emotional sometimes, when he gets really high. I reach out for his hand.

"What are you talking about? You know as well as I do, there's no way to fight him."

"He's a human being, Tav. He isn't immortal. He can die just like everyone else."

I pull away from him as my heart drops to my stomach. "What are you saying?"

A number is announced over the intercom and Toben stands up. "That's ours. I'll be right back."

He can't be talking about what I think he's talking about. I know Logan has done terrible and horrible things to us, but Toben isn't a killer. He's just upset. My leg shakes as I wait for him to come back and tell me what's going on in his head.

Carrying the tray with our food, he returns to our table and hands me my fries.

"Here you go. And I got tons of ketchup."

I wait for him to sit before I push for him to tell me what he means. "Toben, what are you thinking?"

He dips a fry in his shake and pops it in his mouth. "I'm

not thinking anything. I've made up my mind."

I copy him because shakes and fries together are one of the best combinations ever. "About what?"

"I'm going to kill Logan."

CHAPTER FIFTEEN
Burn

Alexander

WELL, TIMOTHY LOOKS LIKE SHIT. I REALIZE Todd is out of town, so I guess there's no reason to dress nice, but Jesus Christ. I step back to let him in and walk back to the kitchen.

"You wanna beer?"

He rubs the back of his neck. "Sure."

Blind Mag's collar jingles somewhere in the room as I open the fridge. "So, when does Todd get back?"

He slides onto a bar stool, resting his massive forearms on the edge of the island. "A couple of days."

Kicking the refrigerator door closed, I hand him his beer and twist the top off mine. "I don't want you to take this the wrong way, I'm glad you asked me, it's only…do you not have friends to keep you company?"

"I do. They're all couples though. It feels weird when I'm by myself." I nod to him because I get that. "Where's Tavin?"

"I decided to loosen up and let her go out with Toben alone. I still want you here when I'm at work, at least for a while, I figure letting her spend some time with her friends alone has to happen at some point." He's quieter than usual as he nods and drinks his beer. "Are you wanting to go out, or would you rather stay here?"

"If it's alright, I'd rather go out. The noise might be nice you know? It's so quiet at my place."

"Sounds good to me. I'll change and we can go."

I let him pick the bar and it's not exactly The Necco Room, but it's not bad. As we take our seat, I realize there isn't a single woman here.

"Seriously Timothy, you brought me to a gay bar?"

He shrugs. "You told me to choose. Besides, they make the drinks strong."

I shake my head even though I'm almost laughing. Our server comes up and smiles at us. "Hello, handsomes. What can I get started for you?"

"I'll have a whiskey on the rocks. The best top shelf you have."

Timothy nods. "Same."

The server lays down two coasters and a food menu. "Got it. My name's Calvin and I'll be right back with those drinks, okay?"

"Thanks." I turn back to Timothy and pick up the menu. "I don't want to discuss business tonight, there's just one thing I want to ask." He gives me a blank stare and I assume that means to continue. "An end date hasn't been decided on your contract yet, so how would you feel about staying on retainer for when the daily protection isn't necessary? Tavin likes you, I trust you, and who knows when I might need someone to protect her when I can't."

"Yeah of course…I would like that."

I know he misses Todd, he just doesn't seem like himself at all. I'm hoping these drinks the server just dropped off will help cheer him up.

I push his toward him. "Are you still taking those

cooking classes?" He nods with a grunt. "How are those going? Good?" Nodding again, he throws back half of his drink and I don't think I particularly like mopey Timothy. I can hold up my end of a conversation no problem, it's carrying the weight of the whole damn thing that I don't particularly like.

Calvin takes the order for our fourth round as I gesture towards the restroom. "I'll be right back."

Of course I don't get a verbal response from Timothy, so I smile at Calvin and scoot out of my seat. The bathrooms are clean, thank God and when I return to our table, I see our drinks have been dropped off.

I throw back half my whiskey and try to move the conversation along by asking him about where he went to college and when he moved to Central California. Still, his answers remain abrupt. Avoiding Todd doesn't seem to be helping, so I give up and ask about him.

"Do you get along with Todd's family?"

I think he cracks a smile. "Yeah, they're fantastic."

"What about your family? Do they like him?"

His face goes back to blank. "They do now, they had a hard time getting over my ex, at first. They loved Melanie."

He's still not...not acting like himself.... but I think it's...I think it's helping.

"Do you...plern on..." God, I'm really messed up all of a sudden...I shouldn't be this drunk. My hand. I can't lift my hand. "Something's wr...wr..." Everything is soft and blurry and I feel like I'm floating, yet my head weighs too much to move. My eyes are all I can lift as I look to Timothy. He stares down at me like he wants to cry.

I think he's saying something...what did he say?

I'm so sorry, Alexander. I had no choice.

Did he...drug me?

I try to jerk my body from the booth when the floor becomes a black hole. I'm too weak to stop myself from falling in.

⌁

Fuck my face hurts.

Smack.

Jesus! Did I just get hit?

"Wake up, Alexander."

The slow, steady voice begins to clear the cobwebs in my head. Where am I?

SMACK!

"Fuck! Stop it!"

The words scratch their way out of my swollen throat, his chuckle echoing in my ears as if I'm in a hallway.

"While we're waiting for our playmates to arrive, would you like to play a game?" There's an excitement in his tone that makes my skin shudder. My body aches, just not as much as my head. I open my heavy eyes and they are met with hazel ones. Logan smiles at me as he takes a drink from a bottle of water. "How about tic-tac-toe?"

I move to lunge at him and I can't. I can't move at all. I blink to clear my vision and the first thing I focus on is Tavin's bed. I'm in her room. What the fuck? Ropes are tied around my torso binding me to something. A chair. My skin is damp with sweat, regardless of the fact it's freezing in this basement. No matter how much I struggle, I can't gain any leverage. I think the chair I'm tied to is attached to the wall.

Laughing in mild amusement, he bends down to be at my eye level. "I'll go first."

He rips apart my shirt, and before I realize he's holding a blade, he slices two horizontal lines beneath my clavicle bone. The pain isn't immediate. It isn't until he swipes the knife down to make two vertical lines that the hot sting blooms across my shoulder.

"Ahh! Are you fucking serious?"

He ignores me as he taps the bloody tip of the blade to his chin. "Hmm."

I'm prepared for him this time, and it doesn't make a damn difference as he slices an *X* into the middle square.

"Why are you doing this?" I growl through clenched teeth, "I paid you for her. This is over!"

He scoffs with a smile that fades as quickly as it arrives. "You inconvenienced and stole from me. Did you really believe that was something you could buy your way out of? No son, you will pay your debt and it won't be with money." He looks at my bleeding shoulder and chuckles to himself, "I suppose I'll have to play for you, won't I?" He points the knife toward the game board carved into my skin. "Where would you like me to put the *O*?"

My mind's still a little hazy from the drugs and is having a hard time playing catch up. "Where's Timothy? Was he working for you the whole time?"

His nostrils flair as he sighs in irritation. "No, he was simply a convenience I had the good fortune to stumble upon." He smacks me in the head with the flat part of the knife. "Now. Where do you want the *O*?"

His calculated and condescending way of speaking makes me grit my teeth. My smart-ass remark is on the tip of my tongue when a crash comes from the stairs. His eyes flash as an impish grin stretches his face.

"No matter. My toys have arrived." He straightens and sets the knife on the nightstand before rubbing his hands together. "It's time to play."

Tavin

"WHAT?!" The couple at the table next to us turns around to give me a dirty look so I lower my voice to a whisper. "Stop it. You aren't going to kill him, Toben. You're not a killer."

His face does that blank thing where I have no idea what he's thinking.

"I've wanted him dead for thirteen years, Tav. I let him fuck with my head and I'm sorry. This was always the only way, I see that now. What he's done has no retribution besides death. He took our lives, I'm gonna take his."

My heart beats faster and faster. He's spoken this way before, but this is different. He isn't just talking this time.

"I know that video was hard to watch, and I know it brought up a lot of…feelings, just think about what you're saying, Tobe."

His finger jabs at the table as he leans toward me. "It's all I've been thinking about."

"Can we just talk to Lex first? He has a plan to get Logan put in jail. He can't do anything to us or anyone else if he is locked up, right?"

"He doesn't fucking deserve prison and I don't think even that will stop him." I give him my best begging face and he finally rolls his eyes. "If it will make you feel better, fine. We'll talk to your boyfriend first."

I sigh with relief and stand up to hug him. "It'll be better this way, you'll see."

We finish our food and take a cab back to Alexander's house. I take the key he gave me, out of my pocket. When we walk in, Blind Mag is sitting at the front door like she's been waiting.

"Hey, girl, where's Lex?" She stands on her hind legs in front of Toben and he leans down to pick her up. "Lex?" The house is quiet and still, so maybe they're by the pool. We walk to the back of the house, even though I can tell before we reach the back door they aren't out there.

I open the basement door and we walk down to the theater room. "Lex? Timothy?"

Toben is petting Blind Mag's ears and she's flicking her tongue out trying to lick him, when he says, "Maybe they went out?"

I take my cell from my pocket and call Lex's phone. He doesn't answer and the same thing happens when I call Timothy.

"Huh. That's weird." I take his hand. "You want some expensive alcohol?"

"Hell yeah." Putting Blind Mag on the floor, he walks behind the bar to make our drinks.

"Do you have any weed?" I ask.

He drops his head to look at me through hooded eyes. "What do you think, Love?"

"Shut up." He pulls out his cigarette pack and gives me my drink. I swallow the whole thing while he lights the joint and hands it to me. I pick up Blind Mag, taking her and the joint to the theater chairs while Toben pours me another drink. "This doesn't feel right. It's the first time Lex has left me alone since he came back, and now he isn't answering my call? It doesn't feel like something he'd do."

"I'm sure he's just wasted. Stop over thinking and do the same."

He hands me my drink as he sits next to me and I force myself to smile. "Maybe you're right."

The room is quiet, so when his phone rings, it makes me, him, and Blind Mag all jump. He chuckles as he takes his phone out and the life melts from his face.

"It's Logan." Somehow, I already knew that. I can't make myself respond as he brings the phone to his ear. "Hello, Logan." He looks at me as he listens. After what I know is only seconds, regardless of how it feels, he finally sighs, "Yes, Logan,"

He hangs up and his silence is torture as his hand squeezes the armrest.

"Well? What did he say?"

He shakes his head and I know it's bad when I see his face. "He has your boyfriend. We need to go home."

"This taxi is taking forever."

If he dies it will be because of you.

I've paced back and forth in front of this stupid gate a hundred times. It's taking too long. Toben pulls my hands apart and slides his fingers into mine. I've been picking at them again and now they're bleeding.

"He won't do anything before we get there. Whatever he has planned, he wants us to see it."

My shoes feel like they're sinking into the concrete. "If that's supposed to make me feel better, it doesn't"

"Look." He points behind me and I turn to see the lime green cab driving over the hill.

"Come on."

I grab his hand so I can pull him to meet the cabbie. I don't even let the tires completely stop rolling before I rip open the back door and jump in, yanking Tobe behind me.

I rush out our destination as the driver turns around to give me a dirty look. "Eighty-three twenty-six South Morningstar Avenue."

He shakes his head as he enters our address. Toben squeezes my hand as I lay my head on his shoulder and silently beg Alexander to be okay.

We turn onto my street and I grip the door handle as Toben tells the driver, "It's the shitty one on the right."

He's not wrong. Maintenance has never really been a priority. The cab comes to a stop and I don't wait for Toben when I push open the car door. Running up the rickety steps, I hear him yelling after me, I just can't make my feet stop moving.

"Tavin, wait!"

The front door bangs against the wall as I throw it open, and it echoes through the empty living room. I run to the basement door as Toben's shoes pound on the hardwood behind me. He catches up to me at the top step as I run down to my room faster than ever before.

Immediately after turning onto the landing, I see him. The air burns its way to my lungs and my heart turns to glass, ready to shatter.

"Lex!"

Screaming for him is useless and as soon as he looks up at me, the tears instantly blur my vision. He's hurt.

The golden eyes that have haunted me my entire life pierce into me.

"Good evening, Playthings."

Toben and I fall to our positions.

"Good evening, Logan."

My eyes are fighting to look at Lex and refusing at the same time. I don't want him to see me here. I don't want him to watch us play.

"Say hello to our guest, Playthings."

My breathing feels chopped up as it climbs up my lungs. I finally allow my gaze to shift over to him. Thoughts of defying Logan and freeing Lex from his bindings pop around my head.

"Hello."

Toben's greeting rings in my ears and I know I must

force my own.

"H—hello."

The hands that have abused and nurtured me, touch my face. They have broken and cleaned me. It feels like I've been gone for so long, I really thought I'd never have to feel the suffocation of his touch ever again.

"Don't you touch her! Do not fucking touch her!"

The agony in Alexander's scream hurts my chest. I wish I could make him be quiet. He doesn't know the rules and he's going to make Logan angry.

"This is our last playdate, my little Lotus," he coos at me with a smile. "We are going to have so much fun."

Fear for myself and Toben has been there from the beginning. It's part of our normal. Fearing for Lex is a whole new flavor of fear. It's thicker.

"Pick a tool." Logan barks at Toben.

My scalp stings as Logan drags me to Alexander and a sharp pain vibrates through my knees as he throws me to the concrete. Once I straighten back into my position, I see his hands undoing his pants in my peripheral.

"Fuck! No!"

Lex's screaming makes my brain have tingles like when my leg falls asleep. He needs to be quiet. He fights so hard to break through the ropes, rocking his body as he tries to get leverage.

Listening to Logan's footsteps as he walks to the tool bag, I wish Alexander could read my thoughts so I could tell him to just obey. To be compliant and things are always much easier. When Logan takes out the scold's bridle, I bite my cheek to stop myself from pleading and making it worse.

Please just stay quiet and you'll be okay.

I wish it like a prayer.

"You aren't playing nice and are being much too loud."

My stomach feels hollowed out and my head shakes

before I can stop it, but Logan is too busy having fun with Alexander to notice. It's not the helmet part that I'm afraid of…it's the spiked mouthpiece.

"Oh, fuck you. Hell no," Alexander barks.

His tone is disrespectful and he's going to make things so much harder on all of us. I chance a glance at Toben. I've never wanted Logan to die before, but if it protects Lex then that's all that matters. The guilt squeezes my heart when I hope Toben does what he said he would.

"Open your mouth or I'll put this on her instead." I want to scream *yes!* at Logan's false threat. The scold's bridle hasn't done anything to me in years. Of course, Alexander doesn't know that and he must comply because I hear the *click* of it closing. "Do not attempt to speak. Doing so will not be pleasant."

Seeing Lex inside that thing causes a sob to escape my throat. I know the pain that tool brings and the tears fall imagining him feeling that. Alexander's strong will has always been attractive to me. Right now though, I wish he would just give in.

Logan stands in front of me and removes his erection. "Your turn, Lotus. Open your mouth." Regardless of my humiliation, I do what I'm meant to. Keeping my hands on my thighs, I take him down my throat. His hand grips my head, shoving himself deeper. I meet each of his violent thrusts as the tears wet my cheeks. "The rules are a little different tonight, Plaything. Instead of looking at me, you will look at him."

He strokes himself as he speaks. He adores my mortification. Sometimes I hate him so much when he pushes me past what my heart can take. Focusing on him and not having to look at Lex was what was going to get me through this. Begging will get me nowhere. He's waited for this and that's not good for us.

I do as I'm told before he becomes impatient, and look to Lex. Even though I hate seeing him in the scold's bridle, I'm grateful for the way it partially blocks his face as I flick my tongue over the tip of Logan's cock. After a moment, he turns away and I slowly let out the breath I was holding, through my nostrils.

Logan slams his abdomen into my face and I do my best to make it feel good. He can always tell when I'm not trying.

"Plaything," Logan calls to Toben, as he yanks my hair by its roots to slide my mouth off of him. "Use your whip."

My disgusting body aches in anticipation for the pain Toben's whip brings. My eyes find Lex's and my heart leaps at the way he looks at me.

The *whoosh* is the precursor to the *snap* that splits the skin across my back. Pulsing between my legs matches the thump of my heart as he hits me again. My fingers squeeze the flesh of my thighs and my breathing causes rogue strands of hair to momentarily flutter from my face. Logan's sneakers are stained with old blood and I keep my stare on them as I'm hit again. I hear myself moan and even though Alexander knows I like pain, I despise him seeing me receive pleasure like this. Beautiful agony bursts across my back as Logan's voice cuts through the room like a knife in icing. "That's enough for now, Plaything. Run upstairs and get me the meat mallet from the kitchen."

"Yes, Logan."

Toben is being submissive and I don't know if that relieves me or if I'm disappointed. He walks past me to climb the stairs and as soon as he gets to the top, he looks down at me and winks before he disappears. He's thinking something.

My stomach suddenly feels impaled, causing me to dry heave and double over. My ribs are attacked next before Logan jabs his sneaker against my back. I crawl in the direction he kicks me until I'm back in front of Alexander. I make

the mistake of lifting my head and looking at him. His eyes
are the only thing not distorted by the mask, allowing me to
see them clearly. I want more than anything to kiss away the
terror and fury blazing within them, as they dart from me
to Logan.

I'm so sorry.

I don't say it loud enough to whisper, I make no sound,
while in my head, I'm screaming it. I'm pleading for him to
forgive me for this.

Logan pushes my forehead to the cool concrete and
chills run across my skin as my dress is moved up my body,
exposing my flesh. The elastic of my panties is stretched
tight against my skin as he pulls them to my knees. Lifting a
leg at a time, I use my foot to scoot them to my ankles so I
can push them off.

His weight presses my knees harder against the concrete, as I fight the urge to repel at his tongue inside my ear.
His fingers spread me open to prepare me for what's about
to come, and I'm grateful for the ability to close my eyes as
he infiltrates my body.

Physically, I'm aware of him shoving in deep and yanking himself out, I'm even wet because I'm sick, I just don't
really feel it. I'm numb to it.

My neck strains when my head snaps forward and Logan
grunts with another deep thrust as he yanks me back against
his chest. He keeps me in place by my hair and I shove my
body onto his, hard and fast.

It's stupid for me to still hope that if we're good and take
our punishment, then this will be the end of it. He said this
was our last playdate. If he gets to make his point, will he let
Lex survive? Let me go with him?

"Tell him, little Lotus, tell him who's property you are."

I smell the cinnamon of Logan's breath as it brushes
against my cheek, and even though I'm confused at what's

true anymore, I know what I'm expected to say.

"Yours, Logan."

"That's right." The cramping in my stomach from him staying so deep causes a dull ache between my thighs and I push myself down further onto him. Hot tears run down my face as my self-disgust intensifies. His teeth dig into my skin and rip at the flesh, sending radiating jolts directly to my cunt. "And who am I, Plaything?"

"My Maker. You're my Maker, Logan."

No matter what happens, that fact will remain. I am who I am because of Logan and part of me will always hate him for that.

"That's fucking right. Now, look at him!" His nails dig into my face and I involuntarily clench my jaw. "Our play-mate needs to understand that."

I do what he says, but Lex's attention is on the staircase. The next thing I know, my body is thrown to the floor as Toben's shoes bang loud on the steps.

Logan pulls up his pants as I tuck my legs beneath me to get back in my kneeling position. This is not an average playdate, I know that, and I wonder since we're being good, if he's going to give us heroin. For the first time in a very long time, that thought scares me. Alexander would never want to do that and I don't ever want him to.

My fear for what could come is overrun by the reality in front of me. Logan is punching Lex in the stomach, over and over. If he keeps at it, Lex is going to vomit and I know from experience how scary that is with the spikes. I have to try to help him.

"Please, Logan! Please! Tell me what to do, I'll do any-thing. Tell me how to stop this!"

He glares down at me, his golden eyes bright with fury as he storms over to me and takes away my airflow. Squeezing my neck, he pulls me to standing.

"There is no stopping this, Plaything." I trip over my feet as he pushes me back to the bed. My hands clutch onto his wrists as he barks, "Toben, be good and share your whip with our playmate."

He throws my body against the blankets, and my throat opens up causing me to gasp as I gulp in the air. Watching Toben set up for the blow lodges the scream in my throat. I've never seen him do this to anyone else before and I don't like it one tiny bit. Lex's bindings are so tight he can barely move, yet when the whips slices across his chest, his body jolts. I see the exact moment the spikes pierce is tongue. His eyes widen with torment as blood drips from the scold's bridle.

"No! Stop!"

I'm still screaming the words as Logan charges toward me. He brings his arm across his chest before he backhands me so hard I fall backward on the bed. The sounds of the leather snapping against flesh are all around me. Logan climbs on top of me. He's heavy as he whispers, "Are you having fun, cunt?"

The familiarity of the needles puncturing my thigh is comforting as I suck in air and respond just as softly, "Yes, Logan."

He pulls, causing the needles to go deeper as he slides back into me. My orgasm is quickly building; the sounds of the whip the only thing keeping it at bay. He shifts around so I will ride him, tapping on my clit as I slide down his length.

"Look at him, let him watch you come on my cock." The warmth of the blood rolling in streams down my thigh makes me ride him harder. The needles burrow deeper and I can't...I can't hold it back any longer. My tears roll down my face as I come in violent pulses. "Tell him Lotus, tell him what you're doing."

"I'm coming. You're making me come, Logan." My body

doesn't know whether to weep or moan. I look to Lex, and as I shudder from the remnants of pleasure, he's getting ripped to shreds.

I. Hate. Who. I. Am.

And it's *his* fault.

He grabs my waist and discards me on the bed as he stands and tugs up his slacks. "Toben. The tenderizer, give it to me."

My chest feels like it's caving in as I imagine the possibilities of what he could do to Lex with that. I've always known Logan could kill us, I'm just not sure if I ever truly believed he would. With Alexander, I know he won't blink.

I squeeze my eyes shut for only a moment. When I hear a *thud*, fear shorts out my heart and it beats in a frenzy. My eyes fly open to see…Logan on the floor?

Toben's arms are flying around as he hits Logan with all his might. How the heck did that happen?

Alexander.

I jump off the bed and run to him, wanting more than anything to hug him.

"I'm so sorry. Are you okay?" His chest is ripped up, his mouth is bleeding, and I know he can't speak, so it's such a stupid question. I need to stop crying. Taking a deep breath, I look at his chest drenched in scarlet. My fingers find the iron latch and the hinges on the mask squeak in protest as I carefully open it. I drop it on the floor and try to untie him.

These stupid ropes are so tight. Alexander silently watches my frustration as I fumble with his bindings. There's no way I can do this with my hands.

"I can't get it untied. Hold on."

There's plenty of things in Logan's bag I can use to cut through rope, so I grab the top knife and hurry back to Lex. I try my best to cut the ropes and not him, but I'm scared, in a hurry, and Toben needs our help.

"Shit! Sorry..."

Finally, the bonds loosen enough for him to help and as soon as he's free, his big, warm hands are holding my face.

I know the wounds make it difficult to speak and, in this moment, I don't need him to. As he looks at me, I know all the way down in the deepest part of me that he's never going to stop loving me. Not ever.

He stands up straight and almost appears to be getting larger as he pushes back his shoulders and takes the knife from my hand. Toben's hits have lost a lot of strength and momentum, so I run over to him. Now that Lex is free, he can help us.

My fingers grasp on to Toben's shirt as I tug him to his feet and back away from Logan. After a quick inspection of my injuries, he jerks his arm free and goes for Lex. For a second, I think he's going to attack him.

"No fucking way! He's ours. Don't touch him." Toben isn't as tall as Lex, but I've seen him take down bigger. His fists are balled up as he leans into Alexander's face. Lex scoffs and brushes past him. Toben's shoulders fall as he shakes his head. "Don't you dare kill him. We deserve that."

Logan pulls himself to his feet as Toben backs up to stand next to me. I look down at his hand and see he took the knife from Lex. I hold him close to me as Logan's bloody face peers past Alexander, to us.

"I must say, I didn't think you had it in you, Plaything. I'm proud of you."

"Fuck you," Toben spats.

His voice is strong while his arm shakes beneath my hands. When Lex goes for Logan, I cringe. I hate seeing him fight. It takes away his brightness. It's not like when he hits the bag in his gym, that's fun for him. This? This is sucking out his sunshine. He takes Logan back to the floor easily and even though Logan is fighting back, he can't keep up.

After a few terrible moments, Toben calls out, "Okay, you had your turn. That's enough." Alexander ignores him, landing hit after hit. "Stop!" he yells this time, and when he still receives no acknowledgment, he rips his arms from my grasp and runs to separate Lex and Logan. "Stop, damn it!"

He pulls him off and for a moment, I think Lex is going to punch him too. I'm too busy watching them, that by the time I notice Logan is standing, he's lunging for me.

Metal slicing through the skin on my arm is such a distinct sensation, I recognize it immediately. I don't need to look at it to know it's deep, and on instinct, I use my hand to add pressure. Blood trickles between my fingers as Toben tackles Logan back to the floor and Lex is next to me in a single stride.

The way he looks down at me is confusing. It's not anger or disgust, it's not even fear. The tears are fighting to fall from his eyes and all his self-assurances are gone. He lifts my hand from my arm to look at my cut before he grips my head tight. This is like after he showed me the video. Does he feel guilt over this? How is any of this his fault? I don't want to make him speak and I know what he wants to know. I touch his cheek and press a soft kiss to the side of his mouth.

"I'm fine. Go, help him."

Determination is beautiful on his face as he turns to the fight on the floor. He walks right up to them and steps on Logan's arm like he's squashing a bug. When the knife falls from Logan's hand and clanks to the floor, Lex picks it up and Toben gives him a smile that makes my stomach queasy. He backs up to stand next to me and give Toben space.

There's never been a time where we were the ones with the advantage, and as much as it makes me feel like a bunch of flies are buzzing under my skin, it's also what I want.

I want this to be over.

"You're done. You've taken everything from me, from

us. It's ending now." Toben straddles Logan's stomach, his fists grip at his shirt, as he spits out the words.

Logan narrows his eyes in mild disappointment. "Oh, come now, Plaything. That isn't true. I gave you your Lotus', didn't I?"

Every bit of air is siphoned from my lungs as an invisible fist punches my stomach. He's lying. He's making this up, trying to turn us against each other like he's always done. Toben jumps up and when I look at him for assurance, there's none.

"What's he talking about?" I don't realize I'm speaking aloud until the question is asked. The sickness has made permanent residence in my stomach while Logan's patronizing laugh makes me want to scream.

My hair hits my face as I shake my head. This can't be right. Toben would never do that. Alexander's fingers slide between mine as he squeezes my hand, silently comforting me.

I want Toben to say something. Tell me this is a trick and what Logan is saying is twisted.

"You have your own girls?" He can't even look at me and I know in my bones, it's true. "Why?" I despise feeling anger towards him, and right now, it's the only thing I feel. He doesn't respond. A hundred unanswered questions still make me want to refuse to believe this. When did this happen? When did he go from tormented to tormentor? "How long have you done this?" Blackness wraps around my brain, taking away everything I thought I knew about my best friend. "Answer me, Toben!"

His eyes are fighting tears while I freely let mine fall. Who is this boy I grew up with? He knows me inside out, yet I feel like I'm looking at a stranger.

"I've had Nikki for six years and Tiffany for about eight months, but neither of them were children when I got them."

He says it as if it makes a difference. It doesn't matter who they were, it doesn't change that he tortured, beat, and raped them.

At some point, Logan pulls himself off the floor because when he speaks, he's back to standing. "You think he's innocent in all this. He's caused you more suffering than you realize, my little Lotus. There's so much you don't know. He helped me play with my Lotus' for years before obtaining his own."

For years? For years they've hid this from me. I feel so stupid. I believed them both.

Wait…Logan has more besides me?

"You have another Lotus?"

"Oh, I've had several."

I was never special to him. I thought I was the only one he did those things to. Knowing this makes me sad, yet somehow, the thought of other girls living a life like mine gives me a comfort that it shouldn't.

"There are more Sweet Girls? There's more like me?"

"Oh no, my Plaything. None have been like you. The others all kept their expiration date." He rolls his head as he takes a drag off the cigarette he started smoking. "Besides Nikki of course."

Everything they're saying is ricocheting in my head and getting tangled. I don't understand. So many questions are bombarding into each other. Why are there other Lotus', and no other Sweet Girls? Does expiration mean death?

"They're dead?" If Toben's been helping him all this time, does that mean… "You've killed people?"

He reaches out for me and I don't want him to lay a hand on me right now. I back away to get closer to Lex. I can't get my emotions to line up and can't make my thoughts settle. I want out of this room.

Toben growls as he clutches the knife. His pleading eyes

turn to hateful ones as he spins around and attacks Logan. As soon as they hit the floor, Toben holds a blade to his throat.

"You made me just like you!"

"I didn't make you who you are, Plaything, I simply brought it out. You love what you do to your Lotus'. You know you do. It makes you feel alive."

Logan has a way of knotting things up and making them seem different than they are. I know in my heart that Toben is a good person, but I don't know what Logan put him through when he took him out of the basement. I don't know a lot of things apparently.

Toben hits himself in the head with the hilt of the knife, as the urge to hold him tight runs through me. I'm angry, betrayed, and confused, and still…he's my Toben.

"No, no, NO! I never would have done those things if it wasn't for you!" He screams as he cuts a gash from Logan's mouth to his ear. He's unraveling and I don't know how to keep him together. There's a cracking sound as Toben grabs Logan's throat and slams his skull against the concrete. "It's my turn to play, Logan," he grates out, as he cuts Logan's shirt. When he turns to Alexander and orders, "Don't let him get up." The empty look on his face makes me flinch.

He's Toben, the other half of me. I thought we knew each other deeper than any two people could. The overwhelming desire to wrap him in my arms until the boy I know comes back, surges through me. His eyes are black and hollow as he makes his way to Logan's bag, immediately finding what he's searching for. The blue torch is in his hand as he storms back to Logan. I can't let him do whatever morbid thing he's thinking of. I urge forward and reach for him, when Alexander grabs my hand to stop me.

"Toben, don't."

I may as well be speaking another language because his steps don't falter. Lex's warm hand squeezes mine, and while

I wish with all my heart I could take back everything he's suffered, I'm so thankful he's here with me.

Toben drops the knife on the floor and the torch makes a *shhhh* noise as he turns it on. Lowering to his knees, he leans over to speak in Logan's ear, "This is the last time I ever kneel for you." As he sits straight, he turns the blowtorch up, causing the flame to grow. "You're so fond of marking your toys, I think it's time you know how it feels."

His back is to me, so I watch his shoulder lift as the first sound, immediate and familiar, fills my ears. I've heard the melody of my own cooking flesh many times. The second sound though, is one I've never heard before. Logan's wails of agony are more gratifying than I'm comfortable admitting. I don't want to watch the way his body flails as Toben holds him down, so I press my face against Lex's chest. It does nothing to quiet his screams or dilute the unmistakable smell of burning skin.

I stay there until the noise of his torture has gone quiet. I know it's going to be horrid, and still, when I see what he's done, my knees wobble. Crude, bright red letters burn down his chest.

PEDO

Toben slowly stands as he walks toward me, holding out a blade. "This is it, Tav. He's used and abused us for over half our lives. He stole who we were supposed to be. It's time he suffers for it. He deserves to die."

I take the knife, but even after everything, the idea of taking someone out of the world, even Logan, is impossible to me.

"I don't know if I can."

"He won't ever stop. If we want this to end, we have to end it."

Alexander releases me and I take Toben's hand, allowing him to lead me to Logan. The bumps of the handle are pressing against my fingers as I slide my leg over Logan's chest and sit on his stomach. He looks at me the way he used to, when he gave me my candy. Almost like he loves me.

He's never loved you.

"I've taken care of you, Tavin, kept you safe. You, Toben, and I are a family."

A family.

I've waited my whole life to hear him say those words and he chooses now, after all this time, to say them. Memories of all the times I prayed for him to say that, to say he loved me, burst around my mind, and I cry harder.

"You've never said we are a family, before."

I squeeze my eyes shut as a hand presses against my chest. I open them to see Toben crouched in front of me.

"He's trying to confuse you. He's a liar, Love. I need you to remember. Please, really remember what he's made you feel like. Here." His hand softly rubs the side of my head and I do what he asks. I think about all the times I was raped and beaten for our disobedience. How he used our fear and love for each other against us. The terrible things that were spit from his mouth.

You're weak.

This is your fault.

You disgust me.

I know you're enjoying this, whore.

"Give me your knife."

Toben's order snaps me back to now, as I watch Lex hand Toben the blade. Alexander's complacency is shocking to me. He's completely on board with this. Toben presses the blade to Logan's throat and looks back to me.

"He's forced us to be with countless men, he's done unspeakable things to you, and he's made me do them to others. I need you to do this with me, Tav. When you bleed, I bleed, right?"

'When you bleed, I bleed'. Our mantra, our promise to each other. And it was Logan who gave us the need to have it. I don't know what would have become of us if we'd never been bought by Logan. For the first time in my life, I know about the things we could have had. The experiences he stole from us. It was all to feed his desires. None of it was ever for us.

"You never loved us. We were always just your toys."

The words fall out as the truth sets into my core. He isn't my savior, he's my tormentor.

The white of his teeth makes the blood covering them seem brighter, as he struggles to speak.

"Though that may be true, Lotus, I've had many toys, and you two were always my favorites. If I could love, I would have loved the both of you."

I look at the man who has raised me, fed me, cleaned me, raped me, abused me and the veil is suddenly ripped away. I see him for the evil man he is. He's right, love isn't something he has the capacity for. The earth will be a safer place for everyone if he isn't in it anymore. I don't want him to take another breath.

No matter how hard you scrub yourself clean, you will always be repulsive. It's in your filthy blood, and still I give you everything. I am your Maker, Lotus. You breathe because I desire you to. No one can love useless things, yet I allow you purpose.

Sticky, hot liquid squishes between my fingers, and when I look down at the knife in my hand, it's also in his chest. He chokes, and blood splatters on his face as he gargles around words.

Toben takes a big breath as his weight shifts to put pressure on his knife. This is really it. It's actually over. I yank my blade out of the closest thing I have to a parent, as Toben rips his across his neck.

Logan's throat spreads open and blood oozes from the wound. Thirteen years of suffering, caused by him, jolts through my body and explodes from my lungs in a scream as I bring down the blade again. And again, and again. Finally, my heart rate slows and I look into his dead eyes. Dropping the knife to the floor, I whisper, "Good bye, Logan."

The moment feels suspended, frozen, until Alexander's voice slowly breaks through like the light of a train in a tunnel.

"We need to go, grab anything important. You need to clean up and change your clothes." He speaks slowly around his wounds and I know that's as painful as it is difficult. He needs me to get up and I still can't lift myself from Logan's body. "I'm sorry, we have to get out of here."

This time, I do as he asks, and look at Toben. I know he had a relationship with Logan that I didn't, and it went even deeper than I originally thought. I'm angry about the Lotus'. I feel confused and betrayed and I'm still struggling to grasp it. Right now though, we just freed ourselves from the captor that has consumed our entire lives, and I need him in my arms.

I put my forehead to his and press our scars together. He's done things I don't want to think about, but I need him to know I will never leave him. No matter what. We stay like that for as long as I think Lex will allow before I stand to follow his request. Toben silently turns to climb the stairs, and though I know my feet are moving, I feel like they're doing it on their own.

I stand in front of my side table and wrap my fingers around the white paint-chipped knob. The drawer sticks, so I jiggle it to pull it open.

"Tavin?"

His voice is like hot chocolate in the winter. He's the light in a dark room of monsters. My lips lift into a smile. I will do everything I can to make sure he knows how grateful I am for it all. He changed my life. In this moment though, I want to be alone with Logan a final time and I don't know how that will make him feel.

"Please give me a minute. I'll be up soon."

Moments pass and even though I can hear that he's gone, the emptiness of the room is much louder. I lift our prince and princess rag dolls from the drawer and press them to my chest. I made these for us the day Logan changed our lives forever. It always meant so much to me that he let me keep them.

I turn to the lifeless body that used to house the man responsible for so much filth and fear. Kneeling next to him, I let my fingers trail across his lifeless cheek. He's gone. I will never hear his voice again. I will never smell him again.

Cinnamon and cigarettes.

Thirteen years ago...

"Again!"

The explosion of heat and pain from Toben's whip spreads up my back just as Logan gives the order. The snap of the whip and Toben's grunt warns me another blow is right behind it. I force my wet eyes to stay open and locked on to Logan's. When his gaze burns into mine this way, the worse thing I could do is look away.

Suddenly, his big hands squeeze my shoulders to shove me off him. He yanks my arm so hard it pops, as he slams my face down into my bloody blankets. He grabs my hips and the cold metal of his knife presses into my spine before the sting of the slicing, burns across my back. I know better than to cry out though. He makes his yucky noises as his movements get faster and I'm grateful I don't have to look at him anymore. Instead, I look at the brown paper bags he brought with him, sitting on the table.

I'm trying not to get too excited…does he somehow know about my birthday? He already put away our food for the week so I know it's not that. I hope with all my might it's a special treat for me.

A few days ago, Toben sang me a 'Happy Birthday' song and gave me some new colored pens and pencils. He even saved a candle from his cake and told me to make a wish and to blow it out.

Oh, I wonder if there's a cake in that bag. I've never had my own cake before.

"Such a disgusting, dirty girl…" Logan groans, and every time a drop of his sweat splashes onto my back, it burns inside the cuts. At least he's getting closer. "Fuck, your filthy little body feels so fucking good!"

He goes still for a minute, then pushes me away, and I stay like that until I hear the bathroom door close.

"Are you alright?"

I roll over and Toben is holding out my blue dress. I nod and take it to slip over my head as he sits next to me on the bed. "What do you think is in the bags?"

His shoulders lift up as he shrugs. "How am I supposed to know?"

He says that, but he's smirking like he really does know. My stomach does that thing with popping bubbles and I clasp my hands together because I just know it's something for me.

"Is it for my birthday?"

He laughs and smiles as he lays his arm across my shoulder. "I guess we'll have to wait and see."

He takes my hand as we get on the floor to kneel in our positions. I wish Logan would hurry up! Why is it, whenever I want him to go fast, he takes forever, and when I want him to slow down and stay with us awhile, he's always fast and in a hurry?

Finally, the bathroom door opens and even though he's back in his suit, his jacket isn't on yet. He walks over to the table and sits down in the chair. The smile he has when he's nice, lifts up his cheeks as he pats his leg.

"Come here, my little Lotus." I try to run to him before I'm fully standing and almost trip. I keep myself from falling and keep going until I'm sitting on his lap. He waves his hand to release Toben from his position. "You may get up as well, Plaything." His hand rubs up and down my thigh, and it's okay because I know he won't play with me again today. "Someone told me today was your eleventh birthday."

My smile is so big my eyes get squinty. "Yes, Logan."

He kisses me and reaches behind me to grab one of the bags. "What do you want first? Presents or cake?"

A cake! He got me my first cake! Sometimes, he makes me so happy. "Cake! Oh, thank you, Logan."

I wrap my arms around his neck and squeeze him. He chuckles and lets me hug him before he grabs my wrists and pulls me away. The sound of the paper bag crinkling as he sets it on the floor has me bouncing on his knee. He reaches in and takes out a white box and sets it on the table. When he lifts the lid, I want to jump up and down and spin in a circle. It's the prettiest cake I've ever seen.

It's square, and white, and sparkly with pale rainbow-colored frosting. There are candy stars and hearts on it and right in the middle, in big, pink letters, is my favorite part.

Happy 11th Birthday, Tavin

It says my name. Not Lotus or Plaything. It says, Tavin.

I look up at Logan and he's smiling at me as he rubs my back. It hurts over my new cuts and slashes, but I don't care one bit.

"Do you like it?"

"Yes, Logan. So, so much."

He scoots me off his lap as he pulls a knife out of the bag.

"Alright, both of you, go sit on the bed."

I hurry to obey, grabbing Toben's hand as I pass him to pull him with me. The bed squeaks as we jump on it and I laugh at Toben's grin. He leans over and kisses my cheek as I whisper, "You told him."

"Of course I told him. You didn't think I'd let you go without having your own birthday cake, did you?"

I grin and lean my head against his shoulder so I can watch Logan put yummy and delicious slices onto our plates. He carries them over and I sit up straight to take my treat. He gave me a corner piece! Those are the best because you get a bunch more frosting. I have the letters H and B on my piece. I stab in my fork and eat a big bite. My cake is vanilla. The taste of the frosting hits my mouth and it's so yummy that it makes me feel good all over. I thought I liked chocolate best, and now I don't know. I look over at Toben's piece and my slice is way bigger.

Logan walks back to the table and reaches into the other brown bag and takes out two packages. I can't believe those are for me! The first one is wrapped in purple wrapping paper and has a white ribbon on it. The second one is smaller and wrapped in green and pink striped paper with a pink bow on it. He didn't tell me to get up, and even though he's being nice, anything can change that, so I make sure not to jump off the bed no matter how excited I am.

He puts them down and brushes my bangs off my forehead. "Open the big one first."

I smile at him and he nods at me, so I dig my fingers into where the paper is folded and rip as hard as I can. The paper tearing to show me the surprise, makes my heart jump up and down. I get the paper all off and see the box, and I can't be excited because I don't know what it is. I hate asking questions because it shows him how stupid I am, but if I don't ask, then I'll stay stupid forever.

"Wh—what is it?"

Logan leans over to pick up the box and begins to open it. He takes out a black, skinny, plastic square that's twice the size of a notebook. There are long chords coming out of the back, so it's something you plug in.

"It's a DVD player."

He walks over to my TV and connects it to the plastic square with the chords. I sigh because I don't know what that is either. "What's a dee-vee-dee player?"

Logan laughs, making me embarrassed, so I decide I'll wait till he's gone to ask Toben my questions later.

"Just open your other gift, Lotus."

This gift is so light, it doesn't feel like it weighs anything. I rip open the paper and I don't exactly know what this is either, and it doesn't even matter. I can't stop looking at it. It's a plastic case bigger than Toben's CDs and has the prettiest picture on it. There's a girl in a blue dress and she has her arms looped with a metal man and a lion! She doesn't even look scared. She looks happy. A giant doll is standing next to the metal man and they are all walking on a yellow street. There's a green castle in the back with red flowers everywhere. I don't know where they are, I just know if I ever get to leave this basement again, I'm going to go there. The words spell out, 'The Wizard of OZ' and there's a little puppy sitting in the O. I know I said I would wait, but I can't. I have to know what this is.

"What does it do?" His shoulders fall as he shakes his head and takes it from me. If it were anyone besides Logan, I wouldn't have let them take it. Before I can apologize for not saying 'thank you', he opens the case like a book and removes a CD. Is it music? It disappears inside the dee-vee-dee player as he turns on my TV.

When the screen flashes on, I hold my hands up in fists. I figured it out!

"It's a movie!"

I realize it as soon as the lion growls inside of the ribbon. Movies play on TV sometimes, and even though I always miss parts of them, it seems like whenever I get to see the beginning of one, they all start with that lion. Logan smiles at me as he situates himself at the head of my bed and wraps his arm around my waist. He pulls me against him so I'm in between him and Toben.

"That's right, Lotus. You can watch it whenever you want, as many times as you want. Now, do you want to go, or do you want to watch the film first?"

I'm so happy he's letting me choose. I do like heroin, especially because it makes me feel nice after he makes me feel so bad, but right now he's making me feel good, so I want to sit here and enjoy it.

"The movie, please, Logan."

He smiles and rubs his hand over my neck before he kisses it. The smell of cigarette smoke sprinkled in cinnamon, tickles my nose. "Did you have a good birthday, Lotus?"

Since it's my first one it's an easy answer. It doesn't make it any less true.

"Yes, Logan. It's the best birthday I've ever had."

He doesn't even touch me as we watch the movie. It's not only the best birthday I've ever had, it might be the best one I'll ever have.

"All I wanted was for you to love me. Why couldn't you love me?" My tears fall on his face, smearing the blood as they roll down his cheek. Scooting down, I lay on his burnt chest. "Why did you choose us?" I allow myself to weep against him knowing I will never get my answers. I don't know how much time passes, but Alexander is waiting on me, so I finally separate myself from him.

I place my dolls, some pictures, clothes, and a few notebooks of my drawings in a bag before putting it at the base of the stairs. I pull the leather through the loop on the belt and slowly pull the needles from my leg, causing more blood to seep out of the puncture wounds. Lifting my torn, bloody dress over my head, I drop it to the floor.

The bathroom light flickers when it turns on and the pipes gurgle as water flows from a rusted faucet. Blood swirls down the drain as I wash my fresh cuts, and when I pat myself dry, some leftover blood stains the towel. Wrapping some gauze around my leg and arm, I pull the green dress Logan bought me for Christmas, over my head and pick up my bag.

I look at my bedroom for the final time, and try to tattoo it into my memory. For better or worse, this was my childhood. I stare at his body, allowing the last tear I will ever cry for him to fall, as I climb the stairs.

Lex and Toben are in the kitchen standing next to the stove that's pulled away from the wall. I can't believe how much Alexander has seemed to age in the last few hours. His torn shirt is sticking to his chest from all the wounds, and there are streaks of blood coming from his mouth. He has to be in so much pain.

"Are you okay? You're still bleeding."

He nods toward the front room and something about his demeanor has changed from moments ago. He's harder. Colder.

"I'm fine. Take your things outside and wait for Silas. I'll be there in a minute"

Toben's lips kiss my head as we do what Lex says. We stop at the bottom porch step and place our things on the ground. Sitting in silence, we watch a few cars drive by before he speaks.

"Do you hate me?"

He saw everything Logan did to me. He held me as I cried and comforted me in the darkness. How could he do those things to other girls?

"I don't know what I feel, Toben. I could never hate you, I just don't understand. How could you?"

He rests his elbows on his knees and drops his head. "He changed me. Made things fucked up in my head. At some point, I loved having the control over them. I've felt helpless every day of my life except for when I'm with them. I never wanted you to know because I was too scared to lose you."

My feelings are jumbled. I want to claw off my face and scream. I lift my head to see Silas roll up in front of us. He opens his door and gets out to holler at us over the hood.

"What's going on?"

Neither of us are able to respond before Lex rushes from the house. "You two, get in the car." He holds out his hand to Silas. "You brought my clothes, right?"

Silas' eyes travel down Lex's body. "What the hell happened?! Is that your blood?!"

"Come on, we gotta go." He snaps his fingers. "Clothes, now." Silas ducks down to reach into his car and tosses a bag to Alexander. "Keep the car running and be ready to go."

"What's wrong with your voice?" Silas calls after him as Lex climbs the steps to go back into the house. He turns to us. "I don't suppose either of you are gonna fill me in?" I just sigh and do as Alexander said and get in the car. Toben climbs in behind me and takes my hand as Silas gets in the driver's seat "That was a lot of blood Alex was sportin'. Is everyone alright?"

Neither of us respond as Silas turns around in his seat and I nod to him. We all remain silent until Lex comes running down the front steps.

He jumps in the front seat and barks, "Drive Silas, now!"

The tires make a shrill sound as the car drives away from the curb. Silas looks around the car and shakes his head in agitation. "Will someone please tell me wha-"

BOOM!

The entire car shakes and when I turn my head to look, I see my house drowning in smoke and flames. Toben and I look at each other before turning to watch it burn.

I say my final goodbye to my home, my Maker, and my life as I know it. Everything will be different now. Nothing will ever be the same again.

"Jesus Christ!" Silas yells, startling Toben and I, to turn back around.

"Where are you keeping these girls, Toben?"

Lex's voice has never sounded so cold before, and I don't like it. He still has to speak slow which makes it even more unnerving. Toben looks out the window and I think it's so he doesn't have to look at me when he answers.

"I'll give you the address."

"And they're both legal right? Tell me I don't need to call Social Services."

Toben sighs and presses his hand to his forehead. "They're both adults. I've never voluntarily done anything to a child."

"Good to know you have standards," Lex snaps.

I can see Silas' eyes are huge as he mouths What. The. Fuck? to Lex, as Alexander just shakes his head and scoffs. His face is hard and blank as he stares silently ahead.

We arrive at Silas' and Lex unbuckles his seat belt. "I need your car." At first Silas looks like he's about to protest, until Alexander jabs a finger at Toben. "Do not let the little fuck leave, and if he tries, call the police."

I use my eyes to beg Toben to not give them a reason to do that. Lex can't send him to jail. I know what he did is bad, and honestly, I'm struggling to grasp it as well, but I still won't let them take him away.

"Lex-"

He glares at me making me sink into the seat, as he

slams the door. Toben looks back at me one last time before he and Silas go inside.

"I know you love him, but he's a murderer and a rapist. It doesn't get much worse than that. Think about his victims. He deserves to pay for his crimes." I'm impressed with how well he's already speaking as he carefully says each word. "Your story is incredible and I do feel for what you went through, especially as children. However, he's an adult now and has made a lot of these choices for himself. He should have to suffer the consequences of those actions."

I don't care about consequences and actions. We are different and I never want him in a cage again.

He types the address Toben gave him into Silas' GPS, and laces his fingers with mine. "I'm sorry, Tavin. I promised you it wouldn't happen again and it did." His voice cracks before he swallows. "Please forgive me for that."

I hate that he's feeling guilty when he is the only reason I have my freedom in the first place. I use both of my hands to hold his as I kiss all of his fingers. He looks at me and I shake my head. "There's nothing to forgive you for, Lex."

He gives me an expression that doesn't quite make it into a smile as he rubs his thumb across mine.

We barely speak on the almost hour-long drive and when we pull up to a cute two story, tan home, he looks through the windshield.

"This is not at all what I was expecting."

We get out of the car and I'm so scared to see what's inside this place, this side of Toben I never knew existed.

Alexander pulls the key Toben gave him, from his pocket, and unlocks the white door. It's completely quiet as we step inside and the carpet keeps it that way as I walk to the kitchen. There isn't a single appliance besides the empty fridge. Everything is bare and there's hardly any furniture.

"I don't think anyone lives here." I'm whispering and I

don't know exactly why, other than the eerie stillness in the air.

He nods down the hall and pauses at the first door. Turning the knob, he slowly opens it. The light is off and when he turns it on, his shoulders slump. "It's only a bathroom."

We creep to the second door to find it's an empty closet. He takes a breath before opening the third door, but when he tries, it's locked. He quirks his lip in a nervous expression and his uneasiness isn't doing anything to help my own.

He softly raps on the door and speaks slightly above a whisper. "Hello? Are you alright in there? We're here to help you." There isn't a single sound or any evidence at all that anyone's here. I shrug at him and he taps again. "Please, we won't hurt you, I promise."

Still there's nothing. He reaches up to run his hand along the door frame and a skeleton key drops on the carpet. I lean down to pick it up and run my finger over the design at the top. It's a very pretty key. I hand it to him and when the lock *clicks* and the door swings open, it's to an empty bedroom.

"Hello?" Lex asks, softly.

The room is clean, with a bed, dresser, closet, books, TV, radio and a few other items. I see a shirt on the floor and when I open the closet there are clothes inside. Lex opens the other door and it's a bathroom. I hear him move the shower curtain and whisper, "It's okay. You're okay. I'm not going to do anything to you."

I enter the bathroom and see a girl with brown hair, a few years younger than me, huddled in the bathtub. She's shaking in tremors, until finally she murmurs, "Where's Toben?"

"He's gone," Lex answers.

"Gone?"

He leans down in front of her. "We just want to help you

and get you out of here, okay?"

"I can go home?" she whispers, like she's scared to hope the words are true.

He nods and when he reaches for her, she tries to push herself harder against the side of the tub. He stands up and backs away to give her space. "Yes, we just need to find the other girl first. Does someone else live here with you?"

She looks up at the ceiling. "Nikki. Her room is upstairs."

He gives her a small smile and stands next to me. "Bring anything you want to keep. We'll get you out of here soon."

I follow him out of the bedroom and up the stairs. He clenches the skeleton key in his hand and as we arrive at the first door, he slides it into the lock and turns it with a *click*.

In this room, a strawberry blonde girl is waiting on her knees. My heart can't take much more breaking. He makes her kneel just like Logan made us. Her head lifts and her face falls with a frown. "Where's Toben?"

Lex tucks the key in his pocket. "He's letting you go."

"What?" Her eyes fill up with tears as she lets her position fall. "Why? What did I do?"

Lex's head cocks to the side in surprise as I step to her. "You didn't do anything, he just doesn't want to hurt you anymore."

"Leaving me is hurting me! I want to talk to him, where is he?"

She cares for him, that much is clear, and I hope it's because he wasn't as cruel to her as Logan made it seem.

"He's gone. I'm sorry," Alexander says.

She shakes her head. "No, he wouldn't leave me alone." As if only seeing me, she scrunches her nose and scowls at me. "Who the fuck are you anyway?"

"My name is Tavin. I—"

She lunges for me. "You bitch!" Her face is inches from mine. "It's your fault he's closed off and won't let himself love me. You're the reason he's gone, aren't you?" She gives me an unimpressed sneer. "I'm not going anywhere with you." She walks over to her bed and sits, leaning against the head board. "I'm waiting for Toben."

Alexander bristles and loosens his fists. "If that's what you want to do, we can't stop you, just know he's not coming back."

He grabs my hand, before I turn back at her. If I did have a part in hurting her, I never wanted to.

"I'm sorry." She looks away from me, so I follow him out.

"Well, good to know he added brainwashing to the list."

I don't know how to respond, so I don't, as we walk back downstairs to Tiffany. She still seems a little hesitant to believe us, until we open the front door, then she runs out and falls to her knees in the grass. She weeps as she scrapes her fingers through the blades.

"I can't believe it's over..." Her shoulders shake as she lifts her head to Lex. "Where are you taking me?"

He kneels down next to her. "Where are you from?"

She wipes her nose and sits back. "Phoenix."

He looks at me with a questioning expression. How the heck am I supposed to know how she got here? I shrug at him and he helps her up. "Are you hungry?"

She shakes her head. "I just want to see my parents."

Lex opens up the car and lets her in. She crawls in the back and I climb up front with him.

"How did you get here? Do you remember?"

She chokes on her sobs. "It was my first day of college. I was walking from my apartment to my first class and the next thing I know, I'm in a dark room. There were other girls there and even more came later. A man came in and tied us all together with a rope. I don't know how many of us there were when they blindfolded us and put us in the back of either a van or a truck. We were in there for a really long time. One of the girls died." I look back at her and she's crying. "We had to stay tied to her for…I don't know…maybe days."

Alexander takes in a big breath and starts the car. "Jesus."

She fidgets with her fingers as she continues. "We were still blindfolded when they walked us into a loud room. I don't know what was going on because all I could hear was voices. So many voices…" I think that's the end of the story because it feels like we're driving in silence for a while before she starts again. "I was cut free from the girls and taken to a quiet room. I was alone for a while, then a man took off my blindfold and told me I was a gift for someone. He seemed nice, so even though I should have been terrified, I was a lot less scared than I had been. He took me on the most gorgeous plane I have ever seen. He let me take a shower and gave me one of the best meals I've ever tasted. Then he took me to Toben…" She shakes her head and whispers, "I should have been more scared."

Neither of us respond, even though I feel like I should. I understand her and I know what she feels, it's just that her captor is my best friend.

I wonder where Lex is driving, right as he says, "How would you feel if we drop you off at the hospital? We won't be able to stay with you and I'm sorry about that. The staff there will help you contact your parents and make sure you're healthy."

She gives a sad smile. "Thank you. You two are my guardian angels. I'll never forget this. What are your names, anyway?"

"If you don't mind, I think it's best if we remain nameless. I don't want us connected to this, so if you really want to thank us, forget all about us."

She nods her agreement as silence wraps itself around us.

I still don't understand how or why Toben would ever want to do this. I look out the window as we drive back and try to go through all my memories. I try to see how I missed this. How I didn't know what he was becoming. I don't know if it scares me more that he isn't who I thought he was, or that I know it doesn't change how I feel about him. He will always be my Toben, my other half. We are half people.

We drop her off at the entrance of St. Macarius Medical Center and Lex's fingers slip between mine as we drive back to Silas'.

I try to think of what in the world I'm going to say to Toben. What was the purpose of it all? Keeping these girls wasn't something Logan forced on him. He wanted it. He chose to inflict the same pain on these girls that Logan caused us.

Lex's cell phone rings and Silas' name is lit up on the screen in front of me.

"Hey—"

"This kid is fucking overdosing! I'm taking him to the E.R."

No screams on repeat in my brain as I shake my head. Silas is mistaken, I bet Toben just got super doped up.

"You cannot be serious with this shit." Alexander's eyes roll back as he lets out a harsh breath. "We'll be there as soon as we can." He hangs up and looks in the rear-view mirror. "It looks like we're headed back to St. Macarius."

Breathing becomes more difficult as I accept that Silas could be right. I clutch the door handle as my eyes fill up with tears. Choking on my prayers to let him be okay, I gasp and Lex grabs my hand. I can't lose him, I need him. I'll always need him. Why the heck would he take so much?

Lex is driving Silas' fancy car so you'd think he'd be able

to go a little faster. I let out a cry of relief when the lit-up sign of St. Macarius is visible. He pulls into a space on the main level parking garage. He doesn't even have the car in park when I jump out, and sprint through the electronic doors. I scan for where I'm supposed to go, seeing someone at the front desk that might know where he is. I'm halfway there when I hear my name.

"Tavin! Over here."

Silas waves at me and Lex runs up behind me, as I ask, "How is he?"

He shakes his head. "I don't know, I was never able to find a pulse. The doctors are working on him now."

My legs feel like putty and Alexander's arms are around me, unknowingly keeping me upright.

We can't see him yet and I hate it. They ask if any of us are family, and I tell them I am his sister, but when I can't prove it, they still won't let me back. I hate sitting out here waiting when he's all alone. He has to be okay. He has to. He can't leave me. I rub my thumb over my tattoo and trace it up my scar. When I tried to kill myself, he did too. He always said if we go, it's together.

I don't know how long we've been sitting here, but Sasha arrived a while ago with coffees, and Marie came in to oversee his care.

Alexander's fingers are combing through my hair when I look up to see Marie walking over to us. She doesn't look worried, if anything she looks relieved. My chest expands as I run up to her.

"Is he okay?"

"He'll be fine. You can go see him now, if you want. He's in room 312."

Running as fast as I can, I push open the doors and sprint down the hall. As the numbers three-one-two come into my line of sight, I could almost cry. I burst through the open door and he's sitting in bed drinking a Sprite. His eyes shift up and as soon as he sees me, his face is soft with a brightness that makes him look so different. He throws his legs off the bed and stands to hug me. "Hello, Love."

I'm so happy and relieved he's alright, that's why I don't understand why I still want to cry. "What were you thinking? Why did you take so much? If anything happened to you…"

He gives me such a soft, sweet smile and cups my face. "I know, and I'm so sorry. It was a selfish reaction done out of fear. I thought you wouldn't love me anymore. I've done horrible things, Tav, but it doesn't have to be the end, you know? I can still change. She said I can still make her proud."

She? What's he talking about? He's never talked like this before. "What do you mean?"

He smiles so big and his happy eyes have a ring of wet around them.

"I saw her, Tav. I saw my mom. She told me she still loves me and she knows her little boy is still in here." He taps his chest. "That I can still make amends for all the suffering I've caused." He grabs my arms and looks so deeply into my eyes, I can feel it in my stomach, "I'm so sorry for everything I've done and lied about. I'll spend the rest of my life making it up to you, but I don't have to be the monster he made me. I can still choose to be me." He has a light in him that's never been there. Not even before Logan. The joy bursting from his skin makes me laugh even though it's weak. "I know it sounds crazy, but for the first time, maybe ever, I feel peace. Real peace."

CHAPTER SIXTEEN
Fallout

Alexander

THE NIGHT HAS EXHAUSTED HER. SHE FALLS ASLEEP before Silas drops us off at home and barely stays awake long enough for Marie to stitch up the cut on her arm.

The hospital wants to keep Toben overnight for observation. They said we can pick him up in the morning. I can't fathom what she must be feeling, and honestly, I can't imagine she's really had the chance to catch her breath enough to process it.

Logan's body needs to be found and identified while making sure there's no connection between me, Tavin, or Toben. I get her put to bed with Blind Mag, and go for a drive. After a few miles, I feel it's safe enough to pull into a gas station and use the pay phone. While I'm sure it's already been done, I report the fire anonymously and hang up.

I slide into my front seat and it's as though everything that's happened the last few months, rains down like a monsoon and since I'm alone, I allow my grief to consume me, and I cry for her. I cry for everything that was stolen from them. Their childhood, their innocence, a normal fucking life. The things Toben did…I truly believe he never would have been able to conceive them had it not been for Logan.

Death was a gift for him. He didn't get what he deserved, and I will make sure people know the kind of man he was. I can take the tapes in now. He isn't around to hire the lawyers to lie for him.

This is really over. There's nothing more he can do to them. Now what's left is the long-term damage this could have on both of them. The whole thing with Toben's 'epiphany' is odd, although I've always been a believer that faith can be a strong thing. If he truly believes that he spoke to his mother, then that could be enough to help him through this. He did almost die. There are tons of stories about people with near death experiences who have professed some type of spiritual calm or tranquility. I just hope at some point, Tavin finds hers.

Monday, July 13th

I take Tav for pancakes before heading back to the hospital to pick up Toben. I don't know what's going to happen with him. He has to suffer the consequences of his crimes. It's the only chance he has at a decent life. While I'll pull the strings I can to keep him out of prison, he definitely needs some type of rehabilitation program.

"Can I order a vanilla bean Frappuccino for Toben? It's his favorite coffee." I smile and nod at her to go ahead.

She gets her drinks in a carrier and gets a container to bring some pancakes to Toben. She holds them tight in her lap and anxiously fidgets in her seat until we arrive at St. Macarius. We walk through the spinning door and I try not to breathe in too deeply. I've never particularly liked the smell of hospitals or the way they make me feel. Too much sickness and loss in one building.

We take the elevator until it *dings,* telling us we've arrived on his floor. The second the doors open, she bursts down the hall with his drink in one hand and pancakes in the other. She comes to such an abrupt stop, I nearly run into her. She's frozen cold, staring at something in front of her. As my eyes follow the direction of her gaze, they land on a man. It takes me a moment because he's older and I've only seen him once on grainy film, but I recognize him.

Kyle.

He keeps walking and smiles at her as he passes by. Loud beeping blares and Tavin's long hair spins around as she turns to Toben's room. She drops the coffee and container of food as she runs through the open door of room 312.

"TOBEN!"

I hear her scream five seconds before I see the blood bath. It's pooled in the sheets and on the floor. Tavin cries as she holds his body to her chest. "NO! Wake up! Please! You're okay, you're okay. Don't leave me, please don't leave me. You promised! YOU CAN'T DO THIS!" The nurses and doctors rush in as they try to pull her off of him. "No!" She grips his shirt and fights them with all she has.

My mind and my heart are fighting over staying with Tavin or chasing after Kyle when finally, they get her off of him and push her toward me. It takes all my strength to hold her against me and keep her out of the room. She screams and falls to the floor as if her legs have stopped working completely. I sit next to her and rock her against my chest. There was too much blood, I saw his face. He's gone. No matter how good these doctors are, they won't be able to bring him back. She wails against my chest as we watch the medical staff try to perform a miracle.

When the doctor walks out covered in blood, he shakes his head. "I'm sorry. There was nothing that could be done."

Tavin pushes me away. "You're a liar! You're a fucking

liar! He wouldn't leave me!" She shoves past the doctor to go back into his room. She climbs up onto the bed and curls up on his chest. I walk in after her, watching her body shake and her tears mix with his blood.

The police arrive and I give them Kyle's description. I'm not sure how helpful it will be without being able to mention his name or his connection to Logan.

The staff allows her as much time with him as they're able, and when they can no longer leave the body in the room, it takes me and five orderlies to pull her away from him. Her agonizing wails cause physical pain in my chest. When is her suffering going to stop? When is life going to give her a fucking break?

I have to literally drag her outside kicking and screaming, while ignoring the alarmed looks I get. She falls asleep in the car and I don't want her alone right now, so I drop her off with Sasha and Silas before making the drive to talk to Nikki.

I find her in the same position as when we left her. When she looks up and sees me, her face falls.

"I told you. I'm not leaving. I'm waiting for Toben."

"Well, Toben is dead."

Maybe I should have been gentler about it, broke it a little easier, I just truly don't have the energy to make the effort.

Her eyes take on a sheen as she shakes her head. "I don't believe you."

"I'm sorry, he's gone." I reach into my pocket and hand her my card. "If you decide you need a place to stay, call me. You're welcome to stay at my home."

She takes the card and holds it to her chest for a moment before falling into the fetal position and crying. I stand there for as long as I can before I feel like a creep watching her. I leave her to be alone and I can hear her sobs all the way down the stairs.

Tuesday, July 21st

Cara Jo's jaw is hanging open as I tell her the cliff notes version of what's really been going on. She arrived back in town last night and called me as soon as she did. She had heard about Logan's death on the news, while she was away. They have found the lockets and the tapes, which is what makes this such a story.

Rissa products are being boycotted everywhere and the name Logan James is now synonymous with pedophile, psychopath, and murderer.

To keep from involving myself, I paid some kid skateboarding outside the police station a hundred dollars to bring the tapes inside and make sure an officer took them. Ever since, the case has been all over the news. Logan's wife and children have left Shadoebox, and Kyle must have skipped the country because he's nowhere to be found. Even though they're still investigating, the news story about searching Logan's home has become all anyone seems to be talking about.

Twelve lockets were on display in a glass box in his office. Each one held the flesh of a different girl, their name, and dates engraved on the back.

I'm able to drink my coffee, though reading Tavin's name among Nikki's and the others, makes eating breakfast impossible.

Meagan West // 1986-1990
Kelly Mickey // 1990-1995
Ashley Evers // 1992-1997
Mia Jones // 1995-2000
Katie Grace // 1997-2002
Morgan Bishop // 2000-2004
Tavin Winters // 2002-

Nikki Thomas // 2004-
Courtney McLaughlin // 2007-2012
Brittany Myers // 2009-2014
Shea Andrews // 2012-
Faith Denman //2014-

Twelve little girls. He did this to twelve children, killing eight of them and leaving the other four with fucked up lives. The only two girls reported as missing were Nikki and Ashley Evers.

Nikki's father was under the impression she had died years ago. Not having a death date on her locket changes that. I hear his plea on the news begging anyone who knows of her whereabouts to please come forward. I want to, I just know I can't.

A few days ago, she showed up at Vulture. She doesn't want to see her father, she told me the little girl he knew is dead. She isn't anywhere near the same person. She's scared, heartbroken, angry, and hates Tavin, but she has nowhere else to go.

Cara Jo shakes her head at the newscast playing on her little kitchen TV. "This is repulsive. I can't keep listening to this. I'm going to take Nikki some breakfast. Hopefully she'll eat it this time."

Nikki refuses to leave her room except to go to the bathroom. I still haven't told Tavin she's here. I haven't been able to have much of a conversation with Tavin at all.

I nod and as I stand to place my mug in the sink, the doorbell rings. Cara Jo's hands are full with Nikki's food so I wave her on.

"I got it."

I pull open the front door and raise my eyebrows in disbelief. "You've got balls coming here, Timothy."

His eyes are red and tired and he's not much more put

together than the last time I saw him. "Alex, please. Just let me say I'm sorry."

"Oh, you're sorry? Well, then no worries about drugging me, getting Tavin raped, and both of us almost killed. Water under the bridge."

I go to slam the door in his face as he holds his hand out, choking on held-in sobs, as he tries to speak. "H—he raped her?"

Shutting the door behind me, I keep my voice as level as possible. "What the fuck did you think would happen? How did he do it? Was it money? Did he pay you to sell us out?"

His hand squeezes his forehead. "Fuck, no, of course not." He takes in a breath and blinks at the sky before making eye contact. "It was Todd. He was going to kill him and I was told it wouldn't be until after extensive torture. I didn't know what to do. He just said he wanted her back. I thought once Todd was safe, I could help you save her. I... I don't have an excuse. I just wanted you to know I will never forgive myself for this, so if you don't either, I understand."

My feelings shift so quickly from anger to concern, I stutter out my response. "Todd was—is he okay?"

Timothy nods. "Minor bumps and bruises, and he's been really stressed, but he'll be alright."

Shoving my hands in my pockets, I lean against the door frame. "That had to be a hard choice to make."

He looks at me through hooded eyes. "You're my friends, I would never want anything to happen to any of you. It's just Todd, he's—"

"You're heart?"

He releases a sad laugh. "Yeah."

I haven't been able to get Tavin out of bed all week. I can't get her to eat and can barely get her to talk to me, except when she begs me to let her escape the pain. All she does is sleep, cry, and sing songs from Toben's lyric book. It was inside the box of things he saved from their house. She sleeps with those things.

I look at the time and it's getting late. Toben's funeral is in an hour and I need to make sure everything's in order. If I don't get Tavin out of the house to go, she'll never forgive herself, or me.

Lightly tapping on her door, I slowly push it open. She's standing in front of her mirror trying to put makeup on her wet face. Her hair is a tangled mess and she has on the black dress I bought her for today. Her hand is shaking terribly, and in her frustration, she throws the makeup bottle across the room.

"Shit!"

I go to her and wrap her in my arms, letting her cry against my chest before I take her hand and sit her in the chair in front of the mirror. A hairbrush and a few hair bands are on the dresser, so I pick them up and gather her hair in my hands. I brush as gently as I can and still get out the tangles.

"Will you talk to me?"

"Are you going to keep making me suffer?" she murmurs.

"Come on, that isn't fair. You know how I feel. The drugs won't take the pain away, they'll only postpone it."

I wrap the ties around her hair in a ponytail, leaving a few strands to frame her face.

"Then there isn't anything to talk about." She stands and takes her rag dolls off the bed. "Let's go."

I'm trying not to take this personally. I know she's in a lot of pain and just lost the one person who could truly understand her in a way no one else ever could. I sigh and follow her downstairs.

She refused to have any type of religious officiant give

the eulogy. She said Toben would have hated it. She and Christopher will each be speaking, and then there will be open time for anyone else who wants to talk.

Funeral homes and graveyards are different than any other places on earth. It's as if there's a veil of heavy sorrow you pass through. The feeling is so instant, it hits you like a fist in the chest.

I park the car, and even though I know we need to get inside, neither of us move.

"I'll speak to the funeral director and make sure she understands the itinerary. If you want a chance to be alone with him, it's now."

She opens the door and walks inside without waiting for me. Even though I know it's still her, I'm scared this will somehow change how she feels about me. What if all I do is remind her of what she lost?

Tavin

Every step hurts. Every breath aches.

It's freezing in here and I don't care. I welcome it. Let me freeze. Let my skin turn to ice and break into a million little, bloody pieces. I know what's behind this door. I know once I see him I can never deny it again. I can never hope that it's only a bad dream or a terrible prank. I will never be able to smell him, or kiss him, or hear his voice singing his songs. Never again will I hear him call me Love.

I pull on the metal handle and the door is heavy. I see the box he will spend forever in, at the end of the room. Every time I put a foot in front of the other, I see further into the box. His face coming into view makes me weigh ten thousand pounds. I can't move. I can't see him like this, but if I don't I'll never see him again.

I take his hand and I long so terribly to feel him squeeze, that I cry out from the agony.

"You can't be gone. Without you I am just a half person. Please, please. I love you, I love you, I love you. I will never love anyone the same way I love you. I'm so sorry for everything. I am so sorry I hurt you. I know this is all my fault. Please forgive me, Tobe. I'm so sorry. I'm so, so sorry."

I can't fix this, I can't do anything besides lay my head against his chest and hold my best friend for as long as I can.

There are so many people here and it makes me feel proud of him. All these people care about him and will miss him. Christopher is sitting next to me holding one hand while Alexander is holding my other. There are the friends we partied with, his old teachers and classmates. Silas, Sasha, and Marie are here, and I see a man that I'm pretty sure is Mr. Stride, one of Toben's regular Clients. I look back to Cara Jo and she's sitting next to Nikki.

Blink 182's *I Miss You* plays while the pictures of our life together flash across a screen. I'm angry at Alexander for making me experience this. I know how to take it away and he won't let me. It feels like I am dying and I hope that I am.

The music fades and Christopher makes his way to the front. He tells the story of how they first met in grade school and different stories of mischief they caused together. He says things I never knew about Toben. I've never seen Christopher cry before.

He holds out his hand and introduces me. Even though I haven't ever spoken in front of so many people, I need them to know how amazing he was. I want people to see him the way I do. I take Christopher's hand and stand behind a tall, skinny, wooden table.

"H—hi. I…uh. I've known Toben almost my whole life. When my parents starved and abused me, he fed me and loved me. No one had ever been nice to me and I certainly had never had a friend before. He taught me things and made me laugh. He made me excited to wake up in the morning. He protected me from my father and did so much more as we grew older. Our life was not what most people would understand. We went through a lot of bad stuff, and because I had him, I was able to survive it. Toben Michaels was my best friend, my protector, my family, and he was…" My voice breaks and I know I need to finish soon, "my Tobe…and I love him and miss him so much, and it hurts so bad." Everyone is looking at me so I pull the piece of paper out of my pocket. "Toben has written songs and poems for as long as I've known him. There's one that I would like to share with you." Even though I don't know the tune he put it to, I do my best.

I don't know what will become of me.
All I know is, you're my eternity.
On our souls, they fucking prey and feed.
Just don't ever forget: when you bleed, I bleed.
You showed a wounded child what real love could be.
It's only you that will ever set me free.
I taste your kiss and I smell you in my dreams.
It hurts so bad, like I'm ripping at the seams.
These words are my world, they are my spoken creed.
I can feel beneath your flesh, and when you bleed, I bleed.

Folding the paper up, I walk off the stage. I can't be in this room any longer so I keep going until I walk out the back doors. I know we still need to bury him and I know I'm supposed to talk to a bunch of people, but I can't. I just keep walking. I don't know to where and it doesn't matter. I least I don't think it does until I end up at the beach. The first place we went together. Our favorite place. I pull off my shoes and dig my toes in the sand, before I lie down. I try to pick out shapes in the clouds like we used to, but I can't see clearly through the tears. I don't know what to do from here.

Half of me is dead.

Wednesday, August 19th

Alexander

I should be working instead of reading every story I can find about Tavin and Nikki's case. I really wish they would speak to each other. Nikki blames Tavin for Toben not saving her and not loving her, and Tavin doesn't know what to think about her.

I log out of my computer as my cell rings, and I see it's Sasha. Since she's the only one Nikki seems to be warming up to, I asked her to take Nikki to the doctor this afternoon for the stomach bug she's had all week.

Standing up, I press the answer button. "Hey. How is Nikki?"

She sighs, "We have an issue."

"Sash, I don't need the suspense. Just tell me."

"She's pregnant."

I drop my head back and groan as I lock my office door. "You've got to be kidding me."

"Yeah, I wish. She's a mess. She doesn't want to keep it."

I hold out my hand to ask the woman in the elevator to keep the door open. "I can't say that I blame her." I keep my voice down as I push the button for the correct floor. "Try to keep this from Tavin until I get home. I don't know how she's going to react when she finds out."

"She can't keep going on like this. It's been a month."

"I know. I just don't know how to help her."

"I'm sorry, Alex. I don't have any answers for you."

"You have no idea how grateful I am for all your help through this whole mess. I'll see you tonight, okay?"

Hanging up, I pull up the map for the restaurant I'm looking for. About a month ago, I got the idea to see what I could find about Tavin's mother's family.

Tavin's biological grandfather, Jeffrey Bellerose, passed away from cancer three years ago, though her grandmother, Margaret is still alive. They had two children. Lacie, of course, and Tavin Bellerose.

It may be overprotective and a little paranoid, but I'm not bringing anyone else into her life that I am not completely certain will have a positive impact, so I've been... observing before reaching out.

Tavin Bellerose is thirty-seven years old and the mother of a six-year-old child named Jonas, though she's not and never has been married. She works full time in a nursing home for people with mental disorders and disabilities. On occasional weekends, she helps counsel a narcotics anonymous group.

After driving three hours to get to the restaurant they visit every Wednesday, I watch her with her son, through the window. It makes me smile with relief to see the way she hugs and kisses him. What really makes me happy though, is the way he looks at her. As if there is nobody more perfect in this world.

Seeing as this is a public place, I 'm hoping I don't make her too uncomfortable by approaching her. I cross the restaurant to their table and she looks up at me with a confused, yet sweet expression.

I smile at her and the little boy. "Hello. My name is Alexander Sørensen. This may be unusual... Would you mind if I ask you a few questions about your sister, Lacie?"

The smile falls from her face as she leans back in her seat. "I don't know what I can tell you. I haven't spoken to her since I was a kid, and she passed away some time ago. Can I ask what this is about?"

The automatic grin that appears when I think about her pulls at my mouth. "It's about her daughter."

Disbelief is the apparent reaction. "I apologize, you must be mistaken. Lacie never had children."

I pull out my phone and show her a picture. "Lacie and Brian never told anyone about her. Her name is Tavin Winters and she's twenty-three years old."

Her hand covers her mouth as she takes the phone from my hand. "Oh my God." She whispers, "She looks just like her…this is impossible." She has no idea how many things about Tavin's existence seem impossible. She looks back up at me in awe. "Where is she?" She gestures to the seat across the table, "Please sit. Would you like anything?"

"You're very kind, but no, thank you." I take a seat and clasp my hands together on the table. "She lives with me. I assume you've heard the Logan James story on the news? She was one of his girls." She nods with wide eyes and I can see so much of Tavin in her. "She's been through a horrific ordeal and I feel I need to prepare you for the fact that she may not be receptive to seeing you…at least not right away. However, I do think it's worth it to try."

"Of course." She shakes her head and laughs as if she is in a bit of a daze. "My mother won't believe this." Her hand reaches across the table and takes a hold of mine. "Thank you. When may I see her?"

I smile. "Whenever you'd like."

Sasha and Cara Jo are in the kitchen when I arrive home.

"Hello, Alex. How was your day?"

I pull off my jacket and fall into the closest chair. "Interesting." I told Sasha when I first found the Belleroses, and not much beyond that. "I met Tavin's aunt today."

Sasha and Cara Jo have matching stretched out eyes and mouths.

"Well, how'd it go?" Sasha's impatience is sweet. I know how much she loves Tavin, too.

"It went really well. She seems like a good person and she wants to meet her. She was thrilled about it, actually."

Sasha sighs and drinks from her coffee mug. "I never knew what to expect out of Tavin before all this, and it's even worse now. Hopefully she'll be open to this"

"It might take time, but I think a family is something she's always wanted." I groan as I move on to a less appealing subject. "Now, what are we gonna do about Nikki? How is she?"

"A fucking mess. She's angry at Toben for leaving her with this. She doesn't want to consider a child when her life is in shambles."

I run my hands over my face and push myself out of the seat. "I'm going to talk to Tavin, how long until dinner is ready?"

I think Cara Jo has been having a hard time with this. She's been quieter than usual since this has all come out. She looks at the clock. "About twenty minutes."

I walk upstairs to her room and her door is closed, which has been the norm the last few weeks. Pushing it open, I find her in her bed once again.

"Tav? Are you awake?"

"Yes," she whispers.

"I need to talk to you. Can you sit up for a second?" Her hair is sticking out everywhere and her eyes are still in their constant state of being puffy and red rimmed. She keeps her chin to her chest as she scoots herself up, refusing to look at me. "Nikki found out something today." She doesn't make a move to respond, so I continue. "She's pregnant."

For the first time in weeks, she looks me in the eye. "What?"

"For now, Nikki's pregnant, and even though I don't think she will be for long, I wanted you to know what's going on."

She jumps up to her knees and is more alert in this conversation than she has been in any, since he died.

"No, she has to keep it. It's his baby."

"Tavin, that's not fair. This is her choice. He was her rapist and captor. Imagine if Logan had gotten you pregnant."

She shakes her head and throws off the sheets. "No. She can't do this." She jumps off the bed and swings open the door. I follow her down the stairs and through the kitchen.

"Tavin, this isn't your decision."

Sasha and Cara Jo watch her as she turns down the back hallway to where Nikki's room is. Although I don't try to physically stop her, that doesn't keep me from trying verbally, as I follow her down the hall. She arrives at Nikki's, and knocks.

"Nikki, it's Tavin. I know you don't like me, but please talk to me about this."

There's no answer at first, and when the door swings open, they stare each other down.

"This has nothing to do with you."

"This has everything to do with me. This is the only thing left of my best friend and you want to take it away. I can't let you do that, Nikki."

"You can't stop me."

She tries to shut the door as Tavin presses her hand against it. "Please, Nikki. Let me have it. You won't have to ever see the baby again, please...don't do this."

"He never loved me and it was because of you. So please, tell me why the fuck I should do this for you?"

Tavin reaches out and takes her hand. "Because I know you loved him. I didn't keep him from being with you. Logan did. All of this is Logan's fault. He hurt me, too. He did horrible things to me and Toben. I'm sorry you think he didn't love you, Nikki. I knew him better than anyone, and I'm sure you're wrong." She actually looks like she may consider this. "This is the only way to keep part of him alive. No matter how much you hate me, please don't make that disappear."

Tears roll down both of their faces. "And once I have it, I'll never have to see it again?"

Tavin shakes her head so hard her bangs flop around. "No, not if you don't want to."

Sasha, Cara Jo, and I are all watching as the silence stretches on so long I don't know if Nikki will respond. Then suddenly, she gives the slightest of nods. Tavin wraps her arms around her and sobs.

"Thank you, Nikki."

Tavin

I stand in the doorway of his office and watch him. He has stuck by me through all this, and I've treated him less than fairly. Even the best of men wouldn't have stayed through all this. The way I've been acting, it's been terrible and he doesn't deserve it. He deserves all the kisses and hugs and love I have.

He's not voiced a single objection about me keeping the baby and I didn't even ask him how he felt about it. It somehow makes me feel like part of Toben is still alive and at the time, that's all that mattered.

His hands wipe over his face as he works hard on his computer. Even though he's busy, I don't want to wait a second longer to apologize. Not only have I been distant, emotionally, I also haven't been with him physically, in weeks.

I miss everything—his touch, his kiss, his scent, his words. He needs to know how much I love him and how much he truly means to me, how much everything he's done for me, means. He's changed my life in the most remarkable way. I owe my freedom and the possibility to a new future, all to him. I owe him everything.

"Lex?"

He looks up at me and smiles at me the same way he always has. His feelings haven't changed and I know in my soul they never will.

He turns his chair and stands. "Are you alright?"

Closing the space between us, I press my hands to his chest, careful to not touch where his tic-tac-toe and whip cuts are. "I will be and that's because of you. I'm so sorry about the way I've been, the things I've said. I've been so difficult and you've stayed next to me and..." My voice cracks from more tears and I try to speak around them. "I love you, Alexander. I will always love you."

His hands grip my waist as he picks me up and puts me on his desk. He touches his nose to mine. "You haven't been difficult, you've been grieving, and I'll never blame you for that. I love you too, Tav. More than I knew I could."

I smile at him as a tear drops off my jaw. "I don't deserve you." He's about to respond when his eyes shift to my fingers undoing his pants. "I miss you," I whisper.

His hands grasp my face and he kisses me with so much intensity it's like I am the only place he can get oxygen. I feel frantic with the need to be a part of him again.

I push down my shorts and he doesn't wait for me to

take off my panties, he just yanks them to the side and shoves himself all the way in with one hard thrust. The moan slides out on its own, as I grip the back of his neck.

"Thank you for staying with me."

He presses his forehead to mine and gives me the most gorgeous smile.

"It's impossible to live without a heart."

Thursday, August 27th

"Come on, Nikki, I know you don't feel good, but you're throwing up everything you've drank. You need more water."

I feel bad for her, she has to go through this every day. I sure hope this doesn't last the whole time. She can't keep anything down and Alexander says the baby eats what she eats, so how is the baby supposed to grow if she can't stop throwing up all her food?

"I've had six glasses already. Can't I take a break?"

I sigh and set the glass on the dresser. I know she's trying. "Okay. Do you want to try a Popsicle?"

She wipes her mouth. "Alright, then I'm taking a bath."

"I'll make you one with bubbles, okay? Then I'll paint your nails. Does that sound good?"

She gives me a forced smile. She's trying really hard to be nice to me. "Sure."

I walk down the hall to the kitchen and open the freezer, as Cara Jo is covering a dish with tin foil.

"Hi, Cara Jo. Did Lex say he was working late tonight? He's usually home by now."

"I actually just heard from him. He's on his way, he said he got caught up."

Turning to head back to Nikki's room, I almost drop the Popsicle when the doorbell rings. I look at Cara Jo.

"I don't think we're expecting anyone. Will you get it?"

Placing the Popsicle back in the freezer, I walk to the entryway and swing open the front door. My stomach slides to my knees as all the air escapes my body, making my voice come out in a squeaky whisper.

"Lacie?"

It can't be her. This is impossible…I've seen her dead body. I can't get myself to breathe, and right when I think my chest might explode, she smiles at me.

"Lacie was my big sister. My name is Tavin." She covers her mouth with an odd laugh. "I'm your aunt." I hear what she says, but…what? Every word I try to pick is wrong. Suddenly, her arms are around me, hugging me. "I'm so sorry for everything she put you through." She straightens herself and smooths out her hair. "This must be such a shock for you. It was for me too, I'm just so happy to meet you. There are a lot of people who want to meet you, actually. Your grandmother is so excited, and so is your cousin. That is, if you're comfortable with that, we don't want to pressure you." She laughs again. "Listen to me, I'm probably freaking you right out."

I have a family? That wants to see me? I don't know what I'm feeling. It isn't bad…just curious and surprised. She said I have a cousin and a grandmother. I can't begin to imagine what that's like.

Cara Jo comes up behind me and opens the door wider. "Would you like to invite your guest in for something to drink?"

"Uh…yeah, sure. Do you want to come in?"

Her head nods so hard her necklace shakes. "I would love that."

EPILOGUE

Four Years and Two Months Later: Friday, December 6th

Alexander

"M R. SØRENSEN, THANK YOU FOR COMING down today. I tried to contact your wife, but her assistant said she was unavailable." My son's principal stacks her papers into a nice pile before leading me into the hall. "Michael is a bright and sweet boy, and we've never had any problems before today, though I do feel we should nip this issue in the bud."

I smile as gracefully as possible, considering I have no idea what this is about. I follow her into her office where Michael is sitting in the chair in front of her desk.

He looks up and gives me that adorable grin.

"Daddy!"

His little legs are going as fast as they can as he runs over to me and wraps his arms around my legs, squeezing me tight.

"Hey, buddy." I lean down and kiss his head before I hand him his phone. "Go out in the hall and play your game while I talk to Ms. Crabtree. I'll be out in a minute."

I don't have to tell him twice. He snatches the phone and

disappears into the hallway.

She smirks at me as she takes a seat and gestures for me to do the same. "If I'm being completely honest, I'm going to tell my friends this story over drinks tonight."

I know at least one eyebrow raises because this isn't going the direction I was prepared for.

"I'm sorry?"

She clearly feels as if she can relax around me because her posture loosens. "Between you and me, on a personal level, I thought this was adorably hilarious, though as the pre-school principal, I need to correct it."

"What exactly did he do?"

She sighs before taking off her glasses and chuckling, "He...he spanked a little girl on the bottom, and said," she can't contain another giggle, "'Damn, that ass.'"

I'm more than slightly mortified. Tavin's been telling me I need to watch what I say around him. I rub my forehead, mostly so I don't have to make eye contact. "Oh, Jesus."

She laughs again and leans back in her chair. "You would be surprised at how much of a glimpse I get into these children's home lives based off things they are obviously mimicking. I wish I could say it's always as innocent as this clearly is. I would just suggest being careful about what you say and do in front of him."

I force a smile and give a curt nod. "Yeah...I do apologize."

Standing, she waves off my comment and holds out a hand. "It was nice to see you again, Mr. Sørensen."

Michael's game is beeping and his tongue is sticking out when I walk into the hall. Ruffling his hair, I pick up his backpack. "Alright, let's go."

He swings his lunch box back and forth as he walks. "Am I in trouble?"

I pick him up and let him ride on my back. "You aren't

in trouble. We will need to talk about it with Mommy later, though."

He sighs, "So, that would be yes."

This kid is always making me laugh. "If you were in trouble would we be getting ice cream?"

"Yay!" I open the car door and let him climb in, when something dawns on him. "Mom will be mad if we go without her."

"You're right about that, so we better bring her something. Do you want to go visit Toben first?"

His dark brown hair flops as he nods. "Can I bring him the picture I drew for him?"

"I think he would like that very much, buddy."

The cemetery plot I chose for Toben is next to a little bridge and a park bench shaded by a tree. It's pretty and secluded, allowing us privacy.

Michael lays his picture on the grave. "Hi, Daddy Toben. I made this for you. Mommy said you had brown hair like me, so that's how I colored you. I also wrote a song for you, it's written on the back." He turns the paper over to show him. "I hope you're having a good day. I love you, Daddy Toben." He gets up before turning back. "Oh, and guess what? Mommy told me that her new art show is all about you! I bet you would like it. She still cries when she misses you, ya know. Okay, bye, Daddy Toben."

Jumping up, he runs back to the car, but not without grabbing a stick and swinging at the air in the process. I have been here hundreds of times, and each time it pulls at the heart strings. If it wasn't for Toben, I wouldn't have my little boy and my wife. In some ways, I owe him everything.

Tavin has blossomed the last few years. She speaks through her art and it's had an effect on quite a few people, because her career has exploded. She's been in magazines and occasionally, she'll do a live interview, although she hates them and they're always a little awkward. All of the money she earns she gives away to various favorite charities and organizations, along with many individual families and children. While her talent is the main reason for her fan base, I believe her kindness draws a large part of her following as well. She doesn't care about being famous. In fact, too much attention can become overwhelming for her. She does it because she loves it, and in my opinion, it has helped in her rehabilitation.

Not to say we haven't struggled…we have. There have been nights I was scared we weren't strong enough to make it through. I will never give up on her, though. My place is and will always be beside her. She's messed up a few times and relapsed, however the effect Michael has had on her is extraordinary. Hell, Michael's had quite the effect on me, too. I've cut back on my drinking and I work daily on controlling my anger.

Counseling helps her learn to cope with her childhood, but I don't expect her to heal. Not completely. I don't mean that in a bad way. She's been through things that are irreversible. I know she'll continue to improve, as she already has exponentially, I simply don't ever expect her to be 'fixed'. All I've ever asked is that she tries her hardest, and she has.

I open the door to her gallery as Michael runs through her exhibit screaming, "Mommy!" Potential clients turn in annoyance, and Tavin doesn't notice or care.

"There's my handsome little prince!" She picks him up and twirls him around before giving him Eskimo kisses.

"We brought you ice cream, Mommy!"

Her eyes widen. "You did?" She looks at me with a grin. "Cotton candy flavor?"

I hold up the bag. "See for yourself."

She peeks inside before looking up at me with those bright eyes. Her little hand strokes my cheek before she kisses me. "Thank you for the ice cream. Was everything okay at the school?"

I know she's going to kill me when she finds out, so I just chuckle, "Yeah, it was nothing." She narrows her eyes at me with a smirk, dropping it for now. "How late will you be tonight?" I ask.

She pulls out her phone. "I'll be sure I'm home before nine. I want to put Michael to bed."

"Alright, *Lille*, see you tonight."

Doing as she says, she's home by eight-forty. She bounds up to me and wraps her arms around my neck, as soon as she's in the door.

"Hey."

"Hey." I enjoy her smell for a moment. "Michael's teeth are brushed. He's in his pajamas, playing in his room."

She lays her head against my chest and takes in a deep breath. "I'm going to go tuck him in."

I lock the doors and turn off the lights before following her upstairs. Michael's bedroom is Tavin's old room and as I push open the door, I hear her singing. She's lying in bed with him and Blind Mag, holding Toben's lyric book, singing his words to her own melodies.

My heart aches as I watch her sing our child to sleep, and as his breathing slows, she creeps out of the bed to meet me in the hallway. As soon as she shuts the door, I pick her up, squeezing her tight ass as I wrap her legs around my waist and slam her against the wall.

"I missed you today, Tavin Sørensen."

She lets her head fall to the side as she laughs. "I missed you too, Lex."

Her lips press hard against mine as I carry the love of my perfectly sweet life, to our room.

Sunday, December 8th

Tavin

"Happy birthday, Mommy!" Michael's precious little voice yells, and I'm smiling before I even open my eyes. He jumps on the bed as Lex carries a tray. "We made you pancakes with sprinkles!"

"You did?!"

Alexander sets the tray down on my lap and the pancakes have whipped cream, rainbow sprinkles, and a bunch of burning candles. There's a glass of strawberry milk and a lotus flower in a vase.

What the lotus means has changed for me. It's no longer a symbol of belonging to Logan, it's a symbol of belonging to me. A reminder of my new life and the person I have become.

The pancakes look delicious and I'm moaning in anticipation, as Alexander sits next to me on the bed. "Mikey was such a big helper. He put the sprinkles and the candles on, all by himself."

My heart feels like it will explode, sometimes, when I look at Michael. I love him more than this life I have. He looks so much like Toben it makes my chest physically ache.

"It's absolutely perfect."

Michael cuddles up next to me. "Make a wish!"

I grin at Lex. What else is there to wish for? I have more than I could have ever dreamed. I squeeze my eyes shut and wish with all my might that things will stay this perfect forever. When I open them, I take a deep breath and blow all the candles out, on my first try.

Michael and I both clap our hands and Lex laughs. Picking up my fork, I cut a scrumptious piece.

"Can I have a bite?" Mikey's mouth is already open waiting for his treat. I giggle and put the fork in his mouth. "Mmmm, yummy!"

I get to eat every other bite of my birthday breakfast before Lex picks Michael up off the bed.

"Why don't you go take a nice bath while we set up for your party tonight?"

I throw the covers off and jump up to wrap my arms around them. "I love you both, more than anything."

"We love you more than anything too, Mommy!"

Lex's eyes shine as he smiles down at me. "Yes, we do."

My chest tightens as I clutch the Tupperware in my hands and weave between the headstones. Every time I see the words, they feel chiseled in my soul just like they are on the granite.

Toben Lee Michaels
10/8/91- 7/13/15
"When you bleed, I bleed."
YOU ARE THE BEST FRIEND I EVER HAD.
I LOVE YOU. I LOVE YOU.

I kneel before what remains of my friend. "I brought you some cake."

Popping open the container, I lay his piece on his grave. "Michael helped Cara Jo make it." I laugh, "He's so much like you, it's ridiculous." I take a bite of my cake and breathe in the winter air. "The art show went amazing. It was my best by far. I couldn't have done it without you, so thank you."

I last longer than I usually do when the tears inevitably fall. I lie down on his grave as I ache for his arms around me. "I miss you so much, Tobe. I wish you could be here to see how perfect Michael is, to see my art, to live this incredible life with me." I feel the anger squeezing me, making me want to scream. "It isn't fair, all you did was suffer! Why didn't you get to live this life? Why can't you be here for the birthday YOU gave me?" I clutch at the dirt because it's the only thing available. "I hope you're with your mom and you get her hugs and kisses every day. I hope you're as happy as I am."

It still hurts so terribly and I know it will never go away, yet I have so many people in my life who love me, that I love. They make life beautiful, and while I would do anything to have Toben back here with me, I have so many reasons to live.

"Kyle's trial finally ended. Three life sentences. He'll never hurt anyone else again." I sigh and draw a heart in the dirt. "I love you so much, Toben." I wipe the tears and sit up. "I need to go. Everyone is coming over for my party!" I lean forward and kiss his gravestone. "Mikey and I will come see you tomorrow, okay?"

I stand and look at his plot for a moment before I walk back to my car. I learned how to drive two years ago. Alexander bought me my lilac Lamborghini last year as a wedding present. I like to drive. It's so fun, and I like being able to go anywhere I want, whenever I want, in a split second.

As I pull through our gate, I see all the cars and my stomach tickles me. All these people are here because they care about me and they want to celebrate my birthday.

I run inside and Blind Mag pops out of the propped-open basement door. I can hear the laughing and talking from up here. Picking her up, I hurry down the stairs. There's music playing and everyone's attention is on Michael as he shows off his sword fighting skills, in his crown and cloak.

He's a dragon hunting prince, you know.

Nikki is sitting on Cain's lap, clapping with glee, and I'm so grateful she changed her mind about being in Michael's life. She kept living with us even after Michael was born. On his first birthday, we went out to celebrate and ran into Cain. I thought it would be awkward, until the moment he laid eyes on Nikki. Not me or any other woman in the world existed after that. He's been perfect for her and he has grown close with Alexander. Lex now considers him one of his closest friends.

Sasha is wearing my princess crown as she hides behind the play castle and says, "If only there was a strong prince to save me!"

Silas jumps up from behind the couch and growls, "RAWR! I'm going to eat the princess up!" He turns to Sasha and winks. "I'm going to eat her up real good."

Lex shakes his head. "Silas, keep it G-rated, alright? I'm still not completely out of the woods for Friday."

I smirk because he's out of the woods just fine. I have the marks on my back to prove it.

Cara Jo laughs as she watches Mikey. I owe so much to her. There's no way I could have gotten through this without her. Michael had a few medical issues when he was born, including jaundice and colic. I didn't know what to do and I felt like a failure, and she was there to help us through it, every step of the way.

My grandmother leans over and laughs with Cara Jo. They have become good friends and she has been a big help as well. She's hilarious. Some of the things that come out of her mouth are crazy. She's one of the kindest people I have ever met and I love her dearly.

I've grown extremely close to my Aunt Tavin. She

understands my feelings even when I can't explain them to myself. She claps along with my cousin Jonas, as Michael slays the Silas dragon. Jonas has been like a big brother to Michael and is very smart. He's two grades ahead of what he is supposed to be and loves to teach Michael things.

Alexander's mother, Caterina, is sitting in a chair drinking her martini and holding Lauralie, Silas and Sasha's little girl. Caterina's somewhat starting to come around to me. I wouldn't say she's warming up to me, but at least she isn't freezing me out anymore. Cooling up to me maybe? At least she talks to me now, and she's nice to Mikey.

Marie smiles and coos at Lauralie. About halfway through Nikki's pregnancy, she reached out to me and apologized. She and Sasha have repaired their friendship and I can honestly say she's my friend too. She's our family doctor and helped assure me, when Michael was a sickly baby.

Benny, Todd, and Timothy are playing poker at the table. I don't play with them anymore because I always lose horribly.

I've been learning so much from Benny's self-defense classes. If I'm ever in another situation that I have to protect myself, I have all the confidence that I could. I even took Lex down once.

A couple years ago, I reached out to Alia and found out her real name is Shelby. We've become extremely close. She and Christopher hit it off at my birthday last year and have been together ever since.

I smile as they down shots at the bar. Even though they're still both heavy into the drug and party scene, they've never broken our 'no drugs in the house' rule, and are usually sober, for the most part, around Mikey. I love Christopher for staying in Michael's life, and we always go to the cemetery together, every year on Toben's birthday.

I let my eyes fill up with tears because the whole scene is

more than I could have ever dreamed.

Michael looks up and sees me, throwing his arms up as he yells, "Mommy!"

Everyone turns, and Lex's whole face still brightens every time he sees me.

"HAPPY BIRTHDAY!"

Everyone yells in unison, making it impossible not to grin. I finally have a family. I'm not a half-person anymore. I'm whole. I no longer spend my days doing anything not to feel. Now, I do everything I can to feel every single moment. I'm not a plaything or a toy.

I am a mother.

I am a friend.

I am a sister.

I am a niece.

I am a granddaughter.

I am his *Lille*.

I am…Tavin.

CHAPTER ONE
Beginning

October 2001

Tavin

S HE'S SLEEPING AGAIN. SHE DOESN'T MOVE EVEN when I poke her with the fork.

"Mommy, wake up!" I yell it in her face, but she stays still. My stomach twists; I'm so hungry.

There's voices. My head whips to the door. Uh oh. Daddy's home and he's with someone.

I better go hide.

I jump off Mommy, rip open my door, and run downstairs to my room. Crawling beneath the stairs, I hold my lips together so I don't make sounds with my breathing. I hug myself tight as the door creaks open from the top of the stairs.

BOOM. BOOM. BOOM. BOOM.

Someone's coming.

"Stay down there, you little fucker. I'll get you when I'm done."

That isn't daddy's voice.

A loud pounding above my head makes me try to shrink smaller, and a big thump lets me know whatever was just thrown down here, has made it to the bottom.

The door slams.

I hear moaning and grumbling. Someone's here. I stay perfectly still as the source of the noise comes into my view.

"Bastard," he mumbles.

It's a boy and I don't know who he's talking to because he doesn't know I'm here. I think he is close to the same age as me. His brown hair falls into his face while he kicks at my floor on his way to my bed. I make sure I stay under the stairs as I move out a little further for a better look. He sits down and bounces a few times before he looks up and sees me.

"Ahh!" He yells and falls back a little. "What are you doing, freak?"

I crawl out. "My name is Tavin."

"I didn't ask you your name, freak, I asked you what you're doing, creepin' under the stairs."

Why is he still calling me 'freak'?

"I was hiding. Why are you in my room?"

"Because my dad wants to get high with yours." He rolls his eyes. "I don't even know why he brought me."

I've never met another kid before. I see them all the time, I've just never talked to one.

"What is your name?"

I stand up to meet him at my bed and look at his clothes. He's wearing a long sleeve black shirt and he has a black hat on.

"Toben."

I like his name, it kind of sounds like mine. The sharp pain turns over. My tummy hurts so badly, I hope I don't throw up in front of him.

"Do you have food?"

He shifts awkwardly. "Uh, no. Sorry."

"Oh, it's okay. You can play with me if you want."

His eyebrows scrunch and he frowns at me. "I don't want."

Oh…dang.

I look at his hands and he's holding a notebook! Maybe he likes to draw, like me. He sets it down on my bed before reaching into his jeans, pulling out two long wires that are attached to a little shiny black box. It lights up when he touches it.

"What is that?" I point to it.

"It's an iPod, duh."

Then he does something so funny, he puts the wires in his ears! "Why did you do that?"

He raises one of his eyebrows and I can see his eyes. They're as dark as night. I bet he's good at drawing.

He takes one of the wires out and hands it to me. "Listen."

I put the wire in my ear like he did. Instantly, loud screaming and banging music fills my head. I rip it back out. "What is that?!"

"It's Behemoth." He sort of smiles. I wonder what a bee-hee-moth is.

"Why is he yelling?"

"I guess because he's mad."

"Why?"

He shrugs. "Maybe because there's no God."

That's the first time he looks at my eyes and I hope he does it again. I like it.

"Oh."

He takes the wires out of the black box. The bee-hee-moth starts coming out of it and I can hear it all over my room.

"I've never see you at lunch or anything, where do you go to school?"

I shake my head. "I don't go anywhere."

He frowns at me. "Everybody has to go to school. You're lying."

"Hey! I'm not lying."

Why would I lie to him?

He crosses his arms. "Then how did you learn to read, and tell time, and write your name?"

I climb off my bed to show him my wall.

"I don't know how to do any of that stuff. Here, stand up, I want to show you my pictures." He gets off so I can move my bed. "I like to draw."

When my bed is out of the way, I look at him and his eyebrows are lifted.

"Obviously."

I kneel by my drawings. "Do you want to help?"

He walks around my room. "Uh, no I'm good." Shoving his hands in his pockets, he blows his hair out of his eyes. "All you have is that little TV and old radio? You don't have an Xbox or anything?"

What is this silly boy talking about? "I don't think so."

He stomps to my bed and falls back onto it. "Great."

I crawl to him and prop my arms on my sheets. I rest my head in my hands as I watch him.

"How old are you?"

He lifts his head. "I turned ten last week. How old are you?"

I want to know so badly! "I don't know, I think I might be nine, but maybe I'm ten too!"

"How do you not know how old you are, freak?"

This boy is making me mad now, he knows my name. I point my finger at him, so he can see I'm serious.

"Hey! My name is Tavin."

He gets off of my bed and sits on the floor with me. "Okay, *Tavin*. What's your deal? You're filthy, you aren't even trying to cover up your bruises, you say you've never been to school, and now you don't even know how old you are?"

I guess I have worn this dress a long time. I don't have very many, though, and the others are just like this. I didn't know it was bad.

"I'm filthy?"

"God, yes. When was the last time you had a bath?"

I close my eyes and try to remember. "I don't know, I think mommy gave me one when there were still kids playing outside all day."

"You haven't had a bath since summer vacation? That was over a month ago!" He brings his knees to his chest. "You're too old for your mom to still be washing you. Why don't you clean yourself?"

I shrug. "I didn't know I was supposed to." I look at the purple marks on my arm. "Why should I hide them?"

I can't help that I get them. Should I be embarrassed? He keeps looking at me funny. Oh, I hope he doesn't think I'm stupid.

"Because then people will know. If they know, then they will call the cops, and you don't want to meet a cop."

I know about police. Daddy says if they find me, they will lock me away in jail and I'll never get out. I've never actually seen them, I just know they are bad.

"Why would they do that?"

"Because people don't know how to mind their own damn business."

"I don't ever see people though. I never leave the house."

"What? What about the dentist and the doctor?"

"Daddy says I don't need a doctor because I should be dead anyway."

I think I did something wrong because he looks mad at me.

"You never leave? Will your parents not let you?"

I'm always too scared to leave. Daddy says there are a lot

of people who will hurt little girls. I don't want him to know I get scared, though.

"They don't care if I leave, I just don't. I like to watch all the people through my window."

He turns his head and points his thumb. "That's a window well, the only thing outside there is a concrete wall."

"You have to climb the ladder, silly."

"Wow, really?" He stands up and hurries to my window. When he opens it, he looks at the ladder. "Well I'll be damned." He turns to me and smiles. His whole face changes when he smiles. "You're weird, but I like you. See you around, Tavin." He climbs out and is gone.

Why did he leave? He said he liked me.

He left his eye pad, I think he called it, and his notebook, on my bed. I bet he will come back for it. Oh, I hope he does!

Toben

Damn it. I left my lyric book and iPod in her room. I'll need to go back to get them, just not tonight. I still don't know why he dragged me over there in the first place, he normally can't wait to get me out of his sight. Is he trying to be an actual parent and punish me for getting suspended today? Why doesn't he just punch me in the stomach like usual and be done with it? Whatever. I don't give a shit. I thought he was bad when he was drinking, now that he has been using, it's as if his hate has become a creature of its own.

That Tavin girl is the oddest person I've ever met. I wonder if she's telling the truth about all that stuff. I've lived two houses down from her my whole life, and I've never seen her before. She doesn't act like she's nine, and she's smaller than the girls in my class. She's covered in dirt and her hair needs washing, but she's interesting. I think I was kind of mean to her, and it's not normal that I care.

I found myself continuously looking at her pretty purple eyes that were out of place with her ragged clothes and tangled hair. I don't understand how her parents have been able to keep her locked up and out of sight for so long, or why they'd want to. Maybe I can ask my dad, if I can catch him on one of his good days.

I'm gonna get the crap beat out of me for leaving. What else is new? At least I don't have to stay in the room that time forgot.

I run back to my house, get my bike, and begin to ride the two blocks to Christopher's, as I breathe in the perfect air.

I love the fall. It's calming to watch the grass and flowers dying. It's the end of stupid pool parties and getting crazy-ass looks from people for wearing long sleeved shirts. It smells cleaner, and the air feels better, than any other time of year.

Christopher is the closest thing to a best friend that I have. His parents think I'm a bad influence on their perfect little boy because my dad's a dick and I listen to metal. If they only knew their angel introduced me to pot, and I'm about to get drunk off the vodka he stole from their liquor cabinet.

I almost told him the last time we drank, about my dad, and I have wanted to tell him on a few other occasions. Then I remind myself of the possible outcomes.

He could try to help by telling his parents, which would most likely mean I'd go into foster care. I definitely don't want that, at least now I pretty much do whatever I want. He could keep quiet, but always pity me and get all weird which would cost me my only real friend. He could ask why my dad does what he does, and when I tell him it's because I killed my mother, he could end up agreeing that I deserve the beatings. The odds of him staying my friend and staying quiet are pretty damn slim, so I keep it to myself.

The thought occurs to me that I could tell Tavin. Just from what I saw, her arms, neck, side of her face, and legs are all covered in either new or healing bruises. I feel bad for her, she's so small. I don't think she can take too much. Her dad is a decent size guy, nothing like my dad, but he could definitely inflict some damage. She doesn't even act like it's a secret. She probably wouldn't bat an eye if I took off my shirt. It would be so nice to just say it aloud. To tell someone.

I'll go see her tomorrow to get my stuff.

I drop my bike in Christopher's yard and knock on his front door. His mom answers, which is better than his dad. I try to be as polite as I can, and they still don't like me. At least she tries to hide it.

She sighs in greeting, "Hello, Toben. Christopher is in his room."

"Thank you, Mrs. Reed."

I give her a big smile and she makes a sad attempt to return it. I pound down the stairs and take the left into Christopher's room. Some top forty shit is playing, and he's propped in bed pounding buttons on his Gameboy.

He turns his head and when he sees me, a huge grin crosses his face.

"Dude, that was seriously legendary. I swear you didn't even look at him the first time, your fist was just punching his face out of nowhere." He starts laughing, "Then you lost it." Shaking his head he adds, "You're crazy."

He reaches under his bed, recovers a bottle, and takes a drink. He hands it to me, and after a burning swig, I tell him why Thomas asked for everything he got.

"He deserved it. He's a dick. He was kicking Michelle

Andrews in the shin and I've seen him pick on other girls before, too. So I thought, if he wants to fight, he can fight me."

"Yeah, well, just give me a chance to explain things if I ever make you mad."

We drink a few more drinks and soon my head is fuzzy. I better stop or I won't be able to make it home.

"Hey, do you have any weed? I can pay you." I reach for the twenty I ripped off from my dad, this morning.

"No, but I get it from the high school kids. Just make sure whoever you ask looks cool."

I'm able to walk up the stairs fairly straight and I only fall off my bike once on my way to the high school. I think the ride clears my head because I can focus better once I get there. Even though they're already out for the day, there are always a few who stay for clubs, or practices, or whatever else they do in senior high. I ride by the football field, to the parking lot. Sure enough, there's a group of them heading to their cars. I scan them and my eyes land on a kid with dreadlocks. There's no way someone that doesn't smoke weed would do that to their hair. I park my bike in the rack and try to hurry without being obvious about it. I catch up to him just as he's getting into his car.

He raises his eyebrows. "Do you need something, little man?"

I reach in my pocket and pull out the twenty, showing it to him, while keeping it in my fist. "I need a quarter."

He laughs at me, "A quarter of what?"

"Of weed."

"Jesus, you're a little young, yeah?" He looks me up and down, sighs, and then nods toward his car. "Fine, get in."

I think for sure he'll rip me off, but he's cool. His name is

Cory Ridge and he tells me to hit him up any time.

When I get back to my house, I still have a great buzz and my dad isn't back yet. Getting some papers from my desk drawer, I roll a joint, and light up. The high is calm and relaxing. I feel my heart rate slow and I close my eyes.

I know that I would want to see Tavin again even if I hadn't left my crap there. I don't have school for three days on account of my suspension, and she apparently doesn't have it at all. I think I'll try to get her to leave tomorrow and take her to the beach. It's the best time of year to go, in my opinion. If she's never left then maybe I can show her some new things. I've never had a girl for a friend before.

I wonder what it will be like.

Sweetened
PLAYLIST

1. *Never Forget You* – Zara Larsson ft. MNEK
2. *Little One* – Highly Suspect
3. *Blood in the Cut* – K. Flay
4. *Bloodstream* – Stateless
5. *Wolves* - Selena Gomez ft. Marshmallow
6. *Sugar* – Maroon 5
7. *High Enough* – K. Flay
8. *Bubblegum Bitch* – Marina and the Diamonds
9. *Not on Drugs*- Tove Lo
10. *Roses* – The Chainsmokers
11. *Broken Girl* – Matthew West
12. *Roots* – In This Moment
13. *Homegrown* - Otep
14. *Beautiful Pain* – Eminem ft. Sia
15. *Flashlight (Sweet Life Remix)* - Hailee Steinfeld

HELPLINES AND WEBSITES

RAINN (Rape, Abuse, and Incest National Network):
1-800-656-HOPE (4673)
www.rainn.org

National Domestic Violence Hotline:
1-800-799- SAFE (7233)
www.ndvh.org

National Child Abuse Hotline:
1-800-422-4453
www.childhelp.org

National Suicide Prevention Lifeline:
1-800-273-8255
www.suicidepreventionlifeline.org

SAMHSA (Substance Abuse and Mental Health Services
Administration)
1-800-662-HELP (4357)
www.samhsa.gov

BOOKS BY
CHARITY B.

The Sweet Treats Trilogy

Candy Coated Chaos
Sweetened Suffering

Acknowledgments

My Beta Readers Elaine Kelly, Danielle Krushel, Lia Covington from Lia's Bookish Obsession, Salina Donovan, Kween Corie, and Terry Rains. I don't know where I would be without you guys and these books wouldn't be what they are without your help. Thank you so much for having my back.

My readers and stalkers. Your support means so much to me and you have made my dreams come true. I do this for you guys. Thank you for all your love.

All the blogs that have posted about these books. You are guys are awesome and I love you all and greatly appreciate you.

Kathi and Maureen from Maureen and Kathi Read and The Dark Angels for being so supportive and taking a chance on me.

All the authors that have helped me by not only talking about the books, but have offered advice and information to help me learn this business.

Stacey with Champagne formats. You have made this book more beautiful than I ever imagined. You have been so understanding and phenomenal through this whole process.

Megan with Mischievous Design. The teasers you have made for this series are still blowing me away. Your work is so incredible and you were a dream to work with.

Indie Solutions Cover Design for giving the covers I fantasized about.

My editor Joanne LaRe Thompson. You have been a dream and I have loved working with you. Thank you so much for everything you have done for this book and series.

ABOUT THE
Author

As an independent author, your ratings and especially reviews mean more than you realize. If you enjoyed the book, please consider lending your support by leaving your thoughts in a review.

Charity B. lives in Salem Oregon with her husband and ornery little boy. She has always loved to read and write, but began her love affair with dark romance when she read C.J. Robert's *The Dark Duet*. She has a passion for the disturbing and sexy and wants nothing more than to give her readers the ultimate book hangover. In her spare time when she's not chasing her son, she enjoys reading, the occasional TV show binge, and is deeply inspired by music.

For news on upcoming releases go to charitybauthor.com

Made in the USA
Monee, IL
01 August 2020